Jacqueline gave a small ga

A chill shivered down Cel
turn and look toward Lord Northington at last, and drew
in a deep breath for courage.

Yet she could not find him. She had thought there would be instant recognition, that the hatred she had nursed all these years would immediately focus on Northington despite the time that had passed. Yet none of the men present had the face of her childhood nightmares.

She had a vague impression of a tall man with dark hair, impeccably dressed and with an air of polite boredom in his movements, but her gaze focused beyond him.

"This must be the young lady who has captured Sir John's instant admiration," a deep voice said, the tone slow, rich, seductive.

He reached for her hand, took it in his broad palm, held her fingers in a light clasp as he bent to place a kiss upon her gloved knuckles.

Celia did not resist. She felt as if all eyes were watching, waiting for her response. Panic swelled, coupled with an overwhelming need to escape. But it was his touch that unnerved her most.

Faintly, she managed to say, "If you will excuse me, I must attend to some personal business."

Celia maneuvered a path through the crowd without taking flight or stumbling. She had to escape that penetrating gaze and the discovery that this Northington was *not* the man she had hated for so long, was *not* the man she had come to ruin.

There had to be *two* Lord Northingtons.

Also available from
ROSEMARY ROGERS
and MIRA Books

SWEET SAVAGE LOVE
SAVAGE DESIRE

Coming soon
WICKED LOVING LIES
August 2002

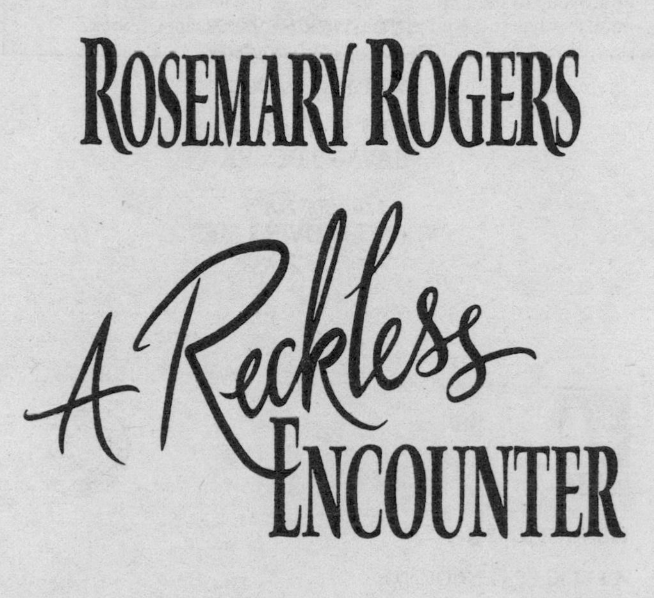
ROSEMARY ROGERS
A Reckless
ENCOUNTER

MIRA

ISBN 1-55166-852-1

A RECKLESS ENCOUNTER

Visit us at www.mirabooks.com

Printed in U.S.A.

To my family

To all my readers, lifelong and new.
I cherish your loyalty much more than I can say. And to my wonderful editors at MIRA Books, Dianne Moggy and Martha Keenan. Here's to a glorious future!

PART I

"The heart has reasons
of which reason has no knowledge."

—Pascal, *Pensées*

Prologue

Georgetown, District of Columbia
1810

Danger wore an elegant coat and arrogance. When twelve-year-old Celia Sinclair opened the door that cool autumn evening, a tall man with features as sharp as a hawk stood on the stoop. His voice was impatient and brusque, the words clipped, the accent unmistakably British.

"I have come to visit Madame."

When she did not reply, but continued to stare at him, he added impatiently, "This is the home of Léonie St. Remy, is it not?"

Celia smoothed her hands over the blue kersey of her dress, suddenly aware of how shabby she must look. "Madame *Sinclair* is busy at the moment, sir. If you will leave your card, I will—"

"My *card?* Rather pretentious of you, considering this humble abode, I think. Go and fetch your mistress, girl." He pushed her hand away when she moved to close the door, and wedged his body inside. "Inform her that Lord Northington wishes to see her at once."

Brown eyes stared down at her from a face pitted with the faint remnants of scars. His mouth was full, his cheekbones high and stark, the slash of black eyebrows a marked contrast to his powdered hair.

This was Lord Northington, the man her mother had once said was a beast!

"Don't stand there gaping at me, girl," he said sharply. "I'll see you're dismissed from your post for this impertinence. Fetch Madame at once!"

"I am not a servant, my lord," she replied, crossing her arms over her chest. "I have no intention of fetching Madame. Leave your card, and when she returns, I shall give it to her."

"Impudent brat," he spat. "I know she's here. I followed her." Even in the gloom, she could see the hot flare of anger in his eyes, the white lines that cut grooves on each side of his mouth as he grated, "It would serve you best to do as you're told. The consequences can so often be...unpleasant."

Celia's brief spurt of courage failed her. She took a backward step, her heart hammering fearfully in her chest.

"You have no authority here!"

"I have no intention of remaining here to bandy words with an insolent brat."

Ignoring her choked cry, he brushed past her. Bootsteps echoed loudly on the bare wooden floors as he moved down the hallway to the tiny parlor. His glance into the empty room was dismissive, his lip curled.

Celia saw it as he must see it, so bare now of the once lovely furnishings; not even linen scarves were left to adorn the single drum table that had yet to be sold, and the upholstered settee looked alone and forlorn in front of the cold fireplace. The years of deprivation since her father's death were obvious, the remnants of their once comfortable life pitiful. Northington moved past the parlor.

"You must not!" she cried as he pushed open the door that led to the kitchen. Panic drove her, and unreasoning fear that he meant to harm her mother. She caught at his sleeve, but he jerked free.

The covered walkway was short, and he closed the distance in only three strides, then pushed open the door. "There you are, Madame!"

His change from contemptuous to beguiling was instant and shocking. Celia hung back, trembling as her mother turned to face the intruder with a serenity that belied the taut set of her mouth. Blond hair waved back from her high, intelligent forehead, and green eyes studied the man with an emotion Celia couldn't interpret. Fear? Disdain?

"Lord Northington. This is certainly a surprise."

"A pleasant one, I trust."

"Would it matter if it were not, my lord?"

It was said lightly, but Celia recognized the steel beneath her mother's velvet tone. Behind her, Old Peter stood silent and stiff, disapproval radiating from his dusky face.

Maman and the viscount spoke French, the language lending itself to subtle nuances that even a child could identify.

"My dear Madame," Northington said with a soft laugh, "I crave your approval as none other."

"Would that were true, my lord. Tell me what brings you to my home."

"Need you ask?"

Celia saw her mother flush.

"Not in front of my daughter, if you please, my lord!"

"Your daughter? This pretty child?" He turned toward Celia. "I should have known. That glorious fair hair and green eyes are too exquisite to be duplicated in mere dross. Come here, child, and tell me your name."

Though she made no effort to move, her mother stepped in front of Celia as if to protect her. She gazed coolly at Northington as she said, "Stay here, little one. Peter will serve your supper."

"But I wish to wait for you, Maman."

"I will return to you soon, my love."

Old Peter put a hand on Celia's shoulder when she would have protested more, and she fell silent as her mother preceded Northington from the kitchen. The clatter of a pot lid made a staccato sound. After a moment, Old Peter said softly, "He is bold, that one. To come here after her—"

"I do not like him." Celia jerked away from Peter's grasp to go to the kitchen door. A hard knot formed in her chest. "He is quite rude. Maman does not like him, either. I saw it in her eyes."

She whirled around to face the old man. "Do you think he'll hurt her?"

Old Peter shook his head, but she noticed that his hand trembled slightly as he ladled soup into a bowl. Steam rose in a thin cloud from the pot.

"He would not dare, lamb. Not even an English lord can escape the law. Here. Come and sit down. Eat your soup, and some of these apples you love. The bread— Did you bring back Madame's market bag from the front room?"

"Oh. I forgot it... Shall I go and fetch it? I left it at the front door when *he* came."

"No. No, I'll get it. You stay here and eat, child."

Celia sat on the long bench drawn up to the scarred oak table that was incongruously set with the silver and a few pieces of china—remnants of better days. She was no longer hungry. Not even the apples were tempting.

Glumly she watched her soup cool, waiting for Old Peter's return with the bread Maman had bought on her way home from teaching French to the children of wealthy townspeople.

Time passed and she began to fret. What could be taking so long? Why had Old Peter not returned? And where was Maman?

Finally, as the fire dimmed and the usually warm

kitchen grew cool, Celia abandoned her untouched soup. It had grown even colder outside; as she crossed the breezeway to the main house, the wind tugged at her blue dress and loosened pale coils of her hair from beneath the white cap she wore. The smell of winter was in the air.

Shivering, she eased into the house and paused, uncertain. It was ominously quiet. The tall case clock that Maman had said now belonged to a new owner ticked softly in the hallway. A lamp had been lit, a thin thread of light from beneath a door guiding her down the hallway.

A feeling of dread enveloped her as she reached the parlor door; it was partially open. She began to shake. It was so quiet, deathly quiet...

"Maman?" Her hand spread on the door and pushed; it didn't move. No sound greeted her as she wedged her body into the parlor. A low lamp burned in a wall sconce, casting the settee into a stark silhouette that seemed suddenly ominous. Her heart thudded painfully as she took a step into the room, glancing down at the obstruction holding the door. A scream locked in her throat.

Old Peter lay there motionless. His mouth was agape, his eyes closed. She knelt beside him, but he made no sound when she whispered his name. His dark face was so still.

Panic nearly paralyzed her, but she rose again and turned, walking toward the settee. Boards creaked beneath her feet, familiar but now much too loud in the soft gloom.

"Maman?"

It was a faint whisper, tentative and afraid. Her hand curled over the back of the settee, the horsehair-stuffed upholstery unyielding beneath the pressure of her clutching fingers. A bundle of rags lay upon the seat, shapeless and bulky.

But when she slipped around the end of the settee to inspect further, the bundle moaned softly.

"Maman! Oh, Maman!"

A feeble hand reached out for her, and then Celia saw that her mother's skirts were up around her waist, her lower body naked. Immediately she pulled the skirts over Maman's legs, then knelt beside her.

"Maman—you're hurt! And Old Peter won't wake. I must fetch the physician."

"No..." The moan formed a refusal.

"But you'll die, and Old Peter is so still...I'm afraid for you and I don't know what to do!" Sobs thickened her words and she felt her mother's hand graze her cheek in a comforting gesture.

"Help...Peter. I'm...fine. Truly. Go to Peter."

But Old Peter was past help, dead from a grievous blow to the side of his head.

Celia spent the next few weeks in a daze. Maman had never been very strong, and now her meager reserves of strength were depleted by Lord Northington's brutal rape. He had hurt much more than just her body; the light had gone from Léonie's eyes, leaving behind an empty shell.

Anger sparked, the helpless rage of a child who has lost all comfort and security.

Léonie tried to recover; she dragged herself from the bed to do the sewing that helped to support them, but her heart was no longer in it. Northington had destroyed something inside her that Celia couldn't understand.

"It is no use, petite," Maman said sadly when Celia insisted she go to the authorities again. "They do not see me, do not care to see me. And it no longer matters. He's gone now, back to England."

"But we have papers. I read them, Maman! Charges were brought—"

"Against a man who is inviolate, a peer of the realm with access to money for bribes. Not even Peter's murder will be avenged, so my *charge* is even less likely to be acknowledged. I am familiar with the advantages of power, my petite. Once, I lived with it. I know what it can do, what it can accomplish. It is no use to fight it."

"No!" Celia raged, her voice almost a howl that alarmed her mother. "He has to pay for what he's done, Maman. He has to be punished! Where is the justice? Why can he escape—"

Léonie grabbed her close, held her as tears wet their cheeks. "Justice is not always in this life," she said at last, stroking Celia's hair with a trembling hand. "I have seen too much to expect evil deeds to always be punished."

Anger and resentment burned inside Celia's breast,

but she held her tongue. It only made things worse to remind Maman of what had happened. But one day—one day she would find a way to make Lord Northington pay for what he had done!

PART II

"And whatever sky's above me,
Here's a heart for any fate."
—Lord Byron

LONDON, ENGLAND
September, 1819

1

Traveling under the name St. Clair, Celia stared over the rail of the ship nosing a watery trough up the Thames. It had been a tedious voyage save for a storm that she'd been convinced would destroy them all. But now she was here at last. At last! She knotted her hands in the folds of the reticule she carried; a letter crackled softly in the velvet bag. It was her future, the letter to Maman's cousin, Jacqueline Fournier Leverton. Jacqueline and Léonie St. Remy had fled Paris during that bloody Revolution that had cost so many lives. Jacqueline had married an English baron, while Léonie wed the dashing American captain Samuel Sinclair and left England behind forever.

Perhaps Léonie had worried what might happen one day, for, when Celia was still an infant, she'd written a letter to her cousin about her daughter. She'd kept Jacqueline's reply, her promise to stand as godmother to the child she hoped to one day meet. That letter was old, the pages yellowed and the ink faint, but it would serve as a letter of introduction to this godmother Celia had never met.

And now the time had come. So many fears, so much pain and heartache behind her...but she would let nothing stand in her way. Not now. Not after so many years.

Coming to England was not just the start of a new life, it was an act of vengeance. For nearly ten years, she had hated Lord Northington. At times, it had been all that let her feel alive.

Celia's hands tightened on the ship rail as the London docks grew sharper in the gray mist that cloaked the river and hazed the forest of tall, swaying masts that looked like so many reeds choking the waterway. Shrouds seemed to part sullenly as the prow eased through debris and water, a lingering fog that diffused the sharper outlines of the city's gray spires and forbidding towers.

So close, so close. It was nearly time now...all the planning, and now she was here at last. Maman would have wanted her to come to England.

Maman....

It was nine years since her death, nine years since Celia had watched helplessly as Léonie bled to death in the childbed. Her infant son had lived only a few minutes more than his mother, Northington's babe drawing only a few gasps of air. They were buried together, a simple grave in a corner of the cemetery where paupers were granted space for their eternity.

At thirteen, Celia had found herself orphaned and alone. There had been no relatives to take her in, no one but the kind nuns at a foundling home. As Léonie had once done, Celia taught French to students, saving every penny she earned through the years. Even after her eighteenth birthday, she'd stayed on, saving her money, a goal firmly fixed in her mind, her sworn revenge keeping her strong.

It was the death of her mother that had formed the need for vengeance, formed the burning desire to find Northington and, if nothing else, confront him with his crimes. Why should he be allowed to forget the woman he had raped or the old man he had killed? Didn't she live with their memories every day, the pain as fresh at times as it had been when she'd lost them? Yes, and Northington would soon find a reminder of what he'd done on his doorstep.

In the reticule with the letter to Lady Leverton was a document with the old charges against the viscount. It bore the seal of the Georgetown magistrate where it had been filed so many years before—the only proof of Northington's crime. A charge of murder still held weight even after so long, though the death of a freed slave had not been important enough to halt Northington's flight.

But it was important to me, Celia thought fiercely as the docks became more visible in the fog. Old Peter was still a sharp memory, she'd never forget him.

It was the careless indifference that rankled most, the viscount's arrogant claim that the old man had assaulted him. It had been a farce, a travesty of justice.

But Celia intended to see that he acknowledged his acts, to expose him for the cruel killer that he was and to seek justice for the wrongs done not only to Old Peter, but to her mother and an innocent babe.

The nuns had taught her a great deal about atonement for sins committed, and she would educate Northington. He would have his name shamed in the society he kept, and endure the scourge of public scorn. I just hope he's still alive to suffer it! she thought fiercely.

A chill wind blew across the decks, but she paid no heed to it, or to the sidelong glances she received from some of the deckhands. Most of the passengers aboard ship were from America, but the *Liberty* had briefly docked in Liverpool the day before, and several men had boarded for the trip around the southern coast of England to London. For the most part, they seemed inoffensive, though she had noticed one man in particular who stood out from the others.

Tall, dark, with an inbred arrogance that reminded her far too clearly of the kind of man she detested, he remained aloof from the others, keeping company instead with the captain of the vessel as if they were old friends. Yet there was an air about him that drew her attention, though she would have denied it if anyone had noticed her interest. It might be his self-assurance, or even his lean good looks, but she found her gaze drawn to him when he came onto the upper deck.

He was dressed casually in tight-fitting buff trousers and knee-high jackboots, his white shirt and open coat giving him the appearance of a country squire.

But there was something primitive, predatory about him, as if he was a man accustomed to command and instant obedience. His lean face was like the blade of a hatchet, the features too well-defined to belong to a simple squire. He seemed—dangerous.

Leaning against the wall of the deckhouse, he was engaged in conversation with the first mate, but happened to glance up and catch her staring at him. A mocking smile tucked the corners of his mouth inward, and he inclined his head in her direction to acknowledge her gaze.

Celia flushed and looked casually away, as if she'd only been searching for a companion.

Fortunately Mister Carlisle, a fellow passenger who had boarded only the day before but had already made himself known to her, chose that moment to approach her at the rail, his smile wide and friendly.

"Miss St. Clair," he said agreeably. "It seems we made it to London in good time."

"Yes, so it does, Mister Carlisle."

As the ship glided down the Thames, the decks were frenetic with activity; ropes hummed through the shrouds and canvas snapped with heavy weight.

A brisk wind tugged at her skirts and threatened to loosen her hat. Celia grabbed at the ribbons to hold her hat in place and managed a smile. If she hadn't been caught staring so rudely at another passenger, she would have been quite cool to Mister Carlisle. Since boarding the *Liberty,* he had seemed to take a special interest in her, dogging her steps every time she came above deck.

Now his smile was ingratiating, his manner a bit too bluff and hearty.

"So, Miss St. Clair, do you have family or friends meeting you?"

"I couldn't say, Mister Carlisle. Arrival dates are so uncertain, you know."

"Yes, it's so easy to miscalculate, especially when the vessel arrives ahead of schedule." He hesitated, his brown eyes observing her with obvious admiration. "London is a huge, busy city, and it's very easy to get lost or taken advantage of if you aren't familiar with the streets and byways. Perhaps I could see you to your destination, if it wouldn't be too presumptuous of me to suggest it."

Her smile cooled. "That really isn't necessary, Mister Carlisle. I'm quite capable of reaching my family on my own, thank you."

"But I thought you'd never been to London—"

"No, but one doesn't have to have lived here to be able to hire a hack, I'm quite certain."

Carlisle shrugged. "True enough, yet a hired hack is hardly suitable for a woman of your presence."

He moved closer, his tone shifting. It became more intimate, husky and cajoling. Just his supposition that she would be susceptible made her answer him sharply when he offered again to take her in his own coach.

"Perhaps you misunderstood me, Mister Carlisle. I do not care to be alone in your company."

Undeterred, he smiled broadly. "You have come all the way across the Atlantic alone. I didn't think you would consider yourself in danger being alone with me in a public carriage. But since you're reluctant—"

"Yes, I am reluctant. I do not really know you. An acquaintance made aboard ship is not really what one could call proper."

He bowed slightly. "I beg your pardon if I offended you, as it seems I have. Here, do let me loan you my city directory. Hired hacks so often take advantage of visitors to London, and he may well try to overcharge you since you are unfamiliar with the streets."

When she hesitated, he smiled disarmingly. "I have a sister I would wish protected, Miss St. Clair. I would hope some gentleman would be so kind as to offer his assistance should she be in need of it. I want nothing in return but your safety.''

''Very well,'' she said, and smiled back at him. ''I'm grateful for your concern. What is this directory?''

''It is a map of main streets and routes in London. See, here is the Tower, and this is Parliament over here....'' He traced the route with his fingertip. ''If you know your destination, you'll be able to find the general area on this map, then not allow any dishonest hackman to take you the long way round.''

''Yes,'' she said. ''Oh my, this map is so detailed and the print so small I don't know if I can find my street.''

''If you'd like, tell me the name of your street and I'll point to it. You don't have to share the address. London is a big city, and it's easy to get lost.''

''Very well,'' she said after a moment, for he was quite right in that it seemed to be much larger than she had anticipated. ''Please show me Bruton Street.''

''Ah, tell the driver to take you to Mayfair. Here. Go by way of these main roads and you should get there quite quickly.'' He traced a route with his finger, then smiled as he pressed the small map into her hand. ''Keep it for now, but do be kind enough to return it to me, if you will, once you've used it. Have it delivered by post, or messenger if you like, to the Carlisle in Shoreditch. It's a public house owned by my brother.''

''Thank you, sir, for your kindness,'' she said as she tucked the directory into her reticule. Perhaps she should not be so suspicious, she thought, but a woman traveling alone dare not attract too much attention.

Why, most of the voyage had been spent in her cabin, a stuffy corner not much larger than a water closet and smelling very similar.

As the *Liberty* edged close to the dock, the decks grew quite crowded and loud, and Celia realized that, in the press of crowd and crew, James Carlisle had vanished. It was faintly surprising. He'd seemed so insistent, and now he'd just disappeared in the chaos, leaving her alone to make her way ashore.

Celia dismissed Carlisle from her mind when the hack rolled to a halt before the buff stone facade of Lord Leverton's Mayfair home. It was imposing, a veritable five-story tower with staircases that curved up each side to the entrance. It was a house that radiated power and position.

It was this kind of house, this kind of wealth, that bred men like Lord Northington....

She was shown into the entrance hall and bade wait, and the butler who greeted her looked down his long thin nose at her as if she were an interloper.

"Lady Leverton is not accepting visitors, I fear," he said coldly. "However, you may leave your card."

But Celia was not to be denied. "I will wait in the parlor." She made her tone as lofty as his, with just a touch of arrogance. "Please be so good as to direct me. Lady Leverton will be pleased to see me, I assure you."

There were, she thought, few things more intimidating than a proper English servant. He regarded her as if she were an insect, but at last briefly inclined his head, and beckoned to a young maid.

"Show Miss—" He studied the card she'd given

him for an instant, then continued, ''St. Clair into the small parlor to wait, Hester.''

The uniformed maid led her to a wide set of double doors that opened into a room much larger than any she'd seen. If it was named the *small parlor,* she would truly be amazed at any larger chamber.

Richly furnished, there was a warm fire in the grate and thick rugs on the floors. Plush settees upholstered in embroidered velvet were placed before the hearth. Ornate vases and Dresden figurines adorned baroque tables that gleamed with the sheen of highly polished mahogany. Fresh flowers spilled from crystal vases.

Celia felt suddenly awkward and graceless in such a room, and wondered with a spurt of panic if she could truly pretend to be what she was not. How could she keep up the masquerade?

And while she may dislike deceiving her own godmother with the charade, she had little choice. She *had* to be the woman she posed herself to be, or she would never be able to fit in the society of those surrounding Northington.

That was, after all, her goal. To do less would be to fail.

But the success in her plan hinged on her acceptance here, with Jacqueline Leverton. Tension made her nerves taut, and she drew in a deep breath to steady herself. What if her godmother should not wish her to stay? She had never met her, after all, and their brief correspondence had been rather stilted.

A light laugh preceded the appearance of a tiny dark-haired woman in the doorway. ''Celia Sinclair? Could it be?'' she cried, and moved swiftly toward her. ''I cannot believe it! You did come, after all. Oh my, you are the very image of your dear mother...my beautiful Léonie.''

Unexpected tears stung her eyes as Celia was drawn into a warm embrace. There was none of the awkwardness of their written correspondence, and no question of being accepted. She found herself seated on the settee answering questions about her mother, telling Jacqueline—''But you must call me Jacque, my dearest, as do all my friends,''—about her mother's death.

She left out the details, saying only that Maman had died of a fever. It was difficult not dissolving in tears, but Jacqueline proved to be more pragmatic than her bubbly nature promised.

''It is a dreadful thing, but life is not always kind, I have learned,'' she sighed in her accented English. ''My poor Léonie. She was always so beautiful, so bright. I adored her, you know. Just as I shall adore you. Your mother's marriage was so romantic, and your father— Ah! So handsome he was,'' Jacqueline said with a smile. ''And so much in love with Léonie! But of course, every man who met her fell in love with her. She was so beautiful, how could they not? Once, before she met your dear papa, she said her face was a curse, not a blessing. But I am glad that it proved not to be true.''

Celia's jaw set. But it had been true, in the end. Her mother's blessing had turned to a curse because of Lord Northington.

''Ah, my lovely one,'' Jacqueline was saying, ''you will be the toast of all London, I am quite certain! With those marvelous green eyes and that lovely blond hair, you shall break the hearts of all the men, and perhaps marry a duke, or even a prince one day!"

She laughed, her dark head tilted to one side like a saucy little bird, and Celia found herself smiling back at her.

"Now come, Celia," Jacqueline said, and held out her hand to draw her with her. "I shall show you to your room and see you settled in until supper. Tomorrow we shall set about showing you London."

"I look forward to it, my lady."

"No, no, *Jacque*. Family is not formal here. I do not like it. Oh, and you must meet my husband and my daughter, for she is to be presented this year. It is so exciting. Now I shall have *two* beautiful young ladies to display!"

The spacious chamber on the third floor was larger than any of Celia's experience. She could scarcely believe that it was to be hers alone, not shared with an entire room full of girls, as she had lived at the foundling home.

"But of course it is just yours," Jacqueline said with a laugh when Celia asked if she was to share the chamber. "And you may have things arranged to suit you. Just tell Lily and she will have a footman come to move furniture about. A chambermaid will tend your fire for you— But where are your trunks? This one cannot be all you have. Are more waiting at the docks with your maid?"

A flush heated her face, but Celia lied smoothly. "My trunks were unfortunately lost, and the one is all I have left. A pity, for I had some beautiful gowns. Oh, and all my jewelry— But now that I am here I don't feel the loss, for your welcome has been so warm I feel only joy at finally meeting you."

That was true enough. Lady Leverton's obvious welcome was much more than Celia had hoped for, and her open nature so warm that Celia felt as if she was closer to her mother just by being with this petite woman. It was also an unexpected complication. She must remain distant, or she would not be able to do what she must do....

"And your maid?" her cousin inquired. "Tell me you did not travel without a maid!"

"I'm afraid that she grew ill and it was too late to find a proper lady's maid." *Another lie... I'm becoming far too proficient at this!*

"Oh, my dear, you traveled all this way alone? It is astounding that you were not accosted by some ruffian along the way. An unaccompanied lady is so at the mercy of rude men. But the loss of a maid is easily remedied. You are here now and shall have all that is necessary. Here. Sit beside me on the chaise while Lily puts away your things for you, and tell me of your plans."

"Plans? I suppose I have none. I've just...just been so unhappy since Maman died." There was no need for subterfuge now, for the tears still came when she spoke of her mother. "You're all the family I know, all I have left. I hope—I hope I am welcome."

"Of course, you poor child! How could you think you would not be? I am just sorry you waited so long to come to us! You are a St. Remy, as am I on my mother's side. We are of the same blood. Odd, that Jarvis said St. Clair instead of Sinclair, but I knew at once who you were, of course. I recognized your father's name.''

''Actually, I have begun using St. Clair instead of Sinclair,'' Celia explained, having carefully rehearsed her intention for using a name that Northington may not easily recognize. ''Maman changed it after Papa died, because she was afraid some of the English officers would attempt vengeance on us for Papa's part in the war.'' She paused, then said, ''The Sinclair family lost everything in the war, and Papa was the only one left. Then he died in a skirmish with one of Napoleon's ships. His ship was later sold, I heard, as were other seized United States ships. Maman said we must learn to adapt. So I have.''

''Léonie always was the practical one, even when we were children. You may now revert to your dear papa's name, of course, for there is no danger to you here.''

''I've used St. Clair so long, it's my name now. It is no insult to Papa, for the original usage was St. Clair, I've been told. Names do not matter so much in America.''

''So true...names there change to suit the bearer. Ah well. *C'est la vie!* We must learn to adapt to all things in time.'' Jacqueline smiled. ''Léonie and I learned that lesson quite early, you know. We changed our names a dozen times during the dark days, but always we knew who we were and our true heritage. That is what matters most.''

''When you speak of her, it's as if Maman is alive for me again.''

''But of course, petite. Our childhoods were glorious. That was before the Terror, when life seemed so bright and promising and France was still so elegant. But the world changed for us, as it has for you. Now, tomorrow will be your first day here, and you will meet my daughter. My son is at Oxford, but Carolyn is more your age, a bit younger than you, but already betrothed. We shall see what we can do about your future!"

"No, please," Celia said with a soft laugh. "I am far too content just being here with you to even consider such a thing."

"So you say now," Jacqueline said slyly. "But that will soon change. Here is Lily with your dressing gown. One of the footmen will bring up hot water for your bath, then you must rest while you can. You look so weary. Would you prefer having a light supper in your room?"

"I…I am rather tired. If it wouldn't offend you—"

"Of course it won't offend me. Just rest this evening. I intend to do all I can for you, just as Léonie would have done for my Caro."

It was a bit overwhelming. Celia found herself whisked to an overheated room off her bedchamber where a huge brass tub was filled with scented water and thick cotton towels warmed before a cheery fire. A ladies' maid waited patiently to assist her in undressing and bathing, but Celia shook her head.

"Please—Lily, is it? I'd rather do it myself."

It was novel, this pampered existence, and she thought again of her mother, and how she had once lived in a lovely château in the French countryside, the pampered, petted daughter of aristocrats. Upheaval and tragedy had displaced her, but she'd finally found happiness, however briefly. Nothing lasted. Everything changed.

Hadn't her own life changed so drastically? Yes, and now it was changed again. After years of watching from the other side while people moved in a privileged world, she was at last part of it. The years of scrimping and saving, planning for this, had come to pass. Could she do it? Could she fit into his world long enough to exact some kind of retribution against Northington? God knows, I've wanted it long enough, she thought fiercely.

And it wasn't just for herself. It was for Maman and Old Peter. They deserved justice.

2

"'Pistols at Chalk Farm? Hardly worth the trouble, I'd think." Robert George Colter Hampton—Lord Northington—regarded Harvey with a cynical smile that didn't quite reach his cold blue eyes.

"So I thought." Sir John Harvey gave his companion a glance of hopeful appeal. "Unfortunately I'm not the marksman you are. 'Pistols for two, breakfast for one' will be my likely fate. Sir Skeffington's liable to call me out about this little tart. Any chance you'll be my second?"

"And take your place when you suddenly fall ill?" Leaning back in his chair, he stretched lazily. "You've played that game before. I have no desire to meet anyone at dawn unless it's a buxom wench with light skirts and a willing smile."

Harvey sighed. "I feared you'd say that."

"No, you knew I'd refuse. I don't interfere in other men's quarrels." Northington downed the last of his brandy to indicate his desire to leave the club.

Raggett, the proprietor of White's, came to sweep ashes and crumbs from the top of the green baize table, obliging and efficient in the art of catering to his patrons—and always on the watch for a stray coin.

Northington stifled a yawn. It was late. Or early, depending upon the point of view. His interest had begun to wane several hours before, but it was bad form to bankrupt a man at cards and not give him at least a small chance to recoup.

The night had been profitable. Not only Harvey, but the young Wharton had lost several thousand pounds on the turn of the cards. Harvey was an inveterate gambler, and no doubt would one day ruin himself.

Wharton was another matter. He was young, with only a pale downy stubble on his jaw, a green youth at both cards and life. Christ. They seemed to get younger every year. Had he ever been this young? Yes, but not this foolish.

More brandy appeared at his elbow, amber fire in cut crystal. He regarded Wharton over the rim of the snifter.

"Are you done, sir?"

Wharton gave a start, pale cheeks flushed with an emotion Northington recognized as extreme distress.

"Done up is more like it, my lord." He attempted a smile that wobbled on his mouth. "I'm under the hatches, I fear. Will you accept my vowels?"

Northington leaned forward, raked the counters toward him with a lazy swipe of one hand. "A man should never bet what he cannot pay, Wharton."

Harvey, who had leaned his chair back on the two rear legs, sat forward with a loud thump.

"Sermons? From *you?* Good God, we must both be foxed!"

Northington spared him a glance. "I assume you speak for yourself. I always pay my debts."

"Yes, and much more quickly since your grandfather's death and your father's newly acquired title—and since *you* became Viscount Northington," Harvey replied with a wry twist of his mouth. "Now, if only my family would be so cooperative as to die off and leave me with a substantial fortune and a bloody title, I'd not worry about a few thousand pounds here and there, either."

"No doubt." Colter's eyes flicked to young Wharton, studied his flushed face, the dissipation that had already begun to distort youthful features.

"I'm done up," Wharton said again, and reached for the cards. He riffled them almost desperately. "You seem to have the devil's own luck, my lord."

"Yes. I do, don't I?" Colter's lazy smile altered to a sharper expression. Impatient now, he raked his fingers through his dark hair, then put out a hand for the deck of cards, sweat-stained from the long night's play.

"One more round, Wharton. You cut."

Wharton stared at him in disbelief. "I doubt I can pay all I owe you now! If I lose...if I lose, my life won't be worth a shilling."

"It's hardly worth that now if you judge yourself by what you owe instead of how you pay." It was said with a mocking twist of his mouth, but he saw that Wharton took his point.

After the barest hesitation, the young man placed the deck of cards in Colter's palm. Shuffling in expert, easy movements, Colter let the soft whisper of pasteboard flow fluidly from hand to hand as Wharton's obvious uncertainty increased.

After a long moment of silence, Wharton made a hoarse sound. "Damn, but it hardly matters if I'm hung for a sheep or a lamb...deal another hand."

"No. The high card takes all." Colter's long fingers arranged the deck in the middle of the green baize table. He tapped it lightly with one finger. "But if I win, your debt to me is satisfied once you give me your oath you'll not play cards here again."

"Not play—you jest!"

"I've never been more serious. Don't look so stricken at my offer. I could always insist upon prompt payment."

Wharton flushed. His jaw set, his mouth a slash that made him look suddenly older.

"Don't gammon me, Northington."

"Cut the cards or make arrangements with the bank to pay me what you owe, Wharton. It's as simple as that."

Indecision clouded his face briefly, but he gave a jerk of his head. "Very well. I'll cut. High card takes all."

A trembling hand reached out, separated the deck and turned it over. A four of spades gleamed in the pale light. Despair quivered on Wharton's mouth, but he looked up to meet Colter's gaze with a steady enough stare.

"It seems you have an excellent chance to win, my lord."

"So it does. I'm used to winning. It's a damn sight better than losing."

Wharton paled even more, but his face was resolute as Colter deftly cut the remaining cards.

"Seven of hearts," someone behind them breathed softly, and Colter was aware they had gathered a crowd. "Northington won, by God!"

"So I did." Colter stood up, pushed his chair back and lifted a brow. "Your debt is satisfied, but you must heed your oath, Wharton. If I ever see or hear of you being here again I shall assume that means you have the means to repay your debt to me, and I shall take steps to collect it."

The youth looked shocked, shaken, but managed to lurch to his feet. "I say! I...I say!"

"Yes, I'm sure you do. Now, if you'll excuse me, I am through playing for the evening."

Harvey rose as well and shot Colter a jaundiced glance as he accompanied him to the front of the establishment. "Well, Northington, I've never known you to cheat at cards before."

Colter shrugged into his coat, flicked lint from the sleeve and looked up at his companion. "Men have been called out for less inflammatory words, Harvey."

"Yes, and I'm well aware you're a dead shot. But I am also a fair hand at cards, and not drunk enough to miss you palm that seven. Why?"

"Why let him cry off? Or why cheat?"

"Both. Either. Wharton's old enough to learn better. He doesn't need a wet nurse."

"No, he doesn't, but a bit of guidance won't hurt him. One chance is more than enough for some."

"I've never known you to be so philanthropic. What in the devil did you drink tonight?"

"A cup too many, it seems. Or maybe I just dislike ruining green boys. Wharton has no business here."

"It could be said that none of us do," Harvey said dryly.

"Yes, it could." Colter blinked against the cold sunlight that struck him as they stepped outside. It was much later than he'd thought. Tradesmen had already made early deliveries and traffic along St. James Street was heavy. A beer cart narrowly missed splashing mud on them as it lumbered past.

"It will be all over London by nightfall that you evicted Wharton from White's, you know." Harvey kept pace, though a bit wobbly. "Bad form, Northington. You should have just ruined him."

"That would be far too easy. I enjoy a challenge."

Puddles of water still stood along the paving stones from the recent rains. A fetid odor lingered in the air. He stepped over a brackish pool and left Harvey trailing behind him as he crossed St. James and turned the corner.

His mind was already on the beguiling prospect of a hot meal and warm bed when Harvey grabbed his arm to pull him to a halt.

"Damn, but that's a prime article! Who is she? Do you know her? I'm sure I know her companion—"

Colter shook loose his hand, impatient and weary, and certainly in no mood to make polite conversation with any female of Harvey's acquaintance. They were usually brainless society belles or women of loose character and looser morals. Not that he had any particular objection to the latter, but Harvey was too damned enthusiastic.

"Leverton. That's her name! Married to Jules Leverton, Lord Sharpton's youngest son and a financial genius. But who is that luscious bit with her?''

''Satisfy your curiosity alone or at some other time.'' Colter hailed a hack, and it rumbled to a halt at the curb. As the door swung open, he put a foot on the narrow rung to step up and glanced down at his companion. ''Do you wish a ride to your lodgings?''

''No.'' Sir John's attention was trained on the approaching women. ''I think it may be time I renewed my acquaintance with Lady Leverton.''

Colter followed Harvey's intent gaze. His brow rose. Jacqueline Leverton was a lovely woman who had kept her beauty through the years. The young lady at her side had her head bent, her hat shadowing her face, but it was her form that drew attention. She was lovely, though not so unusual as to warrant such rapt admiration, in his opinion.

''Harvey, you've always been an easy mark when it comes to women. Have a go at her. Spare me all the details when next I see you. Curzon Street, driver. And take the shortest route, not the most profitable.''

The driver slammed the hack door closed, and Harvey stepped away from the vehicle, his attention already returned to the women down the street.

''A prime article, don't you think?'' Harvey said again, and grinned up at Colter. ''An introduction can't hurt.''

''As so many fools before you have also said, to their collective destruction. Keep your head.'' Colter waved a dismissive hand as the hack lurched forward, then leaned back against the worn squabs that held strong hints of previous occupants. He was getting too old for this. Long nights were the mark of a jaded man. At thirty-one, he knew better.

Harvey was incorrigible; he could see him out the window as the hack drew closer, its progress obstructed by a draft wagon blocking the road. Propping a boot against the far seat, Colter watched idly as Harvey approached the two women accompanied by their maid. They paused to speak to him, crisp morning light at last revealing their faces.

He frowned, struck by a sudden memory. Lady Leverton's companion was the woman from the ship—the *Liberty.* He'd seen her staring at him, and then he'd seen her talking to James Carlisle. So, she was acquainted with Leverton, was she? A curious coincidence. But he wasn't a man who believed much in coincidences and this one seemed far too unlikely.

Yet she was a striking woman, with pale hair beneath a wide-brimmed bonnet and elegant bone structure. Tall and slender, she moved with languid grace as she turned to regard Harvey with polite attention.

Colter watched closely. She'd kept dangerous company for a woman new to London. Carlisle was not an innocuous acquaintance. How well did she know him? It was a question that begged an answer. She'd come from America, and he'd noticed her aboard ship. How could he not? While he'd kept a close eye on Carlisle, the woman had seemed to keep an eye on him in return.

Now she was staying in Jules Leverton's home, a man known to be a fervent Tory, a contradiction at best if she was acquainted with Carlisle. Perhaps there was much more to what had appeared to be a casual shipboard acquaintance than he'd first thought. This situation required a closer investigation.

Like Harvey, he wanted to know more about her—but not for the same reasons.

3

Celia eyed Sir John with a mixture of amusement and suspicion. He was handsome enough, she supposed, with fair hair and a rakish charm, but he reeked of cigar smoke and brandy. She had no intention of allowing herself to be even slightly involved with him despite his boyish appeal.

A gentle pressure of her fingers on Jacqueline's arm was a broad hint that she wished to move on, and her cousin took the cue at once, ending the conversation.

"It is so very pleasant to see you again, sir. Do leave your calling card. As I wished to show my cousin London, we made an appointment at the dressmaker's instead of having her to the house as usual. I insist upon being punctual."

Harvey said hastily, "Yes, yes, of course, Lady Leverton, but I do wish to say again how fortuitous this meeting is for me. I am planning a soirée, you see, and need expert advice. Your affairs are legend for being the most popular, and if it is not too bold, I thought perhaps you would be so kind as to make suggestions...."

He let his sentence trail hopefully, and Celia hid a smile. This Sir John was much too obvious. He'd not taken his gaze from her since hailing them, and now his hazel eyes were intent as he regarded her.

"How flattering, Sir John," Jacqueline said. "Of course, I will be most pleased to lend my aid. When do you plan your affair?"

"When? Oh, I hadn't thought that far ahead yet. Shall I come round tomorrow morning, perhaps, and we can discuss details? I am certain Miss St. Clair will have some superb suggestions as well."

"You are a brash, forward young man, aren't you?" Jacqueline's voice held a hint of reproof that finally penetrated Harvey's intensity, and he gave her a startled glance, then a disarming smile and impudent honesty.

"Not always. Only when I see a beautiful young woman I wish to know."

"I see." Jacqueline lifted a disapproving brow. "And you hope to make a good impression, I presume."

"It had occurred to me."

"Then you will be most dismayed to learn that you have not, sir. My *petite cousine* is not impressed with men who behave boorishly."

Jacqueline took Celia's arm and led her around him, turning back only when Harvey said lamely, "I would still like to leave my card tomorrow."

"Only if your manners improve, sir."

As they left him standing staring after them, Celia said faintly, "Oh my! That was rather ruthless of you."

"Do you think so? But Harvey will not overstep his

boundaries now, and word will be out that no liberties are to be taken with you. Believe me, it is a much better lesson than one could hope for, and to have Harvey at our beck and call could be beneficial. Too bad Northington did not join us.''

''Northington?'' Celia's hand shook slightly, and she curled her fingers more tightly around the strings of her small reticule. A chill wind smelled of the streets, rife with debris. She put a hand to her nose as if to ward off the stench while Jacqueline continued blithely.

''Yes, I saw him get into a hired hack, but he moved on. A pity. It would have been delightful to introduce you to him.''

A feeling of nausea swept over Celia, and her fingers were clumsy as she fumbled in her reticule for a linen scarf to press to her nose. *Northington!* He'd been that close and she hadn't even known it....

''Harvey is an intimate of Lord Northington, who is far too elusive, I fear,'' Jacqueline was saying, oblivious to Celia's reaction.

She cleared her throat. ''Why is this Northington so elusive?''

''Probably because he's weary of being pursued by so many marriageable women.'' Jacqueline laughed softly. ''His reputation leans toward rakish, but if a hostess manages to get him to attend an affair, success is assured. He is quite sought after—an unmarried viscount usually is these days. You'd be amazed at the lengths some hostesses go to in order to secure his presence at a ball or soirée. But a man who is heir to an earldom can take his time to wed, it seems.''

Celia sidestepped a clod of debris on the walkway, her tone calm. "So he will be an earl one day."

"Yes, and perhaps sooner than one would think, as his father has been an invalid for several years now...a most unpleasant man— Do be careful *ma petite,* and beware of where you step. What was I saying? Oh, yes, Northington is very closely acquainted with Harvey. They seem to attend many of the same functions."

"Is he?" She cleared her throat. "And you aspire to have Northington in attendance?"

"It would be a social coup. But never fear. I have already taken steps to ensure his attendance. Ah, here we are. Madame Dupre is most strict about punctuality. She's much sought after as a seamstress and will be able to fashion you some flattering gowns. Oh, this is going to be so amusing, Celia! I'm so glad you've come to visit. I needed a new venture to occupy my time now that Carolyn's future is assured."

Celia smiled, and during the next two hours endured the prodding and poking of the seamstress as she measured her for new gowns, exclaiming over her unusual height and slender proportions.

"But you are so tall, mademoiselle! And such long legs. Rarely have I seen a woman with your proportions. It is a pleasure to fit you for gowns. So many of these English misses have figures like boards, so petite and with no female curves. Made like boys, they are, But you! Ah, you are magnificent!"

Feeling awkward, Celia managed an appropriate murmur in reply, and caught Jacqueline's amused gaze on her.

"She is not accustomed to such praise, Madame

Dupre," Jacqueline said briskly. "But it is good for her to hear it. She must realize her worth."

Celia's chin came up. "I know my worth," she said quietly.

Jacqueline laughed. "Yes, I believe you do. Very good! No unnecessary modesty, I'm pleased to see. But she is correct, you know, Celia. You are most unusual. I predict you will be a success."

"Are you certain you wish to do this? I had not thought it important." Celia frowned slightly. "It seems a great deal of trouble just to introduce me to your friends."

"Ah, but it is not just to introduce you to my friends, my dear. We intend to snare you a wealthy husband, just as my own Caro has done. Of course, her marriage was arranged years ago, but before she settles into married life, I wish her to enjoy herself. But you—you have so much promise! Already there is interest. You saw your effect on Sir John, did you not? He was absolutely tripping over his own feet to talk to you. And as I said, he has extensive connections of the right sort. In London, it is imperative to be well connected." She paused, glanced at Madame Dupre and said a bit wistfully, "In France, it was much the same. But we did not worry about appearances so much as they do here, for we were all secure in our proper places. And, of course, we all *knew* we were lovely and well dressed!"

Madame Dupre joined her in soft laughter, and Celia let her mind wander. If Sir John was close companions with Lord Northington, she fully intended to expand upon their brief acquaintance. Through Harvey, she could learn much about her quarry. And quarry he was, though Northington may not know it. Would he remember her? Would he even recognize the woman in the girl he had once known? Did he ever think about Léonie Sinclair, or had she been only one more woman he'd used and cast aside as unimportant.

Anger burned deeply, a low, smoldering blaze that never eased, never altered, and she thought of how delicious it would be to ruin Northington. He would pay, in whatever way she could manage, for Old Peter's death as well as her mother's. Everyone in London would know what he had done. If she could, she would see him hanged for murder. But that was unlikely. Vengeance would have to be tempered with practicality.

"Child," Madame Dupre said with a puzzled look on her face, "you are so stiff, like a board! Please, you must not worry that I will stick you with a pin. I've not wounded many of my clients."

Celia managed a laugh. "Forgive me, madame. I was thinking of something else. A sudden memory."

"It must be something dreadful, to make you so stiff."

"Yes. It was."

"Poor child," Jacqueline said. "You have suffered so much sorrow."

"Not so very much," Celia said. "Not as much as many others have suffered."

"Perhaps you are right." Jacqueline lapsed into a sorrowful silence that was shared by Madame Dupre, another French emigré who had fled Paris during the terrible revolution.

So many, Celia had learned during her short time

here, had survived horrors. It was no wonder her mother had shied away from discussing those dark days, but spoke instead of the happier times—her love for her husband and their meeting in London.

"But come," Madame Dupre said briskly after a moment, "we must not dwell on those things. They are past now, and we must think only of the coming Season. It will be most exciting this year, I believe, as the Prince of Wales has already begun making preparations for a grand fête...."

As the two women chattered in French about the coming galas, Celia lifted her arms obediently as she was measured and turned this way and that, while the talk turned to silk versus satin for evening, and of course, how low should the décolletage be this year without inviting scandal.

"But I think, with her height, that she should wear the newest fashion," Madame Dupre announced. "Waists are dropping, but necklines are still low enough to tempt the eye without being *too* risqué. A pointed bodice perhaps. Off the shoulders, of course, with long gloves to the elbow. No oversleeves are necessary, for she has such lovely slender arms. For this ball, tulle over white satin, do you not think? Four rouleaux?"

"No," Jacqueline said thoughtfully. "I think perhaps flounces edged with a rollio, and the underskirt with a rouleau...definitely white for her first ball, though not that *glaring* white against her pale skin. And a sash of celestial blue would be so lovely...a complement to Caro's gown as well. What a striking pair they will be!"

Jacqueline's daughter had already been fitted for her

gowns, and she had declined to accompany them for Celia's fittings. Though not antagonistic, Carolyn was very reserved in her welcome, and there had been a certain restraint between them at first.

It had been Carolyn who dictated the rudiments of proper address, the tangle of titles so confusing that Celia made her laugh with her errors.

"No, no," Caro had said when she mistakenly referred to a duke as Sir Charles. "Dukes are always your grace, or the duke of Marlborough, never Sir. His son would be called my lord, as would a viscount, marquess or earl. And never call anyone Lord John unless he is a younger son of a duke or marquess. It's simple, really, if you can remember that the only nobles are princes and dukes. Everyone else, even earls, are commoners. All male peers except dukes are called Lord whatever their title name is, do you see?"

"No," Celia said frankly, and Carolyn had laughed, easing some of the first tension between them.

"We shall continue our lessons until you know it all very well," Caro had assured her, and the past week had been devoted to lessons in protocol as well as titles.

Oh, it was all so much to learn, and nothing could have properly prepared her for the vast differences. Soon it would all be put to the test.

After her first resistance, Celia was now glad she had yielded to the inevitable. It would give her access to Northington.

"And it is, after all, only the small Season, so you need not feel overwhelmed," Jacqueline had said gaily. "It is quite entertaining with everyone arriving back in London after the summer heat."

So it would be endured to achieve her goal. After that, obscurity, no doubt, and a return to America where her services would always be in demand as a French tutor. As long as she allowed no scandal to follow her…

The fickle vagaries of human nature allowed a man like Northington to ignore murder yet condemned a woman who was innocent of all crime. The memory of Maman's shame would haunt Celia for the rest of her life.

A pregnant widow of two years was not allowed in *decent* homes, regardless of the circumstances. At times Celia thought bitterly that what had really killed Maman was the humiliation she had suffered.

It was true Celia was only a child then, but she'd been old enough to recognize her mother's torment, and old enough to vow vengeance on the man responsible….

Now, at last, she was old enough to carry out that vengeance….

4

"Why must you take such vulgar modes of transport, Colter? You have a perfectly lovely carriage-and-four at your disposal. It's unseemly to travel about London in hired hacks."

Colter leaned forward, gave his mother the customary peck on her cheek. She smelled of lavender, a familiar, powdery fragrance he always associated with her. He straightened, a dark brow cocked.

"You make it sound as if I arrived in the butcher's cart."

"You might as well have." Lady Moreland flicked an elegant hand at the maid to indicate where she wished her breakfast tray set. When the servant had gone, she turned to regard her son with an arched brow. "I'm pleased you found time to visit me. I began to wonder if I had offended you in some way."

Colter braced one arm atop the mantel where a cheery fire burned behind brass firedogs. "You know why I don't come more often."

"Yes. I do." She perched daintily upon an upholstered settee, still youthful and graceful despite her years. "Your father has inquired about you."

"Has he." Colter shifted restlessly. "Why?"

"Can a father not inquire about his son without undue suspicion?"

"Other fathers, perhaps. Not mine." Colter moved past his mother to stare out the window into the gardens below. Stone statuary graced fading flower beds, and a fountain trickled cold water from a jug held by a Grecian goddess. Venus, he thought, though Attila the Hun would be more appropriate for the Moreland garden.

"Really, Colter," his mother said behind him. "You should make more effort to compromise."

He turned to face her. Thin sunlight streamed through the windows, creating an aura around Lady Moreland that was almost ethereal. She resembled an elegant stone angel, save for the faint lines of strain that fanned from the corners of her eyes. Her hand shook slightly as she poured hot chocolate into a cup; rich aromatic steam rose in wispy tendrils. She didn't look at him, her attention focused upon the silver tray laden with biscuits, cake and serving ware.

He scowled at her obvious tension.

"What has he been on at you about? Don't deny it. You can't even look at me. Christ above, what tear is he on now that he's upset you?"

Anger edged his words, made them hard and brittle so that his mother set down the china pot and folded her hands in her lap before she looked up at him.

"It's that business with the East India company. The new docks that he's financing have gone beyond the budget, and he's convinced that his uncle is involved in a scheme to ruin him."

"Given Philip's propensity for idleness, I find that accusation unlikely." Colter shrugged when his mother made a small sound of dismay. "You must admit all the animosity seems to come from my father. While Philip may resent the fact that my father inherited when fever took the first heir, he hides it well enough. And he's too bloody lazy to scheme."

"You shouldn't talk about your great-uncle that way. Or your father, for that matter. Really, whatever has gotten into you lately? You were once quite pleasant. Now—"

"Now I'm the reckless Lord Northington, heir to a title and my father's reputation. I can no longer afford to be pleasant. If Grandfather had only lived awhile longer, perhaps we could have all been set free. It was a damned nuisance that he contracted a fever and shared it with the only heir capable of decency. My father's lucky star again, that he inherited after all."

The countess looked distressed, and Colter cursed his harsh tongue. The same fever that had taken the sixth earl and an uncle had also taken his older brother Anthony, the heir, an unexpected death his mother still deeply mourned and his father cursed.

He crossed the small sitting room and sat beside his mother on the striped brocade settee in front of the fire.

"I'm in a wicked mood, *ma mére*. It has nothing to do with you. I'll go up and see him before I leave. I always do, don't I?"

"Yes." Blue eyes not quite as bright as his stared

at him with a searching penetration. "You always do your duty. You're an honorable man."

"Don't let that get about. I want nothing to sully my reputation as a scoundrel and a rake, if you don't mind. It's much more convenient to have anxious mamas avoid me rather than push their horse-faced daughters in my direction."

A faint smile touched the corners of her lips. "Not even your sullied reputation will divert some, I'm afraid. Your presence at a fête has been requested by one of my dearest friends, and I trust you won't disappoint me."

Colter lifted an ironic brow. "How grim."

"Just make an appearance. You aren't required to stay long."

"Which of your friends is ruining my evening with a room filled with chattering ninnies, may I ask? Or do you intend to surprise me— God, it's not Lady Throgmorton, I trust."

"No, not even I would be so cruel as to make that demand of you. It's Lady Leverton. She's been my dear friend for some time. Her daughter was just presented to the prince and is to be wed next summer, but apparently wishes to enjoy the small Season. She also mentioned that her cousin's daughter from the Colonies will be presented. A charming girl, I understand. Quiet, and not prone to giggling or stammering. I find that refreshing these days."

Colter thought of Harvey and the young woman who had accompanied Lady Leverton. He was wrong. London was small enough for coincidences, after all.

And it couldn't have come at a more perfect time.

"Since you ask it of me," he said, and saw his

mother's surprise, "I'll let you fling me to the wolves. Just don't expect me to linger for the coup de grace."

"Really, Colter."

"Ah, now I've earned your reproach. I should offer my apologies to you."

"Yes, you should. But all will be forgiven if you pay particular attention to Lady Leverton's cousin. I've been assured she has excellent manners. Be charming enough to assure her success, but do not be *too* charming. No sense in giving the wrong impression to either the young lady or to Lady Leverton."

"Now I see your plot. You're a disgraceful schemer, and should be ashamed, but I see that you have no scruples at all. You know I hate to be charming."

"But you do it so effortlessly when you choose." Her smile was serene. "You surprise me, Colter. I thought it would take much more to wring an agreement from you."

"You know I've never been able to refuse anything you ask of me."

"Then I ask that you be agreeable to your father. Ah. I see that doesn't get an immediate response from you. Are you more able to refuse me now?"

"Let's just say I'd rather clean the Aegean stables. It would be less messy, and far more successful."

Unperturbed by his observation, she said, "Excellent. Now, be so good as to visit your father before he sends Brewster down to fetch you. He's already in a rare mood. Try not to quarrel with him."

Rising to his feet, Colter regarded his mother for a brief moment. She sat erect as she always did, her bearing innately aristocratic. It was a posture he had come to associate with times of duress, an indication that the earl was behaving toward her with more than just his usual perversity. He bent over the hand she held out to him.

"I'll visit the dragon, but I make no promises. He can hire whipping boys. I refuse to be one."

"Just—" She paused, then said softly, "Just try to remember his illness."

"His *illness* has little to do with his nature. If you prefer to forget that, I choose to remember."

The countess said nothing, but her eyes held a sorrowful recognition of the truth. He felt like a bloody bastard reminding her of it.

The earl was irascible as always, made even more petulant by his chafing against the infirmity that kept him confined to his chamber most of the time. His valet, Brewster, hovered nearby, tending him solicitously despite the old man's impatience.

"It's about time you had the decency to answer my summons," Moreland growled, glaring at Colter from beneath a heavy shelf of brow. "You've become damned insolent."

"Yes. Is there something specific you wished to speak with me about?"

Moreland's glare held evidence of his old vigor, but his hand shook as he gripped the coverlet over his legs with a knotted fist. "It may interest you to learn that one of our ships is apparently lost at sea with a valuable cargo. Or perhaps your business acumen isn't sharp enough to understand what that means to our financial interests."

The earl glared up at him, his insult left hanging in the air. Colter shrugged.

"No, probably not. Will it affect my inheritance?"

The earl's jaw clenched; a muscle leaped beneath his pitted skin. "It should have been you who died instead of Anthony. He was a fitting heir, with a true sense of his heritage. Damn you, you're your mother's son—a weakling, a profligate without proper appreciation for the Moreland heritage!"

"Yes, I certainly agree with that. Tony should have been your heir. He aspired to your legacy, after all, while I prefer my amusements to be willing."

Colter's gaze was riveted on his father, but he heard the soft click of the closing door that indicated Brewster had deemed it wise not to be privy to this particular conversation. The valet was noted for his discretion, a wise habit that had kept him in the earl's employ for the past twenty years.

"I never know what the bloody hell you're talking about these days," Moreland snapped. The bank of windows behind him filtered light that softened the earl's sagging features but not his harsh tone. "You make these obscure remarks that are completely incomprehensible."

"Yes, so it seems. Do you refer to the *India*, by any chance? It is reported to have gone down off the islands near Lubang. She was carrying a full cargo of spices and specie, according to my sources."

Moreland snorted. "Which we can ill afford to lose. As you are a major shareholder in the company, and now the family representative, you must meet with the board. A cursed business. First, the docks have gone beyond budget and now this! We have creditors who'll want an explanation for the ship's loss."

"No doubt. The obvious explanation will certainly not suffice. I presume Leatherwood has the ship's manifests and budget reports I'll need."

"Yes. Placate the board, Northington. We must have time to recover from this loss. We can't risk losing investors. It would cause far too many complications." The earl squinted up at his son, his mouth set in a bitter slash. "I've often wondered if my father somehow knew the trouble it would cause me to have you on the board. If he'd only left *me* those crucial shares..."

As the earl's voice trailed into silence, Colter reflected that his grandfather had certainly known what he was doing. The former earl had done what he could to curtail his heir's access to the family fortune. As no doubt the present earl would continue to do to his own heir.

"Do not," the earl added tersely, "speak of this to my uncle. The less Philip knows at the moment, the better I like it."

"I wasn't aware Philip was involved."

"He's not. Or shouldn't be. But curse him, he manages to find out about my business affairs far too often, and I don't trust him."

"Such familial devotion," Colter observed dryly.

"No more so than he's exhibited for me. He has always thought the title should belong to him upon the death of my grandfather. 'The younger son should inherit his father's estate, not the grandson,' he said. Rubbish!"

"So you claim, yet I've never heard a word spoken

about it from Philip. He seems quite content with his inheritance. He enjoys being an idle gentleman.''

Moreland snorted. ''Don't be fooled by his pretense of complacence. You consider me ruthless, but I assure you that my uncle has refined the art.''

Colter didn't reply. There had always been rivalry between the two men, and though Philip Worth—Lord Easton—may indeed be the epitome of a wastrel, Colter had never known him to act with any malice.

Unlike his father, who had acted with malice too many times to count.

The earl flapped a hand at his son, an indication he was being dismissed. Brewster returned to tend him, a silent, efficient valet fussing over the blanket draped over the earl as if there was no one else in the room, as if Colter had already departed.

He left the house without seeing his mother again, his boots echoing in the wide, empty cavern of the entrance hall, the gleaming black-and-white marble floors spotless and sterile. The quiet peace of the house was deceptive. Beneath the facade of serenity lurked a cesspool of anger and corruption. The earl thrived on it. Until his illness, he had instigated scandal and schemes without a shred of restraint. Only his wealth and title had saved him from ruin.

It fell to his son and heir—the unwanted heir—to walk a fine line between his father's tainted reputation and the necessity of maintaining the facade without being tarnished by the same brush. Publicly he would not denounce his father, but privately, he did all he could to show his contempt for the man the earl had become. It had become a game of sorts between them. A serious game in which winner took all.

Christ, it was just as bitter a regret for him as for his father that Anthony had died from that fever. There were times he felt trapped, imprisoned and raging against the invisible bars of his cell.

He welcomed strife, welcomed a challenge, welcomed anything that would distract him. Why not? It was better than the reality of his situation, the trap that closed in around him a little more every day.

It wasn't the mechanics entailed in the myriad technicalities of a vast shipping business that he found stifling, for that could be energizing if he was left to his own devices and decisions. But it was intolerable to be in the position of having his every decision supervised and examined as if he was still a schoolboy at Eton.

If not for his mother, he would have damned the title and the money and left long ago, taken the Grand Tour that Napoleon had denied him until His Majesty's invitation to lead an army against the Corsican. It was not as he had first envisioned touring the Continent, with the smell of gunpowder and stench of death in his nostrils, the screams of dying men drowning out everything but the instinct to survive. He had learned the art of killing, refined it, then been sent home to be civilized once the war ended.

It was difficult. Acquired savagery still surfaced at times, still seethed beneath the thin veneer of civility. So he'd left England for a while, traveled, seen places in the world that were exotic and dangerous. He'd gone to South America, Spanish California and New Orleans in the American South, and when he'd come home at last, it was to find his entire life irrevocably changed.

Had he remained in England, he would probably have died of the same fever that had killed his brother. It was an ironic twist of fate that he'd survived legions of French while Anthony—the heir, the golden son—had died at home in his bed.

There were times Colter almost envied him.

5

Light from thousands of candles and wall sconces illuminated the vast ballroom. Glittering jewels sparkled on bare bosoms and elegant coiffures. Music soared above the chatter and laughter of hundreds of guests, linen-draped tables lined walls and potted plants cast feathery shadows on polished floors. Celia scarcely recognized her cousin's ballroom. It exceeded her childhood dreams.

It had seemed immense when vacant, but now the ballroom had shrunk to a suffocating constriction of space. For a brief moment, she was slightly panicked. How had she ever thought for a single instant that she could manage this? She was out of her depths here among these people far too accustomed to the trappings of wealth and polite society. Since arriving in London she had realized how far apart her world was from this glittering society. The chasm was wide. Almost too wide.

Nervously she ran a swift hand over the skirts of her new gown, the satin and tulle embroidered with tiny gold stars and ending in a graceful train. It was caught just beneath her breasts with a wide sash also embroidered with gold stars upon lush blue velvet. Matching slippers were adorned with stars sewn in glittering gold threads. The only concession to the cool night was a silk shawl of sheer white, spangled with more gold stars.

Lily had dressed her hair, piling it in luxuriant curls atop her crown and allowing artful tendrils to fall over her forehead, temples and neck. A wreath of gold stars was placed upon her brow, with a matching piece that was attached to the comb securing her curls.

"It is the *à l'enfant* style," Lily said, gazing at her with approval when Celia had stared at her reflection in the mirror. *"Ravissante!"*

Astonished at the transformation, Celia hadn't even heard Jacqueline come into the room until she came up behind her, saying with delight, "How beautiful you are, petite. But you should hurry, for we must form the receiving line."

"I...I'll be down very soon, I promise," she'd said, and saw that Jacqueline understood.

The light hand on her shoulder squeezed tightly. "You will be quite the thing tonight. No one will be able resist not only your beauty, but your sweet charm. Just be yourself, and all will be well."

But would it? Celia thought distractedly that if Jacqueline knew the truth she would not be so certain of success. There were moments she considered leaving rather than disappointing her cousin, but still she stayed. She must face Northington again, must *see* for herself the man who had brought so much pain into her life. She could never be free until he paid for his injustice.

Now that the moment was here, she wavered between anticipation and stark fear. Yet the face in her mirror looked composed, showed nothing of her inner turmoil.

At last she took the wide, curved staircase to the ballroom on the second floor. She waited, heart thumping an erratic rhythm. It was so crowded, a whirl of men in evening breeches and elegant coats, a glitter of jewels and flashing smiles in a sea of strange faces.

Finally she spied Jacqueline in the receiving line. She was in her clement, laughing gaily, reveling in the success of her first ball of the Season. The guest list included most of the upper strata of society, and quite a few were in attendance. Ladies Jersey and Cowper formed a gracious quartet with Jacqueline and Carolyn. Celia knew them by reputation only. The formidable ladies could ruin a young lady's aspirations with a simple rejection to the inclusion of Almacks, their vaunted club, and it was the single-minded goal of many London mamas to have their daughters accepted into that desired society.

Celia had no illusions about her future. Yet her desire to please Jacqueline made her dutifully agree to all the preparations. It was necessary to feign interest in a suitable marriage in order to achieve her true goal.

Oh, but she truly felt guilty over the subterfuge. Jacqueline was far too kind and loving to be duped in this manner, and several times Celia had hovered on the verge of confession. Only the memories of Maman's tragic death and the man responsible kept her still silent.

And now she would once more face Lord Northington. Fingers gripped her ivory fan so tightly it crackled a protest, and she relaxed before it broke.

I must remain calm. It is the moment I've waited for all these years....

Would Northington recognize her? Remember the little girl whose mother he had killed as surely as if he had plunged a dagger into her heart?

"Celia dear," Jacqueline beckoned, a gloved hand urging her forward. "Come and meet Lady Jersey and Lady Cowper."

Pasting a smile on her face, Celia moved forward to greet the two formidable grande dames of London society. Oh, she thought in surprise when they greeted her quite graciously, they are very pleasant. Perhaps it is just their reputations that are intimidating, though they *are* assessing me quite openly.

"Will you remain long in our fair city?" Lady Jersey inquired, her lace-and-ivory fan wafting a slight breeze over elegant features as she gazed at Celia. "Lady Leverton informs me that you've only recently arrived from the Colonies."

"Yes. I'm not at all certain how long I'll remain in London. I suppose that depends upon the kindness of my godmother and her husband. Lady Leverton has been far too good to me, and I'm truly enjoying London sights."

Emily Cowper leaned forward, fascination evident in her round face. Rumored to be the most accommodating of Almack's patronesses, she seemed genuinely interested in the American colonies. "Tell me, how does our city compare to the Colonies? Is it true that wild savages roam the streets of cities in America, or is that only one of those ridiculous rumors that so often abound?''

Celia snagged a glass of champagne punch from the tray carried by a passing footman, and smiled brightly over the rim.

''As it happens, it's partially true. On occasion the natives have been known to visit the city, but for the most part, they prefer their own company. Can you blame them? However, it wasn't so long ago that uprisings and massacres indeed were visited upon American cities. The retaliation was quite harsh.''

''Ah, I do not understand this American penchant for hostility,'' Lady Jersey remarked, blithely ignoring the recent war with France. She flicked her fingers in the air to indicate contempt. ''One would think they would be too busy rebuilding their primitive capital to even consider retaliation upon savages.''

Celia delicately refrained from mentioning that it had been British soldiers who had burned Washington and the Capitol before ravaging the countryside only five years before. She said instead, ''There are hostile tribes of natives still inhabiting the wilderness, but they remain distant for the most part.''

''How terrifying!'' Lady Cowper gave a delicious shiver. ''I cannot imagine such a horrid fate. All those brown men running about half-naked and abducting females—they have been known to do that, no?''

Celia nodded. ''It has happened.''

''How terrible! I'm so glad I live where it's quite civilized.''

''You wouldn't think it so civilized if you were to walk past St. Giles Cathedral,'' Lady Jersey said dryly. ''All those wretched women hanging about, and even the children ready to cut your purse—or throat—without blinking...."

As the conversation turned to other subjects, Lady Cowper's gaze drifted across the ballroom and her brow shot up. "Oh my, *do* look who has arrived!"

Turning, Jacqueline gave a small gasp of delight. "It is Northington!"

A chill shivered down Celia's spine, and she could not at once bring herself to turn and look at the man who had destroyed her childhood. She emptied her champagne and gave the glass to a footman. Her fingers tightened on the bone handle of her fan. She waved it idly back and forth, rigidly waiting. Hairs on the back of her neck tightened; it felt as if the careful cluster of artfully arranged curls on her crown were standing erect.

Lady Jersey said, "He arrives late, and does not even acknowledge the receiving line. Is that Sir John Harvey with him? Perhaps I missed his name on the guest list..."

Jacqueline's chin lifted slightly at the implication, and though her mouth was smiling, there was a glint in her eyes. "I don't turn away pleasant company. Harvey's father is a baron, and Sir John I find quite charming."

"Yes, perhaps. His father is a member of the Carlton House set and quite fast, you know. A gambler, as is his son, but neither is as proficient as Northington."

"Neither man has the *best* reputation," Lady Cowper said with a flutter of her fan, and her eyes held a speculative glow. "Yet he is so attractive, for all that he seems so...well, *dangerous,* I suppose you could say."

Lady Jersey lifted her lorgnette to gaze across the room. "You must mean Northington. A handsome man, and yes, so dangerous. Quite the rogue, they say. Very adept with the pistol and the sword, and has been known to walk away from several duels, though of course, that's still frowned upon these days. How many commendations did he receive for his military service?"

A gleam of naked excitement brightened Lady Cowper's eyes. "One commendation was awarded for Northington's courage in leading a charge against Napoleon's right flank in which nearly every man of his squad was killed but him. But, of course, I'm not surprised that he survived. He has a certain *air* about him...not just dangerous, but—savage. Yes, that's it! His skin is nearly as dark as one of Miss St. Clair's savages, don't you think? Oh, I wonder what he would look like half-naked. I'd allow him to ravish *me,* I vow!"

They all laughed but Celia, who managed to force a stiff smile. No one even noticed her silence. But how could they know what had happened to Maman? Or that she was near dizzy with suppressed anger, anticipation and nausea at this reminder of it?

Oh, I cannot do this! she thought. I cannot stand and listen to them talk about him as if he's gallant or brave, or even *human!*

But, of course, she could say nothing, and the talk of Northington continued, Lady Jersey once more ignoring the feelings of her companions as she said, "It was reported that Northington disposed of the French at an alarming rate. A bold soldier—and an even bolder rake. He's cut quite a swath through not only actresses, but several high-born ladies. You *do* recall that scandal two years ago with Letitia Goodridge? She's still in seclusion, I understand. Quite heartbroken, they say. Apparently Sir Lawrence has locked her away in the country since she was so imprudent as to make a public scene with Northington. Foolish chit. At least Lady Katherine was discreet. Discretion is everything."

The ladies nodded approval and agreement, a silent pact that set the standard of the day.

"But do look at him," Jacqueline said in a whisper that reeked of triumph. "Northington could persuade any woman to folly if he chose. I think he's a devastatingly handsome man, and from one of the oldest families. Scandal barely touches them."

"I would think," Lady Jersey observed, "that would depend upon the nature of the scandal. Ah. He sees us. I expect he will properly present himself now."

Celia steeled herself to turn and look toward Lord Northington at last, and drew in a deep breath for courage. Surely he was not truly handsome after ten years, when he had not been what she recalled as very appealing even in his younger days. Indeed, if not for his lineage and family's influence in the shipping industry, even Americans would not have found his company especially desirable.

Nerves jangled, her stomach throbbed and there was a loud humming in her ears as she turned at last to look once more upon the man she hated.

Yet she could not find him in the throng of satins,

jewels and lamplight. She had thought there would be instant recognition, that the hatred she had nursed all these years would immediately focus on Northington despite the time that had passed. Yet none of the men present had the face of her childhood nightmares.

Bewildered, she stood stiffly as her cousin moved forward to greet another man. She had a vague impression of a tall man with dark hair, impeccably dressed and with an air of polite boredom in his movements, but her gaze focused beyond him.

Celia searched the crowd for Northington, her eyes scanning faces restlessly, barely paying attention as Jacqueline began the introductions. Only when the hated name penetrated her distraction did she realize that the man before her bore the same name.

"Lord Northington," she repeated tonelessly, and saw from the corner of her eye her cousin's slight frown.

"Yes, dear." Jacqueline stressed the first word. "Surely you recall his name on the guest list. Northington has honored us with his presence this evening, and we are most delighted."

"This must be the young lady who has captured Sir John's instant admiration," a deep voice said, the tone slow, rich, seductive.

She turned her gaze to look fully at the man before her. Her breath caught.

Eyes of a startling blue gazed down at her from beneath black lashes, and Celia recognized him at once as the man she had seen aboard the *Liberty*. Confused, it took a moment to find her voice.

"Sir John is most flattering if he has indeed expressed admiration for me, my lord," she finally said.

"I would say he has been truthful, for a refreshing change of pace. Flattery imparts insincerity, but in this case he's quite correct. You are indeed lovely."

His sensual voice had a husky, mocking quality that sent a shiver down her spine. He reached for her hand, took it in his broad palm, held her fingers in a light clasp as he bent to place a kiss upon her gloved knuckles. Celia did not resist. She felt as if all eyes were watching, waiting for her response.

Panic swelled, coupled with an overpowering need to escape this room that had suddenly grown far too stifling; the music and laughter and smell of perfume threatened to suffocate her.

But it was his touch that unnerved her most, burning into her skin even through the gloves. She snatched her hand away, saw the leap of surprise in his eyes, heard Carolyn's soft gasp.

Faintly, she managed to say, "How kind of you. If you will excuse me, I must attend some personal business."

Aware of Jacqueline's disconcerted stare and Carolyn's gaping expression, Celia maneuvered a path through the crowd without taking flight or stumbling. She had to escape that penetrating gaze and the discovery that this Northington was *not* the man she had hated for so long. But who was he? A brother? Cousin? Or perhaps he was a son... Whoever he was, he wasn't the man she had come to ruin.

There had to be two Lord Northingtons.

And she had to collect her wits before she said or did something else foolish. Already, she had risked offending her cousin as well as Northington. Her direct cut would not go unnoticed, nor would her ill-bred behavior. It was nearly unforgivable, and she must seek a way to make amends or she may ruin everything.

Celia sought a quiet corner away from the crowd and din of revelry, and sank down upon a cushioned bench in an alcove across the hall. Her lovely gown was not made for sitting at all but for dancing and standing, yet at the moment she didn't care. Her head throbbed and nausea churned so that she felt as if she would truly be sick at any moment. She should leave, but how could she? To go upstairs now would be an insult to Jacqueline after all she'd done, all the preparations she'd made and her hopes for her beloved Léonie's daughter to make a decent match.

A burble of hysterical laughter caught in her throat. How can I tell her that's the farthest thing from my mind? No. I must remain. Ah, I'm such a coward to flee....

She drew in a deep breath to calm herself. After all this time, if she was undone by so trivial a setback as the wrong Lord Northington, then she might as well have remained in America and let Maman's death go unavenged.

Rising to her feet, she put a hand against the wall to brace herself as she smoothed her skirts and collected her wits. It was fashionable for females to swoon. Perhaps she would use that excuse, though she detested those who yielded to such feeble behavior.

"Are you ill, Miss St. Clair?"

Celia's head jerked up. Northington stood before her, his dark visage a mask of polite concern. She considered briefly, then stifled the impulse to flee, and nodded.

"I fear I felt a bit overwhelmed by all the noise. I'm accustomed to a more quiet life."

"So I understand. Lady Leverton informs me that you're from Georgetown in the American capital."

"Yes. Yes, I lived there with my parents until their deaths." She said it calmly, but inside, a volley of angry, baffling emotions seethed.

How distressing to be reminded—and how dare he stand there staring down at her with that cool, confident smile on his handsome face, as if he knew how attractive he was, how intimidated he made her feel...how his voice seemed to reach down into her with the potent heat of fine brandy...

"My father once lived in Georgetown," he was saying, "but it was over ten years ago. He rarely speaks of his travels, but my mother tells me it's a lovely region."

His father...his father... God, it's his father who raped and murdered...

"Yes," she said when the silence stretched too long, aware of his narrowed stare, the cock of his black brow and his faintly sardonic smile. "Parts of it are certainly lovely, though much of it is giving way to new buildings and construction... If you will pardon me, my lord, I do feel a bit unsteady yet."

I have to escape him, she thought distractedly. Oh, why won't he go away?

But Northington moved swiftly to cup her elbow, his hand easily supporting her as she eased back to the bench cushions. His hand lingered, fingers strong and demanding upon her arm.

"You didn't seem the type to swoon, Miss St. Clair," he said with a tilt of his dark brow.

Perhaps swooning would have to remain the convenient excuse for her peculiar behavior, she thought with angry distraction. She took several deep breaths to clear her head, aware of him so close to her, his hand upon her arm, the heat from his body a raw force that threatened to suffocate her. He was unnerving. And he was the wrong man.

Yet he was Lord Northington's son... Perhaps not all was lost. Through the son, she might yet reach the father.

Yes...

A faint smile curved her lips as she tilted back her head to look up at Northington through her lashes.

6

Shadows draped the recess beneath the stairs, and light filtered through potted palms into the alcove to barely illuminate Celia St. Clair's face. Wide-eyed, she stared up at Colter in the thin light. A delicate fineness of bone structure rescued her features from the ordinary and made them striking. High cheekbones, a full mouth with well-shaped lips, a hint of cleft in her chin, and wide-spaced gray—no, green eyes were made unusual by a trick of fate. Harvey was right. She was a prime article.

She was also feigning a swoon and doing very badly at it.

"I've seen better actresses in the pit at Covent Garden," he said when she did not reply to his observation, and saw her eyes widen, absorbing dull light like a cheap mirror.

"No doubt you have, my lord," she said with a lift of perfectly arched eyebrows. "But what has that to do with me?"

"Your swoon. You're not faint."

A smile curved her mouth into a tempting bow, and she met his gaze boldly. "Not in the least bit."

Her voice was husky, low-pitched and slow, each word a rich drawl. He smiled.

"Ah, then I am to understand that you wished to avoid my company."

"You're very astute, my lord."

Little baggage! It was an unexpected response. He had anticipated the usual demur, the protests that she truly was of delicate constitution—or maybe even a shy confession that she had wished to speak with him alone—but not this frank surrender and even more blunt admission that she did not desire his company.

His suspicions may be wrong; her acquaintance with James Carlisle could be as innocent as it had seemed.

"Am I that heinous?" He moved to sit beside her on the bench. She did not move coyly away, but gazed at him with a steady stare. A pulse beat in the hollow of her throat, ivory skin gleaming softly in the pale light as she seemed to consider his question.

"Having just made your acquaintance, I could hardly come to such a conclusion so rapidly. Did you follow me just to ask that question, my lord?"

"No." He observed her with growing amusement. "Your cousin sent me after you. A rather obvious ploy to extend our acquaintance."

"Then I trust you are now convinced I had nothing to do with that."

"Not entirely." His eyes narrowed, noting that brown lashes lowered over a gleam in her eyes she couldn't quite hide. For the first time that he could recall, he wasn't certain of a woman's motives. It was intriguing.

He leaned closer, saw her involuntary recoil. "It could be a conspiracy between you to compromise me. You needn't work so hard at it. I can be quite adaptable."

"That's very enlightened of you, my lord, but I fear you overrate your charms."

She turned slightly, giving him an excellent view of the tops of her breasts above the edge of her bodice—a deliberate ploy that revealed an enticing shadow between them. Tempting. Provocative. And damned distracting.

He dragged his attention slowly away when she said in husky, beguiling tones, "Now, if you'll excuse me, I do not wish to court unnecessary gossip or nasty speculation as to our activities in a dark corner. Your reputation may thrive on such, but mine, I assure you, will not."

She rose from the bench and he rose with her, putting out his arm to delay her progress, stretching it in front of her so that she halted and turned to look up at him with a haughtily lifted brow.

"You are impeding me, my lord."

"Only for a moment." He resisted the sudden impulse to touch a single golden curl that draped over her bare shoulder; it drew his attention back to the pale gleaming breasts, rounded and perfect above her demure bodice.

"If you are through ogling me, my lord, I wish to pass. Please move aside."

A slow smile curved his mouth. "But perhaps I'm

not through *ogling* you, Miss St. Clair. I find the view most enticing.''

''And I find you boorish. Step aside or I shall call for a footman to remove you from my path.''

She meant it. There was determination in her eyes, a hot, fierce gleam that convinced him. He let his arm drop and she moved past him without a backward glance to glide gracefully across the hallway and toward the ballroom.

Colter crossed his arms and leaned against the wall. Twice in the space of a few minutes, she had given him the cut direct. It was as irritating as it was intriguing.

''I say, old man, looks as if the lady ain't that interested. I'm shocked.'' Harvey loomed out of the dim alcove shadows, grinning like an idiot. ''My first opinion of her intelligence has just been proven.''

''Devil take you, Harvey.'' Colter watched as she moved across the hallway to enter the ballroom. ''You're enjoying this far too much.''

Harvey glanced after Miss St. Clair with a thoughtful expression. ''Not at all,'' he said with a shrug. ''But the lady certainly is. If I were as plump in the pocket as you are, I'd have a go at her myself, but I need a wealthy wife instead of a beauty.''

It would do no good to remind Harvey that he had only himself to blame for his lack of coin; gambling whittled away what fortune he had inherited from his mother, while his father, the Baron Leawood, habitually gambled away his own bank account. ''You should make wise investments,'' he said, ''so you can afford her.''

''What of your shipping investments?'' Harvey

asked, hazel eyes reflecting the dim glow of a wall sconce that barely lightened the alcove shadows. "Is it true that one of your ships went down with all hands and cargo aboard?"

"It's always possible. Nothing is known for certain yet."

"Rumor has it that you're negotiating to purchase a fleet of steamships now that a vessel has successfully navigated the Atlantic. Deuced amazing thing, the powering of ships by steam instead of sail, but efficient enough, I suppose. These iron monsters are said to be safer, more reliable in storms without the weight of top masts and sails, but bloody strange looking."

Colter regarded him with a lifted brow. "Where did you hear that rumor?"

Those negotiations were private, and still not yet completed. It was his own venture, since his father and the board were reluctant to take on any new, unproven mode of transport yet. A foolish failure to seize new opportunity in his opinion. How the hell did Harvey know of it?

Startled, Harvey shrugged. "It's just a vague rumor I heard at White's—or maybe it was Brooks's. Damned if I can remember who said it or when. Been meaning to ask you about it. Intriguing business, these new inventions, but risky at times."

"Any business venture is risky. Without risk, there's little profit."

"And you're a master at taking risks, old boy." A faint smile curled his mouth. "A hero with a drawer full of commendations and medals. The risk of investing funds in precarious ventures does not compare."

"I never knew you to be so interested in my business affairs, Harvey." It was said softly, but there was a steely warning beneath the comment that was obvious even to the baronet.

Harvey shrugged.

"Not so much interested as intrigued, on an idle basis. You know where my interests lie for the most part. I merely envy your ability to spin gold from straw."

Amused, Colter drawled, "It still takes effort on my part to do the spinning, Harvey. Think of something other than cards and drink and your fortunes will change quickly enough. Marry a wealthy widow."

"That's easy enough for you to say, when all you have to do is crook your finger and females flock to you. It'd be simpler to understand if it was only your money, but from the sighs and moans of unrequited love I hear, you've something more to offer than mere coin."

"Yes. It's called a title. Women may claim to want only love, but beneath the simpering sighs and fluttering hearts you'll find a tenacious desire for control. They just cloak it in vows of passion and loyalty."

"Cynical bastard, aren't you."

"I prefer to think of it as cautious."

"You would, of course, deny any involvement with the luscious Countess D'Argent, for instance? Or the ever so lovely Lady Montravers, neither of whom need another title when they have their husbands' names and money?"

Harvey laughed when Colter merely cocked a brow at him, then inclined his head toward the ballroom and said with a meaningful glance, "Here comes one of your former *involvements* now. It's time for me to disappear."

A whiff of perfume caught Colter's attention and diverted it to the lovely brunette crossing the foyer.

"Northington, what a delight to see you again. It's been far too long."

Lady Katherine, daughter of an earl, wife of the earl of Cresswood, glided toward him on an inexorable course, her scent and smile promising pleasant diversions.

An insatiable lover, Katherine was still a beauty. It had been three years since they'd slept together. The parting had been amicable enough, with both moving on to other partners. Now she was wed to an earl, her goal at last attained.

"Lady Cresswood," he said politely, and bowed over the hand she held out to him as if they were the barest of acquaintances.

She tapped him with her folded fan. "Rogue. Don't pretend you scarcely know me. *I've* not forgotten former—pleasures—even if you seem to have done so."

"I never forget beautiful women or fast horses," he said with a faint smile, and would have released her hand had she not gripped him tightly in her fingers.

"Sir John," she said without looking at Harvey. "How pleasant to see you again."

Harvey promptly took his cue. "And you, my lady. Pardon me, if you will, as I see some old friends beckoning me."

Katherine didn't bother to acknowledge his departure, but kept her amber gaze on Colter.

"It's been far too long, you wicked scoundrel. Are you avoiding me?"

"Not you, but I've no desire to meet your husband at dawn under the oaks in Hyde Park."

She laughed, a throaty sound, her husky voice a purr when she said softly, "Am I not worth risking your life?"

"Decidedly. But no woman is worth prison."

Another playful tap of her fan on his arm, and she released his hand to run her fingers up his sleeve in a light caress. "My my, we do have our preferences straight. What makes you so certain you would kill my husband in a duel? You might—" she leaned close, her breath a warmth against his cheek "—only wound him."

"If I'm put to the trouble of meeting a man with weapons, my sweet, I do not leave him alive to try again."

"I always said you were a dangerous beast." She drew back slightly. Excitement gleamed in those amber eyes, a golden glow that couldn't hide the sheen of barely concealed lust. Many were their nights together when he'd left her bed with claw marks on his back, marks she'd made in the heat of passion until he'd sworn at her, jerked her hands over her head to take her roughly, as she liked him to do. Lady Katherine preferred her sexual encounters to be contests, and bloodletting was expected. He had learned quickly enough to treat her as a whore and not a lady. It heightened her passion.

Now she leaned even closer, displaying the generous swells of her breasts. She'd rouged her nipples; they were clearly visible beneath the low bodice of her gown, an invitation and promise.

"I've missed you," she murmured, and he took her

hand from his sleeve to bring it to his mouth, lips grazing her knuckles lightly at first, then with his teeth. She drew in a sharp, excited breath.

"You've not had a dearth of admirers in your bed from what I hear, Katherine," he said, and she pursed her lips in a pretense of pouting.

"None as formidable as you, Colter. You're the only man capable of earning my respect."

"You mean obedience. Give them a whip to stripe your lovely backside, and they'll earn your respect quickly enough."

"Oh, that's something to consider."

He smiled, a sardonic twist of his mouth. No doubt, Lady Katherine already owned silken whips and ropes and other toys to play the games she liked. She was a feral creature, with tiger eyes and a body made for pleasure, not for the demure social life a title and money required.

"You'd do well as a bird of paradise," he drawled. Instead of being insulted, she agreed.

"I've thought of it. If I could manage it without anyone knowing my identity, I swear I'd enjoy it. I'd be the most sought after demimonde in all of England."

"I've no doubt of that, little cat. But behave yourself here. Eyes and ears are everywhere."

She'd slipped her hand between their bodies to run her fingers over his belly and lower, practiced strokes of her hand that summoned an instant erection.

"Damn you," he said calmly, and grasped her wrist in a steely grip. She only laughed, brows arching.

"It's dark in this corner, Colter. Let's step back a bit. I'll lift my skirts and you—"

"Require much more time than we'd have here," he cut in. He flicked the backs of his fingers against the soft curve of her cheek in a light rebuke. "Don't tempt me. I've enough temptations."

"Yes, so I saw earlier." Unperturbed by his refusal, quite confident in her own beauty and ability to arouse him, she tilted her head toward the ballroom. "That milk and water Colonial with no manners. Lady Leverton presents her as her protégé, but it's doubtful she'll be accepted. It will be most surprising if Lady Jersey grants her a voucher to Almack's."

"I doubt Miss St. Clair will feel the lack. I've not noticed many men here asking Lady Jersey's opinion."

"No? Perhaps you're right." Katherine glanced toward the ballroom again, her gaze narrowed and thoughtful. "Do you intend to pursue Miss St. Clair?"

"Pursue is hardly the word I'd use, but I've never been one to turn down an invitation from a lovely lady. Do you have any objections?"

"Several hundred, but all purely personal. Do give it a try. It should be amusing to observe. I predict she will be quite overcome by your attentions, but hardly swept away."

Again the folded fan tapped against his chest playfully. "I recognize her type, Colter. Ice runs in her veins instead of hot blood as in mine. You'll grow weary of trying to thaw her out and seek warmer beds quite soon. My bed is always...very...warm."

The last was said huskily as she drew her hand from the slim column of her throat to toy with an ornate ruby-and-gold necklace circling her neck. Long fingers idly twisted the ruby pendant that dangled between her breasts, dragging it over plump swells to caress the rouged nipples so easily visible beneath her plunging bodice.

"Ever subtle, aren't you," he observed, and her smile widened.

"Subtlety is overrated, my lord Northington. Too bad I didn't know your brother would die and you would be in line for the title. I might have waited for you."

"You wouldn't like marriage to me," he said bluntly. "I'd beat you every time you were unfaithful."

She shivered. "A delicious temptation."

"You'd tire of it soon enough."

"What you really mean is *you* would tire of it soon enough."

"You know me much better than I thought, Katherine."

"Yes, my handsome, dangerous cavalier, I certainly do. Go now, for I see that the little Colonial has presented you with a challenge you're determined to meet. When you tire of the cold, I'll be waiting."

Colter left the alcove and reentered the ballroom. He hadn't bothered correcting Katherine. Let her think what she would. He had no intention of explaining his true reasons for being here. He just wished he knew what to think of Celia St. Clair.

Was she a green-eyed little witch who had managed to wheedle her way into a society where she didn't quite fit? Or were there darker secrets that lay beneath the facade of a guileless American? Was she involved in conspiracy and anarchy with James Carlisle? He was a rum one, and the reason for Colter's brief voyage on the bucket known as the *Liberty.* Yet it didn't seem likely that Celia St. Clair was a part of the conspiracy. What would she have to gain? She wasn't English and had no vested interest.

Yet there had been deceit in those wide green eyes, a glint that promised hell to pay for the man so bold or foolish enough to try to peel away the layers of guile to get to the truth.

It should be easy enough to do. Yet it should have been easy enough to intimidate her.

But Celia St. Clair had not been intimidated, nor even interested. She had been—indifferent.

He saw her on the dance floor, where she stood out in an endless sea of females clad in pale muslin or silk or satin. She wasn't the tallest woman there, nor even the most beautiful, but she was definitely intriguing.

She had accepted a dance with Reginald Harwood, the youngest son of a landed baron, and Colter watched as she performed the steps of the contredanse with fluid grace. The hem of her gown lifted around trim ankles as her feet moved across the floor, slippers glittering with golden threads that caught the light.

When Harwood returned her to Lady Leverton and bowed over her hand, Colter moved forward. It was time to get the obligatory dance out of the way, then he would leave.

As the musicians ensconced upon a dais at the far end of the ballroom began playing a waltz, he approached Lady Leverton and her charges, a colorful flock of silken birds still chattering like guinea hens when he reached them.

"Do you waltz, Miss St. Clair?" His question cut across their chatter like a knife. Instant silence ensued at the breach of etiquette in directing his request to her instead of her chaperone.

Slowly turning from her cousin to look at him, Celia made no reply for a long moment, but simply gazed at him as if she had never before seen him.

Lady Leverton spoke up in a bright chirp. "Miss St. Clair performs *all* dances beautifully, my lord."

"Then I claim this waltz with her."

Celia began, "Oh, but I believe that Lord Harwood is—"

"Is dancing with Miss Grantham at the moment. Shall we?" He put out his hand, a challenge in his eyes.

As he'd suspected she would, Miss St. Clair accepted his challenge and allowed him to take her arm and lead her onto the dance floor. She moved a bit stiffly in his arms, obviously uncomfortable, but kept a smile on her face as she gracefully followed his steps. The waltz allowed him to hold her hand and put his free hand on her back, though social protocol demanded that he not slide it any lower than her shoulder blades. The waltz was scandalous enough, but without drawing attention to them, there was little she could do if he *did* let his hand move lower.

Deliberately he slid it to the small of her back, fingers a light pressure against firm flesh instead of one of those damn corsets women had taken to wearing again. A bloody nuisance, in his opinion, and damned inconvenient to remove. Warm female flesh beneath thin silk instead of stiff whalebone was much more enticing.

He heard a quickly inhaled breath, felt a vibration of suppressed indignation quiver through her.

"Be so kind as to move your hand, my lord."

"You don't really want me to do that."

"Yes, I do!"

He pressed it even lower and she took a jerky step away from him. Not releasing her hand, he turned her in the steps, at last moving his hand up her back again.

She was stiff, unyielding, her face a set mask of white fury and blazing green eyes that narrowed up at him like a cat, spitting fury and uncertainty. Her tawny hair was piled atop her head in an intricate style, fastened with some kind of comb made of gold wire and stars. It glittered in the reflected light of crystal chandeliers.

What would she look like with her hair tumbled across a pillow, those lips parted and her eyes half-closed... A tempting thought.

"You move most agilely for a marionette," he observed when she resisted his effort to turn her.

"Your meaning escapes me, my lord."

"Does it? You move as stiff and wooden as a puppet jerked by strings." He swung her about before she could pull away. "Relax. I don't intend to eat you."

Her head tilted back smoothly, so that her eyes met his in a steady gaze. "If you find me unresponsive to your charms, my lord, I can only assume that you wish to charm me. Is that the case?"

Amused, he deliberately studied her upturned face until she looked away. "Are all Americans as direct as you, Miss St. Clair?"

"I have no idea. Do you find me too forthright in my replies?"

"To the point of rudeness." He smiled at her angry gasp. "Perhaps it's the custom in America."

"No," she said after a moment. "It's not the custom. I have behaved badly, my lord, and I apologize."

His eyes narrowed slightly. Her apology was too ready and too glib; he didn't believe it for an instant.

"Apologies are easy, Miss St. Clair. What restitution do you offer?"

"Restitution? You expect too much, my lord."

"I disagree."

The waltz would be ending soon. He steered her toward the far end of the ballroom, a subtle curve that she had not yet noticed. She arched her head to look up at him.

"Your arrogance is outrageous, my lord. It's easy to see that you have earned your wicked reputation."

"May I ask why you took a sudden dislike to me?"

For a moment he thought she would not answer, then she said, "Perhaps I do not wish my name added to your long list of conquests."

"A list that is long in supposition and short in actuality."

"Nonetheless, your attentions can both elevate and ruin a lady's reputation. Discretion, it is said, is everything."

"And so it is. Then it would be indiscreet to dance with you again."

Her upward glance was oblique. "More than four dances in an evening and my reputation will be in tatters."

"If that's the case, I'll dance with Lady Jersey five times. That would set tongues wagging and add to my wicked reputation."

"You jest, my lord!"

"Yes, Miss St. Clair, I jest." She was light on his

arm, tall enough that her eyes were level with his jaw, taller than most women of his acquaintance. A faint smile curved her mouth and laughter gleamed in her eyes.

They had reached the far end of the ballroom where a chill breeze filtered in through doors that led onto a wide terrace. Two steps took them through it, and they were outside. She didn't seem surprised.

"Why did you bring me out here, my lord?"

She eased free of his loose embrace and moved to the wide balustrade that edged the terrace. Reflected light streamed through windows in ragged squares to illuminate her face as she turned toward him, draped gracefully upon the stone ledge. The gown she wore was a virginal white spangled with gold, demure in style yet unable to disguise the lush curves of her slender body.

"I think you know why I brought you out here," he said, and saw that she did. It was in her eyes, the aware gleam of a female certain of her allure.

Green-eyed little witch. He should give her what she so prettily expected. Lady Katherine's brazen touch had reminded him it had been too long since he had been with a woman, and now the silent invitation in Miss St. Clair's wide eyes was instantly arousing. His arm snaked out to pull her close, to hold her against his chest and press her against him. She made some kind of soft sound—protest? Pleasure?—but made no effort to push him away. His hand tangled in the hair on her nape, pulled her head back to give him access to her lips as he brought his mouth down over hers.

She tasted as he'd known she would, hot and sweet and willing. Her lips opened from the pressure of his mouth on hers and he took instant advantage. His tongue slid inside the heated velvet of her mouth, taking complete possession as she made a soft, choked sound like a moan.

He felt her shiver, moved harder against her, so they fit from chest to hips. Deliberately leaning into her, he pinned her between the balustrade and the rigid pressure of his erection. It prodded against the soft swell of her belly, an insistent persuasion, and for a moment, he felt her yield.

An instant later she wrenched free and would have pulled away if he had not held her. His hand curled around her wrist, the other cupped the back of her neck. His thumb rubbed idly over the silky skin of her jawline.

Her lips were slightly swollen from the force of his kiss, wet and enticing. He was tempted to kiss her again.

"Penance, Miss St. Clair," he said softly instead. "Retribution is now paid in full. Care to sin again? I rather like this form of atonement."

"No," she said coolly, more coolly than he'd thought she felt, standing and staring at him with the light from the ballroom full on her face, no sign of passion in her eyes as she regarded him. "I find I'm not as interested as I thought I would be. Now that I have been absolved of my earlier transgression, be so good as to allow me to pass, my lord. I feel a bit chilled out here. No," she added when he started to take her arm. "Your escort will only cause more comment. My cousin is looking for me, and I do not intend to invite gossip. I'll go back alone, please."

"For now, Miss St. Clair."

Stepping aside, he let her pass. There was more to this "milk and water Colonial" than even Katherine had guessed. His eyes narrowed slightly as he watched her return to the ballroom. This was not the end of it. She was no missish virgin playing a game, but a woman who knew what she wanted.

Just as he knew what he wanted from her.

7

Jacqueline paced the floor of Celia's chamber with small, energetic steps. Her hair was awry, straggling from the usually neat coil atop her head; the curls she liked to wear in ringlets on her forehead dangled in her eyes rather than the usual tidy coils. She was distraught as she passed beneath the soft glow of a wall sconce, still wearing a ballgown that dragged across the Aubusson carpet in a satin trail.

"Whatever were you thinking, Celia?" she moaned. "To so insult Lord Northington—what mischief made you do it?"

Celia sighed. "After what Lady Jersey said..."

"My God, do you think any of that matters? Lord Northington is a member of the peerage! And it is only gossip. Oh, if he is offended enough he can ruin your chances—"

"He is not offended." Celia dragged a brush through her loose hair; it crackled slightly, fine filaments arcing to meet the silver-backed hairbrush like a pale cloud of lightning. "He is intrigued."

Jacqueline paused in midstep and turned to stare at her. "What do you mean?"

"I mean that, instead of fawning over him as were all the other young ladies and their mamas, I presented him with a challenge. It has not escaped my notice that there are men who prefer challenges to easy conquests. Did you not notice that his eyes did not leave me the rest of the evening?" A slight lie; she'd been well aware of him, but he had seemed content enough to ignore her for the short time he had remained. What would Jacqueline say if she knew what he'd done on the terrace?

She turned on the dressing stool to face her cousin. "I find him—aggressive."

Jacqueline was staring at her with an arrested expression.

"What is it, petite? Did—did Northington insult you when you felt faint? He didn't say anything—"

"No, no, nothing like that, I swear it, but he did approach me again before he left the ball, and I agreed to ride with him in the park Tuesday. So you see, I have piqued his interest with indifference."

Gaping at her, Jacqueline finally nodded. "Yes, but it is true! Oh, how foolish I have been. You are right, my little one," she babbled in French, half-laughing. "You have managed what most have not! To snare the attentions of the elusive Lord Northington."

"If only half the rumors are true, there are many who have managed to snare his attention for a while."

"But you, my clever little pigeon, will manage to hold his attention. How stupid I have been! An imbecile!"

Celia's smile felt stiff on her lips. What had she

done? Oh, she must be utterly mad to have agreed to ride with him in the park, for he'd made it plain enough that he had more on his mind than a mere sedate tour. And the invitation had seemed more of an afterthought, for he was leaving while she was being escorted onto the dance floor by Sir John.

"Northington," Harvey had said, halting him, "you've met Miss St. Clair, have you not?"

"I have." Blue eyes had skimmed her briefly with an air of polite boredom, as if he had not been so bold as to kiss her on the terrace.

"Miss St. Clair has informed me that she's not yet been for a turn in Hyde Park," Harvey had continued with a smile that could only be described as wicked. "And, as my carriage is unfortunately in disrepair at the moment, I assured her you would be so kind as to escort her one day."

"I hardly think Miss St. Clair will lack for offers," Northington drawled, but his eyes rested on her face with a glint of amusement, as if he suspected she had engineered the invitation.

Trapped, Celia could only return his stare with a cool gaze of her own. "Indeed, my lord, your confidence is uplifting."

"My tours of Hyde Park are always very extensive," he had said then, "but should Miss St. Clair wish, I would be more than happy to escort her."

If not for Harvey's interference, she suspected Lord Northington would not have suggested it at all. Indeed, a faintly sardonic smile had accompanied that overly polite invitation, so that she'd almost refused.

He expects me to refuse, she'd realized, and to be perverse, had said sweetly that she would be honored.

What have I done? she thought now, despairingly. Oh, why did I have to be so perverse?

"But you must be cautious," Jacqueline was saying, her mood buoyed now, "and not be *too* much of a challenge. You do not wish to truly offend him. There is a fine line you must walk if you wish to succeed. Remember, my sweet, Northington is quite accustomed to having his own way. Ah, but he is so handsome, yes, and despite his reputation he is quite a catch. One day he will be earl of Moreland. How lovely it would be if you were to marry him. Lady Moreland is one of my dearest friends. I have known her for years."

"You never told me that," Celia said quietly, and placed her hairbrush on the dresser. "I had no idea."

"Yes, it was Margaret who introduced me to my husband so long ago. I was only a penniless emigré then, so young and afraid. Your dear mama and I barely escaped with our lives, you know, and we had so little money. We came to London to stay with friends who had fled France before that terrible time."

She never referred to it as the Revolution, but as that "terrible time" or "the Terror." Now she looked up at Celia, eyes wide with memories.

"Some were fortunate and clever enough to escape with some of their wealth. So many did not, so many died...but Léonie and I, we were young, and pretty if penniless, so were offered refuge. Lady Moreland—she was Lady Northington then—was my patroness. I shall never be able to repay her for all her kindnesses to me."

Celia was silent. God, perhaps...should she tell Jacqueline how Léonie had really died? Should she tell her that the husband of her dearest friend was responsible for her death? *Oh God.*

Jacqueline came to her, put a hand on her shoulder. "Do not look so sad, my dear. It is behind us now. And I am quite content with my Jules, and your mama was so very happy with her handsome American. Shall I tell you again how they met? And how he was so enchanted with her, he took her from the arms of a baron and swept her away out onto the terrace where they danced alone? It was so romantic despite the scandal, and even though I thought Léonie could have married any man in London, she fell in love with her sea captain."

"Yes. They were very much in love."

Leaning close, her cousin whispered, "There are so many in this world who never know that kind of love, my child. Do not grieve so very much for them. They were more fortunate than most."

"Yes." Celia swallowed the surge of emotion in her throat, the impulse to confess all. "Yes, they were very fortunate."

"And if the good God wills it, so will you be. Ah, you are so very like your mother, you know. There are times I look at you and it is like seeing Léonie again, when she was very young and we had first come to England." Reaching out, Jacqueline lifted a skein of Celia's hair, let it slide through her fingers, a silky tumble. "Do not cut your hair. It may be the style now, but this suits you. So soft, and such a lovely shade of dark gold—"

"No. No, I won't." Celia rose from the small stool set before the dresser, suddenly restless, unable to bear another moment of guilt. How could she even contemplate an act that may very well disgrace Jacqueline? The stain of her sin would spread, like ink on a clean blotter, ruining all it touched. She felt sick.

"Oh, when Northington waltzed you out onto the terrace I thought I would faint, too," Jacqueline was saying with a smile. "But now—now perhaps it is as it was with your dear mama and papa, eh? Could it be that he has formed an attachment for you already? And, perhaps, you for him?"

"No." The denial was jerked from her, an instant reaction, and she put a hand over her mouth to halt more betraying words.

"Are you unwell?" Jacqueline frowned at her, then gave a nod of her head. "Ah, it is the excitement of the evening. It's too much for you. I should have thought of that. Well, my dear, you are a success. Lady Jersey and Lady Cowper thought you enchanting, and Lord Northington singled you out for a dance. Sleep well, knowing that the world is before you. You can do anything with it you wish."

Celia swallowed hard. The enormity of her betrayal loomed before her eyes, Jacqueline's kindness and love like a raw wound that wouldn't heal. How could she keep it to herself, not confide in this woman who was so good to her? Oh God, it was so confusing, so...perilous.

She leaned forward, wanting to say so much yet not quite daring to say too much, the words coming out shaky and not sounding like herself.

"It is not always so easy to do. There are times— There are things that make people do what they wouldn't ordinarily do, you know. I may fail you."

"My child, failure is impossible. Whatever you

choose to do, it will be right." Jacqueline smiled. "I have faith in you."

"Don't—oh, don't have faith in me!" Celia blurted, then stopped when her cousin just stared at her. Shaking her head, Celia managed a light laugh. "I'm afraid the champagne punch went to my head. You're right, of course. I shall do what I must."

"And now you must rest. It has been a long evening, and soon the sun will be up. I shall instruct Lily not to wake you. Rest, my dearest. You and Carolyn were the toast of the ton this evening. I am so fortunate to have two such lovely young ladies in my household!"

Once in bed, with only the glow from the coals in the grate to light the room, Celia was consumed by anguish. Hot tears wet her cheeks, grief for her parents and guilt for the treachery with which she returned her cousin's affection. If only she dared confide in her, tell her what had happened so long ago. But she did not dare. And to learn that Jacqueline's dearest friend was Lady Moreland—no, she would never understand or approve.

And I could not expect her to, Celia thought sadly. It was so unexpected that she would feel such affection for Jacqueline. It overshadowed everything.

Yet I cannot let it deter me from exacting justice on Moreland! she thought fiercely. Nor will I trust his son. Despite his invitation for an innocent ride in the park, Lord Northington was dangerous.

That was clear enough. She hadn't expected him to be so determined, so forceful, on the terrace. Nor had she expected him to be aroused, but she had been well aware of his hard arousal pressing against her belly, the strength of it shocking. It had alarmed her, but even more alarming was her response to him. For a moment, just a brief instant, she had found herself kissing him back.

Dieu! But it had taken all her strength of will to walk away, to pretend a coolness and indifference she certainly had not felt at the moment. It was surprising he hadn't seen through her effort, for she'd thought at any moment that her knees would buckle and she'd sink to the floor.

Yet she hadn't.

And in a few days, she would be forced to spend time with him, to continue the deception. God, if only there was another way, but she saw none. What else could she do? It made her head hurt to even think of it anymore, to even try to form a cohesive plan. Putting her fingers to her temples, she squeezed her eyes tightly shut.

It was Northington's father she wanted to ruin. If she had to use his son, she would. It might even be justice of a sort.

Why waste pity on a man who thought it appropriate to seduce young women on their very own terraces? If she had given him more encouragement, no doubt he would have lifted her skirts. No, she wouldn't lose a moment's sleep over either Northington, young or old.

Yet when she succumbed at last to sleep, it was a troubled slumber with vivid dreams and haunting images.

Jacqueline Leverton sat at her dressing table and frowned slightly at her reflection as the maid brushed out her hair. Celia seemed so...so *grieved* about something, but she could not learn what it might be. The poor child. Of course, with both her parents dead now she must feel terribly alone. At least when she and Léonie had fled France they'd had each other.

Now Celia was here, and she owed it to Léonie to do all she could for her daughter. They'd made a pact during those dark days, that they would always be there for each other. This was the only way she had now of keeping that pact with her cousin.

But even if she did not do it for any other reason, she would do it for Celia. There was a melancholy quality to her that exuded from every pore, sad lights in her eyes even when she laughed. Oh, to wipe away that sadness, to give Celia the happiness that Carolyn had, the same sense of safety and serenity she gave to her daughter.

Jules chose that moment to appear at her door, his brisk knock the usual signal.

Dismissing her maid with a wave of one hand, she turned with a smile as her husband entered the chamber and came straight to her.

"It was a brilliant success, my sweet, but then, your affairs always are." He bent, his hand gentle on her shoulder as he pressed a kiss upon her cheek. He smelled faintly of tobacco and brandy. So familiar, so beloved. It was still a miracle to her that they were married, that he loved her after so many years.

"If they are a success," she said lightly, "it is all due to you."

"To me?" Jules feigned amazement, and they both laughed. "Why would you say that, my love?"

"Because it is due to your generosity and kindness that I am able to spend so lavishly."

"My darling, I would give my entire fortune to make you happy, and would give dear Caro anything, as you well know."

"Yes, and you are so generous to my beloved Léonie's daughter, just as you are to our own. For that, I can never thank you enough."

"My dearest wife, I would be generous to a dozen of your orphaned relatives if it pleased you, but I genuinely like Celia. She's a lovely young woman, though very sad."

"Oh, you see it, too!" Jacqueline stared up at him. Short and balding, with luxurious side whiskers that he thought made his face seem leaner, Jules Leverton seemed to some as a genial aristocrat, but in fact he was a shrewd judge of character and a canny businessman. He had rescued his family's failing fortunes from calamity, and never failed to help those he could. He was, Jacqueline thought, the most wonderful man she had ever known.

"Of course I see it," Jules said softly. "Celia bears a great weight on her young shoulders. There's more than sadness in her eyes. There's something akin to dread that I've glimpsed on occasion. Do what you can for her, my dearest."

"I will," Jacqueline promised. "I will."

And she would. She would do her best to learn what lay in Celia's past that could make her fear the future.

8

Hyde Park dipped in hills and greenswards that were still bright with fading summer flowers. Braving the capricious weather, open carriages took advantage of the sunny day to fill the park's roads.

Celia St. Clair blinked against the press of light in her eyes, and tugged at the brim of her fashionable bonnet to shade her face. She wore a bonnet of green satin lined with white; a full plume of snowy ostrich feathers curled in graceful dips on the crown. As the gleaming curricle wheeled swiftly down the pathway, feathers fluttered as if about to take wing and fly.

Colter eyed them with a lifted brow. "Enjoy the sun's warmth while you can," he said to the lofty plumes that covered Celia's head and part of her face. "It will disappear soon enough."

Her chin tilted upward, the feathers bobbing. "Such an optimist. Are you always so cheerful, my lord?"

"Not always. On occasion I'm quite surly." Handling the reins of the spirited horses, he slid a glance toward her and saw the faintest smile on her mouth.

"If that is indeed true, be so kind as not to inflict

your presence upon me at those dismal moments of choler,'' she replied with a coolness that belied her amusement. Colter smiled his appreciation of her retort.

''Your lack of tolerance is shocking, Miss St. Clair.''

''I doubt that. You don't seem to be a man who is easily shocked.''

''I could tell you some tales—''

''I'm sure you could. Please spare me.''

She turned her head slightly, a glance from green eyes that could alter from warm to frigid in an instant. A smile lingered at the corners of her mouth, a tempting curve that was inviting and rejecting at the same time.

Little baggage. He should kiss her again, if for no other reason than to prove to her how much she liked it. She may feign indifference but she hadn't been indifferent the last time. And no damned ladies' maid would keep him from it, so she needn't have gone to the trouble of bringing one along.

The maid, a thin little thing with the look of a determined sparrow, clung to the sides of the curricle as if she feared being thrown out at any moment. He curbed a perverse impulse to increase his speed.

''Very well,'' he said, handling the ribbons and horses with efficient ease as he deftly took a curve in the road. ''Entertain me with lively tales of your own.''

''Really, I cannot imagine you would be interested in any tales I could tell, my lord.''

''I might surprise you. If you lack ideas, tell me

about your home in Georgetown. You lived there for some time?''

''Yes.''

When she said nothing else, he glanced at her again. Her face was shadowed by the brim of her bonnet as she tilted her head downward, but her hands were tightly clenched around the velvet cords of the reticule she held in her lap. She vibrated with sudden tension.

''If you'd rather speak of something else, Miss St. Clair—''

Her head came up. ''No. What would you like to know? And I was really born in Virginia. We moved to Georgetown when I was very small.''

''Then your parents are from Virginia, I presume.''

There was a brief hesitation before she said, ''Yes. My father's family owned land along the Chesapeake Bay.''

''So what brings you alone to England?''

She turned to stare at him, eyes boring into his face as if trying to decide what to say next. ''How do you know I arrived alone, my lord? Because you saw me alone on the ship?''

''No, because your cousin hasn't mentioned anyone else as a guest. A simple enough deduction, but I'm sure you'll tell me if I'm wrong.''

''No, you aren't wrong. My parents died some time ago, my father killed when his vessel was seized by a French warship. I'm the only member of my immediate family left.''

''I see.'' There was no hint of emotion in her voice, only a calm recital of facts, yet her gaze on him was intent. He glanced back at the road. ''And so you came to visit your mother's relatives here. England has a lot to answer for, it seems, in colonizing America."

When she shifted slightly, he caught a whiff of delicate scent. Verbena? He wasn't certain. It was light, elusive, inviting—as alluring as her voice, a seductive blend of female innocence and wisdom borne in the husky, drawling tones of a Colonial. Enticing little chit.

"I bear no grudges. America won its independence in the end. A humiliating defeat for England, it seems."

Amused, he said, "Perhaps just a concession instead of a victory. England has too many Colonies to waste far too much time on insurgents."

"Yes, such as India, I presume. Yet oddly enough, it seems worth the expense, time and life to continue there."

"India is proving to be more profitable and even less civilized, despite our best efforts."

"Ah, the British are so *aggressive.*"

"Yes. You might keep that in mind should you ever plan a small revolution of your own."

She gave him an arch look, eyes innocently wide. "If memory serves, my lord, England didn't do so well in the last great revolution with the American Colonies."

"A slight case of miscalculation. We do learn from our mistakes, however."

"Apparently there are lapses in memory, as it was not so very long ago that there was another war with America. It was in 1812 and didn't end well for you then, either."

"Touché, Miss St. Clair. I yield to the victorious Colonist."

She laughed, a soft sound of amusement, genuine and contagious. "You yield so easily, my lord. I'm surprised. And a bit disappointed. I thought you a more worthy foe."

"I am a worthy foe in more *intimate* matters, Miss St. Clair." He smiled at her when she gave him a startled glance, and had the satisfaction of seeing color flood her cheeks.

It was only a matter of time. He'd give her today, by God, with her damned lady's maid and chaperon sitting like a watchful cat in the boot of the curricle, but the next time he took her for a ride, it would be under his terms.

She was a mystery, an intrigue, a lovely, sensual female. He was developing a ferocious itch for her. It was damned inconvenient.

"America," she said with a betraying tremor in her lovely lilting drawl, an obvious attempt to ease the tension between them, "is very different from England. It's so *vast*. I think that's what first strikes visitors. One can go afoot for months and not reach the distant shores. It's so large, no road exists from one coast to the other. To reach Spanish California one must travel months by ship."

Amused by her effort, he said, "I've been to Spanish California, but it was a long time ago, when I was barely out of Oxford. Now the United States and Spain have an ongoing quarrel with Mexico over the territory. It makes it inconvenient to visit."

"Then describe it for me, since you've seen it." Her glance at him was speculative. "I was told it's a marvelous place with constant sunshine, soft winds and lush grass for miles and miles.''

''An apt description. A vast wilderness, but excellent for cattle and hermits.''

''That sounds a bit prejudicial.''

''It wasn't what I expected but I wasn't disappointed. I found California to be—a challenge. Wild. A place where a man's past doesn't matter, only his ability to survive.''

''You seem adept at survival.''

''So do you, Miss St. Clair.''

With a light shrug, she turned her head to gaze at the much tamer aspect of flower beds and tree-lined drive. He had the sense there was much she didn't say.

Colter guided the horses more slowly along the curve of the path. It was more crowded in this part of the park, with curricles, landaus and horsemen exhibiting not only equestrian skill, but excellent horseflesh and lovely riding apparel. Nobility rubbed elbows with riffraff.

Madame Poirier, procurer of prostitutes, had several of her newest recruits decked out in all their finery and parading the park in a gleaming brougham with gilded harness and trappings. The ladybirds were near as lovely as the horses, and he recognized several of the men eyeing them appraisingly.

''Isn't that Sir John?''

He followed Celia's gaze and saw Harvey approach Madame Poirier's carriage; sunlight gilded his hair with the same bright glints as the brass harness. An elegant horseman, the baronet rode a flashy bay from his father's stables. Colter recognized it, remembered Baron Leawood at Tattersall's purchasing the mare.

He'd almost tried to outbid him, but decided against it. If Harvey was riding his father's mounts, his own stable must be depleted. It was a matter of pride for a man to parade his own cattle through the park.

"Yes," he said, "Harvey seems to be showing off his fine horsemanship."

"And his fine horse as well as his diverse tastes."

"Ah, do I detect jealousy?"

"Only of the horse, my lord. It's a beautiful beast. I imagine such a lovely animal is quite costly."

"Yes, as a matter of fact, it was. I was there when it was first shown at Tattersall's. Do you ride, Miss St. Clair?"

There was a brief pause before she said, "Not well. I much prefer my riding to be done in a well-sprung landau."

"Your riding instructors must be most distressed to hear it."

She turned on her seat to face him. He felt the press of her knee against his thigh, a gentle nudge that sent a flash of fire through him. If it wasn't for the watchful maid in the rear, he'd take Celia St. Clair to the nearest privacy he could find.

"What is it you want from me, my lord? A recitation of my qualities? My education? What I know and what I don't know? Shall I confess all my secrets, or do you wish to continue trying to coax them out of me one by one?"

"Have you never heard of discretion?" He slanted her an amused glance, his brow lifted. Angry spots of color glowed on her high cheekbones, made her green eyes seem even brighter.

"Yes, I have, my lord. Have you?"

"Are you speaking of now, or of the night of your cousin's ball? I seem to recall a lack of discretion on your part, as well."

It was a telling reply. Her flush deepened and she looked away from him, staring at the tall sycamores that lined the drive. He focused on the horses, set their pace a bit slower as the well-oiled wheels of the curricle took a neat curve in the serpentine lane.

"Please be so good as to take me back to my cousin's house, my lord."

He'd been expecting the demand. "You're not weary of my company already?"

"No. I—feel faint."

"Ah. I see."

He guided the curricle to a little-traveled lane that led around the lake the prince regent had insisted upon expanding. Swans floated serenely on the surface and ducks nested among reeds. Sunlight reflected on placid water as smooth as a mirror. A stone bench was screened by bushes.

It took just a moment to set the brake and climb down from the seat, another moment to move to the other side of the curricle and reach in for Celia. She made a sound of protest as he put his hands on her waist and lifted her down. He turned to the wide-eyed maid. "Stay here. If you thrash about, the horses might bolt."

A muffled shriek was quickly swallowed as she gripped the side of the curricle with both hands and held tightly.

"Really, my lord," Celia said coldly, "this is not at all necessary."

"If you're faint, you should lie down." He ignored

her resistance as he escorted her with an arm behind her back to the stone bench. She moved stiffly. The muscles beneath his hand contracted in a shudder as he slid his arm more securely around her waist.

"Here," he said with a wicked smile. "Let me help you onto the bench since you're so faint."

He lifted her effortlessly into his arms, held her a long moment over the stone seat, then slowly lowered her until she was in a reclining position with her feet on the ground.

"Let go of me at once," she hissed through clenched teeth, "or I'll scream for help!"

"From that timid bird of a maid? She'd be of little help to anyone. Be still. If anyone should notice us, why give them something to gossip about? A simple conversation by the lake is much different from an amorous struggle that could so easily be misinterpreted, I'd think."

"You are a rogue, sir!" Her eyes narrowed angrily, and she sat up, looking up at him as he propped a boot on the seat of the bench and leaned an arm on his knee. It brought him closer to her, a posture meant to intimidate.

"That's better, Miss St. Clair."

"How long do you intend to continue this farce?"

"As long as it takes."

"As long as it takes for *what* to happen?" She snapped open a fan, then closed it again, ivory spindles a soft click of sound. "If you intend to ravish me, either do it or take me home. I wish an end to this afternoon."

He slid a finger along the curve of her shoulder up

to her jawline, a light caress that summoned a shiver from her.

''I think,'' he said softly, ''that you're in a hurry to be ravished. Ah-ah—slapping won't do anything but annoy me. It certainly won't stop me if I don't want to be stopped.''

''A pity my fencing master did not warn me to always carry a saber,'' she snapped.

''Fencing? How modern of you. Are you expert, or is it on a level with your riding ability?''

''You would make an excellent foil, my lord. Too bad you aren't available as a target.''

''And it's too bad that you're not being honest with me or with yourself. I don't remember that you fought me this hard the last time we were alone. In fact, I seem to recall you kissing me back.''

Her face flamed. Her gaze slipped from his. ''You have a vivid imagination, sir.''

''No, I'm much too pragmatic to waste time imagining kisses. I prefer—'' he paused, dragged a fingertip along the curve of her jawline, watched a pulse beat madly in the hollow of her throat ''—the real to the imagined,'' he ended softly, and bent to kiss her.

His finger beneath her chin held her in a light grip, lifted her face slightly to his. He heard her quick inhalation just before his mouth covered her half-open lips.

Warm, sweet, tempting, she made no effort to pull away, but allowed him to kiss her. This time, there was no response, no participation. She offered no resistance, but no reaction. He slid an arm behind her back to hold her.

''It won't work,'' he said against her mouth.

Bringing her hands up between them, she balled them into fists and wedged some distance between their bodies. "I don't know what you're talking about," she said in a voice that held only a slight quiver.

"Oh, you do." He tucked a curl back beneath the sash of her bonnet, let his hand linger on the delicate whorl of her ear, a slight feathery brush of his finger over the seashell curves that summoned a shudder from her. He smiled. "Oh, yes, you most certainly know what I'm talking about. This pretense that you don't want me to kiss you is a waste of time at best, bad acting at the worst."

She relaxed slightly, let his arm bear her weight as she looked up into his eyes. "You have a marvelous opinion of your effect on females, I see. How pitiful that is for you. Do you truly think that all you have to do is kiss a woman and she will fall into your arms? Ignore her station in life, her reputation, her family? I think you're far too accustomed to your little actresses who must use the few advantages life has given them to get ahead. They must suffer the attentions of arrogant men just to survive. I, however, have other alternatives. Release me at once, or I will scream so loudly everyone in this park will come to my rescue."

"I'm tempted to test you," he said, "but there's time enough for that."

She stared at him, obviously taken aback. "Does nothing prick your insufferable ego, my lord?"

"Many things. Protests from females who enjoy being kissed are not among them, however. I didn't imagine your response."

"No," she once more surprised him by saying.

"You did not imagine it. You simply attached more importance to it than it deserves. Now if you will please escort me back to your carriage, I want to go home."

She pushed him away and stood up, brushed imaginary wrinkles from her smooth satin skirts and gave him a stare so cool and detached that he let her win this point. For today. Only for today. He swept her an ironic bow.

"Your carriage awaits, Miss St. Clair." He put out his arm as if they were in a ballroom. After the briefest hesitation, she tucked her gloved fingers into the crook of his elbow and accompanied him back to the curricle.

The vehicle dipped as he lifted her into it, let his hands linger long enough around her waist to make his own point, then he rounded the boot to climb up and take the reins and release the brake.

"It has been an interesting afternoon," he said as the horses moved forward, hooves digging into the dirt and gravel of the road. "I trust you've enjoyed it as much as I have."

"Probably not," she replied serenely, and stared out over the open side of the curricle as if he no longer existed for her.

"I think," he said bluntly, "that you are taking your charade too far."

"Do you? Shall I tell you what I think, my lord?"

"By all means."

"I think," she said softly as he turned his head to meet her gaze, "that you will never forget me."

"And I think," he replied with an intent stare, "that I will not intend to try."

9

It was a dangerous game she played, and she knew it. For a few panicked moments, Celia thought she'd overplayed her hand. He was so...so *predatory,* that she'd wanted to erase his smug confidence, prick his arrogance.

Yet he was swift enough to take up her challenge.

Oh God, this was so unexpected! She hadn't bargained for this, hadn't thought it through well enough. Consumed by the need for vengeance, she had blithely assumed that she could arrive in London, confront Lord Northington and ruin him with her accusations and documents. But her plans were coming unraveled before her eyes.

Now she realized that it would be much more difficult than she had ever considered. The peerage formed a united front against outsiders even though they harshly judged them on their own terms. The earl's undoing must be more carefully structured, or she would lose any chance at all of getting what she wanted.

What *did* she want? The complete annihilation of

the man who had caused her mother's death. Justice demanded it.

But realistically, what could she do? Raise enough doubts to damage his reputation, such as it was? Create a scandal he could never escape? Cause him humiliation?

It was not enough, but it would have to serve.

And this Lord Northington was crucial to his father's downfall. She must not make any more mistakes.

The movement of the curricle had slowed in the congestion of traffic in the park. Celia studied Lord Northington as he handled the horses with expert efficiency, though she did so discreetly. It was rather like gauging an opponent, an odd dance around the truth while she considered her next move.

Sunlight gleamed on his dark hair; he wore it casually feathered over his ears and below his collar in the popular style, with short side-whiskers that ended at his earlobe. Strong bones delineated a forceful nature corroborated by a firm mouth and square jaw. In daylight, he was even more striking than he had been in the diffused glow of candles and crystal chandeliers. It was unnerving. How could this man be the son of the man she hated so badly? There should be a sign of some sort, a mark of the beast to signify his heritage.

But there was nothing other than his dark good looks to recommend him, and she turned her gaze to the passing landscape of mottled trees. It reminded her of home, the crisp air of autumn that was always so invigorating and so lovely. She and Maman and Old Peter had often gone together to lie in grassy meadows on the fringe of Georgetown, where they would take a basket of food and while away the day with memories and plans for the future.

That had been before, of course, before Papa had died and the world had gone dark, before Lord Northington had come into their lives and poisoned the past and the future.

"You have proven to be more intriguing than I first thought you would be, Miss St. Clair."

Northington sounded cynically amused, and she shot him a furtive glance. A faint, knowing smile curled his mouth. Her heart thumped in alarm. She'd gone too far. Jacqueline had warned her of the fine line between propriety and presumption.

"Have I, my lord? You sound disapproving."

"Surprised, perhaps. A milk and water miss from the Colonies is hardly common in London, especially one who claims to be descended from French royalty."

Her mouth tightened. "*Claims?* I've said nothing to that effect."

"No, but your cousin certainly has. Do you disagree with her on that subject?"

"Why would I? Lady Leverton is in a much better position to know the truth than I am. She was there in—"

"Another revolution that left behind widows, orphans and impostors."

"Into which category do you think I belong?" Anger made her voice sharp.

His gaze was bland. "That is something only you know, Miss St. Clair."

"You speak of rudeness on my part, but your manners lack even the most rudimentary courtesies! Breeding is not an acquired virtue, but something one is born with. It can exist in a lowly milkmaid or an aristocrat, but it is certainly not found in men who behave like rutting boars. I resent your inferences."

"And am I to infer that you're comparing me to a rutting boar?"

"If you like!" Beyond anger, beyond caution, she gave him a furious stare that seemed to have no effect on him whatsoever. He merely smiled, an infuriating, maddening smile that didn't quite reach his eyes. A small muscle leaped in his jaw, as if he was clenching his teeth. With a start, Celia recognized his fury.

At last. She had reached him, managed to elicit an honest emotion from him even though he suppressed it. A cold light gleamed in eyes that had turned an ice-blue, narrowed at her now, the tautness of his mouth more of a grimace than the smile he was obviously attempting. A chill of sudden apprehension clutched at her.

Until now, he had seemed dangerous in a distant, safe kind of way, but at the moment she felt threatened. He said nothing, did nothing, but there was a taut, wolfish look to him, as if he sensed easy prey.

She felt hot and cold at the same time. What had she been thinking? This man was, after all, Northington's son. His father had been capable of rape and murder, why should his son be any different?

With a hand that visibly shook, she put her fingers to her throat, an instinctive gesture of self-protection. She was glad for the maid still in the boot—a witness, a deterrent.

If Northington noticed her distress, he ignored it.

His hands were capable, steady on the long reins as the matched bays picked up a brisk pace. The streets of London were no less crowded than Hyde Park. It took longer than usual to reach Bruton Street, and by the time the curricle halted before the five-story house, Celia had composed herself.

"Good day, my lord," she said coolly, not waiting for him to help her step down from the vehicle. She swung open the low door and dropped to the ground, but her skirt hung up on the seat, catching on the latch. Cold air assaulted her legs, clad only in clocked stockings. She twisted to free herself, glared at the maid sitting bug-eyed in the boot and said, "Get out and help me, Janey."

To her chagrin, Northington leaned across the seat before the maid could move, easily disengaging the velvet and braid hem. "An enticing view, Miss St. Clair," he said with a wicked lift of his brow, and only laughed when she jerked her skirt free of his grasp.

An ignominious end to an afternoon that was already difficult.

It would be a miracle if she ever saw him again. Oh, not that she minded *that* so very much! But without Lord Northington, she must plan another way to reach the earl.

Celia St. Clair eased from his mind when Colter reached the offices of Messrs. Guiterrez and Barclay. A most unlikely pair to be in business together, they were quite successful. Their office overlooked the East India Dock, a massive stretch of warehouses and swaying ships' masts. It was noisy, crowded, and already the area was overflowing. There was talk of new docks to be built in the area now housing St. Katherine's Hospital east of the Tower. It would ease some of the congestion, and get rid of the wretched slums. Shipping interests thrived.

"My lord," Barclay greeted him, "we've been expecting your arrival."

Colter took the chair he was offered, but declined a glass of port. Leaning back, he stretched out long legs and regarded Barclay. "Tell me what you've found. In detail."

"Ah, yes." Barclay, a short, florid man of Scottish descent, cleared his throat. Red hair liberally streaked with gray stuck up in odd tufts atop his head, and he had the expression of a perpetually doleful spaniel. "It's quite perplexing. The *India* is reported to have been lost with all hands and cargo, yet some items have recently reached a Paris shop. The cargo was mostly specie, but some very costly pieces were included in the hold. Most perplexing is how the ancient Chinese vases survived to be offered for sale—privately, it seems—in a small shop off the Rue de Ile. It would seem impossible. How would the vases survive such a storm, yet no sailor? Most unusual."

"Do you have a list of the items offered for sale? It is certain they are the same as those on the manifest my steward delivered to you?"

"Oh, yes, my lord. No mistake about that. While the currency might be unidentifiable, the vases are unique. The Ming dynasty, I believe, and quite rare. It's a miracle they survived intact." He blew out a thoughtful sigh. "Of course, I suppose it's not impossible. Wooden packing crates, a great deal of straw—

When the ship went down, perhaps the hold broke open and these miraculously floated free."

"I don't believe in miracles, Mister Barclay."

He looked up, startled. "Oh, no. Of course not. I see what you mean." Bright blue eyes fringed with red lashes narrowed slightly. "Yes, I believe you and Monsieur Guiterrez are of the same mind on that. He has been most adamant that it's too great a coincidence to be believed. He has come to some conclusions of his own, though I must say that I don't fully agree. It's too unlikely."

"My question is how and where it was done. I was told that the ship went down off the coast of Lubang. If it did not, or if it went down after it was relieved of cargo, it stands to reason that there would be some record of debris washing ashore. I was told there was none."

"Quite right. None at all. No sign of drowned men or even a plank. All that is available are several witnesses to the ship's sinking."

"These witnesses were questioned thoroughly?"

"Very thoroughly. They all told the same tale of seeing the ship attempt to ride out the storm at sea, of seeing it offshore as it broke apart and sank."

"Yet now some of the lost cargo is offered for sale in Paris."

Barclay shuffled through some papers on his desk, and held up several sheafs. "Here is the complete manifest and the list of what was discovered in Paris. The name of the shop is listed, as well as the names of the witnesses in Lubang." A brief smile momentarily brightened his dismal expression. "Odd names, but the translator carefully took down their reports."

Colter scanned the pages. Then he looked up. "They all tell the same tale to the letter. It doesn't vary."

"Yes, my lord. That has been noted. It could be due to the translator."

"Or it could be that these witnesses were told what to say. Moonrakers." He tossed the pages to the desk-top. "I presume you're investigating that possibility."

"Yes, my lord. We sent men to make our own in-quiries as soon as we received these rather peculiar reports."

"Efficient of you, Barclay."

"We do try to be on the spot, my lord." Barclay's nod reeked of satisfaction. "If I do say so myself, we have excellent employees who are very thorough. Nasty business, luring ships onto the rocks just to get the cargo. Utter disregard for human life and the prop-erty of others."

Rising to his feet, Colter picked up the reports. "I would appreciate it if you said nothing of this to either my father or any member of the board. My father has been ill, and the board need not be bothered with un-supported rumors at this point. When the time comes, I'll present them with the facts."

The facts, Colter recognized as rife with deceit. If ships were being reported as lost with all cargo, then that cargo was being sold elsewhere, someone was reaping a great deal of profit. Only the investors lost money, as Lloyd's of London paid but a percentage of the loss.

It was too costly to insure ships and cargo, the earl had argued, save for the barest amount. The board agreed. For the most part, they were right. But if one of the investors had decided to arrange matters to his own benefit, it was time to change that.

He would conduct his own investigations. And he'd start with his own father.

10

Jacqueline leaned forward to place her china cup back on the silver tray arranged on a small table set before the sofa, then turned to face Celia, who sat huddled in a wing chair near the fire. Outside a cold wind blew, the capricious London weather once more asserting itself, but here in her cousin's sitting room, it was warm and cheery with a fire in the grate and lamps lit. It was a vivid contrast to the day before—as Northington had accurately and cynically predicted, Celia thought irritably.

Her irritation must be obvious to Jacqueline, for her cousin frowned though her tone was comforting as she said, "You must not fret, *cherie*. Northington is most adept at evasion. He is far too accustomed to getting his own way with ladies, so do not be gulled by his presumption. It is an insult, yes, an affront that he considered you to be vulnerable to his suggestions. And you may be assured that he was indeed suggesting that you be agreeable to advances from him. You were not mistaken in that assumption."

Celia had confided her doubts about the afternoon

she had spent with Lord Northington, revealing some details but not all, of course.

How could she confess the sleepless nights, the way she had allowed him to coax a response from her? Perhaps she had not surrendered, but she had not expected the wild turbulence of her reaction to his touch, either. It was as mystifying as it was tantalizing. Oh, it was plain to see that he intended to seduce her if he could, that he only played a game that he was confident of winning. But there had been no mistaking his naked desire. She'd seen it in his eyes, felt it in his touch, tasted it in his kiss. He had been as affected as she. While Northington wasn't the first man to kiss her, he was the first to ignite such restless yearnings, such a heated response that she was left tossing and turning in her bed at night.

Now she said frankly, "I had the understanding that it was improper to be too forward, that here in England as in America men regard loose women with no respect and would never make a serious offer."

"Yes and no." Jacqueline shrugged, laughing ruefully. "It is as I told you—one must balance upon the wall that separates eligible ladies from courtesans. It is a skilled woman who can be seductive and demure at the same time."

"That requires the ability to play a part, as a stage actress would do," Celia said with some exasperation. "It is all so unnecessary."

"Ah, but it is a game, my love. Do you not recognize it now? Northington is oh so playful, but beneath his words lie a very real intent—he wishes to learn if you are agreeable to occupying his bed. You say 'No no' while you lean close to him and your eyes say 'Yes yes,' and he is confused and intrigued by it all. He must learn which you mean, the *no* on your lips, or the *yes* in your eyes. The trick is to keep him interested yet hold him at bay until he has made a commitment to you."

Celia laughed softly. "How do you make it seem so plausible when the entire thing sounds so ludicrous?"

"Because it is true. Men in England are only as bold as they are allowed to be. It is the woman who must set the boundaries." Jacqueline paused, lifted a deep china cup and sipped sweet, hot chocolate before saying over the rim, "It is not a game for the timid. Ladies are expected to be virgins on their wedding nights, yet seductive enough to lure a man to their bed. A contradiction. Arranged marriages are much safer, and once wed—ah, then can come the affairs of the heart, as long as one is discreet and has already provided the necessary heirs for her husband."

"A rather jaded view of marriage, I think."

"Because you are American in nature. I've noticed that Americans regard personal freedoms as their right instead of as a luxury. Yet in America, marriages are still arranged for daughters of distinction. After the marriage there can be no affairs of the heart without such dire consequences that I marvel at the restraint of the poor creatures trapped in those situations."

"What of you? Have you had an 'affair of the heart' since your marriage?"

"Yes, but fortunately, it has been with my husband. My circumstances were so different—as were Léonie's. We had nothing but aristocratic blood as our dowries, so we were able to wed men who sought us for reasons other than to increase their estates. If we had remained in France we would have wed men chosen for us by our parents, men who would have been wealthy, titled and able to add to the family fortunes in some way. So out of the Terror came small compensations for all that we lost. Both Léonie and I married for love. Perhaps it has not been such a terrible thing, though I shall always grieve for those who were taken from me."

"As do I," Celia said quietly. Her hands knotted into fists in her lap, and she took a deep breath. Poor Maman. To have survived the terror of the Revolution and then die because of a man like Northington—no, Moreland now, a man who had received an earldom instead of true justice.

And justice must be served. She was the only one capable of visiting it upon him, the only one who still cared that he walked freely in the world. Yet her options were limited, her power to affect the earl insignificant. Before coming to England she had thought the papers she brought would be sufficient to lodge a complaint. Now she realized just how naive she'd been. She had few choices left.

But there is still one way to reach the earl, one way to make him face what he's done....

Celia looked up at her cousin.

"After our ride in the park, Lord Northington was quite angry, though he wouldn't admit it. He may have lost interest. If I should wish to regain that interest..."

Jacqueline smiled. "It requires a delicate balance, my dear. Lord Northington is a rake, a man who prefers mistresses to any kind of emotional entanglement. You must seduce him into making an offer using much more than social graces. He has had his fill of those through the years, even before he came into the title of viscount. Every mama in London pursued him for their daughters at one time, and it has only made them more determined now that he is in line to become earl upon his father's death.''

''He is the eldest son?''

''No. There was another son, Anthony, who was the heir until he contracted a fever that took the old earl and his eldest son as well. Now Northington is the heir.''

Setting her cup in its saucer on the table, Jacqueline leaned back against the cushions of the sofa to study Celia. Long pale fingers toyed with the fringe on a pillow. ''There are certain rules of society that cannot be flaunted, petite, and there are rules that can be bent if not broken, I have observed. One must know which rules are which, however. A single misstep will see a young lady ruined, her reputation shattered and her aspirations doomed. It can be so trivial a violation as dancing too closely, or being seen out without a maid in attendance, or even being seen driving down St. James Street. Those who choose to flaunt the rules soon find, to their dismay, how unforgiving society can be.''

Celia froze, incapable of immediate response, the memory of her mother's shame and isolation in her final days a sharp reminder of how unforgiving society could be.

''I see,'' she finally said, and regarded her cousin quietly. Coal hissed in the grate and rain tickled glass windowpanes outside. It was risky to continue, but how could she live with herself if she allowed Moreland to go unpunished?

Finally she leaned forward to say softly, "If Lord Northington seeks a new mistress instead of a wife, perhaps that is what he shall have."

Jacqueline looked at her, wide-eyed and horrified. "But *no!* You must not—"

"Oh, I have no intention of yielding easily what he covets, but if I must give him the impression that he can attain his desires, then I shall gladly do so. Will you help me?"

"Help? But how can I help you do something that may well ruin you! No, I cannot. Do not ask it of me, *ma chèrie,* for it is too wicked a thing to even consider. Oh, I cannot imagine how you could think I would help you ruin yourself!"

"But you could, *ma cousine,* advise me how far I am able to go without breaking these rules you list. I wish to tantalize him but not antagonize him, lure him without ruining myself. Is it possible?"

Jacqueline had risen to her feet, distress creasing her face, but now she turned to gaze thoughtfully at Celia. Finally a faint smile curved her mouth, and the lines of distress eased.

"Yes, it is possible, of course. Wicked girl! What do you have in mind to lure this *raffiné?*"

"There is another ball which we are to attend next week, is there not?"

"Yes, Lady Stratton presents her youngest daughter, a rather plain girl in my opinion, but as she is so well connected, she has high hopes of making a good match. Her uncle is most influential— How does this matter?"

"Did you not say earlier that Lord Northington may attend Lady Stratton's ball, that he has accepted an invitation? I'm sure I heard you mention it to Caro—"

Jacqueline's smile widened, and her eyes gleamed with anticipation. "Clever girl, yes. Yes, I said that very thing and it is true. Northington sent his card to signify that he will attend. What do you plan?"

"I plan," Celia said, "to seduce Lord Northington into a marriage proposal."

11

Lady Cresswood had engineered his appearance at yet another ball, and Colter toyed with the idea of making her pay for it later.

"Really darling," she'd teased, "you have no choice but to accommodate me. I promised my husband an heir, and since I must somehow whet my appetite for his attentions, I chose you. Don't be cruel enough to deny me."

"Dammit, Katherine, I'm in no mood for your tricks. I am not in a mood for another boring evening, either."

"The only trick will be finding a few minutes to be alone with you before I must apply myself to Cresswood."

She'd draped herself around him, pressed her body so close to him there was no need to hide his reaction. But he hadn't taken what she so freely offered, and ignored her pouting face when he pushed her away.

"How novel," she murmured with an arch of her brow. "For the best, I suppose. How awkward it would be to present Cresswood with a blue-eyed, rake-hell heir."

"It's been done by more than one titled lady. I'm sure you'd find a way around it."

Her laugh was throaty, her gaze speculative. "Yes, I can only imagine my dear husband's chagrin should I be foolish enough to do so. However, back to the ball. The prince will be in attendance, and a certain Lord Mowry wishes to meet with you. Do say you'll be there, Colter, for I should so hate to disappoint Mowry."

Mowry—Lord Liverpool's hireling, a man far too comfortable with political intrigues for his liking. He had never quite trusted the man, but he was the prime minister's agent and those who weren't careful often found themselves suffering repercussions that were never successfully traced to the source.

"So now you're doing Mowry's dirty work. I'll attend the damn ball," he'd said, "but when my business with Mowry is done, I'm leaving. A word of warning—you're keeping bad company when you dally with Mowry."

Katherine was one of those completely amoral females who could be as entertaining as she was dangerous.

"But of course you can leave, darling," she'd said with a guileless smile that hadn't fooled him at all. "And I fancy bad company, as *you* should well know."

Lady Stafford's expansive home was in the heart of Mayfair, a regal dwelling that hosted affairs attended by kings and princes. Tonight was no exception. The regent was to appear with his usual retinue, sycophants and beleaguered officials of his realm trotting at his heels like well-trained dogs.

Lord Mowry arrived well before the prince regent, as was his wont. A tall, thin man with a gaunt face and intense dark eyes, he moved casually through the crowd, pausing to speak to acquaintances.

Colter watched Mowry approach; his air of geniality was deceptive. Beneath the ill-fitting coat and baggy breeches he wore, lurked the soul of a politician, glib and given to sharp, perceptive judgments. Mowry was ruthless in his goals, remorseless in his ambition.

"My lord Northington," he greeted him finally, "it is a pleasant surprise to see you here."

"Hardly a surprise, I would think, since you had Lady Cresswood summon me." Colter eyed him over the rim of his half-empty glass.

Mowry gave him a sharp glance. "Perhaps it is a surprise that you agreed to come. You have not always been so amenable."

"If I haven't always been *amenable,* it may have something to do with the fact that you haven't always been honest with me."

A negligent wave of his hand dismissed Colter's reply as Mowry said, "Politics often breeds the necessity for a swift change of plans. It's not always possible to notify those involved."

"That can be damned inconvenient for a man expecting an agreement to be honored."

"You refer to that Saint Peter's Field business, I presume."

"Hardly a *business,* Mowry. It was a damned massacre."

Mowry regarded him blandly. "Only eleven were killed. It could have ended much worse."

"It could have been avoided entirely."

"Yes, but unfortunately, those idiotic rabble-rousers resisted the constable's demands to disperse."

"It was a meeting, for Christ's sake, and bloodshed could have been prevented if you'd listened to me in the first place. I warned you."

"You are not infallible, Northington, though you seem to think so. Hunt, Carlisle and the others incited a riot. They will be tried before the proper magistrates and duly sentenced. That will be an end to it."

"No reformers are welcome in England, I see. I find that view most unsurprising, but shortsighted."

"My dear lord Northington, I expect only cooperation from you. Your Whig notions are not my concern, nor of any interest to me." Thin lips twitched in an imitation of a smile. "What is of interest to me is your expertise in certain areas. As you know, the king is very ill and not expected to live long. After the recent attempt on the regent's life, we must always be prepared."

"Prepared for what? An insurrection?"

Mowry's lips tightened. "When the Six Acts are passed, as they surely will be, we expect rebellion from certain factions. Lord Sidmouth is most concerned, and has written a letter to Lord Liverpool regarding this matter."

"Christ, government creates resentment and then sets about suppressing any protest. Didn't the American Revolution teach us anything?"

"Ah, Whig sentiments running rife, my lord?"

"I prefer to consider my views as Liberal instead of Whig. As does any man capable of free thought."

"Are you suggesting we allow the rabble to run the country?"

"No. I'm suggesting we not alienate the citizens. The Six Acts Parliament proposes will only create rebellion. I promise you, there will be an unpleasant reaction."

"And that is what Liverpool wishes you to prevent, my lord. Either you work with us or against us." Mowry's gaze was darkly cold. "Your cooperation is required. Need I remind you of your duty?"

"I know my duty. It does not require me to dance at your pleasure. If you'll remember, for all intents and purposes, I'm nothing more than an idle buck concerned only with gambling and horses."

"Ah, yes, and of course, the occasional feminine conquest." Mowry's smile didn't reach his eyes. "Never fear, Northington, your masquerade is not endangered. Nor is it far off the mark, in my opinion. We simply request that you use your talents to discover any rebellions that may occur in reaction to Parliament's taking a stern stand on this matter."

"Christ, any yeoman with a pikestaff can do the same thing," Colter said. "What do you really want from me."

"There has been talk. Henry Hunt, the Orator, is stirring up sedition. James Wroe described the incident at Saint Peter's Field in the *Manchester Observer* as The Peterloo Massacre. We do not need another misstep."

Mowry used *we* as a reminder that he had the government behind him, an implication that the regent confided in him. It was more likely that Prinny was fairly oblivious to anything in regard to politics, and it was certain that his father was too caught up in his own fatal madness to care.

"You," Mowry continued, "have been seen too much lately and are in danger of coming under suspicion. It's been suggested that you *retire* from public light for a short time. Tyler will make investigations and report to you what he learns. When you return to London, you'll operate under the guise you've been using. It's proven quite effective so far." His mouth curled. "Whig sentiments have earned you a certain amount of trust from the radicals."

"And suspicion from the Tories." Colter shrugged. "I'll go to Kent, but when I return I intend to conduct matters my own way. No interference from you this time."

"My dear lord Northington, I wouldn't dream of interfering with your plans. Do remember to keep us advised, however. It wouldn't do to counteract your efforts or ours again."

Mowry drifted away, melding into the guests who were still arriving and queuing up in the receiving line to be graciously greeted and announced before descending into the ballroom.

Restless now, Colter considered leaving. He'd had his meeting with Mowry. His reason for lingering was gone. The desire for fresh air increased with each passing moment, and he made his way toward the doors.

"Northington, do come here. I believe you know Lady Leverton, do you not? Oh, of course you've met her daughter, Miss Carolyn Leverton, I'm certain. Have you been introduced to Miss St. Clair yet?"

Katherine's wickedly amused introduction was made with an expression so innocent, it would be difficult to believe she had any intention in mind but civility if he didn't know better. He turned to face the inevitable.

Lady Leverton and her daughter offered gracious replies to his greeting, but it was Celia St. Clair who caught his instant attention.

No virginal white gown tonight, but a gown of a deep scarlet trimmed in gold, vivid in color and seductive in style as it clung to her curves more closely than fashion dictated. She was creating quite a sensation in it, too, as men craned to view this lovely creature who trod very close to the line between respectability and indecency.

Her every movement made the gold-and-crimson silk shimmer with reflected light, giving the appearance of a flame. The little vixen had to be aware of the glances of admiration, the murmurs of appreciation cast her way, for she wore a small, satisfied smile as she met his gaze and held it, cool green eyes regarding him with speculation. Or was that anticipation?

A gauntlet had been thrown down.

"Miss St. Clair," he drawled, "you do waltz, as I recall."

"I do, my lord."

She gave a small gasp when he gripped her hand a bit too tightly. It was time he let her know that he had no intention of being maneuvered, either by her or by Katherine—who would definitely pay later for her malice.

"You needn't have gone to so much trouble, Miss St. Clair," he said softly as he swung her into the pattern of the waltz. "I would have been glad to play your game as long as it's done by my rules."

"Then it would be *your* game, my lord," she replied, unperturbed, her arm held stiffly to keep him at a proper distance. "My rules are more negotiable."

Lemon verbena was a faint, teasing fragrance that radiated upward as he held her lightly, his hand pressed against her upper back. Christ, the gown revealed every sleek line and curve of her body. It wasn't a dress, it was a proposition. His eyes narrowed slightly.

"Do your rules include seduction, Miss St. Clair?"

Her head tilted as she looked up at him. Lamplight glittered on the rich lustre of rubies nestled in the curls piled artfully atop her head.

"A presumptuous question, my lord."

"I prefer to think it astute. You've set a trap for someone tonight."

"Have I? Perhaps you're right. But if so, why would I be so foolish as to confide in you?"

Celia St. Clair turned gracefully in the steps of the dance, a movement that brought her even closer, the swoosh of her skirts a crimson and gold complement to her cool blond beauty. Her flowery fragrance was delicate and arousing. He was tempted to scoop her into his arms and carry her from the ballroom to the nearest bed.

As her lashes lifted and she tilted her head to gaze up into his eyes, temptation coalesced into firm resolve. She played a game with the wrong man. Someone should have warned her.

The lilting melody of a waltz caressed the air as he steered her smoothly toward an alcove at the far end of the wide ballroom. If she noticed she made no protest.

The music ended briefly just as they reached a curtained recess half-hidden by potted palms behind serving tables for the use of footmen—a private nook once the doors closed.

She gave him a startled glance when he swept her into the shadowed corner and shut the doors. "Sir! This is—"

"Now," he said softly, cutting off her protest, "I'll acquaint you with my rules. I think you must already be familiar with a few of them." His arms shot out to imprison her when she tried to leave, trapping her with his hands against the wall, his body a hard force leaning against her. "Ladies who tempt men with fluttering lashes and scarlet gowns are either foolish, or not ladies. I can't decide which you are, foolish with your big cat eyes and ingenuous chatter, or available as that dress suggests so eloquently. Which is it?"

"I—you are too forward, sir!"

"Oh, no, this is what you wanted, isn't it? With your knowing glances and simpering sighs. It's all been a ruse. I don't know what your goal is, but I assure you that if it's only an idle flirtation, I'm not in the mood. I take this sort of thing seriously, Miss St. Clair, so don't tease the tiger unless you're willing to risk the full consequences."

Her chin tilted, mouth thinning into a taut line as her eyes glinted with anger. "You give yourself far too much credit, my lord! Do you think you're so irresistible that all women must pursue you?"

"No, but by God I know when a woman makes

herself available, and you've done everything but leap naked into my bed."

"Your imagination is vivid, but quite mistaken. Let me go before I scream."

"Scream. It will bring attention to the fact that you've been compromised. I imagine your cousin will be delighted by the scandal, while it won't affect my already tarnished reputation. So do that, Miss St. Clair, scream and bring the entire room running to your aid."

"You—you *bastard!*"

His lips curled into a sardonic smile. "Ah, that's better. Now I see the real person instead of this mirage you've tried so hard to keep intact."

Celia tried to twist free but he dropped his hands to her shoulders, fingers digging into bare skin to hold her. "Ah, no, it's time to give you what you've been so prettily asking for, I think—or at least a preview of future interludes."

Oh, he sounded so...so harsh! Her heart pounded fiercely as his mouth came down over hers with brutal force. His hand cupped behind her neck to hold her head still for his kiss though she offered no struggle. This kiss was different than the last. This was more like an invasion, an assault on her senses that was overpowering.

There was no gentleness in him as he held her pinned against the length of his body, his kiss savage and thorough and almost frightening. His tongue was in her mouth, a heated intrusion that left her light-headed, with a pounding pulse loud in her ears.

The wall was unyielding behind her, his hard body a relentless pressure against her chest, belly and thighs. Oh God, his hand had moved to her breast, shaping it in his palm, fingers stroking in sly circles beneath the braided edge of her bodice, a riveting sensation that shot bolts of fire through her entire body.

What was he...? Oh, it was insane, but a strange heat seared her skin, quivered inside her, the stroke of his tongue in her mouth coaxing a response despite her intention of remaining coy and detached. How could she be detached when he did *that* with his hand, on so intimate a place!

Rolling her nipple between his thumb and finger, he seemed to know how it made her feel, how that awful and delicious throb ignited in her belly and between her thighs, for he deepened his kiss until she truly felt faint this time, as if the floor was dipping away from her and the entire world had faded into a heated mist. She was clutching at him, both hands somehow tangled in the front of his elegant evening coat, clinging to him as if she could no longer stand.

''Christ...Celia,'' he muttered thickly, the words sounding almost like a groan.

Suddenly his head bent and he was kissing her breast, his tongue tracing erotic patterns over the sensitive peak as she shuddered and clung to him and made little whimpering sounds in the back of her throat.

She gave a halfhearted protest, though it sounded muffled and more like a moan. His arms were so strong, insistent, and she closed her eyes and yielded to the intensity that raged inside her, a tight, burning knot that spread fire through her entire body.

Celia arched against him, seeking an elusive release from the torment, far too conscious of the pressure of his long, hard-muscled legs against hers, of the abrasion of his elegant evening jacket against her bare breasts.

Everything had disappeared around her, the shadowed alcove, the filtered strains of a waltz, the laughter and conversation of hundreds of guests beyond the flimsy wall disappearing as if never in existence. All that was real was the pulse, like a heartbeat, that urged her to lean into him, to allow him to take these indecent liberties.

Celia didn't know what would have happened had he not suddenly pulled away, leaving her feeling strangely bruised and aching inside, bereft.

As if through a fog she heard him say, "As much as I'd like to continue this, it's neither the time nor place."

He stepped back, his hands on her shoulders again, a steady pressure to hold her. "Fix your dress. For God's sake, don't look at me like that," he said more harshly when she didn't move, shocking her into response.

She jerked at her bodice to cover her breasts, her face flaming. "If you do not like how I'm looking at you, my lord, that can be easily remedied."

Wrenching away from him, she almost ran out of the alcove, pausing behind the screen of palms to wipe her mouth and rearrange her bodice, her fingers trembling so badly it was difficult.

Damn him! He had so effortlessly unraveled her plans, sweeping them away with no trouble at all. And he had shown her how foolish she'd been to think she could control him.

Celia managed to compose herself, and was glad for

her years of training under the nuns at St. Mary's, for she betrayed no sign of turmoil when Northington appeared at her elbow, his voice a low command.

"For God's sake, behave as though nothing is wrong, then no one will notice. I'll escort you to your cousin."

"That's the least you can do," she returned coolly. Oh, it wasn't so difficult if she concentrated on anything but him. She was aware of the crowd as they passed through women garbed in diamonds, rubies and sapphires, aware of the interested glances from men in knee breeches and dark evening coats such as Northington wore.

"Don't play with fire, Miss St. Clair," he said just before they reached Jacqueline, "unless you know how to keep from being burned."

Turning toward him, she smiled, and saw his eyes narrow. "Your warning is appreciated, but as you can see, I'm not even singed, my lord."

An appreciative smile curled his mouth. "Ever the surprise with you, I see. Perhaps I misjudged you."

"Oh, no. I think your judgment is astute."

"You do like taking risks, then. We'll see how you fare when the stakes are much higher."

"Is that a challenge, my lord Northington?"

"Think of it as—an invitation."

They had reached Jacqueline and Carolyn, and with a sardonic bow, Northington presented her to her cousin and murmured his gratitude for the dance.

Lady Leverton fixed him with a rather cool eye as she said, "Your impetuous conduct has disappointed several of the gentlemen present tonight, Lord Northington. By claiming the first dance with Miss St. Clair, you have dashed numerous hopes.''

''Have I? My apologies, Lady Leverton. As you can see, I have returned her to you in excellent condition.''

''As you found her,'' was the tart reply, and Colter's brow rose.

''Her reputation is intact, my lady. She merely felt a bit faint and I revived her.''

Colter took Celia's hand, lifted it to his lips and murmured in French, ''Until we meet again,'' then left them.

''Are you all right?'' Jacqueline leaned close to murmur in her ear, and Celia nodded.

''Yes. Though I do think,'' she replied with a shaky smile, ''that he is definitely dangerous.''

12

Celia looked shaken, Jacqueline thought, though she behaved as if all were perfectly tranquil. She drank cups of champagne punch, danced with knights, barons and even an earl, laughed and flirted and seemed not to notice that Lord Northington had not returned.

It had not escaped *her* notice that Northington and Celia had disappeared for a short length of time, however, nor that Celia was definitely flustered when she returned. It was so like the viscount to do such a thing, and she worried that Celia—so young and innocent, for all that she seemed capable of handling herself well—would find him too experienced to be seduced into a marriage proposal.

She suppressed a light shiver. Northington wasn't very much like his father had been—a terrible man, the new earl, with no scruples at all. At least the viscount had a sense of decency. Should she tell Celia about the earl and Léonie, how he had pursued her so intently many years before? Oh, the man then known as Lord Northington had been absolutely *furious* when Léonie wed her American and left London.

She had spurned his advances and he'd sworn vengeance on her, but thankfully, she had escaped him unscathed. It had been rumored that then viscount Northington could be quite cruel, and oh, she had been so glad Léonie left England before he could exact his retaliation on her for her refusal of him.

But really, what had he expected? Everyone whispered of his excesses, his depravities and membership in that terrible club where men treated women with such awful indifference. Jules had told her of it—a wicked group of men dedicated to appeasing perverted sexual desires with willing—and unwilling—women. Yet all that was gone now, she thought, for there had been no mention of it in so very long a time.

And now perhaps it would be vindication of a sort if Léonie's daughter *did* wed Northington, for after all, he was not the dissolute rake that his father had been, regardless of the gossip. Even Jules thought highly of him, despite their political differences, and Jules was rarely wrong about a person.

Ah, it was so difficult to know what to do. But at the moment Celia was enjoying herself, and if the viscount was immune to her charm, he was practically the only man there who was. Men buzzed around Celia in her scarlet gown as if bees around a lovely flower, fetching more champagne punch and asking her to dance, promising to leave their cards the very next morning.

Yes, she was a success again tonight, and her lack of a dowry seemed not to matter when it came to men willing to fall at her feet and promise undying devotion.

Practicality dictated that few of them would actually

make an offer, for most needed a profitable alliance to increase family lands or wealth, yet Jacqueline thought with a great deal of satisfaction that her *petite cousine* would make a very good match indeed before this Season ended. There would be no need to worry about presenting her in the spring!

Just like my Caro, she thought fondly as she turned her gaze toward her daughter, who was dancing primly with her betrothed, a rather plain but very good-hearted young man with impeccable antecedents and an excellent future. Lord Melwyn was destined to be influential one day, she was certain of it. With Carolyn at his side, he would lack for nothing. Certainly the ample dowry she brought would be quite beneficial.

What, I wonder, Jacqueline mused, would Jules say if I wished to set aside at least a small portion to offer with Celia? A woman shouldn't ever feel deficient, as if she brought nothing to the marriage but her beauty, for there would always be a niggling worry that her husband had wed beneath him. She knew that feeling well enough. Always, she had worried that Jules regretted not marrying a wealthy bride, and it had taken years to finally believe that he truly loved her.

It would be so wonderful to know Cclia had thc same assurance.

"But here you are again," she said as Celia's partner returned her, both of thcm flushed and smiling from the lively contredanse that had just ended. "And not a moment too soon. We are to go into supper."

"I am not at all hungry," Celia said a little breathlessly as a cup was pressed into her hand. "But I think I have drank too much champagne tonight!"

"My dear, are you unwell?"

Jacqueline leaned close and put a hand on her arm, and Celia realized belatedly that she gripped her crystal glass so tightly the stem had cracked. She managed a light laugh.

"Exhausted, but quite well."

Maneuvering her away from the overattentive ears of those near them, Jacqueline murmured, "Whatever did Lord Northington say to you tonight?"

"Why do you think he said something?"

"I *know* he said something, but what? You look...you look almost angry."

"Oh, I am just weary from all the dancing. Why ever would you think I'm angry?"

"No one has such a fierce expression unless they are, my dear, and it seems that Northington has left without claiming another dance with you. Oh." She drew back a little to peer into Celia's face. "Did you perhaps make *him* angry?"

"How would I know? It would be most difficult to distinguish his moods if I cared to dwell on them." She drained the last of her punch, a less potent drink than the champagne. "I find him quite irritating."

"Most men are irritating. That has nothing to do with being eligible. Northington will be earl one day. He is still young and handsome and has a title. While his father may have an unsavory reputation, that is all in the past. And really, it hardly matters what the father is, as long as the son is his own man."

"But is he? *Is* Lord Northington his own man? He seems as brutal as the father."

"Oh my child, so much gossip is based on false facts, it is difficult to say what is true and what is untrue. But my Jules holds the viscount in high regard so I cannot think he is so very wicked after all."

"I begin to think that there must be something more to life than catching a husband." Celia managed a light tone though she was unsettled and on edge, uncertain what to do next. Nothing had gone as she envisioned, for Northington was not at all malleable, or even predictable.

Jacqueline shook her head. "Only after the wedding, my little cabbage. Then life begins. Until then, it is a time of preparation. I am surprised that Léonie did not instruct you more fully, but then, you were still so young when she died."

"Yes." Celia inhaled sharply. She needed no reminders of her mother tonight; Northington had provided far too many reservations that would haunt her when she lay awake later. It had been years since she'd slept an entire night through without waking several times, sometimes to lie awake for hours staring at a dark ceiling, watching the fire die down and reliving old nightmares while plotting new ones.

"You have a restless spirit," Sister Berthilde had told her once, after finding her wandering the halls of the home a few hours before daybreak.

The good sister's recommendation had been to ease the night with earnest prayer, but Celia had never found that successful. She'd tried. Some nights she'd knelt beside her bed so long that her knees were sore and bruised the next day. Nothing had ever eased her *restless spirit.* Until justice was served, nothing ever would.

Now Jacqueline said, "Your dress certainly intrigued Northington, though I thought him a bit—well, *brazen.*"

"Yes, he was. He has earned his reputation as a rake, it seems. It's not idle gossip at all."

"You must be cautious, Celia, or you'll give him the impression that you're wanton."

"Yes, it seems I have." She gave a little laugh at Jacqueline's expression of dismay. "Oh, I've no intention of allowing him too many liberties, but with a man like the viscount, subtlety has no effect."

Jacqueline's fan fluttered briskly. "He doesn't seem to be the kind of man to be teased, petite. I urge you to caution— Oh God, here comes Sir John to dance with you again, I suspect. I believe he has quite a *thing* for you, but keep in mind, he is an intimate of Northington's and anything you say might be repeated—"

She put a hand on Celia's arm and her voice lifted as Harvey drew closer. "But, of course, you must not weary yourself too greatly, Celia, for there is more dancing after our late supper."

Sir John greeted them with a wide smile, but his eyes did not leave Celia as he murmured an appropriate greeting, then said, "I have come to dance with you and then take you into supper, if you consent, Miss St. Clair."

"Of course, my lord. I shall be delighted," she said with a smile. "But you must be warned that I've already trod upon the toes of two poor gentlemen who've danced with me this evening."

"I feel my luck has changed, and am willing to risk my toes." He put out an arm, and Celia put her hand on it to be led onto the dance floor. A quadrille was forming sets and there was no opportunity to talk during the dance as they glided from partner to partner. It wasn't until he escorted her into the late supper that Celia noted his intensity.

"You are a most lovely young woman, Miss St. Clair, and I imagine you have many admirers," he said as they entered the dining room.

"Not so very many, my lord, though your high esteem is very flattering." She smiled at him. His hazel eyes were fastened on her face as if in rapt attention, but there was a strange tautness to his mouth that stirred her curiosity. "You are being very kind tonight, Sir John."

"Not kind, but rather optimistic, is more like it, Miss St. Clair." His shoulders lifted in a light shrug, and his boyish face creased into a rueful smile. "I have the bad habit of yearning for what I can never have, it seems, and that extends to more than limitless pockets and well-bred horses."

"Ah, but I saw you last week in Hyde Park, and your horse seemed very well-bred to me."

"You saw me?" He looked faintly startled, then waved away any explanation with a laugh and observation, "I seem to be unable to skulk about unnoticed. Not that I was trying, I'm certain, but I do recall riding in the park. It's too bad that I didn't see you, or I could have been a gallant escort."

"Oh, I was already escorted by Lord Northington."

"Ah, I'd forgotten. A social coup for you, it seems, for Northington is hardly the man to issue invitations to innocent rides in the park."

"He would not have done so then," she replied, "if you had not teased him into it."

Harvey grinned. "He needed a taste of civility, and I was certain you would provide him with it. I knew he would never be able to resist such a lovely challenge."

"Challenge, my lord?" Celia frowned slightly. Had they been talking about her? If so, it certainly meant that Northington was more intrigued than she had guessed.

"Yes, I have a confession to make—" He paused beneath the glittering light of a wall sconce dripping with crystals that radiated tiny rainbows of color. "I was in the alcove that evening at the Leverton ball, and heard what transpired between you. Forgive me. I hope you don't think I'm a meddler in your affairs, but I couldn't help but overhear. It was deuced awkward, and I didn't know if I should betray my presence or simply hope that you would not notice me there."

"How embarrassing," she said frankly. "I'm afraid that I've made a terrible impression. You must think me a complete idiot."

"Not at all. I find you disarmingly lovely and very charming, Miss St. Clair. Your arrival in London has graced our stifling society with a freshness that is most welcome in all circles."

There was a sudden commotion, and Harvey turned her toward the dining-room entrance, whispering to her that the prince had finally arrived.

"Have you been presented yet, Miss St. Clair?"

"No—oh, do not, my lord, for I don't know what I would say to him."

"You need only be your charming self, for Prinny loves a beautiful woman nearly as much as he loves himself most of the time. Oh, pay no attention to me. I admit to being jaded, but here...come with me.''

Celia's heart pounded furiously, so that her mouth was quite dry and her knees were quivering when Harvey was greeted by the prince.

''Harvey,'' was the affable acknowledgment, and large eyes turned toward her with an appraising stare. ''Who is this exquisite creature?''

''May I present Miss St. Clair, the newest export from the Colonies.''

''From the Colonies, you say?'' His brow lifted, but a smile curved his rather petulant mouth. ''Indeed, if this is an example of American exports, I am very glad we are continuing our trade.''

Despite his bulk, there was an air of majesty to him that had nothing to do with his birth. An innate sense of position was evident in his tone and obvious expectation of command, though Celia had heard all the gossip of his excesses, his affairs and often ridiculous attachments to unsuitable causes.

Yet beneath that bloated form and face, she sensed a careless kindness.

Lifted from her deep curtsy, she returned his smile. ''I am honored to meet you, Your Grace,'' she said, and hoped that her address was appropriate. What was it that Jacqueline had told her she should say if ever she was introduced to the prince? Oh God, but she could scarcely think tonight, with all that had happened. And now he was gazing at her with obvious assessment, his eyes lingering on her bosom displayed in the scarlet gown.

''I find you enchanting,'' he said, ''and insist that you join our party for supper this evening.''

"Sire," a tall, thin man at his side stepped close to say softly, "we have already made arrangements for you."

"Mowry, you're like a damned hound, always baying at the wrong moment. I wish Miss St. Clair to dine with us."

A flash of resentment lit the man's dark eyes, and his glance at Celia was speculative and not at all kind. But he inclined his head in agreement and stepped back, and Celia found herself escorted by none other than the prince regent.

Nearly giddy with apprehension, she saw Jacqueline's astonished, ecstatic face, and was relieved when she was included in their party, a careless invitation issued by the man called Mowry.

Jacqueline was shaking with excitement, but was very charming as she chatted with a man introduced to Celia as Sir Skeffington, "a veritable fount of information about the theater, and he writes his own plays, my dear."

Celia listened politely as Sir Skeffington regaled them with details of his works; she was fascinated to see he wore paint on his face, discreet rouge and powder, but startling nonetheless.

"Yes," Jacqueline was saying, "I did indeed attend your production of *The Sleeping Beauty,* Sir Skeffington, and found it most delightful."

"Alas," he replied with a wry smile, "you are among the few in that case. It was not well received by most."

"A damned dreadful play," the prince said bluntly, "but with a lovely actress—what was her name again?"

"Siddons, sire,"

"No, not that one, the young one, the lively dark-haired chit."

"Maria Wilson, sire." Mowry's smile did not reach his eyes, and gave him the appearance of a rather crafty fox, Celia thought. He was a bit unnerving, seeming like a dark presence hovering over them. "Before she wed, of course."

It was an awkward moment when the king frowned, then Sir Skeffington tactfully observed that there were few actresses as talented as Sarah Siddons, though there was a new play opening soon with an actress who promised to rival any yet presented.

"Another actress," Mowry said, "is just what England needs. We have far too many in politics alone."

Celia felt the undercurrents, yet didn't comprehend the meaning behind them. This lord Mowry seemed determined to be unpleasant, and he really did make her uncomfortable with his innuendoes. Why didn't the prince reprimand him? Was Mowry so influential that he was above reproof?

"And you, Miss St. Clair," Mowry turned abruptly to say, catching her off guard. "How did you come to visit Lady Leverton? A rather sudden decision, I presume."

"No, not sudden. She is, after all, my godmother. I have always longed to meet her."

Hooded eyes seemed to seek out all her secrets, a penetrating dark gaze that was alarming. She suppressed a shiver as he continued, "How fortunate that you were able to arrive in time for the small Season. There will be weeks of celebrations to attend."

"A most fortunate coincidence, Lord Mowry," she

said. He would not intimidate her with sly insinuations, nor would she give him any information about her reasons!

''Indeed,'' he said smoothly, ''and most welcome after your long voyage. I trust the accommodations aboard the *Liberty* were comfortable?''

''Fairly comfortable, thank you.'' How did he know which ship had brought her to England? It was startling.

And frightening.

''Then I trust your shipboard companions were pleasant,'' he continued, still with that same dark smile that summoned images of shadows and secrecy.

''I'm afraid I spent most of my time in my cabin. *Mal de mer.* I'm not a seasoned traveler.''

''A pity. I happen to know a gentleman who returned to London aboard the *Liberty.* I'm certain he would have been most pleased to have made your acquaintance. He has always appreciated lovely ladies.''

''While I'm flattered at your inference, my lord, I made few acquaintances aboard ship.''

Mowry only smiled, but there was a glint in his eyes as he appraised her that made Celia feel oddly threatened. Why she should, she had no idea, but it was disconcerting.

It wasn't until their return home that Celia recalled the directory loaned her by the man she'd met aboard ship—Mister Carlisle. What he must think of her for not returning it as she'd promised! Oh, she would have to find where she'd put it, and see that it was delivered to him at the public house in Shoreditch. It was the least she could do in exchange for his kindness.

Jacqueline came to her bedchamber just as Lily was helping to unpin Celia's hair. The ruby hairpins were placed carefully back into a velvet-lined box and loops of thick pale hair were released to dangle down her back in curling waves.

Celia saw Jacqueline's reflection in the mirror, and braced herself for the inevitable questions. As long as the maid was still in the room, Jacqueline would not speak too freely, even in French. Lily understood far too much to be trusted. Few secrets were safe from servants under the best circumstances.

When Lily was gone, Celia rose from the stool, the silk hem of her dressing gown wafting about her ankles as she turned to face her cousin.

''Who is this Lord Mowry? I found him to be quite unpleasant, and rather...furtive, in an odd kind of way.''

''Mowry? Oh, he works with Lord Liverpool, I believe.'' Jacqueline's eyes narrowed slightly. ''Jules is a devout Tory, but there are times lately that he says Liverpool is taking the country toward a revolution if he doesn't alter his position even slightly. After that horrid massacre this summer—be so glad you weren't here, dear, as it was a terrible thing to even read about in the papers! So many injured, women and children among them, and all because those Manchester constables were ordered to disperse the large crowd who had come to hear men speak in favor of government reform. Dangerous, I say, but why do you want to know about Mowry?''

''He...oh, I don't know, except that he stared at me so very *intently,* and asked about my voyage, and knew what ship I was on. Why would he even know that? Or care to know it?''

''Oh my...I cannot imagine. He is Liverpool's chief minister in charge of security, I believe, but still...it's not something that threatens national security, I would think. Perhaps he's just being cautious because of the assassination attempt on the prince regent's life after the opening of Parliament two years ago. Perhaps it's now the policy to investigate all those who may chance to meet with the prince as tonight— Whatever is the matter, Celia? You look white as a ghost!''

An investigation! Oh God...she was no threat to the national security, of course, but if Mowry discovered the truth behind what brought her here, he may well distort it into something else. The importance of what had happened to Maman would be negated, just as it had been in Georgetown.

Jacqueline frowned. ''What is it you're not telling me, my dear? Don't be so unkind as to pretend it's nothing for I can see that you are not telling me everything.''

Celia said flatly, ''You're right. I have not told you all. I thought it kinder to keep some things to myself.''

A flicker of uncertainty crossed Jacqueline's face. ''Is there a good reason Lord Mowry would know about you?''

''I have never met the man, and there is no reason I can imagine why he would know about me, unless it is, as you said, his business to know everything that may affect the prince.''

''Celia, petite, why did you alter your last name? Is it truly just to honor my dear Léonie's request, or do you have another reason?''

"Yes, I do have another reason, but I would prefer not to confide in you at this time. I will tell you all one day, I swear it, but please do not ask it of me now."

For a long moment Jacqueline said nothing. Concern was obvious in her still pretty features, the furrow of her brow a clear indicator of her distress. Finally she sighed.

"Tell me, does this have anything to do with your decision to encourage the attentions of Lord Northington?"

It was a perceptive speculation, and Celia answered honestly. "Yes, it does, but not, perhaps, as you may think."

"Ah, I do not know *what* to think!" Jacqueline threw her hands up, laughing uncertainly. "But I will trust you to do what is right. You are Léonie's daughter, and I know you would never betray your dear mother's memory."

It was both a conviction and a warning.

13

Colter stretched his legs out toward the fire to warm the soles of his stockinged feet, while a snifter of good French brandy warmed his belly. He contemplated the evening and the paradoxical lady who both intrigued and irritated him. He should have visited Daphne, the latest actress to catch his eye. Instead his early arrival home had startled his valet.

"My lord," Beaton said as he retrieved discarded evening clothes from the bench, "I did not expect you this early."

Colter regarded him through eyes narrowed against the bright glare of the fire. "And I did not expect to return this early," he said shortly, and Beaton wisely lapsed into silence.

Imperturbable, George Beaton had been with him for nearly fifteen years, a loyal servant who probably knew more about him than anyone else. They rarely discussed personal issues, but he'd found Beaton to be intelligent and well-read, a man who enjoyed life to the fullest.

Colter lifted the snifter, took another sip. Brandy heated his throat, pooled in his belly like liquid fire.

"Can I get you anything, my lord?"

"Where the devil is Martin?"

"I took the liberty of giving him a night out to visit his family, since I assumed you would be gone for the evening. If there is anything you need, I'm available to procure it for you."

"No, there's nothing you can get for me. I've endured enough good intentions tonight."

"Very good, my lord."

After lighting another lamp and turning down the covers of his bed in the adjoining room, Beaton tactfully withdrew from Colter's sitting room just off the main bedchamber, and left him alone with his dark thoughts.

Orange and gold light danced across the ceiling and walls. His mind drifted again to Celia St. Clair. He hated mysteries, and she was proving to be one. Was she what she seemed, or was she somehow involved with men like James Carlisle? It just didn't make sense, dammit. She had little to gain from being involved, Mowry's sly innuendoes be damned. He could smell radicals a mile away, and while Celia may be as patriotic as the next young woman, she was no fervent zealot out to bring down the monarchy.

Nor was she as indifferent to him as she pretended. Another sip of brandy rolled on his tongue as he smiled.

Beneath her cool exterior lurked a sensuality that was promising. She was too young and inexperienced to hide her interest or her response, but not too naive to make it clear she was interested in a casual tryst. A disparity of character.

No innocent miss at all, but a woman aware of a man's touch and needs. He'd wager a thousand pounds on it. He'd never been a particularly patient man and the pursuit of a woman's favors held no allure for him. He rarely bet on the uncertainties in life, preferring guarantees.

Celia St. Clair was an uncertainty, a contradiction to herself, and he was damned if he knew why she intrigued him. Yes, he hated unanswered questions. Trouble always came hand in hand with them.

And trouble attended the inevitably tense interview with the earl of Moreland the following day, a discussion that began, as usual, with his father's verbal assault.

"Bloody hell, man, you spend more time with idle pursuits than you do with business. A poor successor to Moreland lands and title, by God!"

"Thank you. Your faith is appreciated." Colter leaned against the fireplace mantel with arms crossed over his chest, a languid pose that conveyed his utter disregard for the earl's opinions.

"You appreciate nothing." Moreland slammed the tip of his cane against the floor, a signal to his long-suffering valet to attend him. Brewster fetched another blanket, and silently positioned the earl's chair nearer the fire.

Cold eyes stared up from beneath a shelf of brow as the earl regarded his only surviving son.

"What did you discover about the lost vessel? Or did you even think of it again after you left me—"

"John Carter has a full report on the sinking of the

India and its cargo, and a manifest of every item aboard. It may be a loss, but not as huge as it could be. All the board members have been notified and mollified and are in complete agreement with me that monies spent on the docks are within acceptable boundaries. Another ship has been dispatched, as the *India* may not have taken on full cargo when the storm struck. It sank just offshore, not off the isle of Lubang, and only three hands were lost.''

Moreland looked taken aback. ''That's not what my report said. By God, if you've discussed it with Philip—''

''Christ, control your bile. Philip isn't involved in construction, nor is he aware of any details concerning the *India.* His interests, as you well know, are with his own branch of another shipping firm, and if I'm not mistaken, he's still traveling on the Continent and not liable to be back anytime soon. Was there anything else you wished me to do?''

Moreland's eyes narrowed. ''It took you a week to find out that little bit of information?''

''No, it took me a week to compile a complete list of the cargo and speak with all fifteen members of the board. Two were in the country.'' Colter pushed away from the mantel, and moved away from the fire and his father. ''I am only a token member of the board. I prefer not to be involved in any of your affairs for obvious reasons. When you're dead, I'll do what must be done. Until then, do as you see fit.''

''I always do.''

''Yes.'' Colter returned the gaze with a steady stare. ''You always do. I'll be going to the country for a few weeks but you know how to reach me if you need me."

"Going to the country now?" Moreland seemed startled. "It's the wrong time of year for it. I won't have it. You are needed here."

"I am not needed here, nor anywhere, for that matter. I have become as you demanded, a lackey at your beck and call. You should be gratified."

"You've never been amenable. Anthony, now, he knew his place, knew what must be done and was man enough to—"

"Anthony was a coward. He could never stand up to you, and in the end, it killed him."

"He died of a fever!"

"Yes, a fever contracted when you sent him to a house sick with fever to steal papers from your dying father. He was warned not to go, but he was afraid of disappointing you, afraid of your anger if he did not. He was barely thirty years of age and had as much spine as a worm."

Pale hands trembled violently, grasping the gold head of his cane, and the earl brought it up in a swift motion to lash out at Colter. It caught him across the chest, a slight brush that did no harm as Colter easily evaded the brunt of the blow. His father's face was contorted in a snarl.

"Curse you! You're a disgrace!"

"Yes. I agree. I've definitely been cursed."

Colter turned on his heel and left with his father's angry words still echoing in the room while Brewster tried to soothe him. A familiar end to their interviews, and as unpleasant as always.

He found the countess in her private sitting room.

"I take it the interview went as usual," she remarked as she closed the book she'd been reading. "Not even an entire wing of rooms can muffle his rage."

"It's always the same," he replied. "What are you reading?"

"*Ivanhoe* by Sir Walter Scott. I find it entertaining. Have you read it?"

"Yes." Too restless to sit, Colter moved to the wide windows and stared out. "I'm leaving tomorrow for the country and will be gone for a week or two."

"At the beginning of winter?"

"It's barely October, and I feel the need of a change of pace. If I remain here much longer, you'll have me attending every ball, rout and soirée given by your untiring friends. Tell me, do you ever run out of women who feel compelled to press their daughters on me?"

The countess laughed. "Never. But you have the solution to that dilemma within your means, you know."

"Yes, I know. If I marry, I'll no longer be expected to dance with nervous, tittering girls who are barely out of the schoolroom. That in itself should inspire me, but I find that choosing which brainless ninny to spend the rest of my life with is something of a problem."

"Then marry an intelligent young lady. There are bluestockings aplenty underfoot if you take the time to look. They don't all have to be Prime Articles or Incomparables, you know, but good breeding is required."

Colter turned to face her again, a dark brow cocked. "You speak the cant much too freely, *ma mère*. There are facets to your character that I'm beginning to think are much more devious than I always suspected.''

''Yes, Colter, I am much more aware of what goes on in this world than even you know.'' She smiled, and suddenly she looked much younger, the light on her face a soft glow reflected in her blue eyes. ''Since you're going to the country, why don't you invite a few companions to join you for a week?''

''What companions do you have in mind, may I ask? Or shall I make a calculated guess—suitable females and their deadly dull chaperones.''

''You're far too clever for me. Yes, suitable females and their deadly dull chaperones sound just the thing. It would please me, Colter. I'm not getting any younger and neither are you. There must be an heir to carry on after we're gone.''

His jaw set. It was a familiar argument.

''There's no guarantee marrying will produce an heir,'' he said. ''Just look at our illustrious prince. Marriage to a shrew and still no surviving heir.''

His mother's soft eyes grew cold and her mouth thinned into a disapproving line.

''Forgive me for saying it so baldly, but our prince is far too busy constructing monstrosities and swilling syllabubs to father a strong child on his wife. He has no sense of proper duty. He prefers actresses to well-born women. I fear you are becoming much too similar, Colter, and I know you resent me saying it. Yet what else am I to think? Your predilections are fairly well-known, though few would dare speak of them to me, of course. And I hardly consider an *actress* to be suitable as your wife. You're thirty-one years of age now, and it's past time you provide an heir for the

Moreland name and title. Whether you appreciate your heritage is not relevant. *I* appreciate your heritage and mine, and wish to see our line continue.''

For the countess, it was quite a speech. She wasn't given to long diatribes, and Colter recognized how much it meant to her that he marry.

''Christ,'' he growled. ''It was much easier on me when Anthony was the heir. I didn't have to be concerned with providing an heir or being involved in my father's eternal machinations. Thank God it was always Anthony, Father and Grandfather in their exclusive little clique. I fully appreciate that now.''

''Your grandfather never excluded you, Northington.''

Her use of his title indicated her displeasure.

He shrugged. ''Not from his life but from their plans, yes. He had other ambitions for me. He taught me a great deal about investments rather than politics. Our time together was not wasted, nor was it unpleasant.''

Lady Moreland ran an idle finger over the binding of the book in her lap. ''Your grandfather was a stern man in many ways, but I always found him to be fair. I think he often wished you were heir instead of Anthony.''

''Being the heir was never an aspiration of mine. I was quite content with being ignored.''

''Why do you resist marriage?'' She looked up at him, a keen-eyed stare that seemed to see into his soul. ''Is it because of your father?''

After a moment he said softly, ''Perhaps it's best if we don't discuss my reasons. I'm not at all certain you'll want to hear them.''

"Perhaps you're right." She lay the book on the table and rose to stand beside him; a gentle scent of lavender enveloped him as she placed her palm on his jaw in a light caress. "You'll do what is right, Colter. You always have. I trust you to respect my wishes."

It was just the sort of comment designed to make him feel like an utter bastard.

Colter left for the country the following day, and as soon as the city was only a distant haze behind him, the chains of civilization seemed to fall away. With London to the north, he took the south road through Rochester at a fast clip.

Harmony Hill in Kent was by turns an inhospitable and welcoming terrain, land where the conqueror had landed his Norman troops eight hundred years before and slaughtered the Saxon king and his army, but where sheep now grazed peacefully on rolling slopes empty of any strife.

Chalky crags and caves lined the seaside of the Kent estate, bounded by the crashing waves of the straits that separated France and England. Less than sixty miles from London, it might as well have been in France for all the privacy it gave him—a welcome refuge.

Solitude there had eased him after his return from His Royal Majesty's service, the fierce battles against Napoleon a grim preparation for the personal conflicts he found at home—Anthony dead, his grandfather dead, an uncle dead, all succumbing to the effects of a fever first contracted in God only knew what hell-hole.

Just beyond the River Buckland, and nestled in a small dip in the hills, the house rose like a shimmering jewel in a green velvet nest as he topped the nearest ridge and paused. His mount snorted restlessly, sensing an end to the journey, hooves pawing at the damp ground.

Colter nudged the horse forward and down the slope. He was met in the stable yard by the head groom, an old man who had been at Harmony Hill his entire life.

Ancient yews shaded the stable yard, dappled light on stone. "All is in readiness, my lord," Smythe reported as he reached for the horse's reins. "I've got a nice stall ready for this beauty and he knows it."

The bay nudged the old man as if in greeting, ears swiveled forward as nickers came from the row of stables that lined the cobbled yard.

"I think he hears old friends calling him," Colter said as he relinquished the reins. "Tomorrow he'll have even more company. Guests are arriving. Make necessary arrangements to stable their cattle."

"Aye, my lord. It will be done."

Entering the house was the closest thing he knew to peace. It was much smaller than even his London town house, a simple half-timbered structure of twenty-four rooms built around a small, cozy court yard. Generations ago a moat had surrounded the house, but time and years of peace had ended the need for it. Now flowers and shrubs shouldered close to stone walls.

Beyond the house lay gardens with wheels of herbs and raised beds of vegetables. Towering sycamores and elms thrust mottled branches skyward, fringing the curved drive that led from the gatehouse. Stretching as far as the eye could see, grassy fields stitched with hedgerows and stone fences provided ample pasture for sheep.

Colter paused on the front step to gaze out across the land a distant ancestor had been granted in gratitude for service to a long dead king. Men were born and died, but the land would always be here. It was a form of immortality.

The front door opened, and he turned as another old retainer greeted him.

"Welcome home, my lord."

"Thank you, Renfroe." Colter moved past the aged butler into the entrance hall. Newly polished dark wood gleamed with dull light, and there was the fresh smell of wax in the air. "I see Mistress Barbara has been busy."

"Yes, my lord. It is first Monday, her day to polish all the furniture and oil the wainscoting. May I take your hat, sir?"

As he put it into his hands and began to strip off his gloves, Colter asked, "Where is James?"

"In the village, sir. Will you be needing him for the week, or is your city valet to arrive?"

A faint note of disdain crept into Renfroe's tone. It was the same here as elsewhere, the distinction between classes. Beaton was not a country man, as was James, who had been born on the estate. Renfroe was James's uncle by marriage and considered family.

"Beaton will arrive tomorrow with the other guests. You did receive my message?"

"Yes, my lord. James is in the village engaging those people we usually use for such occasions. I trust that meets with your approval." Renfroe followed

Colter across the entrance hall and into the small study. ''I understand there will be six guests arriving.''

''With their staff.'' Colter paused. ''One of the guests, Miss St. Clair, is to be given the green room.''

''I understand, sir.''

He probably understood very well. The green room was set apart from the other guest rooms, a lovely room that looked out over the rear gardens and was quite close to Colter's own bedchamber.

He had little doubt Celia St. Clair would accept his invitation. He had not invited her alone, of course, but included Lady Leverton and her daughter as well, and also sent an invitation to Harvey, Mrs. Pemberton and her niece, Olivia Freestone. Olivia was a calculated invitation, meant to provide Harvey with feminine diversion and also give the appearance of propriety to the visit. The news should please his mother when she heard it, as she no doubt would very soon. An invitation to his country house would be spread about by city gossips soon enough.

Outwardly all was more than proper. A few days in the country, a respite from the hectic chaos of the autumn Season with Lord Northington. An opportunity to view the lovely changing colors of the trees. What could be more respectable?

Except that he intended for Celia St. Clair to enjoy far more than autumn at Harmony Hill.

PART III

"But love is blind, and lovers cannot see
The pretty follies that themselves commit."
—Shakespeare, *Merchant of Venice*

14

Celia stared at her cousin incredulously. "But you cannot mean it! Oh, why did you accept Lord Northington's invitation?"

"Isn't it obvious? He's invited us there for reasons that are quite transparent. If we refuse, he will know why."

"If we accept, he will assume the worst. Really, I think you underestimate Lord Northington."

"If he has wicked designs on you, we are there to see he does not succeed," Jacqueline replied tranquilly. "Oh, it cannot be as bad as that, petite. I doubt he will risk ravishing you within earshot of your family. Besides, it is quite a social coup to be invited to his country house. Very few have ever been—why, I don't think *any* female has been invited before!"

Celia jerked at the ribbons in her hair. It was going into the lion's den, but how could she confide that to her cousin without betraying her own reaction to his touch? It was true that this would be an excellent opportunity, but for whom?

"Very well," she said aloud. "If you think it proper for us to visit, I'll go."

"Brilliant! Carolyn will be delighted at the prospect of a visit to the country. Oh, Northington is intrigued by you. Yes, you were so right, it's obvious he is quite interested, for he never would invite us if he didn't have serious intentions."

"Perhaps, but it's which of his intentions are so serious that concerns me," Celia replied lightly to hide her apprehension.

"Do you think— But no, he would not be so bold. Not even Northington would risk angering Jules." Jacqueline lifted one shoulder in a shrug. "I do not mean to sound so confident, but it is true that Jules is very influential. He has many business interests, and has been involved with the Moreland shipping concern for many years."

"Yes, I'm sure you're right." Celia managed a smile.

"And Mrs. Pemberton has also been invited, with her niece Olivia," Jacqueline said thoughtfully, a frown on her brow as she read again the penned invitation that had been delivered—and answered—that morning. "I'm not at all certain why. For appearance's sake, do you think? It's just that Mrs. Pemberton is easily influenced and quite desperate to make a good match for Olivia. Surely he does not entertain a desire for Miss Freestone!"

"It's possible," Celia said, but Jacqueline was shaking her head.

"No, no, I don't think so. Mrs. Pemberton is only a ruse. She's too determined to snag a title for Olivia, and has become completely obsessed with the notion.

Not that it's easy having a young lady who is still on the shelf at twenty-four, but one should not allow disappointment and despair to overcome breeding and decorum."

"I am twenty-one," Celia pointed out wryly, and her cousin looked momentarily startled.

Then she said, "Yes, but you have not been presented, and Olivia Freestone has had several Seasons."

"Then she deserves our compassion instead of pity, I suspect, especially if she has earned the attentions of Northington."

Jacqueline laughed softly. "You can be most cynical at times, Celia. Lord Northington has met his match in you, I vow. Ah, it promises to be a most *entertaining* few days. I'll inform Jules that we will need the carriage on Thursday."

Harmony Hill was a pleasant surprise. Celia saw it in the valley as their landau crested the hill. By the time the vehicle paused at the gatehouse, she realized that the house itself was actually perched upon a hill slope. Beyond green meadows was a blue-gray haze that was the Straits of Dover, the channel separating England from Calais, chalky-white cliffs that plummeted into a frothy wash of surf.

"Oh, it is a lovely sight," Jacqueline said. "I shall never forget when I first saw those white cliffs. At the time, they represented freedom to me. Now, of course, they represent home."

"Yes, I recall seeing the cliffs when my ship first neared land," Celia replied. Her hands clenched in her lap, fingers knotted together. Had she made a mistake?

Agreeing to come here could set her on a dangerous course, but how could she refuse?

Thank God I am not alone, she thought, but there was little comfort in the reminder. If Northington was bold enough to take liberties in an alcove outside a crowded ballroom, what hope had she of keeping him at bay on his own estate?

Lord Northington was not there to greet them when they disembarked from the landau, but they were told he would arrive soon to welcome his guests.

The ancient butler moved with slow grace as he showed them to their rooms, and Celia learned that they were the first to arrive. Apparently Mrs. Pemberton and her niece had been delayed.

Exchanging a potent glance with her cousin, Celia was shown to her chamber first, a lovely room on the second floor with green silk-striped wallpaper and billowing drapes over windows with a view of the surrounding valley. A massive, ornately carved bed dominated the chamber, and thick carpets lay upon the floor. Freshly cut flowers spilled from a crystal vase atop a baroque table, stalks of lavender vying with roses for color and fragrance, lush blooms a vivid touch to grace the chamber.

"Oh my," she said softly, and saw Jacqueline's self-satisfied smile.

"You are being welcomed, petite."

"So it seems."

"My lady, this way please," Jacqueline was told, and she and Caro were led by the servant down the long hall to another flight of stairs.

Jacqueline was given a room on the courtyard side of the house, right next to Carolyn's bedchamber, but above Celia's chamber. It didn't escape Celia's notice that they were separated by distance though still in the same house. Whose bedchamber lay just beyond hers? She'd wager a solid gold guinea it belonged to Northington!

By dinner that evening, Mrs. Pemberton and her niece had arrived, as well as Sir John. Footmen served dishes to the guests continental style, and Jacqueline remarked how civilized it was to find a host acquainted with the elegant nuances of hospitality.

"So many," she said with a sigh, "simply place the food in the middle of the table or rely upon guests to pass it to one another. By the time it reaches one, it can be quite cold. It is so much more gracious to send footmen round with the dishes."

Lord Northington, seated at the far end of the table behind a bank of flickering candle stands, cocked a dark brow, his smile somewhat mocking, Celia thought. She could barely see him down the length of the table, but was far too aware of his presence. He'd dominated the dining room since the moment he'd entered, with no apologies for his absence or tardiness.

"Dinner requires some formality," he replied smoothly to Jacqueline on his left, "but here in the country I lean toward more simple customs. I rise early and may be gone by the time breakfast is served, so it will be informal, the sideboard set for your convenience. Renfroe will see to your needs."

Aware of Sir John's attention on her, Celia turned to her side. He had been seated next to her instead of beside Lord Northington—a surprise.

"It is very good to see you again, sir," she said politely, and he grinned.

"Unexpected, I imagine."

"I beg your pardon?"

Indicating the others at the table with a careless wave of one hand, he explained, "I imagine you weren't expecting a crowd."

"I hardly think a half-dozen people qualify as a crowd, Sir John."

"That depends on your perspective, I assume." Harvey lifted his wineglass. He hadn't touched his food, she noticed, but drank several glasses of port instead. "Have you ever considered how easily things come to some people?"

"I'm afraid I don't understand." Celia drew back. It was obvious Sir John had imbibed more wine than necessary and he seemed surly beneath his urbane facade.

Shrugging, he turned his attention to the half-empty glass, twirling it between his fingers. She regarded him closely as he seemed about to say something, then obviously decided against it. He glanced up at her with a smile that didn't reach his eyes. Light glinted on his blond hair and in his hazel eyes as he said softly, "I have never been comfortable with losing."

"What have you lost, sir?" She took a sip of sherry to give the impression of nonchalance, even though Harvey was beginning to annoy her. It wasn't only bad manners to be a surly drunk, it caused an uneasy suspicion to form.

"One cannot lose what one never possessed, I suppose. Yet I have managed it. 'She's beautiful and therefore to be woo'd: She's a woman, therefore to be won.' As you may have guessed, I'm cup-shot and quite incoherent."

"Shakespeare is rarely incoherent."

"You are familiar with the play—"

"Henry VI, first act." Celia paused. Harvey seemed more sad than drunk, but another emotion seethed beneath his surface that made her uneasy. She leaned forward to say softly, "May I suggest that you partake of your excellent meal? It should make you feel much better."

"You mean, dilute the port." His smile was a bit wry and self-mocking. "You're right, of course. If I make an ass of myself Northington will not be pleased."

"I'm certain he would forgive you."

"He always does, curse him."

Perplexed, Celia was relieved when the meal finally ended and Sir John maneuvered a path toward Miss Olivia Freestone. She was young, dark-haired and very sweet in an innocent way. And she seemed quite flattered by the attentions of Sir John, though intimidated by her aunt's stern presence. Mrs. Pemberton kept a close eye on her niece, as if afraid she would be abducted.

No doubt, it was that protectiveness that enabled Miss Freestone to retain her air of virginal naivete.

Have I ever been so naive? Perhaps once, but that was so long ago. Oh, she felt so old at times, much older than even her cousin Carolyn, who was basking in the triumph of having been invited to Northington's country home. It was a social coup of sorts, even though Caro had no particular need to expand her social reputation. Her wedding was to be in the summer, and her future was secured.

Celia wandered onto the terrace lit by flickering lanterns that cast wavering pools of light on trees, vines and pots of flowers. Jacqueline and Mrs. Pemberton were deep in conversation, no doubt plotting the demise of the viscount's bachelor days, each with their own goal in mind, and Carolyn had gone upstairs to freshen up after the evening meal.

Lately she had noticed a difference in Carolyn, as if she had gained confidence in the past few weeks. What would it be like to feel as Caro must feel? To *know* that life was safely planned, that there would be no worries other than the proper gown to wear at social functions, or the more important need for an heir. To know that one's life held no uncertainties save the everyday dilemmas that few escaped?

My life has been so different. To be so protected seems like a fiction, a far distant dream as vague as a shadow.

There were times she couldn't even remember what her father had looked like, save for a blurry impression of a tall man with dark hair and brown eyes that were always filled with laughter. They had all been content then, and even when Maman had no more children, Papa had not seemed to mind. He'd said he had two beautiful women in his life and needed no more to make him happy. And it had been enough.

Yet it had ended so soon, their lives changed forever when he died aboard that American warship.

"Hello, cat-eyes," the mocking drawl she'd been half expecting all evening said behind her. Celia turned to face Lord Northington.

Her heart beat a rapid thunder as she met his eyes, and a little shock rippled through her at the intensity of his dark blue gaze.

I'd forgotten how intimidating his stare can be....

"Good evening, my lord," she said in what she hoped was a cool tone.

"How very polite you are—no, don't retreat now, the evening is still so new. We have time enough to explore all our possibilities later."

He stepped in front of her, blocking her progress, and leaned one arm against the vine-covered wall behind her head. It was disconcerting; instead of evening clothes, he now wore a loose white shirt open at the throat and snug-fitting trousers with knee-high black boots.

He radiated masculine power and sensuality, the strong column of his throat a dark contrast to the white cotton shirt, his fitted trousers clinging to muscled legs. Celia averted her eyes from his penetrating gaze.

"What?" he murmured, and drew the backs of his fingers over her cheek in a light caress. "No cutting comments? I'm amazed. And a little disappointed. I had rather looked forward to our usual disagreement."

"I'm sure you have, my lord. My restraint must be very upsetting for you."

"Ah well, we have plenty of time to try again. There is to be music this evening. I expect you and your cousins will enjoy it."

To her faint surprise, he did not try to kiss her, but pushed away from the wall and stepped back. Always the unexpected! She had been sure he meant to kiss her again, and braced herself to resist any response.

But as if he'd anticipated her reaction, he merely smiled that slow, sardonic smile she was growing used to seeing, and left the terrace. He walks like a tiger, she thought distractedly, as quiet and lithe as one of the huge beasts at the Tower menagerie.

And as restless, with the same predatory stride.

She reminded herself how dangerous he could be, how easily he could upset her careful plans. Yes, she must be on her guard.

Oh, but he is maddening! Celia thought later as she perched primly on the cushions of a large settee and listened to Olivia Freestone play yet one more piece on the pianoforte, a mangled version of a lovely French tune. Northington arrived late, coming into the music room just before the butchered tune ended.

He'd had no intention of being present for such tame and irritating entertainment, of course, but certainly didn't mind inflicting it on his guests, she fumed. She saw with some satisfaction that Sir John was as annoyed as she was, his voice tight when he spoke to Northington.

"You've missed some very nice melodies," Harvey said with a glint in his eyes, "but I am certain Miss Freestone will be delighted to give you a private concert."

"I wouldn't dream of tiring her with such a request." Northington's smile betrayed nothing as he moved to the now flustered Olivia Freestone and took her hand to lift her from the seat. "She's been very accommodating as it is. Refreshments are being served on the terrace."

"Bloody bastard," Harvey muttered under his breath, and looked startled when Celia leaned close and agreed.

"Yes. I suggest we tie him to a chair, then have

Miss Freestone play the entire score of Beethoven's Fifth."

A grin squared Harvey's mouth. "But who would stay to ensure she complied? No volunteers here."

They both laughed softly, and she took Harvey's arm as he escorted her to the torch-lit terrace. Linen-draped tables were laid with delicacies, but Harvey made straight for the decanters of port. "A good host would provide something stronger," he said lightly. "A little Blue Ruin wouldn't be taken amiss."

"So it seems, Harvey," Northington drawled softly.

Celia's heart skipped a beat, and she was suddenly fully aware of him behind her, his presence as forceful as a blow. She turned slowly, but Northington's eyes were on Sir John, his voice deceptively soft.

"I have stronger drink in my library, but ladies don't usually swill gin."

Harvey lifted a brimming glass, saluted Northington with a mocking bow. "Then port it shall be, so as not to offend the ladies or dilute the evening's diversions."

"I do have some more *lively* entertainment for the evening," Northington said, and his eyes slid to Celia as he lifted a brow. "Ladies always enjoy dancing."

"Dancing?" Harvey snorted. "Hardly what I'd call more lively, old boy."

"You might change your mind before the night's over."

"That's possible but hardly probable." Harvey drained his glass in a single gulp, then poured another. "But I'm willing to be wrong."

Celia didn't resist when Northington took her arm. His touch was light, impersonal but commanding.

"I think you'll enjoy this, too," he said.

"Will I? A waltz by torchlight hardly seems exciting enough for Sir John."

"I'm sure it's not. However, I've engaged dancers for all of us to enjoy."

She shot him a glance, then turned when she heard the light tinkling of tiny bells and a spate of rapid thrums from a fiddle. Into the middle of the terrace swarmed a group of brightly clad men and women. The women wore full skirts of polished cotton in red and blue and yellow, and bangles on slender arms that jingled with every movement. The men were clad in dark, fitted trousers, scarlet shirts and brilliant blue vests. Their music was loud, lively, and they immediately began to stamp their feet, the women tossing long black hair with obvious abandon and pleasure.

Celia forgot what she was about to say, captured by the primitive, earthy music and graceful abandon of the dancers. Never had she dreamed there could be such dancing as this! One of the women, bolder, younger and more supple than the others, whirled so fiercely that her skirts swung high above her knees, displaying long brown legs. Her hair was loose, save for a knot piled atop her crown and fastened with glittering combs. These she pulled out one by one, tossed them aside as she danced.

"Spanish gypsies," Northington murmured in Celia's ear, his warm breath on her neck summoning a shiver. "They camp on my land every year."

"And you allow them to do so?" It was unnerving, him leaning so close to her, the steady beat of gypsy drums a pounding match to the thud of her heart as she tried to maintain composure.

"It's a cordial agreement. They camp here without fear of persecution in return for helping Smythe train my horses. Santiago, the older one with the gray hair playing the fiddle, is a master with horses. It takes him no time to train them."

"I see." She ignored his hand on her arm, and the suggestive caress of his fingers. "I had no idea you were such a philanthropist, my lord."

"Hardly. I require a fair return on my investment, whether it be with gypsies, or lovely ladies."

She turned to meet his gaze. "So everything is only a business arrangement with you."

"Not everything." He drew his thumb along the curve of her jaw. "Not everything, pretty lady."

It was suddenly too warm, the air stifling as she met that dark blue gaze. He expected more of her than social conversation. But hadn't she known that? Yes, she'd known all along that he wanted her, and she still wasn't certain how she felt—a strange kind of excitement, anticipation—when she should feel only resentment for the son of the man who had killed her mother. Why didn't she hate him as well as his father? She should. Oh yes, she should. But it was unsettling to realize her feelings for him were much different.

Someone pressed a glass of wine in her hands and she took it, looking up to see Harvey's eyes on her with an expression of—sympathy? But why?

Defiantly she smiled at him, upset that he would see her distress. He was far too astute for a man who drank so much and seemed so shallow.

"There is more wine," Harvey said mildly when she drained her glass. "Would you care for another glass?"

Aware of Northington's attention on her, she held out her empty glass and smiled her thanks.

"Harvey seems to be rubbing off on you," he drawled, but she shrugged off his comment. Let him think what he wanted!

The music was loud, crashing around her, a cascade of sound that meant little, so she was startled when suddenly one of the dark-haired gypsies presented herself in front of them, hands on her hips and her black eyes narrowed in a sultry challenge as she smiled at Northington.

"My lord, you want us to play yet you do not listen. Come, dance with me again."

Again? Celia's eyes jerked to the woman, who met her gaze with a lifted brow and knowing smile.

"He dances beautifully, does he not, *señorita?* Like a gypsy, though he swears he is not. Well, will you dance, my lord?"

"Teach the *señorita* to dance, Marita, for it is she who dances beautifully."

"No!" Celia burst out. "I...I do not care to dance."

"Do you not?" The girl he'd called Marita tossed back her long loose hair like a dark cloud, and lifted her slim shoulders in a shrug. "It is truc that few can dance like a gypsy. We are more graceful, have more passion. I have never seen a clumsy Englishwoman who can compare."

"I'm not English," Celia said stiffly, and recognized the challenge in the girl's black eyes. "Nor am I clumsy."

"No?" Red lips parted in a grin. "Yet you stand there as stiff as an English oak, unyielding and with as little grace. No, I say, you do not care to try because you know you cannot learn our dances."

All eyes were on them now, and Celia flushed when her cousin urged her to try. Jacqueline laughed gaily.

"Oh, do give it a try, Celia. I think it would be quite entertaining."

Mrs. Pemberton snorted. "I daresay, a proper lady does not indulge in such...such *heathen* activities. My niece would never be so heedless of her position."

"But, Aunt Agatha," Olivia said softly, "I do not think it would be so terrible. And they *do* look so graceful and lovely, and the music is quite lively."

"I'll try it," Celia said, "if Carolyn and Miss Freestone join me."

Marita clapped her hands, and two of the young men joined them, hot-eyed and eager, with broad white grins on dark faces. She spoke to them in what sounded like Spanish but must be a different dialect, then one of the men took Celia's hand and drew her out onto the cleared paving stones, while another young man escorted Carolyn and Miss Freestone.

Mrs. Pemberton looked disgruntled, but Jacqueline only smiled as the music began again.

Celia's partner put an arm around her waist, and when she drew away, he shook his head and said something in his own language. She looked down at his feet when he pointed to them, and studied the brief steps he showed her. It was very simple, really, a combination of several dances. What made it seem so different was the movement of the body and the stamping of the feet.

Fascinated, she watched Marita, saw that she put her entire body into the dance, eyes half-closed, a teasing smile on her lips as she swayed, turned, then stamped her feet to the beat of the fiddle, guitar and drums. Bells attached to the many bracelets on her arms jangled as she lifted her arms over her head, whirled around, bare feet a blur and her body lithe. She shook her head, and her hair swung down her back to her waist in a silky mass.

Marita looked as if she danced for a man, a lover, her slender body moving in blatant seduction. Snapping fingers over her head, she danced toward Northington, lips half-parted, eyes glistening an invitation as her hips undulated provocatively, skirts whirling up above bare knees. Celia heard her partner make some kind of low sound in the back of his throat as Marita pressed her body against Northington briefly, then whirled away in a teasing summons for him to follow.

To Celia's surprise, he did, eyes narrow and focused on the girl's face, his step matching hers, heels slamming down one after the other, his lean body powerful and graceful at the same time. It was obvious he had done this before, and Celia was shocked by the realization that the gypsy girl was very familiar with him. It was in her eyes, in the laughing curve of her lips, in the dark gleam of triumph she threw toward Celia.

They have been together, she thought then, and was startled by the pang of anger that knifed through her. Why should she care what woman had caught his eye? It didn't matter in the least.

She must have stumbled, for her partner caught her by the elbow to steady her.

"*Señorita,*" he said softly, a question in the dark eyes fastened on her face.

Smiling, he urged her to follow his steps, and Celia forced a smile as she obliged.

Damn Northington, this was just another of his games, an attempt to prove his masculine appeal. She would ignore him, as he well deserved, and pretend that she hadn't noticed at all, or even cared.

She danced with the young gypsy, and discovered that once she concentrated, she could mimic his moves quite well. Her feet flew over the stones and her body seemed to move of its own volition to the driving tempo of the music that soared beneath the lanterns. The music went faster and faster and so did her feet as she twisted, turned, let her arms go above her head as she had seen Marita do. It was suddenly liberating to dance so freely, as if she cared for nothing but the moment.

And maybe that's partly true, she thought as she let the music direct her feet. Maybe I should think of nothing but this very moment, right now, and not remember anything or think of what I must do tomorrow... I'm so weary of it all, the hurting and the frustration. And yes, the desperation. Oh, why did I ever think I could manage this?

It was hopeless. The earl of Moreland was too far out of her reach, beyond any justice she could exact. How silly it all was, to think she could come to England and somehow ruin a man like Moreland.

Hot tears stung her eyes, half-blinding her as she danced, losing herself in the music instead of despair, pushing all from her mind as her breath came in harsh pants and perspiration dampened her clothes.

As she had seen Marita do, she reached up to free her hair, tossing aside the pretty hairpins as carelessly as if they were worthless, shaking her head to let her pale hair cascade around her shoulders and in her face. Nothing mattered at this moment but relief from constant tension, from all restrictions.

From Northington...

Colter was very much aware of her, startled and angrily amused by her display. Bloody hell, he had only himself to blame for it, for goading her into some kind of reaction, something other than the stiff, cool composure that he knew she didn't feel. But this! Christ, Harvey was nearly choking on his port, staring at Celia as if he'd never seen her before, and the gypsies— He'd put an end to this before it went too far, for the young man, Mario, who danced with Celia was getting much too close to her.

Lady Leverton watched Celia with wide eyes and an expression of dismay, while Mrs. Pemberton had risen to her feet and snapped a command for her niece to stop that nonsense at once.

Colter reached Celia in two long strides, his glance at the startled Mario a warning the young man immediately understood. Silently he stepped back.

"What in hell do you think you're doing?" Colter asked Celia softly, but she was obviously impervious to his anger or intimidation.

"Dancing, my lord." A misty sheen made her face glow, and her eyes were very green and bright. "Is this not what you wanted? Your guests to enjoy themselves?"

She whirled away from him before he could reply, and he moved after her, catching her against the far wall, all too aware that they were being observed, that

Santiago was grinning widely. Damn her! The little cat knew what she was doing.

The movements of the dance brought her close to him and she moved her body in a deliberate brush against his. Her arms swept upward, slowly and sinuously, to lift the mass of honey-colored hair away from her neck, then let it drop again as Marita had done earlier, a provocative ploy meant to entice.

"Stop it," he said quietly, the steely note in his voice making her eyes widen at him, "or I'll give you what you're so prettily asking for. If that's what you want, by God, I can oblige. Don't tempt me!"

She came to an abrupt halt as the music ended, her chest heaving from her exertions, green eyes sparkling angrily at him.

"Oh, I've no doubt you will do just what you say, my lord. You seem quite adept at being an autocrat. Is that why you invited me here? You needn't have gone to so much trouble. I was well aware of your inclinations before I arrived."

"I think," he said slowly, eyes narrowed at her, "that you know very well why I invited you here. Don't pretend otherwise."

"Yes," she said in almost a whisper, lips slightly trembling, whether with anger or emotion he couldn't tell, "I know very well why you invited me."

"Then we needn't delay any longer."

15

All the noise, the music and the laughter, even Mrs. Pemberton's shocked disapproval and her not so very quiet scolding of Olivia, faded into a blur of sound as Celia stared up at him. Here it was, the moment she'd been half expecting since she arrived, afraid of it yet anticipating it at the same time, strangely enough. Yet it was a shock, after all, for it wasn't done quietly or privately, but in front of a dozen people and in full view of her cousin.

"Am I expected to fall into your arms now?" she hissed angrily. "Or can you wait until we are alone? Tell me what you expect, my lord, for it's obvious you think I am eager for you."

"Aren't you?" He smiled at her angry hiss. "It wasn't my idea to make a public display."

"Display? I thought it was dancing."

"Not the way you were moving. It was an invitation and I accept. Christ, you can't be that naive to think I'm the only man here who wants you. Look at Mario. And Harvey. If you so much as give either of them the slightest nod of encouragement they'll be more than happy to toss your skirts and take you against the wall. Isn't that what you wanted to prove? That you're desirable? You should be well satisfied with the results, for even old Santiago wouldn't mind tumbling you if you gave him the opportunity. No.'' His hand flashed out to grab her wrist, holding it tightly in a steely grip. ''If you run away now, what have you proven? Only that you're a teasing little gypsy like Marita.''

''If I stay, my lord,'' she managed to say calmly, ''I have the inescapable feeling that I'll end up proving I'm as available as Marita.''

Lights exploded in the dark blue of his eyes, and his smile thinned. ''Ever a surprise,'' he said at last. ''You waver between honesty and deceit at an alarming rate.''

''Do you expect me to deny my attraction to you? I admit I find you—seductive. I'm intrigued, and yes, I'm curious, too. Are you what you seem to be? Or are you only a charlatan beneath all your bluster.'' She lifted one shoulder in a light shrug. ''It would be intriguing to discover the truth, but not at the expense of my good reputation.''

''Take it from a man of experience, a reputation is as fleeting as the seasons, gone in an instant even if it's undeserved. And a *reputation* is damn cold comfort on long winter nights.''

''Perhaps, but you speak from a man's point of view, and as a member of the peerage. Even a bad reputation doesn't keep you from being received in society.''

''Doesn't it? Even an earl can be ostracized. But

you aren't really worried about your reputation. If you were, you wouldn't have danced as you did tonight."

"I hardly think that will keep me from being accepted in society, my lord. Unless you choose to make it greater than it is."

"I'll leave that to Mrs. Pemberton."

Celia smiled. "I doubt she'll betray her own niece, who was also learning the gypsy dances."

"None of which matters." His hand slid down her arm to her elbow, cupped it in his palm to turn her toward the others. "We can discuss all the reasons why you shouldn't be here later, and then I'll give you all the reasons why you should."

There was no need to ask what he meant.

It was unnerving, but Celia managed a careless laugh and shrug when they joined the others. Carolyn and even Olivia expressed admiration for her daring.

"But you are every bit as agile as the gypsy girl," Carolyn said with enthusiasm, and her eyes were admiring. "I am too clumsy to dance so beautifully."

The gypsy girl, Marita, was not as complimentary. She shrugged, and her tone was grudging. "You would never be mistaken for me or Rosa, but you are not so very bad."

Celia met the girl's narrowed gaze with a coolly lifted brow and smile. "I don't think you have to worry about me trying to take your place," she said, and saw that Marita understood her meaning.

She slid a sly glance toward Northington, and leaned close to say softly, "The *señor* seems to prefer women of fire, not ice, so I do not think you will be given a chance to take my place, *señorita!*"

Celia was saved from a reply by Jacqueline, who

put a hand upon her arm and said, "We're going inside where it's warmer, my dear. Do come and join us, for the night is growing quite cool."

Damn him, Celia thought angrily as Northington took Marita's arm to join Santiago and the others, all speaking in that strange sort of Spanish. It was obvious they were all very familiar with one another. He even looked like one of them, with his dark skin and hair, garbed in snug trousers and a loose white shirt. And he had looked as if he enjoyed the dance with Marita, as lithe as she, and with the same kind of casual sensuality.

Celia followed her cousin and Mrs. Pemberton and her niece inside, glad that Northington stayed out on the terrace with the gypsies. Why should I care what he does? It was so ridiculous, and she wished now that she hadn't agreed to come. Olivia Freestone was fraying her temper, and even sweet Caro, with her big eyes and lively nature, was making her fret with her ingenuous chatter.

"Oh, how lovely it is here," Carolyn said as she sank into a chair and sipped a cup of mulled wine. "Don't you think so, Celia?"

"Yes. It's quite lovely. But I'm tired after all that dancing. I think I'll retire for the evening. You'll forgive me for abandoning you, I hope. Please make my apologies to Lord Northington."

Though she said it with a smile, she had no intention of being coaxed to remain, and despite Jacqueline's faint protest and worried eyes, she made her way up the stairs to the chamber she had been given to use. Janey was there, Lily having remained in London, and Celia was tempted to send her away. The girl was inept at best but tried hard, so she bit her lip and allowed Janey to help her.

"I saw you out the window," Janey offered shyly, "and I thought you were the best one, Miss St. Clair."

"Did you? I'm sure there are others who'll disagree with you, but thank you for your kind words, Janey. No, I'll brush my own hair. Later, please go down and retrieve my hairpins from the terrace."

"Yes, Miss. The pearl ones?"

"Yes. After you turn down my bed, you're free to go for the evening. You must be very tired."

She wanted only to be alone, to think, to reflect on how best to extract herself gracefully from this awkward situation. It had been very foolish to come here, where she knew he would be waiting for her to let down her guard, yet she'd allowed Jacqueline to talk her into it.

And, she realized with a shock, she had let down her guard more than she'd ever thought she would. She'd felt not just anger, but a spark of jealousy when he'd danced with Marita, that swift, encompassing pang of realization that they knew one another far better than she knew him.

"But I've ordered hot water for your bath," Janey said, reminding Celia she had earlier expressed a desire to bathe before bed. "And the footmen will be bringing up the water soon."

"Oh. Very well. I'd forgotten...the tub is in this next room?"

Janey nodded. "And a large room it is, with a huge tub that's partway in the floor, Miss! James, the footman, said it was called a Roman tub, and that the lord had it put in himself. Shocking, I say."

"Yes. Very shocking. Let me know when the water is ready."

"Yes, miss."

Janey opened the door just as a light knock sounded on it, and Carolyn peered into Celia's room.

"Are you well, Celia?" she asked.

"Yes, yes, I'm just tired. Aren't you?"

"Yes—and no." Carolyn's pretty face was alight with laughter, and she stepped inside when Celia beckoned.

This was the most exuberant Celia had seen Carolyn since she'd arrived in England, and she felt almost ashamed that she hadn't become better acquainted with her.

"Carolyn," she asked when it became obvious that she wished to linger. "Would you like to talk?"

Relief flickered on Carolyn's face for a moment, then she nodded almost eagerly.

"Yes, I would like to. We haven't really spent much time together, and I know we're only here this week because Lord Northington had to include us so you would come, and I—well, I'm curious about his intentions, I admit it!"

"So am I," Celia said frankly, and they both laughed.

It was wiser to change the subject, and Celia took a seat on an upholstered settee placed before a marble hearth. A fire burned brightly in the grate.

"Tell me all about the plans for your wedding this summer," she said, "and of course, your betrothed. Are you excited about your future, Caro?"

Shrugging, Carolyn reclined on the lounge chair near the fire and said, "Melwyn is pleasant enough.

I've known him since I was very young. It's all been arranged for so long that I suppose I never thought about any other future. I'm content enough.'' She smiled slightly. ''What of you? What is in your future?''

''My future? I hadn't thought about it beyond the next year, I suppose.'' Celia smoothed a hand over her skirts. It wouldn't do to think about Northington, or Moreland. Or what she would do once she had achieved her goal.

''I envy you,'' Carolyn surprised her by saying. ''You are so brave, and so—adventurous! I could never have done what you've done, traveled so far and seen the things you must have seen.''

''But you've been to France, and I've only come from America. I've not done the things you must have done.''

Carolyn waved a hand airily. ''Oh, everyone goes to France. And it's not so very far, though I did get a little green on the Channel crossing. We shopped mostly, hardly an *adventure,* such as coming to live in a new land where everything and everyone must seem so strange to you. I could never be so brave. My life has always been boring and staid. I know what I'll be doing tomorrow, and it's the same thing I did yesterday.''

Celia couldn't answer for a moment. How could she confess how much she envied her that boring life?

''It doesn't seem so very adventurous to me,'' she said at last, ''but rather frightening at times. If not for your mother, I don't know what I would have done.''

''Yes, Mama is very generous. I suppose I take her for granted, when I shouldn't.''

"Yes, be very glad you have your mother," Celia said softly, and looked away from the sudden sympathy she saw in Carolyn's face. "Is she still on the terrace?"

"No, she came up with me. Celia, I must ask, have you set your cap for Lord Northington?" Carolyn laughed softly when Celia merely lifted a brow. "Oh, it's none of my business, but why shouldn't you? He's a splendid match for any woman, and all of London knows that every eligible female over the age of ten has been after him even before he became heir to the Moreland title. It'd be a feather in your cap to be the countess one day, don't you think?"

"I'm sure it would be." Celia smiled. "I hardly think it a possibility, however."

"Don't tell me you haven't thought of it!" Carolyn sat up, staring at her with interest. "Why do you think he has invited us all here this week? Certainly not to woo Miss Freestone. Mama and I were only invited so that you could come without risk of scandal. I think it's simply delightful."

"I think you are mistaken."

"No, I don't think I am. Oh, Celia, I saw him looking at you at the last ball, and then only a day later came the invitation to join him here at his country home. You *do* know that very few people have been invited—or perhaps I should say *respectable* people."

"That bodes well for his intentions," Celia said dryly, and Carolyn giggled.

"Tell me—" she leaned forward to stare intently at Celia "—have you ever...ever...*been* with a man?"

"Been where? Oh, you mean—Caro, what a question to ask!"

"Well? Have you?"

Celia was beginning to regret the impulse to invite her in for a talk.

"No," she said, "not in the way that you mean."

"Is there—how many ways *are* there?"

Really, what a naive little goose Carolyn was. But it was probable that she was as innocent as she seemed.

"Perhaps you should ask your mother these questions," she hedged, but Carolyn shook her head.

"I would be mortified. For all that Mama is so sophisticated, she isn't at all comfortable talking with me about certain things. I haven't known *who* to ask. Once, I asked my old nurse about...about my wedding night, but she said that it's not something decent girls think about. And when I asked Charlotte—my friend who married only a few months ago—about it, she made a face and said it was dark and she just closed her eyes and tried to pretend she was at Brighton, as her mother had advised her to do."

"Hardly helpful," Celia said faintly, and Carolyn agreed.

"Yes. But you seem so *wise* about everything, Celia. I'm sure you must know more than Charlotte. Oh, not that you're experienced, but you do seem resourceful."

"Resourceful." Celia stared at her, uncertain whether she should be amused or insulted. She thought suddenly of her years at the foundling home, and how the girls had all gathered into whispering, giggling groups at night to talk. The conversations had inevitably turned to boys, and the wisest of the group had enlightened them on matters of sex in the most graphic terms. Some of the girls had even practiced kissing, though Celia refrained. It had been a most illuminating education she would never have learned from the nuns.

Now, gazing at Carolyn's expectant, hopeful face, she said slowly, "I suppose I know more than Charlotte."

It was awkward at first, but Celia explained the basics as succinctly as she could, recognizing from Carolyn's wide eyes and disbelieving gaze that she knew absolutely nothing about sexual matters.

"Has no one ever told you *any*thing?" she asked bluntly, and Carolyn shook her head.

"No. Oh my. It's—it's much more *intimate* than I had thought it would be."

"But if you love Melwyn, you won't mind that. You'll be glad to have him hold you, kiss you and I'm certain he'll be tender and gentle."

Not savage and ruthless like Northington....

Carolyn frowned, looking down at her hands as she pleated folds of her skirt between her fingers. "I don't really know Edwin. How can I love him enough to do—do *that?*"

For a moment Celia was silent. It was true that she had little experience with the physical aspects of love. But when Northington had held her against him, she'd felt the surge of his desire and her own quivering response. Heat and confusion had churned inside her until she could barely think coherently.

It had shocked her. Never had she suspected she would feel that way with a man. Especially with Northington.

"I think," she said slowly, and felt Carolyn looking

at her, "that there must be some natural instinct that takes over."

It was the only logical explanation for returning Northington's kiss, for allowing him to haunt her dreams and even her waking thoughts.

"Yes," Carolyn said with a sigh. "I suppose that's true. I'll hope my natural instincts come to my rescue."

Their discussion was interrupted by Janey's return, and Carolyn rose at once, yawning. "I'll leave you to your bath, Celia. I hope your sleep is restful."

"It will certainly be welcome," she replied, and was relieved when Carolyn was gone at last. The turmoil of the evening had left her tense, and after Janey laid out her silk dressing gown and the towels, she told her she could go.

"There's no point in you staying up late just to help with my bath." Clad in just her muslin shift, she waved a dismissal. "I've spent years washing my own back, and will manage quite nicely tonight. Go to bed, Janey."

It was a relief to be alone again, and once the door was closed behind the maid, Celia quickly untied the sash to her dressing gown and draped it over a chair, then stepped into the tub, her toes curling into deliciously hot water. As she sank down into the huge tub that was indeed sunk into the floor save for a wide rim, she breathed in the luxuriant heat of fragrant bath salts.

Reaching behind her, she twisted her hair into a coil atop her head, tucking the ends beneath the knot to secure it, then scooted down to rest against the back of the tub. Slowly the hot water eased her tension, and she closed her eyes, reveling in the release as water lapped around her shoulders. Across the spacious room, a fire burned in the grate, crackling with a comforting sound.

It was the first time she'd been able to relax, truly relax, in some time, and maybe it was the combination of wine and weariness, but whatever it was, she drifted in a pleasant haze.

Nothing else seemed to matter, not the past or the present or even tomorrow.

Oh, the water was so nice and warm, the scent so soothing...

Something warm and solid brushed over her cheek and she sat up with a start, splashing water into her eyes.

"Hello, mermaid," Northington said softly. His face was blurred through the water that clung to her lashes but there was no mistaking the knowing curve of his mouth.

And there was no mistaking his intent, for he wore nothing other than that damned insolent smile.

16

Vapors rose from the hot water, wreathing his face. He didn't move, but leaned on the wide ledge of the tub only a few inches from her. Shocked, Celia crossed her arms over her chest and quickly slid down in the water. She stared at him for a long moment before finding her voice.

"What are you doing in here?"

It came out all wrong, a husky whisper instead of an angry demand, but she was far too aware of him, the golden sheen of his skin, the dark blue of his eyes and the smile that seemed to reach inside her soul.

Feverishly she thought that he was far too close to her, and if he stood up, she would see more of him than she needed to see. Panic rose to clog her throat.

"You know why I'm here," he said softly, and it sounded so ordinary, the way he said it without his usual mockery, that she couldn't contradict him.

It was true. She knew why he was there. The knowledge made her heart beat faster.

"Yes," she finally managed to say. "I suppose I do know why you're here."

"I didn't expect to find a mermaid in my tub, but I'm pleasantly surprised—no, don't turn shy on me now. It's too late for that. Clear water doesn't hide much." He put his hand beneath her chin, and pulled her face gently back to him as she drew her knees toward her chest.

He was being gentle, not harsh or aggressive, and she fought the urge to leap from the tub.

"Please," she said, her voice a shaky whisper. "I'm not—please leave me alone."

"Ah no, you don't mean that." Long fingers shifted, traced a path along her jaw. She shivered, and he smiled. "You know you don't mean that, my pretty lady."

"I do, oh, yes, I do...."

But there was no time for more denials, for forming proper refusals. He was leaning closer, his face so near she felt the heat from him. It was all so confusing, so strange. It didn't seem at all improper for him to kiss her, his mouth lingering on her lips, moving then to her earlobe to blow softly and make her shiver again, and all the while the hot scented water enveloping her like a blanket.

"Such a pleasant surprise," he murmured against her ear while his hand moved over her shoulder down to her breast, "to find a beautiful mermaid in my tub."

"I didn't plan to surprise you, I only wanted a bath. Oh, no...don't do that...."

"This?" His hand had slipped beneath the water to cup her breast in his palm, fingers tugging at her nipple. It was erotic, arousing, and she began to tremble. Any shreds of resistance she still possessed were fading. There was a steamy sensuality to the moment that was inevitable, as if she had only been waiting for the right moment to arrive, as if she had waited for him all her life. Perhaps she had in a way, though the reasons were all tangled up with so many other emotions that she couldn't unravel them right now. All she could do was *feel*.

It was a relief not to think, to allow him to make the decision for her.

He was kissing her again, his hands moving over her body in seductive exploration, slipping beneath the water to caress her breasts, then move between her thighs, slow and so exciting...cool air and heated water. The sensuous stroke of his hands over that aching, melting pulse sent spears of white-hot reaction through her so that she arched upward, her arms curling around his neck as he kept kissing her.

Somehow he was in the water with her, holding her against him while his mouth was on her breasts, his lips and tongue teasing her nipples until she moaned restlessly. It was so intensely erotic and arousing, the silky feel of hot water lapping about their bodies while his hands touched and teased, slid back between her thighs to the soft inner folds to summon such sweet, wild reaction that she suddenly clutched at him with both hands, fingers slipping on his wet skin, his hard muscled arms sliding beneath her palms as she grasped wildly at him.

"Oh God oh God," she said over and over, a panting plea that he seemed to understand when she wasn't certain she did. She arched into his hands, moaning softly as his strokes created a growing tension that was exciting, an elusive promise that seemed to hover just out of reach. She wanted to close her eyes, but she didn't. Instead she stared up at him as her body responded to his erotic caresses, watched the muscled curves of his chest and shoulders flex, powerful yet somehow more vulnerable than she'd ever dreamed. Then the tension burst into searing release that took her beyond the moment into a shuddering oblivion that seemed endless.

Drifting, she was only vaguely aware that she still clung to him, her arms loose around his neck as his mouth found hers in another kiss.

Then he was on his knees, straddling her, lean and dark and so intent, his hands beneath her hips to lift her slightly so that her legs were on each side of him and he fit between her thighs. The hard, thick shaft of his erection replaced his hands, caressing her intimate folds as he slid it across that aching point of sweet pleasure, summoning another shudder and soft cry from her. Her fingers opened and closed on his shoulders. The muscles beneath her hands shook with strain as he braced himself against the edge of the tub, his hands on each side of her head, his gaze dark blue and hot as he watched her.

His breath was harsh and swift, contradicting the slow torment as he moved up and over her, slipping easily through the water to push against her. A dull pressure increased between her legs as he leaned forward, sliding inside the tiniest bit, a surprising invasion.

Even more surprising, he didn't press harder, but pulled back after a moment. He paused, then moved again, slowly pressing forward, the scented water slapping around them. Instinctively she arched into the pressure.

"Christ," he muttered, "don't move, love. Not yet."

With her hands still on his shoulders, slipping a little on his damp skin, she closed her eyes and gave herself up to the unfamiliar sensations that coursed through her body. It was nothing like she'd thought, nothing like she'd told Caro. This was so different, more of an inevitability than a natural instinct.

It was encompassing, a sweeping away of everything she'd always expected, the reality much more overwhelming than the imagined....

He kissed her again, then slid his arms beneath her to lift her as if she was no more than a doll, rising from the tub with her against his chest, water dripping on the floor.

Celia shuddered as cool air whisked over her naked body; she was so hot where his body pressed against her, and so cold where it did not.

"What are you... My lord, where are we going?"

He spoke to her softly, his breath warm against her cheek as he carried her across the room to another door. It didn't lead to her chamber, but to another chamber that she knew must be his own, for it was very masculine, with heavy furniture and rich, dark draperies over the bed.

"You're shivering. I'm going to get you warm. No, it's all right...no one will bother us, love. Here..."

He'd put her on his bed and followed her down, his body over hers now, thick velvet beneath her, cushioning her as tremors made her body quake. Gently, as if tending an invalid, he drew the velvet covers over her, cradling her next to him as she shook uncontrollably. It wasn't the cold, but reaction that made her tremble. Celia started to tell him that but he didn't give her the chance.

"I'm not going to hurt you," he said softly as he tucked the velvet around her, "so you don't need to be afraid."

"I'm...not afraid, it's just that—"

"Yes, I know." He shifted position; she felt him rest on his right side and elbow, his left arm lying across her body. He kissed her brow, then her closed eyelids, then the sensitive spot below her ear, his breath a warm caress. "Celia love, open your eyes. You can look at me, can't you?"

"Yes, of course I can, but I'm not sure I should."

She heard him laugh softly. His finger moved along her cheek, then over her lips. "Contrary little vixen. I think it's your prickly nature that intrigues me most."

Her eyes opened. "Liar."

"Yes, that was a gross exaggeration. I find this most intriguing..." His hand moved beneath velvet to shape her breast, his palm covering it with heat. "And this..." Slowly drawing his hand over her ribs, he caressed the flat plane of her belly and moved even lower, his fingers tugging gently at the nest of curls at the juncture of her thighs. "So lovely! I knew your skin would be this soft...."

Her heart pounded fiercely as he stroked her, and the spark he'd ignited earlier flared again, beating heat through her veins as his fingers worked their clever magic and he whispered to her how beautiful she was, and how he'd wanted her from the moment she had insulted him.

"It was obvious you're more perceptive than most," he murmured lazily as he slid his finger over damp curls and into her quivering flesh. "How could I resist you?"

"My lord—"

"Colter. It's less formal, don't you think, love?"

Oh God, yes, of course it was. And this was definitely an *informal* occasion, she thought a bit wildly, torn between the driving need for him to continue and the warning voice in the back of her brain that told her she'd gone too far now. At least he seemed to know what he was doing, how to calm her fears and doubts, his tone gentle and his hands so skillful. Despite his previous roughness, and the times she'd thought him so dangerous, he was only gentle now, patient with her as he coaxed a response from her body and her soul.

"Ah, no, love," he murmured when he moved over her and she instinctively closed her legs against him. "This is no time for doubts. Not now, when we've come so far. Open for me...yes, like that, like that...it's not so bad, is it?"

"No...no, but—I can't think when you do that!"

"This isn't the time for thinking. Just let me make you feel..."

He kissed her again, until at last she began to relax and kiss him back. His knees were between her thighs, firm pressure keeping them apart. Somehow his hands were on her wrists, pressing her arms into the pillows over her head as he rested his body against hers for a moment. He was swollen and hard, nudging into the vee of her legs, hot and impatient, and Celia caught her breath.

This was all so instinctive, the parting of her legs, the heavy pressure of his penetration and her answering lift into the burn, but she still wasn't prepared for the swift forward thrust of his final invasion. A cry escaped her as her body contorted, and she heard his startled curse against her ear.

"Christ!" He drew back slightly, his body still imbedded inside her, and swore again. "Jesus, what the hell is this?"

Panting a little from the pain, she focused on his face above hers, dark and angry and incredulous as he stared down at her.

"You're a damn virgin," he said when she didn't reply at once. "You should have told me."

"Would it have made any difference?"

"Of course it would. I'm not in the habit of ravishing innocent females."

"I beg to differ," she murmured. "It seems that you have formed a habit of it after all."

Silence greeted her reply, and after a moment, he blew out a harsh breath. "So it seems. Christ above, Celia, you should have warned me."

"Yes, I suppose I should have."

"An understatement." Another pause, then he laughed softly, a resigned sound. "I'm sure I'll regret this, but since the damage is already done..."

He'd freed her arms, and now he moved his hands over her breasts in a leisurely glide, then bent to take first one, then the other nipple into his mouth, sucking gently until she began to writhe beneath him, her breathing swift and labored. The first discomfort had faded to a dull ache and was now replaced with a growing anticipation, the hard knot inside her spreading into heated response. She felt him grow harder, a heavy fullness inside her, but he still didn't move.

"Put your arms around me, love," he murmured when she moaned softly, and when she did, he began at last to move. It was a harsh friction, abrasive on still tender flesh, but not uncomfortable. His movements quickened, and gradually she began to meet his thrusts, matching his pace as the urgency grew hotter and higher. The rhythm of his breathing and thrusting increased until he gave a final hard thrust and a guttural groan, and abruptly withdrew. He held her fiercely, crushing her into the velvet with his weight, his rigid member prodding her belly. There was a peculiar throb as he gave a harsh groan, then he was still and heavy atop her as his breathing gradually slowed.

There was none of the singing elation of earlier, for her body was still unaccustomed to the intrusion, but she knew that the next time would be different. God, would there be a next time? Oh, this was all so confusing, and she felt so uncertain—

He caught her hand and rolled to one side, tucking her against him. "As tempted as I am to keep you with me all night, love," he said against her hair, "there's no reason to risk it. It would be impossible to explain. I find it impossible to explain to myself, and don't exactly relish the thought of having to explain to your cousin. Do you understand?"

He leaned over her, turned her to face him, and she managed a nod and agreement.

"Of course I understand. Do you think I want to risk my reputation?"

"You have strange standards, to yield your virginity but worry about your reputation. No, don't misunderstand, but I have to ask you a question. Under the circumstances, I think it rather a legitimate concern. Why are you here?"

"You invited me—"

His fingers tightened on her face, not harshly but with steely intent. A muscle leaped in his jaw, and his gaze was intent.

"Don't play coy, Celia. You know what I mean. You've been flirting with me since the first time we met, and I was led to believe you were—experienced. Unless this is no trick, I can only assume that you have ulterior motives."

"If we're being honest here, I think we both have to admit to ulterior motives," she said bluntly. "You wanted to bed me, and I allowed it."

"And in return?" His eyes were slightly narrowed, and a mocking smile touched the corners of his mouth as he let his hand rest upon her belly.

"And in return, I expect you to respect my wishes and keep this private between us. Can you do that?"

In the close confines of the velvet bed hangings, his face was shadowed. Light from a lamp on a table across the chamber barely relieved the gloom, but she could see the disbelief in his eyes.

"That is all you expect?"

"Yes," she said. "That is all I want or expect from you, my lord."

"Colter," he reminded, and drew his hand up and over her rib cage. "You are ever a surprise, it seems. I never know what to expect from you."

Feeling bolder, and realizing she had caught him off guard, Celia reached up to pull his head down until her lips were only a fraction away from his mouth.

"Expect the unexpected, Colter. Always."

She kissed him, and after a moment, he kissed her back again, fiercely and with rising passion. Her hands slid over his back; fingers grazed tensed muscles as he moved over her, then moved up again to curl around his neck and tangle in his dark hair as he slid inside her in a long, slow pressure.

It wasn't as abrasive this time but just as potent, and Celia gave herself up to the breathless anticipation he created with hot, turbulent friction, the thrust and drag of his body eliciting unexpected release. It was more violent this time, fierce as he pounded inside her, an unyielding force that took her to sweet oblivion.

Afterward, she allowed him to take her back into the room with the tub of cooling water, his touch gentle and somehow comforting as he sponged her body with a cloth dipped in the scented water. His movements were impersonal and efficient, as if he'd done this very thing a hundred times before, and it was oddly comforting.

When he walked her the few steps to her bedroom door, he paused and put her face up with his hand beneath her chin, then kissed her gently.

He'd pulled her silk dressing gown around her body but he wore nothing, a powerful reminder of what they'd just shared. Celia looked away, suddenly and inexplicably shy.

"I have a feeling," he said softly in a teasing tone, "that there's a lot more to tonight than I want to know. We'll worry about that tomorrow. Now you need to rest."

Tomorrow would come too soon. How would she be able to face him again? With Jacqueline watching, and all that had gone between them still so fresh in her mind, she was liable to betray herself.

Oh God, she hoped it would be worth it in the end, for she felt as if she'd just stepped off a ledge into empty air.

17

"Celia dear, you look so pale." Jacqueline leaned forward with a slight frown. "Are you unwell?"

"No—just a headache."

"Didn't you sleep well?"

Celia forced a smile. "Everything is fine, truly it is. It's just this beastly headache—"

"Shall I have Janey fetch one of my little powders for you?"

They were seated on the terrace, where the morning sun had not yet burned off all the mist beyond the brick wheels of flowers; tables had been set with fine white linen and extravagant vases of late blooms, and sideboards groaned beneath silver platters. It was warmer in Kent than in London, the seasonable weather a welcome change. Celia squinted against the bright light as she shook her head. "Really, it will be fine. Too much wine last night is no doubt the cause. I'm not accustomed to it."

"Ah, but it was a lovely evening. And you danced so well! Quite surprisingly, you looked almost as one of the gypsies, and I thought it was most entertaining."

"Mrs. Pemberton didn't approve," Carolyn said, a faint smile on her lips as she sipped hot chocolate. "I heard her late into the night scolding poor Olivia. You're fortunate that your room is some distance from ours Celia, or you would have been treated to her scold as well."

"Do you think so?" Celia lifted her cup to hide the sudden tremor of her hands. Any reminder of the previous night left her unnerved. What would she do—say—when she saw him again? Thank God he wasn't here this morning, but was out somewhere on the estate, Renfroe had informed them when they came down for breakfast.

"His lordship tenders his regrets, but will see you later in the day. Those of you who wish to ride, or take a trap into the village, are welcome to do so," he'd added, and Mrs. Pemberton had immediately expressed a strong desire to go into Houghan with her niece.

"I admit I'm glad they've gone for a while. I shall go up to my room and write some letters," Jacqueline said when they had finished a lavish breakfast. "You two are free to do as you wish, of course."

"What do you intend to do, Celia?" Carolyn regarded her with a rather wistful expression. "Do you ride?"

Celia recognized the appeal in her cousin's eyes. "I suppose I could try, though it's too bad Mrs. Pemberton already took the pony trap."

"Oh, I'll be glad to show you, and I'm sure there

is a suitable mare that will be quite tame enough for you to ride, Celia. How lovely!''

''Perhaps a turn in the fresh air will clear out any cobwebs from my brain,'' Celia sighed as she rose.

Eagerly, Carolyn joined her, and they strolled slowly along a path of crushed stone to the stables. It was a crisp, cool morning with promising sunlight seeping through tree branches to banish any lingering shrouds of mist, and as she tied the pink strings of her bonnet beneath her chin, Celia was suddenly glad Carolyn had suggested the ride. It would be a relief to think of something other than last night. She'd lain awake until almost dawn, then slept only fitfully until Janey had come in to awaken her.

Strange, she should feel so different, when she had noticed nothing unusual in her appearance that morning, though she'd stared into the mirror for what seemed ages trying to see if she had changed. She should have. There should be some sign, a mark, perhaps, of a fallen woman. Only her normal face had stared back at her, eyes wide and dark with tension in a face that looked paler than usual but without a betraying stamp of guilt.

''Oh look, Celia!'' Carolyn moved eagerly forward as they neared the paddock where horses milled about. ''What absolutely lovely animals!''

Celia eyed them less appreciatively. It was easy to admire their beauty, but she'd never ridden one, despite her claims to Northington. Papa had owned a horse, but it had been sold along with everything else when he died. Her recent experience with horses was limited to carriage rides.

''Isn't that Santiago, the gypsy from last night?''

Caro whispered, nudging Celia. ''Oh it is... Why is he still here, I wonder.''

''He trains the horses.''

Santiago was in the paddock with several sleek-coated animals, talking in soft low tones in his lyrical language and didn't even glance up when Carolyn and Celia leaned on the fence to watch. He was gentle with them, and oblivious to those watching. There was a grace in his movements that reminded Celia of the music he'd played the night before, a kind of rhythm that seemed to transfer to the horses.

One of the other gypsies, Mario she thought, leaned against a far post, and beside him stood Marita. She saw them, and after a moment, Marita came around the paddock to speak to them.

''You admire Santiago's gift with the horses, I see.'' Red lips curved in a smile that seemed more mocking than friendly, and though she spoke to both of them, her gaze remained more on Celia. ''We all learn to ride when we are still children. Not many have the same way with horses as Santiago. It is a talent.''

''Yes,'' Carolyn said admiringly, ''it certainly is.''

''Do you ride?'' Marita addressed the question to Carolyn but still studied Celia with a dark-eyed gaze that held taunting lights.

''Oh, yes, of course,'' Carolyn replied at once. ''I've always ridden, but Celia—''

''I choose my own mounts,'' Celia interrupted coolly, loathe to give Marita even the smallest satisfaction of besting her. Marita's brow lifted.

''So, you do ride, heh? Then you must admire these horses tremendously, for they are very spirited beasts and not for *inexperienced* riders.'' Her shoulders lifted in a slight shrug. "I ride them, but I am much more used to it than you would be." Her eyes narrowed slyly. "Sometimes I ride with his lordship. He is very complimentary of my—skills."

"Yes, I'm certain he is," Celia replied casually, though a little twinge made her add, "It must impress him that you're able to ride like a lady."

"Like a lady?" She laughed, anger sparking in her eyes. "No, no, not so tame as that! He is not so impressed with *ladies,* I think, but admires how I ride like a man. Yes, and he said I make him think of a centaur, for I ride so well."

"Indeed." Celia was aware of Carolyn's curious gaze, but managed an indifferent shrug. "I prefer not to be so manly, but perhaps you do not mind."

"No, and neither does the *señor!*" Marita's gaze was openly hostile now, dark eyes thinned to angry slits as she glared at Celia. "But what would you know, a pale copy of a woman that you are, like ice!"

"Really," Carolyn began faintly, sounding aghast at Marita's vehemence. "I hardly think it your place to be saying these things to a guest of Northington's. He'll be very displeased."

Marita tossed her head. "No, he will not. I know him much better than you—either of you! He admires spirit and fire, not some…some—"

"Marita!" Santiago loomed over them suddenly, coming up without any of them realizing it, his face dark with anger as he spoke sharply to the gypsy girl in their own language. An argument raged briefly, ending with Marita flouncing away with a resentful glance at Celia.

"Forgive my daughter," Santiago turned to say,

"for she is very impetuous and speaks rashly. You have come to ride, yes?"

"Yes," Carolyn said when Celia didn't reply. "We were told there are suitable mounts for us to ride."

Santiago took them to the stables, clapped his hands sharply together, and after a moment, Mario appeared with two horses saddled and ready.

"Oh," Carolyn said, "I prefer sidesaddle, please."

Santiago looked nonplussed. "There is only one here, I'm afraid. The other saddle needs repair."

"I'll ride with this saddle," Celia said quickly, and stepped forward to stroke the muzzle of the small gray that stood docilely by the gate. Riding astride would be much easier than managing a sidesaddle, and besides, now there was no risk of damaging herself, was there? No, not since last night....

"Celia!" Carolyn looked worried. "Are you certain? I don't know if it's safe...."

"It's much safer than trying to balance sidesaddle," she replied, "and I've ridden this way before."

That was true enough, though it had been when she was only a little girl and Papa had put her atop his own horse to ride while he walked her about.

Mario brought forward the platform used for ladies to mount their horses, and Celia took his hand as she stepped atop the gray mare. It was a beautiful animal with dark liquid eyes that were half-closed, the sleek charcoal coat well brushed and gleaming. Gingerly she settled into the saddle, legs straddling the horse and her skirts hiked up a bit, showing her ankles. While Mario held the bridle, she managed to cover her legs, then sat up and took the reins in both hands. When she glanced up, she happened to meet Marita's sullen gaze, but looked away.

Carolyn's mount was brought out after a few minutes, and she settled into the sidesaddle with obvious ease, hooking her leg over the horn and arranging her skirts in a graceful drape.

"I'm ready," she announced gaily, and Celia mimicked her actions, touching her heels lightly to the gray's sides like Carolyn did as they took off at a sedate walk.

It wasn't so difficult, she thought as they rode down the curved drive toward the gatehouse, though a bit more bumpy than she'd thought it would be. She watched Carolyn closely, and kept the same firm grip on the reins, elbows held close to her body, spine erect. When she felt more comfortable, she actually began to enjoy the ride, the freedom of being independent, with the wind in her face and the sunlight warm on her head. Slowly the tension in her stomach eased.

The little mare seemed quite docile, and willing to follow Carolyn's horse as they rode along the dusty track that wound in front of the estate. Brisk air smelled of the sea, that inimitable scent of salt and wind and faraway places. An occasional house crouched beside the road, stone or half-timbered, but always shielded by fence and hedge. Trees twisted by constant sea winds thrust huge gnarled branches into the air, bright red autumn leaves whirling as gaily as gypsy skirts, Celia thought.

Half-formed thoughts tumbled in her mind, images of Marita dancing with Northington, of their easy familiarity with one another, and then later—

God, she just couldn't keep from thinking about it! Hadn't she lain awake all night remembering his hands on her, his mouth, and her own response to him? Yes, and it was with her still, those searing memories that had the power to make her ache. There was no retreat now; she'd gone too far, let him take her too far. And she could blame only herself for it. *How weak I am...*

Just ahead of her, Carolyn pulled her horse to the side, turning with a smile to wait for Celia to catch up. Her bonnet was awry, ribbons half-undone, and her eyes were alight with excitement.

How innocent Caro was, and how carefree, riding her borrowed mount with no thoughts other than the lovely day and the serenity of her life. It had been amusing to hear her speak of her tedious existence—amusing and maddening.

But it was understandable. What else had she known?

"Isn't this glorious, Celia?" Carolyn enthused when she reached her. "A most magnificent day! The sea makes me want to run out into it."

Celia pulled back on the leather reins, and the gray mare halted beside Carolyn's horse. Perched daintily atop the horse, Carolyn's gaze shifted to a thin path that ran parallel to a line of chalky ridges.

"There's a path, and I think it leads down to the water, Celia. Shall we try it?"

Uncertain of her riding ability, Celia hesitated. It had been easy enough on a relatively flat plain, but how would she do on a steep decline?

"Carolyn, really, I'm not at all sure if I want to go that far," she began, but her cousin had already turned her mount toward the trail threading between a line of trees. After a moment's hesitation, Celia muttered, "Damn!" and followed Carolyn.

It wasn't steep at first; stunted bushes grew in haphazard clumps along the pocked slopes. Seagulls wheeled overhead, drifting on air currents, their cries seeping down through the noise of the wind in her ears. The ribbons of her hat fluttered, pink tongues licking at the air. Ahead of her, Carolyn maneuvered her mount down the descent.

Beyond the trail, the gleaming expanse of blue-gray water stretched, blurring to an indistinct haze on the horizon. A salty tang filled the air. Sunlight gleamed on stark white cliffs, porous surfaces absorbing slanted heat and giving it back. The sea was a steady rush of sound.

Celia's mount snorted, tossed its head in a jangle of bridle chains, and she tightened her grip on the reins. It wasn't much farther now to the bottom; Carolyn was well ahead of her, the blue of her skirts flapping as the wind caught them.

The day was truly beautiful. The sky was a polished blue, so bright it hurt the eyes, and lazy clouds puffed overhead. Carolyn had reached the beach.

Just as Celia hit a level stretch of dirt and rock, a sudden loud popping exploded in the air. The mare leaped forward, almost unseating her, and she just barely managed to cling to the neck, the coarse mane whipping against her face as the horse bolted down the narrow stretch of beach.

She was only vaguely aware of Carolyn's open mouth and shocked face as she swept past her, the words obliterated by the rushing wind in her ears. A sense of panic kept her clutching the damp neck, her fingers tangled in reins and the mane.

How had this happened? God, everything was going so fast and she couldn't stop the horse. Nothing was working as it should, not pulling on the reins or shouting—she was sure she was shouting, but heard only wind and the pounding rush of white-laced waves against the shore. Hot tears stung her eyes from the wind, the white cliffs at her side were a blur and the smell of sea and dirt rose around her as she sawed at the reins.

The pounding beat of the horse didn't slow, and she felt her grip loosening. A terrified scream locked in her throat as a solid white wall loomed just ahead. Oh God, she would never be able to turn the horse....

Everything was such a blur as terror and desperation prodded her into dangerous choices—leap, or risk being thrown against that wall? The stark chalk was broken up slightly by something dark against it, a movement like a shadow over the pale surface. Recognition struck, giving her sudden courage.

Afterward, she could never quite recall just how it had happened, but suddenly she was free of the horse, abruptly and gratefully on solid ground again, her brutally rough fall cushioned by unyielding arms and a gruff voice in her ear.

"Christ, do you want to get killed!"

Northington.

The impact of her body against his took him to his knees, slamming them both against the ground. He grunted harshly.

"Stay down!" His sharp order was accompanied by his hand spread against the back of her head, crushing the ridiculous looking bonnet she wore. When she gave an angry gasp, he clamped an arm around her waist to hold her, his mouth against her ear as he grated out an order.

"I said stay down! Do you want to get us both killed? Don't you hear that?" He held her next to him and behind the shelter of a knobby rock.

"Hear...hear what! I don't hear anything but you—oh!"

Another shot rang out, this time the bullet smacking into the wall behind them, spraying chalky splinters through the air like snowfall. She threw herself to the ground immediately.

"Apparently you heard that one," he muttered, cursing softly beneath his breath. "Christ, a devil of a fix to be in, and you aren't helping any. Where the hell did you come from? And why?"

Frightened green eyes stared up at him through the mess of her disheveled bonnet and hair.

"I...the horse bolted. Is someone shooting at us?"

"You're more astute than you look right now. Yes, and I'm damned if I know who or why. At least your cousin had enough sense to know to retreat instead of riding right into the middle of some kind of battle. Be still! You've got rock on your face."

He picked off a shard of pale rock, saw her flinch beneath his touch and smiled grimly. "Fine time to be scared. Why didn't you go the other way like Carolyn?"

"I told you, my horse bolted!" She shoved at him, and indignation welled in her eyes. "This wasn't my choice!"

"It's not mine, either." He drew his pistol from his

belt, saw Celia's eyes widen as he put his hand on her shoulder to keep her behind the rock. "Watch your head. Stay here until I get back."

"Where are you going?" She clutched at him, fright replacing the anger in her eyes. "Oh, don't leave me if someone's shooting at us!"

"You're safer here. I don't intend to spend the night waiting for them to go away. Christ, Celia, do you think I want to risk one hair on that pretty head of yours? Do as I ask without argument. There's no time for this."

Though her clamped lips quivered slightly, she gave a terse nod of her head to indicate acquiescence. A slight grin tugged at the corners of his mouth. Little cat, she had sense enough not to argue too much. He hadn't been able to believe his eyes when she'd come barreling toward him across the rocky beach, halfway off the gray mare he could have sworn was still too green to be ridden.

He left her behind the rock. The shots had come from the mouth of a cave that opened into the Straits. Keeping close to the chalk cliff at his back, he moved along the edge in a crouching run. The shooting had stopped.

Sea spume dampened his face and clothes when he got close to the cave opening, the roar loud and inexorable. A tide line was visible on the white face of the chalky crag just above his head. On the other side of the churning seawater that had cut this cave into the cliff thousands of years before, a track spiraled upward, accessible only when the tide was out.

Now there was barely room for him to make his way on a narrow ledge, his boots slipping a little on damp chalk that broke off if he trod too close to the edge. It was dark, dank inside this cave, the soft sticky bottom of the floor showing evidence of recent passage.

Visibility deep inside the cave was impenetrable; he felt along the wall, and encountered high up on a ledge several wood and leather trunks that deserved a return visit with torches. Whoever had left these here had decided not to risk being seen. The cave echoed emptily.

Sticking his pistol back into his belt, he raked a hand through his damp hair and swore softly. No point in trying to follow them now, especially when he was saddled with Celia. He needed to get her back to the house, and find out what the hell she was doing out here.

It could be just coincidence that she'd shown up at the same time he'd seen trespassers, men who didn't mind shooting at him, but the string of coincidences was growing far too long.

Celia was where he'd left her, huddled behind a hump of rock. She'd taken off her bonnet and sunlight glinted on her hair and face. He noted a very faint sprinkle of freckles across the bridge of her nose. Somehow, it gave her an ingenuous look. He knelt one leg beside her, his knee digging into the rocky ground.

"They're gone. I'll take you back to the house."

She nodded. "Who—why were they shooting at us?"

"I think I interrupted something." An ugly suspicion had begun to form in the back of his mind. It wouldn't surprise him if those trunks held smuggled goods. This part of the coast was pocked with caves, and France was only across the Channel. It wouldn't be the first time smugglers had operated in this area.

"What did you interrupt?" Celia rose and brushed at her skirts with one hand, fingering a small tear in the rose-colored material. "Poachers?"

"Of a sort. Here." He shoved her bonnet into her hand and said curtly, "We'll have to take my horse. The Barb is probably halfway to London by now."

"The Barb?"

"Barbary mare—a special breed of Arabian." He shot her a narrow glance. "The gray horse you rode."

"I realize what you mean now. You needn't speak to me as if I'm a child!" She brushed angrily at the bonnet; one of the pink strings hung by a thread.

"Needn't I? Never mind. Can you walk?"

"Yes, of course I can walk. I'm bruised, but nothing is broken."

She wouldn't meet his gaze, but averted her eyes.

"What were you doing here, Celia? No, don't tell me it's none of my business. It *is* my business. Christ, you could have been killed."

"I hardly expected to be taken as a target," she shot back at him. "Your hospitality leaves much to be desired."

"You should have kept to the road. Or taken the pony trap."

"Mrs. Pemberton and Miss Freestone took the trap into the village—"

"You should have gone with them. I certainly didn't mean for you to ride a mare that's barely been ridden."

She looked startled, then her eyes darkened. "Oh, I

see what happened now. It was your lovely gypsy who saw to it that I rode that mare, I'm certain of it."

"Marita?" He grinned. "It sounds like a trick she might play."

"Yes." She snapped her hat in the air, then crammed it on her head. It hung awry, the brim shading her face and the ribbons dangling. "Your gypsy has a rather strange sense of humor!"

"I don't own Marita."

"She seems to think she belongs to you. Or perhaps you belong to her."

"Jealous, my sweet?"

"Of you?" She laughed, a harsh sound. "You flatter yourself, my lord."

"I don't think so. Christ, Celia, don't look at me as if you don't know me."

"I...I don't know you. Not really. Last night...what we did...what happened between us—"

"If you're expecting an apology, you won't get one from me. Maybe if I'd known you weren't experienced I wouldn't have taken it so far, but you didn't think it was important enough to tell me."

Even in the shadow of the hat brim, he saw bright color flag her cheeks. He knew how it sounded, but he'd sat up all night thinking about her, wondering why she'd yielded something so precious to him. There was no good reason that he could see, unless she had motives that wouldn't bear close inspection.

"There's no point in talking about this now," he said as he took her arm. "It's a long walk back to the house if my horse is gone the same way as yours."

She didn't say a word, even when he found his horse where he'd left it and lifted her up into the saddle. He mounted, holding her in front of him, his arms around her and her hat blocking his view.

"Take off that damned hat," he said finally, and she jerked at the strings.

Her hair had come loose from the braids she usually wore, pale strands like a cape around her shoulders. She leaned into him, warm against his chest, soft and somehow vulnerable despite her prickly manner.

It would be easy to believe she was honest, but long experience had taught him to recognize when people held secrets. And Celia St. Clair had secrets behind those lovely sea-green eyes.

18

Celia looked white as milk, Jacqueline thought as she knelt beside her to put a snifter of brandy into her trembling hand and close her fingers around it. Carolyn was near tears again, her earlier hysterics calmed at last by a sharp word from Northington.

Scowling blackly, the viscount leaned against the mantel in the parlor, arms crossed over his chest as he regarded them all.

"Tell me again why you were there," he said, his brow cocked when Jacqueline threw him a frowning glance. His mouth quirked in a sardonic smile. "Humor me."

"No, I don't mind," Celia said when Jacqueline began to protest, and stared at Northington. "As we told you, we only wanted to ride along the beach. Carolyn saw the trail leading down, and we took it. And as you surely saw, my horse bolted when those shots were fired."

Jacqueline shuddered. "Why was someone shooting at you, my lord? And are you certain they were truly shooting *at* you, or was it perhaps a hunter?"

"Unless he was hunting fish with a rifle, I doubt seriously that it was a hunter, madam."

He pushed away from the mantel, two long strides taking him to stare down at Celia. "I find it strange that you didn't see anyone from atop the ridge. Your cousin had sense enough to ride out of danger's way. Why didn't you?"

Celia's chin came up, and a stubborn light that Jacqueline was beginning to recognize sparked in her eyes as she glared at him.

"You know very well why! I was given an untrained mount, and no one bothered to inform me that she wasn't docile. I could have been killed, yet I don't hear any concern from you about that."

His eyes were hooded, the faint smile on his mouth cynical. "It seems you don't have a habit of being very confiding, Miss St. Clair. You should have told Santiago you were an inexperienced rider. That mare is too damned blooded to be ridden by a novice."

Celia rose to her feet, still holding the brandy in one hand. "You need not worry about me any longer, for I intend to leave early in the morning. My visit is ended." She paused, then said softly, "It was a mistake to come here at all."

"But Celia dear," Jacqueline started to protest, then halted when she saw the determined set of Celia's mouth. A glance at Northington convinced her it was for the best; he wore a dark, thunderous expression on his handsome face that didn't bode well for a congenial stay.

"Yes," she agreed. "Perhaps it's best if we return to the city, my lord. Celia and Caro are quite upset by the day's events, though that is certainly no fault of yours."

Sir John, who had been sitting in a chair by the window, said mildly, "No need to run away. I daresay once the shock has abated, you'll all feel much better."

"They're free to leave," Northington said. "Miss St. Clair is right. It would be a mistake for them to stay."

There were undercurrents to his tone that Jacqueline heard but could not identify. Anger? Regret? Oh, it was so difficult to tell with him, his face was such a mask of impassivity. But surely he was just worried about their safety.

And Celia looked so...so distraught, and unusually disheveled. Of course, after falling from her horse and then having to lie on the ground to avoid being shot, she could certainly be excused for her distress and appearance. But Mrs. Pemberton had looked quite askance at her when the viscount had dismounted in front of the house and then lifted Celia down, his hands lingering a shade too long around her waist, his touch somehow—familiar. Yes, that was it. *Familiar.*

Jacqueline's eyes narrowed thoughtfully. There was much more to this than it seemed on the surface, and trust that wretched gossip Agatha Pemberton to ferret it out. If her tongue wagged freely once they returned to London, it may very well do great damage. Oh, *why* had Northington invited the old tabby!

When Celia moved toward the parlor door, Renfroe appeared with a discreet cough to snare Northington's attention.

"My lord," he said. "You have another visitor."

"No need to announce me, Renfroe," a voice said behind him, and a tall, silver-haired man Jacqueline recognized at once entered the parlor. "Though I am a bit surprised to find guests here this time of year. Hullo, Colter, glad to see you in residence."

Lord Easton, Northington's uncle, strode across the floor to greet his nephew, the very model of urbanity and sophistication as always. Attired immaculately, high-point collars and an intricately tied neckcloth suited more for the city than the country, he smiled upon them all with the obvious expectations of a man assured of his welcome.

"I see we have a lovely gathering. Do make the introductions, Northington, though I am well acquainted with Lady Leverton, of course."

"How pleasant it is to see you again, Lord Easton," Jacqueline said. "And what a lovely surprise."

Northington introduced Celia and Carolyn, then Harvey, whom Easton already seemed to know. Mrs. Pemberton and Olivia Freestone chose that moment to arrive and they were also introduced, Mrs. Pemberton beaming her delight.

"Lord Easton, it is so charming to finally meet you, though I daresay you do not remember our connection. My husband is Clive Pemberton of—"

"Of Exchequer Bank of England. Yes, of course, I am well aware of that connection, Mrs. Pemberton. I see that my nephew is keeping good company after all, and I need not worry."

"I wasn't aware you were prone to worrying about my companions," Northington said dryly, and his uncle turned to him with a grin.

"I always worry about you, my boy. You're my favorite nephew."

"Your only surviving nephew," Northington replied, and Easton laughed.

"Trust you to make that distinction."

"So what brings you back from the Continent?"

"Boring details that we can discuss later." Easton dismissed it with a smile, his attention turning toward Celia. "Miss—St. Clair, you said? You seem quite familiar to me. Have we met before?"

"No, my lord," Celia said stiffly. "I don't believe we have."

"Yet you seem so familiar to me. Perhaps in Paris?"

"I've never been to France, my lord." Celia's smile seemed rather brittle, and Jacqueline gave her a concerned glance.

"Celia is from America," Jacqueline explained, "and has only been in England for the past two months. She's my cousin's child, and my goddaughter."

"Oh, I see." Easton smiled, but his dark eyes were sharp and thoughtful, holding more than admiration in their depths as he regarded Celia for another moment before turning his attention to Miss Freestone.

Celia stood still and silent, but her heart pounded furiously. She was sore from the fall, residual terror at the danger leaving her temper frayed and her stomach all in knots. And now this man—Colter's uncle!—seemed far too acquainted with her cousin. Would he remember Maman? He was old enough to have known her.

As graciously as she could manage, she excused

herself and fled to her room. Nothing was as it should be. She felt so uncertain, as if all was about to fall apart around her.

Perhaps she should never have come to England for vengeance. If she'd only realized how different it was here, how unified the peerage was, she would have known better than to entertain such a foolish notion. In theory it had seemed so simple, gaining justice by presenting the documents charging Northington with Old Peter's murder. Yet now that she was here, she saw that it would make no difference. Old Peter's death had mattered to no one but her and Maman.

The small trunk she'd brought from London was tucked into an alcove, and Celia knelt in front of it to unlock the clasp. The papers were in the reticule she'd brought from Georgetown; it was too risky leaving them behind to chance their discovery by Lily or another maid. They were all the evidence she had, the only proof that the earl of Moreland had committed such a heinous crime. Now the only option left was to confront the earl with this reminder of what he'd done.

But now even that satisfaction would be diluted. If Lord Easton recognized her, then Moreland would know why she was there, and the shock of her charge would lose any surprise and effect she'd hoped to gain.

Opening the velvet reticule, she pulled out the old document and unfolded it, her fingers smoothing the yellowed page. It crackled dully in her hands. The ink was faded but still legible. Perhaps if she could not have complete vengeance, she would get a private audience with the earl. A confrontation, the sight of his face when she reminded him of her mother and what he had done. But did a man like Moreland even have a conscience?

Celia refolded the document and slid it back into the reticule. When it resisted, she peered inside. It was wedged against the directory she'd borrowed from Mister Carlisle. Oh, she'd forgotten it again. The directory really should have been returned by now. He would think she was completely ungrateful and rude. As soon as she got back to London, she would send it immediately to Carlisle's brother's pub in Shoreditch. And she'd write a nice note of gratitude for its loan, and her apologies for being so late in returning it to him after his kindness in lending it to her. It had been of some use, after all, for the hired hack had indeed been a rather crafty man who had tried to take her on a tour rather than straight to the Leverton house.

She thumbed it idly. The directory was a thin pamphlet, and Mister Carlisle had underlined in ink several streets, with faint X's marked along the map at intervals. Well used, it seemed. She tucked it back with the documents and pulled tight the strings to close it, then replaced it in the chest and rang for Janey.

"Help me pack, please," she said when the little maid answered her summons. "We'll be leaving early tomorrow."

"Yes, miss." Janey asked no questions; like all servants worth a shilling, she no doubt knew all about the shots fired earlier, and suspected that was the reason for an early departure.

It was only partially true.

"It would be a mistake for them to stay," he'd said, his eyes hard and blue as he looked at her. She'd known then that what had happened between them the night before was only one more conquest, as she'd once told him she'd never be. How foolish she'd been!

It was the same with most men. They put women up on pedestals as long as they conformed to the masculine ideal of what a woman should be and do and say. Any woman who dared stray from that ideal was regarded as a demi-rep, a courtesan accustomed to the touch of many men. And she had been careless enough to let—no, invite—his touch.

She couldn't return to London fast enough. It was too much to stay and endure his company. How could she? There had been no words of love between them, and really, she didn't know how she felt about him. How should she feel? It was so confusing. At first she'd thought she could use him to get to his father, but now...now her emotions were so tangled, everything she felt for him and about his father a contradiction. How could she reconcile strong hatred with such vulnerability?

Thank God she had very little time to brood on the injustices in the days that followed their return to London, days turning into weeks that were filled with activity. Penned invitations piled high on the silver tray in the entrance hall every morning were brought to her at breakfast with Jacqueline and Carolyn. As she drank hot chocolate, she read them aloud to her delighted cousins. There were invitations to this or that ball or soirée, gala or opera, but not a word from the one man she had thought would at least send a note.

She didn't know whether to be glad or sorry that Northington ignored her. Feminine pride would have liked at least an acknowledgment. After all, much more had passed between them than mere conversation! But there was nothing. Was he even back from the country? Perhaps he'd been shot by whoever had been out on the seaside that day. Irrationally she prayed that he was alive, and in the next instant, thought it would serve him right to be shot!

And then she saw him at an affair one evening not long before Christmas. It was crowded with the ton and as noisy as always, reeking of perfume and the press of too many bodies packed into limited space. Her heart leaped, and her stomach twisted into a tight knot of—misery?

He was with another woman, a gorgeous dark-haired creature that seemed familiar and very possessive, and it wasn't until Jacqueline reminded her that Celia recalled Lady Cresswood, who was married to an earl.

Until that moment Celia hadn't considered how jarring it would be to look up and meet those cold sapphire-blue eyes, to be jolted to the very core by a strange, unthinkable yearning to feel his mouth against hers again, to hear his voice in her ear, husky and soft, calling her "love."

It had all been a lie, his tender touch and the words in her ear—even her own response to him. A masquerade that had been perpetuated by the myth that she could fall in love with the son of the man responsible for Maman's death.

Colter was very polite, remote as they spoke briefly the casual words of courteous strangers, but underneath the civility was a thin thread of tension. She saw it in his eyes, a flicker of light as he regarded her. It was too much to bear.

"Forgive me if I seem rude," she said quickly, "but I promised this dance to Mister Harwood."

She felt his gaze on her as she moved away, and saw a small, curious smile on Lady Cresswood's mouth. No doubt she thought her a complete idiot. She would ignore them both, and pretend that she didn't care.

Yet, even though she danced with Harwood and countless others that night, she was far too aware of Northington, and could have wept when he left with Lady Cresswood.

It was the most difficult thing she had ever done, to dance and smile throughout the long evening, laugh at witticisms, when inside she felt cold and dead. She was relieved when they finally left for home.

Not even the warmth of a cheery fire in her bedchamber eased her chill, and Celia sat up long after Jacqueline and all in the house were asleep. No maid attended her as she sat at the carved mahogany dresser, a hairbrush in her hand, her thick mane of hair in a tangle down her back. She didn't have the energy to brush it, but stared at her reflection and the stranger she had become.

When had it all happened? When had she become this lost person? She looked the same outwardly: wide green eyes, pale hair, mouth a little too generous, her cheekbones high and defined like Maman's...*Maman.*

Despair rose in a choking knot to lodge in her throat. Once it had seemed so simple to avenge Maman's memory, to face the earl with her knowledge of his crime and see the shame in his eyes, or at least the realization that it had not gone unnoticed and was not forgotten. But now...now it was so futile. All her hopes had come unraveled by her own actions. Could she still confront the earl when she had been intimate with his son?

But this was different, she told herself fiercely. It was an act of love and not brutality!

Love. It could be love she'd felt. She'd thought it was at the time, an excitement that she'd never experienced before with any man. And she'd thought he felt the same.

Oh God, it was all so mixed up now. It was obvious that Colter did not love her. She'd been a fool to think it even for an instant.

Her hand throbbed and she looked down, noting with some surprise that she'd almost bent the silver handle of the brush she still held. Red marks creased her palm and fingers. She slowly flexed her hand, easing the sting. The pain cleared her head, and oddly, cemented her resolve.

My God, she thought fiercely, I've spent half my life in pursuit of justice for Maman, and I will not stop now that I'm so close. There must be a way to confront the earl with what he did! If there is— If there is, I'll find it. I will find it and I will at last have the satisfaction of keeping my vow, no matter the cost!

19

It was pitch-dark in this section of London, the slum alleys near St. Giles littered with ramshackle buildings and gin shops. No light penetrated even during the day, and with the setting of the sun, the shadows were impenetrable. A fetid stink permeated the dense January night.

Colter carried a loaded pistol tucked into his belt, easily accessible, and a lethal dagger was stuck in the cuff of his knee-boot. The latent violence learned in warfare was unacceptable in a civilized society, but had saved his life more times than he could remember. Years spent fighting Napoleon's forces had taught him a lot. Fighting in South America and Spanish California had honed his instincts, taught him a different kind of warfare—taught him survival.

This was survival of a different sort, with a different kind of enemy lurking in the shadows; there was no grand and glorious cause, nothing other than idle viciousness or empty bellies driving men to cut throats and purses with equal indifference. Even the children had the same empty look in their eyes, a total lack of compassion or humanity in faces pinched with years of depravity.

Tyler was late and looked disheveled when he finally arrived. Torchlight from the end of the alley shed a fitful glow that silhouetted him in hazy shadow.

Another recruit, the man known only as Tyler was one of their best. Though he preferred to remain anonymous, Colter recognized that he was educated, a man familiar with elegant drawing rooms as well as the slums of St. Giles.

"The Runners are out," Tyler muttered, "and looking for me."

"They won't come here."

A grin split Tyler's face, a muted gleam in the dark. "That's right, mate, they won't. Not even the Bow Street Runners dare enter this hell."

"What news?"

"It's a conspiracy, right enough. The Spenceans. With the radical Thistlewood in control now and Watson demoted, they're planning some kind of vengeance for the Peterloo Massacre. Thistlewood is even talking revolution. He claims he can raise fifteen thousand men in half an hour."

"Are they armed?"

Tyler nodded. "They've got munitions stashed all over London. Ruthven reports there's some kind of log with all the hiding places listed, but he hasn't seen it."

George Ruthven had been recruited by police to join the group as a spy, along with several other men.

"Where is this log kept?"

Tyler shifted, glanced over his shoulder as a burst of raucous laughter came from the far end of the alley, then turned back with a shake of his head.

"We don't know. Carlisle was the last one known to have it in his possession."

"John Carlisle?"

"No, his brother James. The log disappeared. Ruthven thinks he hid it somewhere a couple of months ago. There was an argument he overheard about the missing log, and it being a possible danger to them."

"And no one has been able to find this log."

Another shake of Tyler's head and a furtive glance down the length of the black alley indicated growing disquiet. "At the last meeting, Thistlewood said high treason had been committed against the people at Manchester. He's resolved that the lives of the instigators of Peterloo shall atone for the souls of those murdered innocents. It's a dangerous situation."

"We have to find the log, Tyler. It's more vital now than ever."

"I'm working on it. Any ideas?"

"We'll both work on it. I'll keep you posted as to what I find out. Check back at the Swan and Stone."

Christ, this news would set Mowry on edge.

White's was a world away from St. Giles, separated by more than just city blocks. The only stench here came from expensive tobacco and even more expensive imported scents men applied far too freely at times. Brummel was right, a man should smell only of clean living. But even the impeccable Beau had his failings, exiled now in France after one too many insults directed at the prince.

Not that they weren't deserved at times. The regent cared more for fine art and architecture than he did the state of the country or his subjects. It wasn't calculated indifference, but hazardous all the same. Men like Lords Castlereagh, Liverpool and Sidmouth were left to make the royal decisions about policy. That kind of power bred dangerous men.

Mowry was seated at a table in the gaming room, alone and waiting.

"Do you have news for me, Northington?" Mowry's cool tone was low, meant to be confidential.

Colter met that opaque gaze with a faint smile. "Yes, but you already know that. You were right about Arthur Thistlewood. The bloody fool has munitions stashed all over London."

Mowry swore softly. "Do we know where? It's vital we learn all we can. This came from the usual source?"

"Yes. Look, you know I don't agree with government policy in regard to some of the social issues, but this is anarchy. He has to be stopped at all costs, or it will end up even worse than Peterloo."

"Those damned Spenceans again! Thomas Spence and his idea of a radical transformation of society incites mobs, not reformation. The fool. He's been dead five years and is still causing trouble."

"Some men just need a cause to excuse their love of brutality. Rather like politicians in that area." When Mowry's eyes narrowed at him, he shrugged. "We've known for years that the Spenceans are radicals in search of social equality. Yet a charge of high treason convicted not one single man of them."

"You know the reason for that. Their defence counsel was able to show that John Castle had a criminal record, and his testimony as a spy in their group was unreliable. That's why you've been employed. You may have a reputation as a buck of the first head, but you've no criminal record in your past." Mowry's smile was sardonic. "A war hero can be forgiven much, it seems."

Ignoring that, Colter said, "There's a log that's turned up missing. Ruthven thinks it's important, perhaps detailing the hiding places of their munitions."

"Then why don't we have it in our possession?"

"Carlisle was the last man known to have it. He was overheard arguing with his brother John about its loss."

Colter fell silent, then he added softly, "I believe I may know what happened to that log. What I don't know is the connection."

Tapping his fingers thoughtfully atop the green baize table, Mowry regarded him through hooded eyes. "You were following Carlisle when he boarded the *Liberty* on its stop in Liverpool this past September. We know he made the acquaintance of Miss St. Clair. You saw them conversing aboard the ship, though they didn't disembark together. It's quite possible that he knew he was being watched. Indeed, when you had him searched as soon as he set foot in London, nothing incriminating was found on him. Yet perhaps you're wrong. I begin to think that their brief shipboard acquaintance was not as innocent as we assumed."

"Miss St. Clair is not involved."

"How can you be so certain?" Mowry's smile was cool, his gaze unreadable. "I'm making inquiries."

"As to—"

"As to her reason for suddenly showing up in London. It's hardly likely she decided to join Lady Leverton after all this time unless there was a decisive reason.''

Colter leaned back, regarded Mowry narrowly. ''It's doubtful she met Carlisle aboard ship and suddenly decided to throw in her lot with men intending to set up their own government. Miss St. Clair may be willful, but she doesn't strike me as stupid.''

''How *does* she strike you, Northington? You spent time with her in the country, I understand.'' He smiled again, a wolfish curve of thin lips in a caricature of humor. ''It was quite—eventful. Was she very impressed with your rescue of her? Grateful enough to share...secrets?''

Mowry knew about the shots fired! The man must have a network of spies in every corner of England. Colter gave a shrug. ''Possibly. But don't expect me to try and get them out of her.''

''Ah, but that's exactly what I do expect. Take advantage of your close acquaintance. If she has no secrets, then there's no harm done. But if she does, I want to know what they are. All of them.''

''I'm not in the habit of seducing secrets from women. You're asking me to betray loyalties, Mowry.''

''No, I'm asking you to prove her innocence and remain true to your first loyalty—England.''

Colter cursed silently. The devil of it was he wasn't at all certain Celia St. Clair was innocent.

He rose to his feet. ''I'll think about it.''

''Yes, Northington, you do that. And so will I.''

20

The opera being presented at the King's Theater in Haymarket was *Faust*, a famous production. The horseshoe-shaped auditorium rose in five tiers of boxes, and the huge gallery seated over three thousand people. It was always crowded, and tonight was no exception.

"Oh look, Celia," Jacqueline said. "I do believe that the prince is here this evening! That's his carriage there with the royal crest."

Celia turned to look out their carriage window as the gleaming brougham rolled to a halt. A footman was there at once to open the door and hand them down, and she focused on the slippery step as she allowed him to take her hand. A cold rain would soon turn to ice, and the January wind pierced the folds of her warm mantle despite her efforts to hold it closed.

Her elegant slippers, embroidered in gilt thread and crusted with tiny gems, were lovely but impractical.

"Yes, it is the prince," Carolyn said. Her eyes were bright and shiny in the sparkle of carriage lamps and lights from the opera house. "I wonder if he'll speak!"

"It will be a miracle if he even sees us in this crush," Celia said, but found once they were inside that the box Jules Leverton had purchased gave them not only an excellent view of the stage, but gave the theater a superb view of the box. It was directly across from the prince's box, on the first tier closest to the stage. Long velvet draperies in deep wine enclosed the box, and in the center of the theater, heavy chandeliers glittered from the high dome ceiling.

Below, the gallery was crowded with spectators, a crush of people all talking at once. Catalani was to sing tonight, a mature opera diva at the very height of her success and fresh from a European tour.

"I last saw her in *Otello.* Desdemona is a demanding role," Jacqueline said, "and only the Italians can do it justice. Oh look, the prince sees us, Celia, and just look who is with him!"

Celia's heart pounded fiercely. Northington was with the prince, his tall dark frame a powerful contrast to the regent's pasty corpulence. Both were attired in evening clothes, elegantly garbed in black coats and breeches, but it was Northington who drew admiring glances from feminine eyes.

Damn him, he knows it, she thought, for he looks so arrogant and...and smug, yes, that's it—with an insolent smile that doesn't fool anyone!

So why did her heart leap so at the sight of him?

As if he sensed her gaze, Northington looked toward the Leverton box, and his eyes found hers even across the wide gallery below. He gave a faintly mocking bow in their direction, a lazy smile on his mouth when she turned away in a deliberate cut.

Did he think all he had to do was smile at her and she'd forget the past months of indifference? Perhaps she hadn't expected vows of undying love or a marriage offer, but neither had she expected him to ignore her as if she no longer existed for him.

"Oh, it is Viscount Northington," Carolyn said in her ear. "And I think he sees us, Celia!"

"Yes, it would be hard to miss us as we're directly across from him. Is that Sir John with him?"

Carolyn nodded. "Yes, it is. An infamous lot, don't you think?" She laughed softly. "Bucks of the first head, a motley group of privileged rogues."

"I thought you liked Sir John," Celia said, turning to look at her cousin."

"Oh, I do, but I can't help think what a waste of money and good blood it is when men do nothing other than amuse themselves all day."

"Yes, I agree. Wastrels are utterly useless no matter what their rank." Celia leaned closer to tease, "I suppose you don't include the prince in that group? Or Edwin?"

"Well, not Edwin, anyway!"

They both laughed, and when Celia glanced back at the ornate box where Northington was with the prince, she saw that he'd gone.

It's just as well, she thought, for I don't think I could bear sitting here all evening with him so close!

Jacqueline pointed out others she knew. "Oh, there's Robert Stewart, Lord Castlereagh. He's more unpopular now than ever before," she said with a frown, "for introducing the Six Acts in the House of

Commons. The people boo him whenever they see him or Lord Liverpool, and all because of that horrid Peterloo business. But it's necessary to curb such lawlessness those public meetings have caused. Perhaps it's because the government is willing to use the same tactics against its own citizens as it used against Napoleon and the French army that it angers the people, yet I cannot help but make a comparison to the Terror."

"So," Celia said, "do you approve or disapprove of the Six Acts?"

"Oh, I do think it's vital not to risk such a thing happening here as it did in France, but the average citizen has no concept of true social reform. All they think of is having their white bread and tea. Ridiculous, really, and not at all necessary."

Celia held her tongue. Jacqueline was basically a kind person, but she didn't realize that the gulf between the rich and the poor was so very wide. It wasn't just white bread and a pot of tea that people wanted, it was security, knowing that their children were safe and fed, a warm, dry place to live.

"Social Reform has become quite popular these days," Jacqueline continued, "but it's dangerous to give too much to people who have no idea how to handle great freedom. Why, just look what happens when they are given too much! That impertinent maid, Janey, whom I gave every opportunity to do well, has abruptly left our employ without so much as a by-your-leave! I had Jarvis investigate to be certain she didn't steal anything, and even though he reports nothing gone, I just know that one day we'll discover the sly chit made off with silver candlesticks or some other items.'' She shook her head vigorously, crimped curls bouncing against her temples. ''These people should know their place, or we're in danger here of another Terror.''

''Mama,'' Carolyn said. ''You are in danger of sounding like a Tory!''

They all laughed, for of course, Jules Leverton was adamantly Tory in his leanings, convinced of the ultimate and complete sovereignty of the crown's authority.

''Do I hear Tory sentiments being voiced?'' a familiar deep voice said behind them, and Celia went very still.

''Viscount Northington, what a pleasure to see you again,'' Jacqueline said. ''Do come and sit with us. We were just discussing the import of the Six Acts passed in the House of Commons last month.''

''And are you for or against them?'' He stood behind Celia's chair and she felt the heat from him as if a blanket over her, reminding her of too many things, of that *night* and the Roman tub and the touch of his hands on her... Of how foolish she had been to give away something she could never recover.

''Oh, for them, of course,'' Jacqueline said. ''But I'm aware that you opposed them.''

''Not for the reason you might think. I just consider it unreasonable to pass national laws dealing with problems that only exist in some areas. It's too universal, and suppresses basic human rights and liberties. I'm sure that, as an American, Miss St. Clair has her own opinions.''

Celia didn't look at him, but nodded. ''Yes, my

lord, I certainly do. I am not, however, as certain that you'd wish to hear them."

"Ah, living in a Tory household has had an astringent effect on you, it seems."

He'd moved from behind her to take an empty seat next to Carolyn, and Celia turned to look at him at last. There was no sign of anything other than polite indifference in his face, nothing to indicate that he remembered that night at Harmony Hill. It had changed her life irrevocably, yet obviously meant nothing to him.

She drew in a deep breath and said calmly, "It's been said that every country has the government it deserves, my lord. I'm sure England is no exception."

"Touché, Miss St. Clair. I believe Maistre was talking about France at the time, but it certainly does fit this discussion as well."

Was that a note of respect in his voice? She must be mistaken, for he had shown nothing but contempt for her opinions thus far. Why would he change now?

Carolyn leaned forward to say to her mother, "Oh do look, it's Lord Liverpool! Melwyn hopes the prime minister will put down the seething rebellion on his Irish estates soon. It's been so very difficult for him."

Carolyn's betrothed had left London to see to his estates in Ireland this past week, and Celia knew Caro worried he would be harmed in the growing civil unrest in that country. She fretted constantly about it, fueled by reminders of the French Revolution and the instability of politics.

Carolyn turned to Northington. "Did you discover who shot at us, my lord? It wasn't some sort of rebellion by your tenants, I do hope!"

"My tenants are mostly farmers with pitchforks. And the local magistrate has most likely already acted on the recent measure to search and seize arms. I doubt any of my tenants have in their possession weapons more powerful than scythes."

"Then who would have shot at us?" Celia asked. "If it wasn't an accident, hunters or the like, who would it be?"

"I don't know the who, but I do know the why," he said with a careless shrug of his shoulders that indicated a reluctance to elaborate. "It will all be settled soon enough so that visitors needn't fear for their lives."

"Then perhaps it was the gypsies," Carolyn said with a shudder. "Do you think it might have been? They are said to be thieves and worse. Do you think it's safe to have them on your estate, my lord?"

"As safe as having you there, Miss Leverton." His smile was cynical, and his gaze shifted to Celia. "I'm not so certain about the safety of your presence, however, Miss St. Clair. You're more reckless than your prudent cousin."

"If you're referring to that untamed horse, you might do well to recall that it was your tame gypsy who saddled it for me," Celia retorted. "But don't be too embarrassed about your failure to provide security for guests, as it's not very safe in London, either."

"That's right," Carolyn said with a shudder. "We were accosted by footpads only last week. It was terrible! Four highwaymen set upon our carriage near Berkley Square, and if not for the footman, we might well have been killed!"

"Highwaymen in London?" Northington's eyes narrowed.

"Not just in London, my lord," Jacqueline said, "but in Mayfair! You can imagine our fright. But for our brave footman's efforts, they might have taken much more than just our purses."

"Then nothing of value was stolen." Northington's gaze shifted back to Celia, a fathomless dark blue regard that made her throat ache.

"Nothing that can't be replaced," she replied.

"Yes, a few jewels—" Jacqueline shook her head with a sad sigh. "Thank heavens I wasn't wearing anything too valuable. We were just starting out and had not yet reached Piccadilly. The constable said it was most curious that they would attack us in daylight, as it was right there not far from home. But what can one expect these days, with brigands running about?"

Celia felt Northington's gaze on her and looked away, unable to face that stare and not demand an explanation, a reason for his indifference after what had been, to her, an extraordinary night. Oh, why wouldn't he go away?

But when the opera started, Northington did not leave at once, remaining as the lights dimmed and everyone's attention was on the stage. She felt his presence acutely.

It was difficult to concentrate on the opera, and she stared down at her programme in the dim light afforded by shaded lamps to follow the thread of the story unfolding onstage.

The tale of a legendary musician who sold his soul to the devil in exchange for knowledge and power was quite familiar to her, yet Northington was too great a distraction for her to enjoy the opera.

"This is where he sells his soul to Satan for twenty-four years of pleasure," Northington leaned close to murmur, and Celia shot him a frowning glance. "A high price for such a short time."

"Indeed, my lord," she said softly, "but I've known men who would sell their souls for less than that."

"You keep villainous company, Miss St. Clair."

She met his gaze. "Not by choice, my lord."

Celia was glad when the intermission finally arrived, and was even more glad when Northington accompanied them only briefly to the lobby. He took his leave with polite apologies to Jacqueline, but not even a glance at Celia.

It was crowded in the lobby, where all came to see and be seen, where jewels glittered beneath brilliant lights and aristocrats rubbed elbows with courtesans.

"I don't believe it," Celia exclaimed when Jacqueline pointed out Madame Poirier, the procuress of fallen women, and her charges all elegantly attired and engaged in open conversation with several men she recognized. "Isn't that Lord Harrow talking to her?"

"It is indeed. But surely you are not shocked! They come here to attract new protectors, of course, and Lord Harrow seems to have found a lady who intrigues him."

Fascinated, Celia was so busy watching the ladies of the night that she didn't at first recognize the man who approached her, until finally Carolyn nudged her and she turned. The fair haired man looked vaguely familiar, but it wasn't until he spoke that she remembered him.

"Miss St. Clair, pardon my interruption, but I wonder if perhaps you remember me?"

"Yes, yes, of course I do. Mister Carlisle from the ship."

James Carlisle looked pleased, a smile brightening his face as he nodded. "I see that you've settled into London life quite happily. Are you enjoying the opera?"

"I have indeed settled in, and am finding the opera to be very entertaining. Mister Carlisle, you no doubt think me the most ungrateful of people, for I haven't yet returned your directory to you. Please forgive me. I'll be most happy to send it to you tomorrow."

"You still have it then. It was a gift from a friend, you understand, and even though I could get another, this one is special to me."

Celia bit her lower lip. "Oh, I am so embarrassed. It wasn't intentional, I assure you, Mister Carlisle. I meant to send it on to you, but I'd put it away and—"

"Miss St. Clair, think nothing of it. Truly, I'd not thought of it myself until I saw you tonight in your box, and then recalled the directory. And to be even more honest, it's an excuse to speak with you again."

His smile was broad, inviting her to indulge him, and she laughed softly.

"You are a dreadful rogue, sir."

"Yes, I'm afraid I am. Could I buy you some punch?"

"You're very kind, but we were just about to return to our box. This is my cousin, Miss Leverton. This is the gentleman I told you about, Carolyn, who was kind enough to see to it that I arrived safely when I first docked in London."

Introductions were exchanged, polite pleasantries passed, then they parted company, Celia once more promising to send the directory by courier early the next morning. The crowd had increased, and she was jostled by a man behind her, so that she stumbled forward and was caught by James Carlisle.

"Here, here," he protested as he held her firmly. A mumbled apology was offered by the clumsy patron before he moved on. "Are you all right, Miss St. Clair?" Carlisle asked.

"Yes, I'm fine. I wasn't hurt, only jostled. I believe the intermission is ended, sir, and I must return."

Carlisle held her hands just a shade too long, his smile very wide and very intimate. "I shall count the days until we meet again, Miss St. Clair."

Disengaging her hands from his grip, she was glad to see him leave.

"A shipboard conquest, Celia?" Carolyn murmured in her ear, and Celia tapped her reprovingly with her fan.

"Just an acquaintance. A rather forward man, I think. Go on to the box without me. I'll join you shortly," she said to her cousins. "I must use the convenience before I come up. I can find my way."

A long corridor led to the ladies' convenience, well lit by lamps high on the walls. Dark panelled wainscoting and flocked wallpaper gave the hall a luxuriant appearance that was both ornate and garish. Two women passed her, and she heard them laughing and talking as they returned to the lobby.

When she left the convenience, she could hear the soaring voice of Catalani, and she hurried down the corridor.

The lamps ahead had gone out, and dark shadows obscured the carpeted floor. She slowed, frowning. An eerie silence descended on the hallway, and her nape tingled with sudden dread.

It all happened so quickly, she wasn't certain where he had come from, but there was no time to scream or do more than struggle as a man shoved her against the wall with harsh, bruising force. The breath was knocked from her by his weight, and then his arm pressed hard against her throat. She clawed at it frantically, unable to breathe, but the relentless pressure didn't lessen. Bright lights exploded in her eyes and there was a ringing in her ears. Somehow she managed to wedge her knee upward, and she heard a rough curse.

Then the pressure was abruptly relieved and she slid to the floor, gasping for breath, holding her aching throat with both hands, aware that she was making horrible noises. Strange, terrifying sounds surrounded her.

A sense of urgency filled her. She knew she must escape before he came after her again but she could barely breathe. Staggering, she lurched to her feet, terror prodding her forward as she stumbled along the dark corridor toward the distant light of the lobby.

When she was grabbed from behind, her bruised throat strangled any cry, so that she was only able to whimper a protest at the rough arm around her waist.

''Be still,'' a familiar voice growled in her ear, ''so I can get you out of here.''

Northington? But what was he doing? Oh, why would he do this to her?

She struggled, but his steely arm was unyielding as he dragged her effortlessly with him, bundling her out a door that she hadn't noticed before. Even though it was pitch-black, she knew they were outside again for she could smell the stink of the alley and feel the cold wind on her bare arms.

"Christ, Celia," he muttered in her ear when she tried to twist free. "Will you be still? There's three of them and only one of me, and I'm in no mood for that kind of fight right now. I need to get you out of here."

Everything was so confused. Her head ached and her throat hurt, and all she could think was that Colter had either rescued her or abducted her. Even if she could talk, she didn't know what to say or ask, or why he was there and what he intended to do next.

After a tumultuous ride in a closed carriage through the London streets, during which he refused to tell her anything other than that she would be safe, they arrived at a narrow house on a dark street. He ushered her inside the back door, through a kitchen and down a hallway, and she glimpsed several women in various stages of undress in what looked to be a parlor.

There was a whispered conversation with someone, then he pulled her with him up a narrow flight of stairs.

A large lavish sitting room was comfortably furnished with two couches upholstered in opulent velvet and tables covered with rich linen and set with silver flatware and gleaming china, as if for an intimate dinner. Through an open door, she saw a huge canopied bed enclosed with opulent hangings. An air of comfortable decadence was rife and as obvious as the unclad females in the downstairs parlor.

It was what she'd heard called a Nunnery or School of Venus—a house of ill repute. A place where men visited women like those she'd seen at the opera, and now he'd brought her here. Oh God, the night had become a horrible nightmare!

"Don't look so shocked," he said softly when she glared at him accusingly. "It's the safest place for you right now. You do realize you're in danger, don't you?"

She could only nod, and stood dazedly when he pulled her with him, not ungently, to seat her on a chair before the fire.

"Your clothes are torn," he said, and she noticed for the first time that her lovely green silk gown was ripped; the sleeve of her Spencer was torn from the armhole, and somehow she had lost one of her lovely slippers. "Madame Poirier no doubt has a gown you can borrow—no, don't turn shy on me, love. It's not as if I haven't seen your charms before, is it? You look as if you've been in a carriage wreck. There are bruises on your face. Can you speak at all? Damn the bastards! There are fingermarks on that lovely white skin of yours. I hope I killed them all."

She stared up at him, shaking. Yes, she remembered now, the grunts, the sounds of a fierce struggle and the still, dark forms left sprawled in the corridor as he'd taken her with him. Why? she wanted to ask, but could only make soft choking sounds.

Kneeling beside her, Colter efficiently and matter-of-factly began peeling away her garments, heedless of buttons and laces, until she was clad only in her silk shift and hose. He lifted her cold feet, rubbed them briskly between his hands, then rose and brought back a blanket to pull around her.

A knock on the door brought hot water and clean clothes, and he motioned for the uniformed maid to leave them. When he came back to where she sat before the fire, he brought Celia a glass of brandy, thrust it into her hands and ordered her to drink it all.

"It will put some color in your face. Jesus, you look like a bruised ghost. You're all right, Celia. When it's safe, I'll take you home. For now, no one will ever think to look for you here." A faint smile crooked his mouth, and his dark blue eyes were unreadable as he stared at her. "I think I rather like your silence. It's refreshing not to deal with your sharp tongue."

While she glared at him, he rose again and returned to her with a hairbrush in his hand.

"Your hair is snarled. I'm not much hand as a lady's maid."

She took the brush, sat still with it in her hand, the brandy a warm glow in the pit of her stomach. It was all such a haze now, the brandy helping but not erasing the images that streamed through her mind in an unending repetition of fear and struggle and shock.

With a shaking hand, she finally lifted the brush to pull it through her hair, but it snagged on a bound coil and she couldn't pull it. Tears started in her eyes at the sudden sharp pain.

When Colter held out his hand, she put the brush into it. He moved behind her, unfastened the intricate curls and ropes of hair atop her crown, and then drew the brush through with long, sure strokes. She sat there, numbed by the heat of the brandy and the fire, by the touch of his hands on her in careless concern.

She wanted to ask why he'd rescued her, how he'd even known she was in danger, but wasn't at all certain she wanted to hear the answer.

Shuddering, she slowly became aware of his hands in her hair instead of the brush, of the leisurely sweep of fingers combing through the heavy mass to lift it from her neck, fisting it in one hand. It was sensuous, a relaxing moment of comfort. Surprisingly gentle.

Then he was pulling her to her feet, turning her into him, his hand on her back a steady pressure.

"No, don't move away," he said softly. "There's not anywhere for you to go tonight. And you don't really want to, do you."

She wanted to say *yes!* but her throat was still too sore to speak. Only mangled sounds were able to escape as he pulled away the blanket, let it puddle on the floor at her feet as he removed the last of her garments, the shift a pale drift atop the blanket. Cool air made her shiver. His hands were firm against her shrinking flesh, hot and far too intimate.

Despite her resistance, he scooped her into his arms and carried her to the tub, lowering her into it until the water level was over her breasts.

It was infuriating, but her attempts to keep him from washing her were futile. He easily evaded her slaps at his hands as he dragged a soapy cloth over her face, then down her throat to her breasts. It was a vivid reminder of the last bath, when he'd made love to her and she'd been foolish enough to think he meant more by it than just the moment.

But this was no time to remember that. He was

touching her intimately, his hands moving over her with brisk efficiency. He held her squirming body still, his grip gentle but firm as he scrubbed the cloth over her back.

"Be still, princess. I'm not much of a hand at this," he muttered when she tried to twist away. "You may not know it, but you've got scratches and bruises all over you. Bloody ones, at that. While you don't think I'm much of a gentleman, those men were certainly not. You look like hell, pardon my bluntness."

She turned to glare at him, and he lifted his brow as a wolfish grin squared his mouth.

"What did you expect? A nice lie? There's a mirror by the wall that would tell you the truth soon enough," he said calmly. "And I seem to recall you stating a decided distaste for liars. Ah ah, no splashing about. You'll get my evening clothes wet and Beaton will be put out about it. A gentleman lives in terror of his valet, you know."

If she could speak, she would tell him that he was certainly no gentleman!

He continued to talk to her while he bathed her, so that she barely winced when he cleaned the cuts that were indeed bleeding. Why hadn't she noticed before? There were bruises that would be quite ugly by morning, and several long scratches on her arms that looked rather deep.

But I don't remember getting these, she thought with a vague frown as she allowed Colter to scoop water over her shoulders to rinse away the soap.

Perhaps it was the brandy, or the hot bath, or even his gentle—if a bit too familiar—touch that soothed her, but by the time the bath was finished, she was almost relaxed.

He lifted her from the tub, wrapped a thick towel around her body and carried her from the sitting room into the bedroom where he put her on the wide canopied bed shrouded by heavy draperies. There was an inevitability to it, to his touch, to what came next and to her own response to him.

Yet tonight she needed this, needed to feel something other than fear, needed to feel…needed to feel what he was doing now, with his hands on her body. Oh God, yes. It was as if she'd been waiting for this moment since the last time….

21

Celia sighed softly. His hands were much more gentle than she remembered, though his caresses were hard and almost painful, thumbs digging into tender skin to rub away the soreness. Fingers spread over her bare skin, kneading flesh with an expertise that was unexpected. How had he learned such a wonderful skill?

The mattress dipped beneath his weight as he shifted, and his hands moved from her shoulders down to the small of her back.

"Your muscles are so tight," he said, and his voice seemed to come through layers of gauze, muffled by her hair and the steady rhythm of her blood in her ears. "You need to relax. You're safe now, and you know that. No one will find you here."

His hands drummed against her sore muscles, pounding away tension as he said, "I learned this from an East Indian holy man, who believed that the body could be cured of most ailments by the mind and simple rituals. He was probably right, but it's taken me a long time to realize that."

It was shadowed in the bed, a lamp across the room the only light. It felt suddenly intimate, familiar, as his hands moved from shoulders to the small of her back, kneading and rubbing away stress. She was lulled by his low, husky voice and soothing hands, drifting on a tide of well-being that must have been summoned by the brandy and hot bath.

"Did you recognize the men who attacked you, Celia? You don't need to talk. Just nod if you did."

She gave a slow shake of her head, tension returning at the memory, and he soothed her with circular motions of his hands across her back, his tone pragmatic and calm.

"I've got my own ideas about who it was, but I need you to be honest with me. If you aren't, you could be in danger yourself, though you may not even know why."

She started to turn over, but he held her still, his knees tightening on each side of her hips, his hands a firm, steady pressure on her back.

"No, lay still for now. Listen to me instead of trying to talk. I know there are some things you aren't telling me, or even your cousin." His hands tightened again when she jerked, his voice relentless. "It would be in your best interests to tell me everything. If I'm wrong, then you'll just have to take my word that I only want to help you."

Help? She strangled a painful laugh. How much help would he be if she told him she wanted to destroy his father?

Oh, she'd had too much brandy, her head hurt and her entire body was sore. She wanted to go to sleep, yet she wanted him to continue rubbing away the aches, wanted his hands on her, needed to feel him close and know that she was safe. Odd, of all men in the world, he was not the one she would have thought she'd feel safe with, yet she did. Yes, it must be the brandy. How else to explain it?

"Celia, I want to know how well-acquainted you are with Carlisle. This isn't the time for secrets."

Carlisle? But what had *he* to do with anything? Unless...oh, he wouldn't have attacked her. She would have recognized him, she was certain. Why on earth did Colter think she was familiar with the man?

"I know," he continued, his hands still massaging her sore body, "that you met him aboard the ship. It couldn't have been a long acquaintance, unless you knew him, or of him, before that. Did you?"

She shook her head slowly, hands kneading the clean white linen sheets that smelled slightly of laundry soap and exotic scents. This house was nothing like she'd imagined a house of ill repute would be, she thought distractedly, with clean sheets and baths available, and rather decadent furnishings, if opulent and luxurious— What was he saying now?

"What did Carlisle give you to hold for him? A book, perhaps, or a package?"

She tried to think through the waves of muddled heat in her brain, her body urging her to oblivion but her mind still straining to hold to coherence. Carlisle's face was a vague blur of memory, his offer to escort her once they disembarked in London summoning a niggling detail that she couldn't quite capture. There was something...yes, he had given her a map, but that wasn't the same thing as a book or a package. Was it important? And why was he asking all these questions... Oh, if only she could think clearly, but her head ached so...

"Celia love, what did Carlisle give you to hold for him? Answer me, and I'll let you go to sleep."

He sounded so demanding, his tone almost harsh now, as if he was irritated. Celia tried to recall what she had been thinking a moment before. Yes, there had been the map. She managed a nod of her head as she ground out, "A map," then heard Colter swear softly before he said, "Go to sleep now. We'll talk more tomorrow."

Tomorrow...yes, tomorrow would be better, for maybe then her head wouldn't hurt so badly and she could focus on what he was asking her—and why. But right now it hurt too badly to think, to do more than just *feel,* and he was being so unusually gentle.

It was almost as if he was a different person, a man who shed personalities the way she changed cloaks.

For the first time in longer than she could remember, she felt safe, as if no harm would come to her while with him. It was as astonishing as it was comforting.

She must have slept, for when she woke it was to an empty bed and thin threads of sunlight piercing heavy drapes over the window. Blinking against streamers of dusty light, Celia took a cautious survey of her aches and pains. Amazingly there was little soreness, though there were thin red scratches on her arms, and the bruises were a deep purple.

At least her throat was no longer sore, but it was very dry and she was thirsty; there was nothing on the bedside table to drink, not even her brandy from the night before. It looked as if the room had been cleaned, for through the open door she saw that the bath had been removed from the sitting room. It was quiet in the house, very still. Where was Colter? Had he just *left* her here?

Groggily she sat up and stuck her legs over the side of the bed, holding the coverlet over her breasts as she slid to her feet to wobble to a small round table nearby. A wave of dizziness made her falter, and she leaned on the top of the table to steady her balance.

A pitcher of water and two glasses sat on a silver tray. The chink of fine crystal sounded quite loud in the room as she poured a drink rather clumsily; she was loathe to release her only covering. What if someone should walk in?

She must find her clothes and manage to leave as discreetly as possible. But her gown had been torn, she remembered, as the events of the night before came rushing back. Her hand shook and water spilled onto a lace cloth arranged over the table. She set down the pitcher before she dropped it.

The water tasted slightly musty, but eased her parched throat, and she drank two glasses before she felt she had had enough.

''Ah, my little camel, I see you're awake,'' Colter said behind her, and she managed to set down the empty glass and turn to look at him without falling over or losing her grip on the bedclothes. Her heart gave an erratic thump. He was leaning negligently against the door frame, regarding her with a faint smile. He'd changed clothes, and now wore a dark coat, snug trousers and boots to his knees.

Must he look so handsome this early in the morning? She probably looked a fright, with her hair all loose and eyes puffy from sleep. Just where did *he* sleep last night, she wondered as she tightened her grip on the downward sliding blanket, chin jutting out when he grinned insolently at her hoarse reply.

"Yes, and it's time for me to leave. My cousin must be worried sick about me, and—"

"And I've taken care of all that. Your reputation is safe, your cousin mollified, and now all we have to do is figure out where to hide you."

"Hide me!" She stared at him. "Have you gone mad? Why on earth should I have to *hide* anywhere, and why did you take it upon yourself to make explanations to Jacqueline? What did you tell her? She must wonder where I am and why I left like I did—which is what I'm wondering myself. Who were those men and why did you bring me here?"

"I brought you here," he said as he crossed the room, "because it's the one place I knew they wouldn't look for you. And even if they did, Webster is armed and capable of keeping secrets."

"Who are *they,* and who is Webster? Really," she said with growing exasperation, "this seems so unnecessary. I've no need to hide from cutpurses, especially not *here.*"

"You don't like it here? Odd, it's one of the most popular, frequently visited spots in London. But perhaps you're right. It's not exactly the sort of establishment you can mention in polite company. As fetching as that blanket is on you, my love, I think you're going to need to wear clothes that cover up all that tempting bare flesh."

His dark blue gaze seemed to penetrate the blanket

she held almost to her chin, and she felt a hot flush scour her face. "I told you," she said sharply to cover her sudden embarrassment, "that I am going home to my cousin. If my clothes are ruined, you can find me another dress."

"I think I liked it better last night when you couldn't speak at all, but at least the medicine worked." His mouth curled in a mocking smile at her angry hiss. "You needed it. It relaxed you, and nothing bad happened. You know, with your green eyes slitted at me like that, you look remarkably like a cat, love. That's good, because you're going to need to put on a show if we're to escape notice."

"What are you talking about now? Escape? A show?"

"I hope your acting has improved." He moved past her to a tall armoire set into the wall, and flung open the doors. A row of gowns dangled from hooks—red silks, satins, demure muslin and a taffeta gown in bright yellow hung like wilted flowers. "Here." He reached inside, grabbed the taffeta gown and tossed it to her. "Put this on and see if it fits. If not, Madame can alter it for you."

She'd caught the dress, a reflexive action, then had to grab at the blanket as it slipped from her breasts.

"I have no intention of wearing this ugly thing!" She threw it to the floor. "If you expect me to go along with whatever scheme you've concocted, you'd best tell me what it is or I refuse to step a foot outside this room."

A dark brow cocked, and his grin widened. "Madame wouldn't mind having a new girl in her stable,

I suppose, though after the first few nights you might change your mind about your new vocation.''

He moved toward her, two steps bringing him close. ''Should I interview you for the position? Which do you prefer, love, on your back or—''

''Stop it!'' She retreated a step, her heart thumping alarm when he followed with a determined glint in his eye. ''Why are you doing this? I don't know what's going on or why I was brought here, or even why those men attacked me. And you aren't making things any clearer.''

''They'll be clear soon enough. I know it's a lot to expect you to trust me, but you really don't have any choice right now, Celia.''

He reached for the blanket she held tightly, and pulled it free despite her grip and protests.

''What are you—oh!''

As the blanket slid to the floor, Colter drew Celia to him, his hands sliding around her back to pull her hard against his body. She felt his muscles tighten when she put her hands on his arms.

''Please,'' she said, and hated the way she sounded so breathless. ''If you'll only tell me what's happening and why I'm here...''

''I will, love. I will.'' He lifted her in his arms, took her the few steps to the wide bed still mussed from the night and dumped her on it. ''Has anyone ever told you how appealing you are with your hair all loose and tumbling over your shoulders like that? It's a bloody shame females keep their hair in tight coils, when it's much more alluring like this...a cloud of raw silk, the same color as honey.''

He'd lifted a curl of her hair in his fist, his hands

not ungentle as his fingers tunneled through to push it back from her face. Leaning over her, there was an intently fierce expression on his face, his eyes a dark, glittering blue as he stared down at her.

"Open your legs for me, Celia," he said softly, and she thought for a moment that her ears were playing tricks on her. But then his hand moved with swift certainty over her body, not as it had the night before, but more intimate now, touching her breasts, moving lower to her belly and then below to tease the nest of curls between her thighs.

"If you're going to play the part, perhaps you should have more instruction first, my sweet." His voice was soft, husky, and he lay down beside her, his weight dipping the mattress so that she slid closer.

It was oddly arousing to lie naked next to him while he was still fully clothed, but she felt vulnerable, too, and began to shake her head uncertainly. He threw his leg across her thighs when she tried to move away.

"No, don't resist. You don't really want to, and we've done this before so there's no harm, is there? You enjoyed it then, didn't you, love. Now it will be even better for you...yes, let me kiss you there..."

His tongue flicked over the taut peak of her breast in a hot, damp stroke, and she sucked in a sharp breath at the piercing sweetness of it. His hand caressed her as his lips closed over her breast, drawing her nipple into his mouth, a strong suction that sent shivers of heat through her entire body. Oh God...it must be the residue of the medicine he'd given her, for she found it difficult to think, to resist as his hands moved over her so intimately, shaping her other breast in his palm, thumb and finger tugging at the nipple in a deliciously erotic play. A pulse began to beat between her thighs, strong and hot, and she moaned softly.

Colter tangled one hand in her hair and kissed her on the lips, fiercely, his mouth a bruising pressure. Then she felt his tongue in her mouth, seeking, and she returned his kiss at last, her hands moving to clutch at him, fingers curled into his shirt to hold him tightly.

Oh, no! What was he doing now? Confused, she felt him move back, part her legs with his hands on her inner thighs, fingers sliding down to touch her, then slip beneath her to lift her slightly. Then, shockingly, he lifted her legs over his shoulders and held her there, his hands moving to her breasts again, fingers teasing her nipples until she muffled a cry with her knuckles pressed against her lips and teeth as his mouth found her.

No, no, no...this was not meant to be... She heard as if from a distance the sounds she made, soft sobbing cries that were somehow mixed up with embarrassment and desire and the need for him to continue. His mouth seared into her, tongue like a flame on soft flesh, and she shuddered at the tight, hot growing pressure forming. It wound tighter and tighter, until finally there was an abrupt release that left her shaking, crying out his name, her hips arching into him as she sobbed helplessly.

This was nothing like the last time, nothing like she had ever dreamed. He seemed to know that for he murmured softly to her, words that made no sense but were intuitively comforting. Eyes closed, she drifted on the tide of this new and unexpected emotion.

Still shuddering, she felt him move over her. His

clothes were gone now, his body bare and hot against her as he moved between her legs. His skin was so dark, almost a bronze color, and there were faint ridges of scars on his chest and arms, pale against the golden sheen. She thought suddenly of one of the statues she had seen, the smooth, carved muscles of chest and belly signifying the leashed power and masculine prowess of a Roman god, a warrior.

His entry was slow, steady, an inexorable pressure that was only slightly uncomfortable at first.

No, it was nothing like her first time with him, nothing like she'd anticipated, for the slow thrust and drag of his body inside her created an exquisite friction that had her once more scaling the heights of sensuality. It was an erotic motion, encompassing, and she surrendered to it completely. Why resist? Despite everything, he had only to begin caressing her and she was lost, inexplicably powerless to refuse him—and powerless against her own reaction to him, the need to be with him, her treacherous body overriding caution and common sense.

It even overrode the knowledge that he lived in the camp of the enemy.

"Kiss me, love," he said softly against her ear. She lifted her lips to his, losing herself in the sweet, driving rhythm of their bodies, in the primitive response that she had never dreamed was so strong, until finally she forgot everything else.

22

It was nearly midnight when Colter escorted Celia from Madame Poirier's establishment, casually putting her into a carriage and taking up the reins as if it was a common occurrence.

Perhaps it is for him, Celia thought, and resisted the urge to see if anyone was watching them. Her hands shook slightly, and the yellow taffeta rustled loudly as she arranged it on the narrow seat of the closed gig. The hat she wore had dark curls peeping from beneath the brim, for though they left by the discreet side door provided for those customers who preferred no one know of their nocturnal visits, there was still the chance they might be seen.

It had been the sauntering stroll through the parlor that had unnerved her most, the few men present with a bevy of unclad females more shocking than she had anticipated. But she had done well, she knew, for Colter squeezed her arm when she leaned into him, feigning a sultry laugh as he slid a hand into her bodice, and one of the men who'd glanced up at them turned away after a moment.

She'd known she must look very much as some of the other women there, her eyes half-lidded with the residue of passion, her lips still swollen and bruised from kisses, and her breasts sensitive in the low-cut gown that revealed the tops of her nipples and the marks left by Colter's hands and mouth on her skin. She'd even *felt* like one of them, her loose hair carelessly held back by a ribbon, mussed as if she'd just risen from bed—which she had. It must show on her face, that passion, the hot, wild ferocity of her response to him that had surprised her with its intensity.

"If I didn't know better," he'd drawled lazily as they lay panting and exhausted in bed earlier in the day, "I'd swear you were an experienced courtesan, love."

Angrily she'd tried to rise from the bed but he'd only laughed and held her down easily, pinning her with his body atop hers, his hands roaming her curves and hollows with growing familiarity until she surrendered once again to the inevitable passion he provoked.

What did the future hold for her? And how had she lost control of it so quickly? Oh, it was all so bewildering, the need to leave London and the dark shadow of danger hovering over her, when she had done nothing to invite it other than accept a map of the city.

But that had been enough, Colter said shortly, and one day he'd explain it to her when he was certain she was safe.

Reaction kept her stomach churning, and even now, as the landau jerked forward and they were at last leaving the house, she could barely control her trembling hands. To her surprise, Colter took one of her hands in his and pressed it to his mouth, his eyes narrowed slightly.

"Don't let down your guard," he murmured. "And keep the hat on. That disguise is only good from a distance."

It was still unbelievable that there were desperate men who would rob and, perhaps even kill for the map that James Carlisle had given her. If that was true, why hadn't they come for it before? she'd asked Colter, and he'd only shrugged. While she didn't know what significance the map held for those who pursued it, and he said that she didn't need to know, she couldn't help but wonder why it was so important.

There was so much he didn't say, but if he truly felt she was unsafe in London, perhaps it was best she leave for a while. Oh, what must Jacqueline think of all this? She must have been horrified last night when she'd realized Celia was gone. It would have been even more mystifying to her once she was told that Celia wouldn't be back for a while.

"Only for a short time," he'd promised her, but there had been a vagueness to the promise that was disquieting.

Beyond the city gates it was pitch-black, the darkness broken only by the lanterns affixed to the carriage. Patches of dense fog shrouded Hounslow Heath, dangerous at this time of night, a warren of footpads and highwaymen.

Colter seemed to know the way, his hands adept on the reins. Cold air swept across the gig, and Celia's teeth began to chatter with the cold despite the thick lap robe she pulled up to her chin. The taffeta dress was much too thin, and she thought longingly of her warm wool redingote trimmed in fur and with braided frogs that fastened it all the way to her throat.

Weariness seeped through her, and the tension of the past twenty-four hours left her numb. But when she tried to fall asleep, oblivion eluded her. There was so much to think about, so much she wanted to know... Surprisingly, despite the occasional jolt when a wheel dipped into one of the ruts on the road, she fell asleep at last.

It was a restless slumber, with vivid dreams and images of masked men and the feeling of imminent danger, so that she woke abruptly when the gig came to a stop. It was black outside the gig window, not even the light from the lantern to brighten the dense turbid blanket of night. She heard a swift, whispered conversation, then the gig door opened and she felt Colter's hands on her, pulling her from the vehicle to stand her on her feet.

"Hurry, we haven't much time, Celia."

Sleepily she protested as he bustled her from the gig and into another coach, this one, thankfully, with warm bricks for her feet and a much thicker lap robe to tuck around her shoulders.

"Don't ask questions, love," he said when she voiced a concern. "Believe me when I tell you this is all necessary."

It seemed now as if they went back in the direction they had come, for the road seemed vaguely familiar, the larger coach well-sprung as it barreled along at a brisk pace. She was still alone inside, though there was another man atop the carriage, a driver, perhaps, who sat next to Colter. They passed an inn she had noticed earlier, and now she was convinced they were going back to London.

An elaborate ruse, perhaps, to convince the men who had attacked her that she was gone from the city. Oddly, she did feel safe with Northington, though once she would have laughed at the very notion of it. The son of the man she'd hated for so long was her lover. Oh, what would Maman think if she were still alive?

But then, if Maman were still alive, perhaps she would never have formed such a hatred that it would direct her life. When she returned to London, she would tell Jacqueline the truth, tell her why she had really come to England after so long. She deserved to hear the truth. Besides, the need for vengeance was somewhat abated. Perhaps life had taken care of that better than she could, for hadn't Jacqueline told her that the earl was an invalid, never able to leave his house, confined to a chair most of his days? Yes, it was a much better judgment than she could pronounce on him. Maybe it was true that fate took care of all.

But if she hadn't come to England, she would never have met Colter. Did she love him? Oh, it was an emotion she hadn't expected to feel, and didn't know how to gauge. She felt something for him, of course, an emotion that was still so new and raw she wasn't certain how to explain it even to herself. How could she know? How could she tell if it was truly love she felt, or maybe just a variation of the desire that she felt when she was with him?

The coach lurched to one side and she grabbed at the handstrap just above her right ear to keep her balance. Their speed had increased, but now nothing outside the window looked familiar to her. In the growing light of early dawn she saw hilly slopes and heaths shrouded by misty streamers of morning fog.

They had been traveling for hours, and soon they stopped again in a remote spot beneath an old wooden bridge, where she was once more put into yet another carriage.

"We'll stop at an inn later," Colter told her when she asked where they were going. "Tonight you'll sleep in a bed and have a hot meal, but for now, you'll have to endure the discomfort. It's not so bad, is it, love?"

Aware of the man atop the driver's box, Celia flushed a little when Colter kissed her quickly, then lifted her into the black lacquered carriage that had seen better days. It had begun to rain, the brief sunshine of earlier vanished behind dark low-lying clouds. The roads swiftly became muddy ruts that sucked at the carriage wheels and slowed their progress.

Celia huddled inside, grateful for the warm bricks but wishing they could stop. It seemed the journey would never end. At last they halted in front of a roadside inn on the outskirts of a tiny village. Postboys scurried to take the horses, while Colter came to take Celia inside, his arm around her shoulders as they ran through the pouring rain.

A bright, warm fire provided a cheery blaze and heat and Celia went at once to stand before it, her hands held out. It wasn't the best of establishments, she could see that, but it was dry and warm and didn't move or jolt like the carriage.

Near frozen, she paid no attention at first to the voices behind her, until she heard a woman's scolding,

"I'll have no doxies in me good inn, sir, and never ye mind the coin!"

Glancing up, Celia saw Colter engaged in conversation with an aproned woman who stood with hands on hips, glaring at Celia across the common room. Belatedly she recalled the dress she wore and the silly hat that she'd put back on her head, and flushed. It was obvious the innkeeper's wife considered her a harlot, and with the other patrons giving her curious looks, she felt suddenly as if she was. Her face was hot with embarrassment, but she refused to retreat.

Let them think what they would! Her spine stiffened, and she turned to watch the fire again, ignoring them.

Apparently Colter soothed the woman's ruffled feathers with coin or intimidation, for a few minutes later the alewife brought two cups of wine to a nearby table, though her lips were pursed in tight disapproval.

"Yer room'll be ready soon enow," she said sullenly, "but it be upstairs at the back."

Overlooking the pigsty no doubt, Celia thought angrily, but held her tongue as the woman flounced away.

Colter brought two platters of beef, bread and kidney pie to the table, and sat down across from Celia. He pushed one toward her.

"You'll never see them again," he said flatly, and she lifted her gaze to his face, knowing what he meant.

"It's the dress," she said. "I should have changed. I don't care what that old cow thinks, but I would rather we not attract attention."

"There hasn't been time for you to change clothes. We only have a few hours for you to rest."

"Why this rush? Why can't we just go to the authorities and have the constable—"

"It's not that simple." Dark blue eyes studied her, then he shrugged. "Tell me everything you remember about the map."

"I told you twice that I don't recall anything about it except that he'd made marks of some kind on it—small *x*'s on some of the streets, but I don't know the names."

"Here. Eat this." He reached across the table to slice her beef, the blade of his knife glinting in the murky light of fire and a flickering lantern. "It's tough but edible. Put it on bread and it might go down easier."

She stared at him. "This has something to do with what I've been reading in the papers, doesn't it? About the Six Acts that Parliament just passed. People are angry."

"We English are always up in arms about something." He slapped a slice of beef on a bread crust and held it out to her. "Keep up your strength. You may need it."

Frustrated, she leaned close, her voice low and fierce. "I want to know just why you're dragging me all over the country! It has something to do with Carlisle and something to do with that map, and I think it has something to do with a brewing rebellion!"

His quick upward glance was abruptly opaque and dangerous. "Keep your bloody voice down, Celia. Unless you intend to have your fencing lessons put to the test in the near future, you'll watch your tongue."

She sat back. "I never took fencing lessons. I lied."

"What a surprise. Eat your dinner. It may be the last hot food we have for a while."

There was no point in badgering him, she saw that now, for he was as obdurate as a mule, his face closed as he ate the tough, stringy beef and hard bread crusts.

"I hope you didn't pay much for this," she muttered.

He grinned. "You're becoming a shrew, love. Considering she wanted to evict us promptly—morality can be so fleeting at times—we're damned lucky to have it. If you can stomach vinegar, you'll enjoy the wine."

The upstairs room at the back of the inn wasn't much better, Celia discovered, but at least the bed had clean linens and an honest mattress instead of a straw-stuffed sack. It felt awkward, standing in the middle of the small room with no fire in the empty grate, drafts seeping through cracks around the window as she shivered.

"I see we must pay extra for a fire," Colter observed, and moved to the window to peer out. "At least the view is free. I trust you like pigs."

"You're in a fine humor for a man who fled London in the middle of the night," she said sourly. "I've had little enough sleep, but you've had none."

"I'm used to it. Soldiers in the field rarely sleep long or well."

"Oh, yes, I'd forgotten that you're a war hero." She sat on the edge of the bed; it creaked slightly beneath her weight. "You've no doubt done more than your share of lying awake plotting your next massacre."

Colter turned from the window to look at her, and in the gray light through dingy panes, his expression was unreadable. "Yes," he said softly, "I have. Not just in France, but in the Americas, too."

Arrested by his tension, she sat with her foot pulled across her knee, the slipper she'd just removed still in her hand. He looked ruthless. The facade of the past days was just that, a thin veneer disguising a man capable of killing and more. How had she forgotten, even for a moment?

That day on the Kentish coast she'd seen the fierce light in his eyes, the reckless deviltry in his face when he had taken a loaded pistol and searched for the men who had shot at them. She had known at once that he was accustomed to danger, thrived on it.

The slipper dropped from her hand and she bent to retrieve it. When she straightened, he was staring out the window again, as trickles of rain made silvery paths on the thick leaded glass.

"Stay inside," he said without turning to look at her, "and get some rest. I'll be back later."

There was no use asking where he was going. He wouldn't tell her, she knew that.

And God help me, I don't think I want to know....

23

A cold rain came down in a fine mist like a cobweb; sticky moisture clung to his hair and face as Colter moved toward the line of stables behind the inn. They were as ramshackle as the half-timbered inn, with the same thatched roof. Beneath his coat he carried two pistols stuck into the waist of his trousers, both primed with dry powder.

Detaching from the deeper shadows at the back of the stable, a man he recognized approached across the littered yard, sidestepping steaming piles of horse manure.

"You've been followed," Tyler said abruptly, and jerked his head toward the north. "Bow Street Runners."

"Are they close?" Colter stepped beneath the overhang of the livery stable.

"Not yet. They will be. These men aren't the regular Runners, but hired by Leverton."

"It would be interesting to know how they found us. See what you can learn."

Nodding, Tyler glanced around the nearly empty

yard. He frowned and looked uneasy. "I think I may already know."

"Mowry."

Tyler looked startled, but nodded. "He's the only man I told of your plans."

"I'll deal with him later. Was the map found?"

"Her room had been ransacked, and the maid swears she knows nothing about it. Ruthven is finding out what he can, and there's to be another meeting in a few days. If the log is in their hands, Carlisle might betray himself."

"Were Celia's assailants found? No, I didn't think they would be. I thought I'd killed at least one of them, but the body could have been removed before it was found. Christ, there was no need for Carlisle to attack her. She'd planned to send back the directory the next day, and had just told him so."

"He gave her the map aboard the *Liberty* because he knew you were watching him and wanted to get it off the ship. He looked to be unpleasantly surprised to discover that she knew you." Tyler leaned back against the wall, eyes narrowed in thought. "It could be that he was afraid you'd get to it first and figure out what it means."

"Maybe. But there's something about this entire affair that doesn't quite fit. Celia's had the map since arriving three months ago. Why wait this long to go after it?"

"Didn't you say they were robbed by footpads a few weeks ago? Maybe this wasn't the first time they'd tried."

"Maybe." He rubbed his thumb across his jaw. "And maybe it wasn't Carlisle's men who attacked her. It occurred to me that it's not what she knows, but rather what they think she knows that's put her in danger.''

Tyler nodded agreement.

Damn Mowry, Colter thought after he parted company with Tyler. He had interfered again. There would be hell to pay for that later, and there would be hell to pay if the Runners caught up with them while he was still with Celia. He should have taken her to Katherine, but he hadn't wanted to leave Celia in the city where she was vulnerable.

Celia. Green-eyed little minx, the only woman who had ever managed to hold his attention even when she wasn't with him. It was the damnedest thing. He dreamed of her at times, of her soft, drawling voice, the curve of her mouth when she smiled, and those eyes... She infuriated him, yet he couldn't get enough of her, of the smell and taste of her, even of her sharp tongue.

Christ, he'd let her get close to him. It was damned inconvenient. It affected his judgment, when he should keep his head clear and his goal primary. Celia St. Clair was an unexpected complication, a danger. He thought of her as he'd seen her earlier, eyes wide and staring at him with trust. It was her trust that affected him, her certainty that he would keep her safe.

Not once on the arduous journey had she complained, done more than sag wearily. There was courage in her that he hadn't suspected, and a fortitude that he'd never thought she had. It was startling. How had he ever put her in the same class as the other women he'd known who accomplished flirts and basically very shallow, intent only upon the moment and their pleasure. There was so much more to Celia.

She was strong, firm to the point of stubbornness and surrender wasn't in her nature. He wished he knew what secret she was keeping from him. It was obvious there was something she wasn't telling him. It had nothing to do with the conspiracy, though. He was sure of that.

Events were moving at a fast pace now, and the prospect of a bloody revolt was more than just possible. It was a certainty. How would he keep her safe when he wasn't sure where the true danger to her lay?

He swore softly and a passing stableboy gave him a wide berth, as if afraid to get too close.

Colter smiled grimly, not blaming him. If Colter looked like he felt at the moment, he must look pretty savage. But Christ, what was he going to do with Celia? Taking her to Harmony Hill was dangerous. Options were few; too far or too obvious. If Tyler was right and Mowry was behind the attempt to abduct her, few places were safe for her right now. Mowry had very disagreeable methods of interrogation.

Rain hissed, pattering atop the stable roof in a drumming rhythm. Music from a fiddle drifted from the Inn's common room when the door opened, and Colter's eyes narrowed into glittering blue slits. She wouldn't like it, but he knew where to hide Celia.

Unfortunately Celia resisted the efforts to keep her safe, struggling against him when Colter dragged her from a nice warm bed in the inn and out into the cold rain. Wrapped in a heavy wool cape over the yellow taffeta, she protested sleepily, "We can wait until daylight, can't we? I don't want to leave now!"

"Christ, keep your voice down, Celia." His harsh voice grated next to her ear, and she shivered at the anger in it. He was so brusque, indifferent, his hands on her impersonal, as if he were tending a horse instead of the woman he'd taken to his bed.

Ignoring her futile resistance, he put her atop a horse instead of in a closed gig, and she grabbed at the saddle to keep her balance. She rode astride like a man, dispensing with any semblance of grace as her skirts bunched up around her knees, but he paid no attention to her efforts as he led their mounts from the dark stableyard and into the night.

It was so cold, the January winds bitter and biting, smelling of rain and mud. She clung to her mount as it stayed close to Colter's larger animal, its hooves a pounding drum against the rutted road. Rain slashed into her face at times even though she ducked her head and pulled the hood to the cape as low as possible. Tremors racked her body and misery made her silent, not that he would have paused to listen to her protests or questions.

How had he changed so suddenly from playful lover to this hard-eyed stranger? It was frightening.

When fuzzy gray daylight came at last, it seemed they'd already been riding forever. Every bone in her body ached with fatigue, and Celia reeled in the saddle by the time Colter finally halted late in the day. They were beneath a rocky overhang, with winter-dead creepers brown traceries against rock walls, leafless trees clacking bare branches with a sound like the rattle of old bones. A soughing wind curled around wooded slopes, caught at the hem of her dress and fluttered her hood. She shivered, muscles protesting the involuntary reaction.

At least the rain couldn't reach them here. She made no sound when Colter pulled her from her horse and led her into what turned out to be a shallow cave hollowed into rock. It smelled dank, and as if it had been used before.

He propped her against the rock wall, where gray light seeped inside. Working with silent efficiency, he rubbed down their horses, fed them grain from a burlap sack, then set about making a fire near the front of the cave. It was necessarily small, the damp wood obviously left behind by former occupants stacked on the pitted floor to one side.

Still crouched on his heels, he pivoted slightly to look at her when a tidy blaze spit sparks toward the low ceiling. "It's smoking too badly to use long. Come get warm before I put it out."

Wordlessly she hunched near the fire, spread her hands out to heat them at the licking flames. In the hellish light cast by burning branches, his face was set in stark relief.

"Take off the cape and I'll dry it for you," he said. When she didn't move—couldn't move for the shivering—he rose and came to her, untied it at the neck and slid it from her shoulders to hold it near the fire. She couldn't help but notice that he didn't seem cold at all, but was impervious to the wet clothes and icy winds.

His black hair was wet enough to drip down his collar, but he ignored it, as he disregarded his own drenched coat, now spread over a rock to dry out.

When she could speak, she asked, "Are we staying here all night?"

He glanced up at her through the smoke. "It seems the driest place for now."

"I never thought England could be such a wilderness. It seemed so small and...and civilized."

"A gratifying surprise for you, no doubt, to discover that we have our own share of uncivilized citizens. What we lack in size, we more than make up for in mettle. Ask any Frenchman."

She shivered. Yellow taffeta clung to her legs in sodden folds. She looked away from him. "Do we have any food?"

"Beef and bread. A limited menu, but preferable to rocks or thistles."

When her cape was nearly dry, he spread it over the same rock that held his coat and rummaged in a sack for food, producing cold meat, cheese and hard bread.

They ate silently as the fire died down and dwindled to only glowing embers, leaving the cave in shadow and cold. Near the entrance, the horses settled, heads lowered, legs braced for sleep. The smell of smoke was faint now, acrid, and left a haze in the damp air.

Celia heard Colter rise, saw his vague shadow move again to the gear he'd removed from their mounts. Then he came to her and reached down.

"We might as well get some sleep for a few hours. It smells like snow, and we need to press on soon."

A few hours? Dismayed, she let him lift her to her feet and guide her to the rear of the hollow, where he spread out wool blankets on a rocky shelf. When she stretched out on the lumpy pallet, he lay beside her, ignoring her suddenly stiff body and tense muscles as he pulled her back against his chest so that they fit snugly together.

"It'll be warmer this way, princess," he said softly, his warm breath against her neck making her shiver. His arms held her tight and close, and shortly the heat began to penetrate despite her reservations.

Outside the wind was constant, a keening sound like strange moans. Inside, the smell of horses, old smoke and dampness permeated everything. She closed her eyes when Colter's hand spread across her abdomen, and a peculiar knot loosened inside, an odd quiver that seemed to ease through her entire body so that the trembling was not from cold, but from reaction.

He must have sensed it, for he began to stroke her with light circular motions, fingers splayed upward to cup her breast in his palm. She recognized the pattern, the steps as of a dance in his caresses, and knew when he would move his hand next. She turned into him as he urged her to her back with a gentle nudge upon her shoulder.

Yes, this was becoming so familiar, the same sweet, wild sensation of his hands on her bare flesh, the thunder of blood through her veins in response to his mouth on her lips, eyes and breasts. As if in a dream, she became aware that they were both undressed again and he was between her thighs, fitting to her as if made just for that very purpose. Perhaps he was. Perhaps this was what life was all about, the coming together of a man and a woman this way, in mutual desire and need, the communion without speech but with touch.

And then it was difficult to think coherently. All she could do was *feel*. Nothing else mattered, not the cold or the isolation, nothing but the intense passion that flared between them.

Despite the cold in the cave, or maybe because of it, she clung to him with an almost desperate intensity, not wanting to think about where they were going or why, wanting only to feel him inside her again, his hard male body so vital and strong. It was all that could take away memories that were too painful to bear at times, this forgetfulness he summoned with his mouth and hands, the plane where she could float as free as a bird on waves of oblivion.

"Hold me, Celia," he muttered against her mouth, and she wrapped her arms around him as he pounded into her with a fierce, driving rhythm that took her beyond the cave and beyond even herself.

It was difficult to breathe, to think, to even hear, and she knew she must be mistaken when she heard him say, just as he went still and deep inside her, "God, I hate to leave you...."

When they slept at last, he held her in his arms so that she was almost a part of him, joined together as one.

Colter woke first, when it was still dark outside and there was nothing to see but shades of black. He nudged her awake, and when she moaned a protest, he pulled her to a sitting position.

"It's nearly daylight. We've slept too long. Come on, princess."

Still grumbling protests, she let him help her dress, but frowned when he held out a pair of trousers.

"What are those?"

He gave them an impatient shake. "Put them on, Celia. I don't have time to argue. That dress is almost in rags, and you need to worry more about warmth than appearances. These are compliments of a stable lad. Put them on so we can go."

They were much too large, and he belted them around her waist to hold them up, stuffing a voluminous shirt into the waist so that she resembled a rather portly lad wearing his father's clothes.

Despite feeling ridiculous, Celia was admittedly warmer in the trousers than the taffeta gown, and had no regrets when Colter wadded it up and stuffed it into a bag they took with them.

The blackness of night slowly lightened to gray as they rode, and she hoped Colter knew where he was going since it seemed to be little more than faint tracks that led through wood and then into marsh. Traces of light snow powdered the ground as the sun rose higher, dull light barely penetrating the clouds that seamed sky and earth together in an unending anonymous horizon.

It smelled of the sea here; terns rode air currents, and the marshy ground gradually changed to harder chalk. Was he taking her to Harmony Hill? It seemed far too obvious.

Hunched against the cold, Celia rode numbly now, and when she saw through the trees faint welcoming lights, she sagged with relief.

But it was no house they approached, only some kind of camp, with wheeled houses shouldering beneath the shelter of spiny leaved yews. Smoke rose from a central fire, flames cheery in the gathering dusk.

She stiffened when she recognized the man who

came out to greet them, and shot Colter an accusing glance.

The gypsy, Santiago, grinned widely, speaking in the dialect that was only partly Spanish, and beckoned them down from their mounts. Celia would have refused, for she saw beyond the fire the gypsy girl Marita staring at her with a strange expression, but Colter lifted her down to stand her beside him, his arm draped in casual possession across her shoulders as if to proclaim that Celia belonged to him.

It was only partly gratifying, and with sudden dread, she knew what he intended. He meant to leave her here with these people who spoke a foreign language, to abandon her.

"No," she said when Colter turned to pull her into one of the brightly painted wagons. "I know what you're going to do and I refuse! Do you hear me? I won't stay here with these people. It doesn't matter what you say."

One of the gypsy men laughed, his teeth a white flash in the gloom, but she ignored him and glared at Colter, a mixture of anger and fear making her heart thump madly. They drew the attention of others in the camp, but she refused to retreat, shaking her head and avoiding his reaching hand.

Colter moved swiftly, like a striking snake, to grab her by the arm, fingers steely even through the thick folds of the wool cape.

"Jesus, it's too damn cold to stand out here and argue, Celia, so just cooperate for the moment while I try to work out something else."

"I won't stay here," she repeated. "You have to think of another plan, Colter, you must."

"Get into the wagon and we'll talk." He pulled her up the four steep steps, then inside, and left her with a promise to come right back. "I'll talk to Santiago. Stay here where it's warm and I'll be back in a moment."

But when he returned, she found to her dismay that the something else he had worked out was not at all agreeable.

"Please," she hissed. "Reconsider! If you leave me here, any hope I ever had of salvaging some of my reputation will be ruined. Isn't it bad enough that you dragged me from the theater, then to a...a house of prostitution? Now you intend to leave me with gypsies and God only knows when I'll see you again. Take me back to London. I'd rather take my chances there!"

They were alone in the cramped quarters of the wagon, a wheeled hut that held a bed, tiny table and storage in drawers built under the bed and along the walls. Windows wore gaily colored curtains, and personal items indicated the owner was a man.

"Be quiet," Colter said with a scowl, "and don't insult Santiago's hospitality. No one will think to look for you here. Christ, Celia, I can't keep you safe in London when I'm not even certain who attacked you. I thought I knew, but I was wrong."

She stared at him, distress making her voice quaver slightly. "How long would I have to stay here?"

One corner of his mouth tucked into a grimace. "Just long enough for me to take care of what I have to do."

"That could be weeks!"

"A lifetime if you're in danger. Look, Celia, I don't

claim that you'll be happy here, but it won't be as bad as you think. Santiago will look after you. He's fiercely loyal to me, and has agreed to keep you out of harm's way."

"I seem to recall his daughter putting me *in* harm's way," she snapped, and when he only looked amused, she added acidly, "But, of course, if you think putting me on a horse that could have very well killed me is keeping me safe, who am I to argue?"

"You're reacting with emotion instead of logic. Marita took you at your word when you said you could ride."

"A horse that wasn't even trained!"

"But you did it." He gave her an odd look, half admiring. "If you hadn't ridden into gunfire, nothing would have happened."

It was obvious he wouldn't listen. She pressed her lips tightly together.

"I'm leaving early in the morning, Celia. You'll stay here," he said shortly, "and I want your word you'll not try to leave until I come back for you."

"I have no intention of promising any such thing!" It wasn't just the fact that he was leaving her behind that was distressing, it was the uncertainty of it, the fear and the knowledge that someone—a complete stranger—wanted to hurt her. How could she ever feel safe again? And, how did she keep from telling him that she felt safe only with him, that if he left her behind she would be afraid?

His hand shot out to grasp her by the wrist, and he held her tightly, his face angry. "Bloody hell, this is no game we're playing. Men attacked you. If given the chance, they may do so again. Is that what you want to risk?"

"No, of course not." Her lower lip trembled slightly before she could stop it. She didn't try to pull away from him but remained still, watching his face as she said softly, "I'd rather risk danger with you if I must risk it at all."

His gaze flickered, but he didn't look away. "I can't do what I have to do if I'm worried about you, Celia. If I know you're safe I can do what must be done. It's quicker this way, believe me."

She did believe him. Even if he hadn't told her everything, he hadn't really lied to her. She was the only one who had been dishonest, and when the time was right, she'd tell him everything, about her mother and his father and the reason she'd come to England. She'd tell him all, sparing no details.

It was burdensome living a lie. These past three months had put her on edge far too often. The risk of being found out, and the necessity of hiding the truth had taken a toll. And there was the guilt over being dishonest with people who cared about her. It was time she stopped it, time she told Jacqueline, and time she told Colter.

But not just yet, not until he came back for her, until she knew he was safe and all this was behind him. Until she knew who had tried to hurt her and why.

"Very well," she said. "I'll stay here and not try to leave. But come back quickly, Colter. I won't be able to bear it while you're gone."

His brow quirked. "Lovely little liar, you won't miss me at all."

Yes, she swore silently. I will miss you more than I want to admit.

It was bittersweet, this coming together when both knew it might be a while before they saw each other again. While she may not know details, she had gleaned enough information to realize that Colter was involved in some sort of espionage, and could only imagine that it entailed danger.

So there was this night with him, a night that may very well be their last. She clung to him with fierce emotion driving her reactions so that when he told her to get on top she did so without question, straddling him as he directed her to do.

It was so erotic, the slow slide of her body onto his, the exquisite intrusion sending shudders through her as she began to rock against him. In the gloom, she could see the sheen of his eyes watching her. That she was in control while he watched was exciting, too.

With her knees bent and legs folded on each side of him, she set the pace, lifting enough to tease him, her head tilted back, loose pale hair like a silken cloud down her bare back, the brush of it against her shoulder blades like a caress. Slowly she lowered her body until she heard him groan. His hands moved to her breasts, his fingers cleverly arousing her so that she gasped as heat spiraled through her veins again.

"Here, love," he said softly when she rocked against him with almost frantic urgency. "Like this." And he taught her the motion, his skilled hands tutoring her so that the point of quivering tension was stroked in a far different way than he'd massaged her before. She strained against his hand, learned that she could adjust the level of pleasure herself. With his whispered instructions in language that was direct but not obscene, he taught her about her own body.

"You're made for pleasure," he murmured. With a wicked smile she could barely see in the dusky shadows, he ran his hands from her breasts over her rib cage to the flat of her belly. "And that's the sweetest part of it, love, that this is the way it's meant to be. You like that, don't you? Yes, I see that you do. God, you drive me crazy. I want to make love to you all night when you look at me like that, your eyes half-closed and that teasing smile on your mouth."

She wanted to tell him that she loved the way he made her feel, loved what his hands were doing—and that she loved him. But all that would come out was a husky moan.

The wagon rocked on its wheels as the world exploded around her and she contracted around him in wave after wave of heated bliss. Then he was rolling over with her beneath him, his mouth on hers as he took her with sweet, fierce possession.

And Celia thought hazily that she heard him whisper her name when he lay at last atop her, spent, his arms around her as if she would flee, murmuring soft endearments. It was reassuring and comforting.

He left early the next morning, abandoning the warmth of the surprisingly comfortable bed they'd shared after a last kiss that only made her feel worse. She turned her face away to the wall so he wouldn't see her tears. Neither of them had slept much, but made love again and again, drawing comfort from each other, and Colter had been more tender than ever before, as if to soothe her fears—or say a final farewell.

24

Jacqueline hadn't slept for two days. Sick with worry, she had finally dozed off when word came that Northington had returned to London.

Sitting up on the lounge where she lay, she burst out, "Where is Celia? Oh, Jules, tell me he has her with him and that she's all right… Oh no, don't shake your head at me, when you know I want the truth—"

"My love, be strong," Jules said, crossing to her and going on one knee beside the low lounge. "He claims not to know where she is. The Runners say they cannot find her, that she was last seen with him, but they cannot be certain it was really her."

A choked sob hung in her throat, and she shook her head wildly. "But the note… it just doesn't sound like her to go off without telling me. I don't believe it! I just don't believe it! He has to know—he was with her. I saw them at the opera together… Oh, and there was another man, if only I could remember his name." She stared beseechingly at her husband. "Do you think this has anything to do with the robbery?"

"It's possible." Jules squeezed her hand tightly. "We have to have faith she's all right, my love. She did send a note—"

"No, no, it wasn't right, it just wasn't right! Oh, won't anyone listen to me? Celia wouldn't have written it that way, wouldn't have just *disappeared* like that unless there's something terribly wrong." She drew in a shaky breath. "No one seems to think the robbery that took place while we were at the opera is important since nothing of value was taken. But Lily says that Celia's trunks were searched, and that Janey is no doubt part of the blame. Oh God." She bit her lip, stared at her husband as if he could magically produce Celia and whispered, "I have a terrible feeling that, despite what the police say, the two things are somehow connected."

Jules didn't believe her. Oh, he didn't say it aloud, but it was plain from his distracted patting of her hand and murmured comfort that he thought she was wrong. Despair was an ache. She'd failed Celia, failed Léonie. Northington must know where she was. Why wouldn't he tell anyone? She had to know—and she intended to know.

Lying back on the lounge, she murmured, "I'm distraught and need to rest, Jules. Please be kind enough to send Hester to me with a soothing drink."

"Yes, yes, my dearest, I will. Right away!"

Once Jules had left the room, Jacqueline rose from the lounge and went to her cherry writing desk. She pulled out a fresh sheet of paper, dipped a new pen into the inkwell and began to scrawl a note, pausing twice to think before she continued.

When Hester arrived with a cup of hot milk and

butter, she was told to post the note at once by messenger.

"Give him a coin to assure its swift delivery," she added, and the maid nodded as she left with the sealed note.

Tomorrow, Jacqueline thought, she would ask Northington herself.

"My lord Northington is not in," the butler said once again, his face impassive as he regarded Jacqueline with an air of polite curiosity, "as I have told you, my lady. Please leave your card and I will—"

"No. He may not wish to speak with me, but I wish to speak with him, and I will not accept a refusal." She peeled off her gloves with abrupt, angry motions, eyeing the butler with determination. "I have faced much worse things than an irate viscount, and I will not be intimidated. Tell your master that I will not go away until he answers my question. He'll see me."

After the barest of hesitations, the man inclined his head and withdrew, leaving her standing in the entrance hall instead of showing her to a parlor. She would not be shunted off to wait in a closed room, but intended to remain visible until he relented.

A few moments later, Northington descended from the upper floor, an expression of mild interest on his handsome face.

"My lady Leverton, I'm afraid your visit is futile. I cannot answer your question because I have nothing to tell you."

"Yes," she said firmly, "you do. I am not a child, sir, and will not be fobbed off. I *hear* things, and I know that you are not quite what you seem."

"How intriguing." His smile did not alter, but a sharp light glittered in his eyes. "Come into my study with me and I'll try to explain to you again that your cousin is not with me."

"But you know where she is. Do not deny it."

Once they were in the study and the door closed behind them, Northington seated her opposite his desk. He leaned back against it, long legs crossed at the ankles, his stance negligent but his eyes wary.

"Your note mentioned a missing purse. Why would you think I want it?"

"Because that's what those men were searching for when they broke into my house the night of the opera. I have it." She smiled when his eyes narrowed dangerously, and leaned forward. "I don't know *why* you want it, or why those men want it, but I do know it must be important or no one would go to so much trouble to find it. I ask you again, does Celia know the importance of what she has?"

"Ah, so that's what you meant. A rather cryptic query, and I had no idea how to answer."

"You prevaricate, my lord. Shall I tell you how I know it must have some value? The footpads who robbed us that day in Berkley Square cared not only for our jewels, but for our reticules, as well. I wore an emerald ring and a diamond pin that should have interested any self-respecting thief. But my reticule? I began to wonder about it later, once the shock had worn off, and came to the realization that they had seemed far more interested in the papers I happened to carry that day. Now, shall you tell me if this has anything at all to do with my goddaughter's disappearance? And more importantly, is she safe?"

Silence fell between them. After a moment, he said softly, "I can tell you she is well and safe. That's all you need to know. I warn you, if you truly hold something that's already spurred men to violence, you'd best put it into the proper hands."

"I thought you might say that. But I have never thought it very fair to make an uneven exchange." She leaned forward to stare at him intently. "It will all come out that Celia has been compromised, then any hope of a good match for her will be ruined. You've tread dangerously close to ruining her yourself and don't think I haven't noticed. It's been by God's own grace that her name hasn't been dragged through the gossip mills by now."

"I perceive that you wish a bargain," he said wryly, but there was a taut set to his mouth. She had the sudden thought that perhaps she had gone too far.

"Yes, I do." She hesitated, but could tell nothing from his face. "In exchange for restoring Celia's good reputation, I will tell you where to find what you're looking for, sir. That's my proposition."

"And if I agree?"

"Then you'll secure what others are willing to kill for, it seems."

"How do I know you have what I've been looking for?"

She drew in another deep breath, then made a decision. With a swift tug, she opened the strings of her reticule and drew out a city directory. She held it out to him, and knew from the sudden opacity of his eyes that she was right.

"Well, my lord," she asked, "do we have a bargain?"

25

It had snowed during the night. Celia pushed aside the flimsy curtain to peer outside, shivering in the cold air inside the wagon. An ingenious little stove that held hot coals usually kept it warm enough, but the embers had died to gray ash now.

She scrubbed a hand through her hair, dyed dark at the insistence of Santiago, and she wore gypsy clothes—bright skirts and blouses—with nothing underneath. She had to admit it was much more comfortable than wearing confining stays. The stain on her hair made it rather stiff and dry, so that she usually wore it loose instead of up on her head or in neat plaits. Thankfully the dye was fading, the pale natural color returning with the passage of time.

Perhaps the danger had faded as well. No one had come near the camp, not in all the weeks she'd been here. It was on Northington land, the estate just beyond the line of woods and hill, and sometimes she thought she could almost see it if she walked to the top of the nearest hill. Most of the time she stayed in the wagon, and her one encounter with Marita had been unpleasant.

And revealing.

Tossing long dark hair, the girl had confronted her when no one else was near, the men gone hunting or into the village to peddle cheap wares.

"So," Marita said, a sneer curling red lips. "Do you think because he has left you here that you are safe?"

"If I'm not, it will be your father who's at fault," Celia countered coolly. "He promised Lord Northington that I would come to no harm here. A matter of pride, he said."

A hiss escaped between her teeth as Marita moved a step closer; tension vibrated through her slender body. She wore no cape or cloak for warmth, only several layers of wool skirts and blouses, her legs bare beneath the folds of striped red-and-blue wool. They stood at the edge of the small wooded copse where the wagons formed a tight circle, and save for a woman by the fire in the center and a string of horses tethered beyond the camp, it was deserted.

"Foolish one," Marita said. "It is not safe anytime you are with us, for the good English citizens find reasons to drive us away whenever they can. We must travel constantly, and find ways to live. Few are like *him.* He has respect for us, and we repay it with honor. My father would never do anything to lose that trust, but even he has no control over men who do not mind destroying their own."

"What are you talking about?" Celia didn't like Marita; the girl was too bold, too arrogant, and she seemed to regard Colter as if he belonged to her.

Swinging her hips, Marita sauntered closer. "You were with him when those men fired at him, were you not? I can remember how angry everyone was and how you were thrown from your horse—"

"I jumped. And it was a horse that hadn't even been trained, as you well know."

Marita grinned impudently, and gave a shrug of her slim shoulders. "You said you could ride, so I believed you. What else was I to think?"

"Never mind that. What do you know about those men who fired at us?"

"Only that they were firing at you, not at the handsome lord. Oh, does that surprise you? Did you think you have no enemies?"

"No one has any reason to fire at me," Celia said curtly, though she couldn't help but recall the evening at the opera. Perhaps they hadn't really tried to kill her, but someone definitely didn't mind harming her. "And how would you know anything about it?"

"Because I am here all the time, and I learn things. I do not stay all day in the camp but go places, and I know. I know more than you, it seems, for you do not even believe me when I tell you this."

But she did believe her. Despite the resentment between them, there was the ring of truth to Marita's claim that she had seen the men that day, and had followed them.

"I meant only to follow *you,* because I knew you had lied and that the horse would throw you," she said slyly. "But then I saw what happened. Men like to drink, and when they drink they often like to talk to beautiful women they think have no brains, or no ears to hear what they say."

She shrugged. "So I listen, and I laugh, and I let them think I do not understand. And that is how I learn what I know—that you are not what you pretend to be." She sidled closer. "And I know *he* does not know it. He thinks you are so honest, but all the time you lie, lie, lie."

"Prove it," she said flatly, and Marita's eyes narrowed angrily.

"Do you think I cannot? I will. Oh, I will prove it to you and you will know I am not what you think—a lying gypsy girl with no honor!"

What could she possibly know? Celia wavered between denial and fear. Not fear for herself, but fear that she would be exposed before she had a chance to explain, to tell Jacqueline, and yes, Colter, that it was true she had come under false pretenses, that she'd lied, but now she wanted to tell the entire truth.

Torn with indecision, she'd spent several sleepless nights agonizing over what to do.

And then last night a message had finally come from Colter that she was to meet him away from the gypsy camp. Bold masculine script was a terse scrawl on paper bearing his seal, and now that the moment she'd been dreading and anticipating was here, she found herself calmly accepting it.

Marita was to take her to him, not to Harmony Hill but to a more private spot, the brief note stated. "Go with Marita. She will bring you to me."

It was signed with just his initials, but the seal pressed into fine parchment was unmistakable. She had seen it on glassware, stationary, even reproduced on towels.

Santiago, who had given her the note, gazed down

at her with something akin to sympathy in his dark eyes, and his usually booming voice was soft.

"You look so sad, but you should not. Are you surprised that I see it? I may not know all the reasons, but I do know that whatever your fear, it can only be conquered with the courage you have inside. It is all that is left us at times, that strength to do what must be done. You are much stronger than you think. And he is more honorable than is said."

He'd not needed to specify who he meant, for they both knew who mattered most to her. Was it that obvious? Yes, it must be, for hadn't Marita known it even before she did? It had gleamed in those exotic black eyes from the very first, the recognition that there was far more in her feelings for Colter than she'd admitted to herself.

And now she would face him at last and tell him the truth of why she had come to England. After that, she would know if she had a place here.

So this morning, as the snow frosted ground and trees, she met Marita at the far edge of the gypsy camp.

"Come along," Marita said softly, and motioned to her from the fringe of trees just beyond the camp when Celia moved toward the horses. "I will choose a horse for you, eh?"

"If you don't mind, I think I'll choose my own," Celia replied tartly, and knew from her disappointed pout that she had foiled another of Marita's tricks.

Mounted upon a rather docile, small mare, she followed the gypsy girl down a winding track; it was so quiet in the trees, snow muffling hoofbeats and even the sounds of birds muted, as if in a church. Peace shrouded the land, so that she could almost hear the whisper of snow striking bare limbs and dead stalks of grass that rustled in a light wind. The air smelled of the sea.

They rode out onto a lane that looked vaguely familiar, and Celia thought it must be very near Harmony Hill. She had ridden this way with Carolyn that day, though it had looked so different in soft sunlight and with gentle breezes. Now it was barren, with leafless trees standing sentinel along the edge. It curved near the top of the cliffs, finally in a thin ribbon.

A stone cottage squatted on a spur of land, remote and almost forlorn by itself. There was no sign of life, so that she frowned when Marita reined in her mount. The girl looked satisfied with herself, her voice loud to be heard over the rushing wind that smelled so strongly of the sea now.

"Not here. There. He waits for you. Oh, do you doubt me still? You will see for yourself that I speak the truth."

"I see only a roofless hut, and no horses—"

"No, no, foolish one, beyond it. Do you not see? It is a good place to hide and wait, there in that granary."

"Really, I do see the granary, but it's as deserted as the hut." Exasperated, she shot the girl a disgusted glance. "It's not in much better condition. I have no intention of waiting in it. Nor do I see Northington's horse. If he was already here, he would have come out to greet me. I'll wait for him where I am."

Marita's eyes narrowed; she rode the horse with no saddle, bare brown legs sticking out from her bunched skirts, her feet clad in scuffed shoes. Now she slid from her horse to the ground, glaring up at Celia.

"Oh, you really are foolish! You are to wait for him, or did the note not say so? Yes, I think it did, but you are so used to your own lies, you think everyone lies."

Celia stared at her. Rushing wind tugged at her skirts and hair, chilled her skin. She shivered. Overhead, a seabird made a piercing cry as it wheeled in the sky, and gray clouds seemed suddenly dark. Black thunderheads bunching on the horizon beyond the point of land marked a threatening storm.

"We should go back," she said, "before it breaks."

Marita reached for her horse's bridle, shaking her head. "You are to wait. Or do you not trust him? Do you think he would lie to you as you have lied to him?"

Sudden premonition made Celia tense, and she turned her horse around. "No, but he should be here. He's not, and I'm going back. Stay here or go with me, I don't care."

"Oh, you are so impatient!" Marita circled in front of her. "If you will only wait, you will see him soon."

"No, I think I've had enough of your tricks for today, and I have no intention of lotting you amuse yourself at my expense any longer."

The small mare danced sideways as Marita snared the bridle with one hand, staring up at Celia with a scowl. "You have come this far. At least wait a few more minutes."

Celia hesitated. Caution bade her flee, but logic told her that this girl couldn't have written the note on Colter's stationery or used his seal, nor could she have composed such a coherent, if terse, letter. Finally, against her better judgment, she dismounted rather clumsily when it began to rain.

"A few minutes more," she said. "But if he doesn't come soon I'm going back to your father's camp."

She tied the horse under the cursory shelter of a wind-twisted yew, then followed Marita to the tumbled-down stone granary behind the cottage. Weeds sprouted between fallen rock, and rubble shifted underfoot. A surprisingly solid door stood ajar, swinging slightly in the wind and rain.

Pale gray light darkened the inside of the round structure, and it took a moment for her eyes to adjust. There was a strong smell of burnt wood, and she frowned as she saw the evidence of a recent fire on a ledge. Wall stones had been removed to form a window of sorts, and charred limbs and bits of brittle black charcoal were scattered about.

Celia crossed to peer out the opening at the gray wind-lashed sea. It stretched endlessly, though a curtain of rain moved across the surface like a creeping beast, stealthy and inexorable. She shivered suddenly, the wet air washing over her like a tide.

Was she being foolish to come here with Marita, who had made it plain how she felt? But even Santiago had expressed no reservations. After all, the note must be from Colter or there would be no seal, no recognized messenger from the estate. Yet she could not help the uneasy feeling that bored into the back of her mind, the premonition that all was not as it should be, that surely Colter would have made other, more suitable arrangements for them to meet. Why had he not come to the camp again?

Marita leaned against the far wall, arms crossed over her chest as she regarded Celia with what seemed to be a smugly satisfied expression on her face.

"Why do you stare at me like that?" Celia asked sharply when she turned to look at her. "You make me think you've another trick in mind for me."

"Perhaps I have," the girl said with a soft laugh. "But I would not be so foolish as to tell you if I did. Is it me you do not trust, or your fine gentleman? I did not write the letter to you, and you must know that."

"Yes, it's obvious you didn't." Irritated, Celia turned back to look out the window. Why had Colter sent *this* girl to bring her here? Surely Santiago, or even Mario, could have brought her so she would not have had to endure this insolent creature's disdain.

Celia crossed her arms over her chest for warmth against the damp wind seeping through cracks and the tiny window, and suppressed another shiver. If only he would come. It was the anticipation, the not knowing what he would say or what she would say that kept her in torment. Would Colter believe that she'd not meant him any harm? Oh, but how could he, when she must tell him that she'd intended his own father a great deal of harm? Even when he knew what Moreland had done, he may not understand, may not even believe her until she showed him the documents that detailed the charge of murder.

When an eerie creak sounded behind her, Celia whirled, but it was too late. The heavy door slammed shut, and the sound of a grating bar was a dull, scraping thud. The granary was plunged into sudden darkness, the only light seeping inside through the small hole in the wall.

"Marita!" She dashed to the door, banged on it with her fists, shouted at the gypsy girl to open the door at once. "Damn you, stop playing your nasty tricks! Open the door or, by God, I'll make you sorry for this. I swear I will, you stupid girl!"

Celia shouted until she was hoarse, until the gray light outside began to dim even more, and she had the horrified thought that this time Marita's vicious trick might truly endanger her life.

But finally she heard a masculine voice over the noise of the wind and rain, and heard the bar slide back. At last! Colter had rescued her yet again, and he would deal with the girl, she hoped grimly, so that she'd never try such a trick again!

Then the door swung open. Silhouetted against the misty glow behind him, she glimpsed Marita's gloating face, and her heart thumped in alarm. There was something triumphant in that expression. Her gaze moved slowly to the man who blocked the opening.

It wasn't Colter.

26

Greasy smoke hovered in gauzy drifts that rose to the low, timbered ceiling of the public house. Green-tinged light filtered through leaded-glass windows, and the air was dense with the smell of wet wool, fish and the press of the Great Unwashed.

Colter recognized Tyler at the end of a long table; he lifted a pewter tankard but did not drink, the signal he was available.

"They took the bait," Tyler said to his tankard when Colter elbowed a path through the crowd and took a place on the long bench next to him. "Edwards showed him the piece in the *New Times*."

George Edwards, also recruited as a spy to infiltrate the Spenceans, was responsible for planting an item in the paper that reported the dinner meeting of several members of the British government. The dinner was to be held at Lord Harrowby's house at 39 Grosvenor Square tomorrow night, the twenty-third—a trap for Thistlewood and his gang.

Tyler eyed him briefly, a grin hovering on his mouth. "You look like a fenman."

Garbed in a blue wool jersey, baggy trousers and coat with the collar up to his ears, Colter blended in with the others in this public house near the riverfront. It was a rough clientele that frequented this part of London. The weight of a pistol in his waistband was a stark reminder of the risk.

He'd let his beard grow out some, and gloved fingers rasped over the stubble as he scratched idly.

"Was the map right?"

Nodding, Tyler gulped a draught of ale, then wiped his mouth on his sleeve and belched. "Every place marked held a cache of weapons, right enough. We're watching."

Colter downed the last of his ale and rose. "You know where to meet me."

The air was cooler and fresher outside the pub, though still smelling of the riverfront and bilge. He walked along the narrow street, then through an even more narrow alley; buildings leaned precariously over the avenue with no apparent reason for remaining upright.

Hard-eyed men prowled these byways, ready to slit a throat for less than a shilling, inured to the suffering of others by their own. Urchins clad in little more than rags stared at him with empty eyes, shivering in the icy cold, watching for a chance to steal a coin, just as dangerous as their older counterparts. Nothing had changed for these, and nothing would as long as radicals like Thistlewood plotted murder and anarchy.

Mowry waited for him in the back room of a pub on the corner of Friday Street, brow lifting when Colter joined him.

"You look as dangerous as any footpad, Northington. I trust you have good news."

"Thistlewood intends to move on the bait tomorrow. He obviously thinks he can raise an army that quickly. Are you ready?"

Nodding, Mowry's thin face creased with satisfaction. "More than ready. All is in place. My other informant tells me that John Harrison has inquired about renting a small building—a stable with a hayloft—in Cato Street. It needs to be investigated, as it's only a short distance from Grosvenor Square and will likely be used as a command post. George Edwards will give us more information as soon as he knows something of value. Meanwhile, I trust you will be setting up your own plans."

"I know the stable. I'll wait at the Horse and Groom, as it overlooks the stable on Cato Street. I'll take Tyler with me, and two others."

Mowry nodded, thin fingers drumming an incessant beat on the surface of the table. A flagon of wine and an empty cup rested near his hand. After a moment, he poured himself a drink.

"We cannot fail," he said tersely, wine gleaming on his lips as his eyes narrowed, "for the consequences would reach much farther than just this rebellion. It will show us to be vulnerable, despite how quickly we are able to quell any violence. They plan," he said softly, "to parade the heads of Lords Castlereagh and Sidmouth on poles around the slums of London as an example."

"And they no doubt assume this will entice eager citizens to join their new government. Christ. An armed uprising may provoke a revolution like that in

France. You do recall that, I presume, and the slaughter of innocents? A government cannot oppress its people forever, for one of these days, there will indeed be an uprising that we cannot prevent if we're not willing to alleviate and mollify their grievances. Honest grievances, Mowry, and you know that."

Hooded eyes regarded him coolly. "Perhaps. But the collapse of the monarchy is not the way to effect change."

"I never said it was." Colter rose to his feet. "But I will make my arguments in the House of Lords when the time comes."

"Yes, do that, and perhaps one day Liberals will run the country, but I wouldn't make wagers on it." A half-mocking smile tilted Mowry's mouth, and he held up his wineglass in a derisive salute. "I drink to your zeal, my lord Northington, and to the idealistic ardor of all your Liberal sympathizers."

"One day," he said softly, "you'll do so in earnest."

It was a bad business, but he had no regrets about his part in stopping Thistlewood. The man was a danger, a zealot who had to be stopped at any cost.

"By the way," Mowry said as Colter reached the door to the back alley, "I trust your Miss St. Clair is doing well."

Colter turned, and his voice was hard enough to wipe the smile from Mowry's face.

"If you ever endanger Celia again as you did at the opera, it may be your head that goes round London on a pole. Keep that in mind the next time you interfere."

"I do not tolerate threats," Mowry said, but there

was a flicker of recognition in his eyes that he had gone too far this time.

"I do not make threats. I state facts."

As he closed the door behind him, he heard Mowry's soft curse. Now he knew for a certainty it had been Mowry who was behind the assault at the opera, a desperate attempt to gain the directory. James Carlisle had no reason to risk an assault when he must have been fairly certain she'd send it to him as promised. Tyler had been near enough to eavesdrop, near enough to hear the conversation and Celia's assurance that she would send the map. If nothing else, he would have ransacked the house for it rather than risk attracting attention by abducting her.

But Mowry hadn't known that then, and his network of spies and thugs was vast and volatile enough to take any risks—including the risk to Celia St. Clair.

Celia. When this was over, as it surely would be in the next two days, he'd go back for her. There were a few more things he needed to know about her. Then there was that damned agreement with Lady Leverton that must be addressed.

A faint, cynical smile curved his mouth. How delighted Lady Moreland would be to learn that her son intended to marry at last.

Would the prospective bride be as delighted?

Colter would have been surprised to know Celia was thinking of him at that very moment, fervently wishing he would arrive. Oh God, how had she become so involved without even knowing it?

Yet this man seemed to think she was a danger, or so he informed her.

"Miss St. Clair, I'm afraid that you've become rather a liability," he said apologetically. "Yet I find your plight regrettable. Perhaps we can come to a compromise of sorts."

Anger didn't dilute her terror, but made it sharper. "I cannot imagine any bargain with a villainous man who would be so insensible to his own nephew's—"

"Great-nephew," Lord Easton corrected mildly. "And I am not at all insensible to Northington's welfare. Indeed, it is my concern for him that prompts me to this rather drastic solution."

Quivering with a mixture of rage and fear, Celia drew a deep breath to regulate her racing heart and sharp tongue. "What *compromise* do you suggest, my lord?"

Philip Worth, Lord Easton, leaned back in the plain wooden chair he'd dragged from beneath the table across the room. Now he smiled at her, nodding approval. Light from a lamp on the table barely illuminated the small room.

"You're proving to be much more intelligent than I had assumed you would be, Miss St. Clair. Let us hope you are as agreeable."

Celia had no idea where they were. She'd been taken from the granary, blindfolded and put into a carriage to be brought to this house, but it had to be fairly close for the journey had not lasted long. Nor was Marita still with them, having returned to the camp, no doubt, with some story about how Celia had escaped her. She hoped no one believed it!

"I can be agreeable," she said, "once I know what I'm to agree to."

"Yes, of course." His smile widened, and his gaze

was thoughtful, that of a kindly older man, his appearance so deceiving, with his shock of white hair and impeccable air of breeding and affluence. How deceptive these English aristocrats could be! Was everyone in this family immoral and wicked?

No, no, not Colter, though she'd thought so at first, thought him just like his father. Yet now another member of that family sought her destruction.

"You are very like your mother, you know," Easton shocked her by saying, his tone conversational. "I imagine you could even be mistaken for her. It's amazing. Léonie St. Remy was one of the most sought-after women in London at one time, and even the lack of a dowry had little effect on many impetuous swains. Ah, I remember her so well… It was nearly a scandal when she ran off with her American." His smile was benign, his eyes hiding his real thoughts as he regarded her as casually as if they were having tea in the parlor at Harmony Hill. "But surely you must know why I have taken such a—shall we say, *personal* interest in your relationship with my nephew."

"No," she said stiffly, "I cannot say I do. Nor do I care to know, my lord, if you will forgive my bluntness."

His smile did not waver, and he made a dismissing gesture with his hand. "That's to be expected, of course. It would be supposed you might feel some resentment."

"Resentment? Resentment, my lord? That hardly describes what I'm feeling at this precise moment! Fury would be a more apt word to use, and determined, perhaps, for I have no intention of making any agreement with you at all!"

"A lamentable decision, Miss St. Clair. Do reconsider, if you will. Life can be singularly unpleasant for those who fail to bend even a little. Trust me on that advice. I've spent an entire lifetime perfecting the art of bending. And bending does not necessarily mean yielding, so that militant light in your eyes need not be extinguished. Indeed, I find it quite flattering to you. It becomes clear what my nephew sees in you, however unwise that may be."

Her eyes narrowed slightly. "Is that what this is about, this abduction and attempt to terrorize me? You want me to stay away from Colter?"

"Abduction is such an ugly word. I much prefer to use *invitation,* for that is, after all, what it is—an invitation to leave England quietly, calmly and with more money than you arrived with in your purse. No need for an unnecessary scene, now, is there?"

"He put you up to this." Emotionless, she stared at him with sudden realization. "Northington—Moreland, the earl. He is behind this, isn't he? He discovered who I am, and he wants me gone before I can cause him trouble." A half laugh escaped her, anguished and bitter. "Oh, no need in denying it, for who else would want me to leave England like this?"

"Who else, indeed," Easton murmured, the small smile a slight curve on his lips. "Who else indeed."

"Well, it only proves that he *knows* why I am here, and that he's afraid of what I'll say, afraid of what I can prove about him!" She surged to her feet, hands knotted into fists at her side, anger and pain vibrating through her body so that she could scarcely stand still.

"I won't do it. I'll be heard, by God, for now I know that I can't keep quiet! I had thought— Oh, I was so stupid, for I should know I could never really forget, not even for him. But I thought I might be able to, so that no one would be hurt—not the earl, no, not him, but those I care about. I didn't want to hurt them, you see. Really, it wouldn't bring them back, would it, if I told? Maman and Old Peter are still dead. But now I know that I can't forget it, can't ignore it, that it was done and justice was thwarted."

Easton merely watched her, an arrested expression on his fine features, his eyes unreadable and hooded. He made no attempt to soothe her, nor even to halt her when she turned to the door. Then she discovered he'd had no need to try, for a guard waited outside, turning quickly when she opened the door.

"My dear Miss St. Clair," Easton said finally when she slammed shut the door and whirled back to face him. "You are overwrought. Perhaps in the morning you will be more aware of your plight and amenable to my suggestions. America is your home, but if you prefer, England has many colonies."

"I'm well aware of that."

Easton rose from the chair, intimidating without being threatening, his smile urbane. "You will find it necessary to choose which option you prefer, or it will be chosen for you, but rest assured that you will not remain in England. It is up to you how you leave here."

"Tell Lord Moreland that removing me will not erase his guilt!"

"Really, Miss St. Clair, I'm not at all certain Moreland even remembers your existence."

With that cryptic statement, Easton left her alone in the small room, though she heard him give instructions to the guard outside the door that she was to be closely watched at all times. Celia sat down, bewildered and more frightened than she had been before.

What did he mean by that? Of course Moreland must remember her, for was he not responsible for this? It could only be him. Unless—unless Colter had decided that he no longer needed her, no longer wanted her. But that couldn't be true. Could it?

No, of course it isn't. He wouldn't do that to me, wouldn't just leave me like this to be transported as if I was a common criminal! she thought wildly, despairingly. She put her face into her palms and shuddered.

Oh, why hadn't he come for her?

27

George Ruthven was already at the Horse and Groom, and had been since two that afternoon. Northington, garbed still in the wool jersey and rough coat, sat with him as they waited. Tyler was posted outside to keep watch on the stable. At the stable across the dark street, lights flickered below and above in the hayloft.

"They've been arriving since early today," Ruthven said calmly. "There's about two dozen men."

"Hardly the fifteen thousand Thistlewood predicted." Colter balanced his chair on its two rear legs, arms crossed over his chest as he and several others took turns watching out the window for the conspirators. "We may not have to wait on the Coldstream Guards to arrive."

Ruthven nodded and slid a glance toward Richard Birnie, who was a Bow Street magistrate in charge of the operations. They had just arrived, a dozen police officers and the magistrate, now staring into the darkness of Cato Street. The was an air of tense excitement in the room.

Tyler slid into the room a few minutes later, his face sharp with tension. He beckoned to Colter and said tautly, "You were right. John Brunt has delivered sabers, swords, pistols and rifles to the stable all day, but I was just told they have armed themselves with a hand grenade."

"Christ," Colter swore softly. "A hand grenade is more than we bargained for. They might as well have cannons sitting in that bloody stable."

"What should I do? Do I tell Birnie?"

Colter glanced over his shoulder. "Yes. Tell him, but wait until I've gone."

Tyler's jaw set. "You're not exactly unknown. If they recognize you, that would destroy any chance of surprise we have."

"Then don't wait long after I'm gone to tell them what you know, Tyler."

It was a risk, but there was little choice. It was all happening too quickly now, and an argument with Birnie would take up valuable time.

It was cold, the night pressing down as he stepped outside. Chimney smoke clogged the air, layering beneath the clouds to burn eyes and nose. Across from the pub, a lamp burned over the stable door; the second floor was darker, with something over the windows. The small stable was near a corner where some five-story brick buildings ran parallel. An arch cut under one of the buildings, and he saw a casual lounger waiting beneath the fitful light of a small lamp.

There would be no second chances.

Darkness greeted him on the first floor of the stable, the smell of hay and dung strong as he slipped inside a side door and paused. Stationed at the main door, a man watched the street intently, the dull light a pale glint along the stock of his weapon.

The old reckless exhilaration was on him now as Colter moved on the balls of his feet across the straw-littered dirt of the stable floor, a knife in one hand. He'd done this kind of thing before, in France and in the steaming swamps of Louisiana, and even in the hot, arid desert of California. This kind of fighting wasn't military precision but guerrilla style, stealthy and devastating to morale if not numerically superior. Nervous sentries never knew from where an enemy would come, rising out of black night to slit a throat or put a blade between the ribs, or hiding behind bushes or walls, lying in wait for an ambush.

It was these times he felt truly alive again. It was a paradox that a man only felt alive when he was in danger of dying, but maybe that was because he felt stifled by the atmosphere in which he found himself most of the time. He hadn't felt this acute sense of danger, of risk, since he'd returned to England.

There were only a few minutes before Ruthven and Birnie acted, and he had to find the hand grenade before any of the conspirators had a chance to use it. Disarming the guard was no challenge, sliding up behind him and putting the tip of his knife to the spot just below his ear, his voice soft as he told him to throw down his weapon.

"Softly now. If my hand slips..."

There was no need to say more. The man nodded silently, terror making him clumsy but obedient.

"What's your name?" The knife prodded slightly when he only stammered.

"Ings...James Ings!" was the hoarse whisper.

"Now, Mister Ings, why don't you show me where you keep the hand grenade and other weapons. You know it's all over now, so no sense in being stubborn. The police will be here any minute, and in any case, there are twice as many of them as there are of you, so you don't have a chance. A trial could go either way, just as the last one. And at least you'd have a chance that way. If you warn Thistlewood, I'll gut you right here."

Reflected light from the lantern outside on the wall betrayed Ings's pasty pallor, and he nodded slowly.

"The...grenade is over there. I was to use it if we were stormed...."

It took only a moment to bind and gag Ings, then find the grenade. Colter stood up when Ruthven led his small force inside. Silently he gestured to the ladder, and Ruthven flashed him a grin.

Colter followed as they swarmed up the ladder to the hayloft. As they burst into the loft Ruthven shouted, "We are peace officers! Lay down your arms!"

Thistlewood and Davidson drew their swords, and were immediately engaged by some of the officers, while several of the conspirators hastily tried to load their pistols. A table was knocked over in the confusion as men scrambled, a lamp landing dangerously close to a mound of straw. Moving swiftly, Colter brought his foot down on one man's arm and bent to pluck the pistol from his hand. There was shouting, but it was over quickly, and officers moved to arrest them, herding them in a group.

Glancing up, Colter shouted "Watch him!" just as

a desperate William Davidson lunged forward with his sword to pierce one officer in the chest.

As the officer reeled, he gasped out, "Oh God, I am..." then collapsed.

Colter leaped over the fallen man and tackled Davidson, taking him to the wooden floor. A vicious blow to the jaw made lights explode, and he countered the next punch with an upraised arm, his free hand slashing out and down, catching the conspirator in the angle of his neck and shoulder, sending him crashing to his knees. Straw chaff flew into the air as they fought, but with the advantage of weight and experience against him, Davidson was quickly subdued.

Panting, Colter hauled him to his feet, a pistol stuck into the man's back as he gave him into the custody of one of the police officers. Then he saw Tyler.

He dragged his sleeve across his jaw as he watched the officers round up the others, and said, "They delivered all the munitions for us. All that has to be done now is deliver them to the magistrate."

"Once we catch those who escaped." Tyler shrugged at Colter's sharp glance. "When Smithers was stabbed, a few of them escaped. Thistlewood took advantage of the confusion, and according to Edwards, so did Brunt, Adams and Harrison."

"How's Smithers?"

"Dying, it looks like."

Colter glanced around the loft; the fallen officer lay on his back, blood seeping to the floor, his breath rattling in his throat, while around him his comrades milled in great distress and anger.

"We need to catch them," Tyler said softly, and Colter nodded.

"They'll be caught. And they'll hang." He looked back at Tyler. "I think I know where they might hide."

It was easy enough to find the men who had fled, and Colter found Tyler an able comrade, quick thinking and even quicker to act. They turned them over to the magistrate, a little worse for their ordeal, defiant to the end and spouting radical speech.

"They'll hang," Tyler predicted laconically, leaning on the pub table, a half-empty tankard in his hand.

"Or be deported." The pub was stuffy and full of smoke, swirling every time the door opened. They were waiting for Mowry, though he would come to the back room instead of the common room. Tyler shook his head.

"Not Thistlewood and Davidson. They'll hang, along with Brunt, who hid the weapons. Too bad we couldn't charge John and James Carlisle with anything."

"Not enough proof. The magistrates aren't anxious to lose another case against the Spenceans, though this time there's more than enough proof on Thistlewood."

Mowry confirmed their conclusions, satisfaction evident as he gloated. "Sidmouth is most pleased. As well he should be, since it would have been his head adorning a pole at the city gates." Leaning back, he twisted the stem of his wineglass between his thumb and fingers, a smile lingering as he said, "It seems disaster has been averted yet again. It's regrettable that not all the men involved can be brought before the courts, but one day they will make a misstep. When they do, I'll have them." His eyes flicked to Colter.

"Even Whigs must recognize men like that are dangerous."

"Danger is in a mind closed to progress and reform. But that's another discussion. I have other business to attend."

"Ah, yes, the matter of Miss St. Clair. I trust that all is well in that quarter."

"It will be when I get there."

"Of course." Mowry's smile sharpened slightly. "She must be waiting for you. I trust she'll be more forthcoming in the future."

Damn Mowry, the man never said things directly but had to be so bloody oblique.

"If you have information to share, I'll be glad to hear it," he said. "But I'm in no mood to play games."

"No, it doesn't sound that way. Any information I have is just rumor. I'm sure you'll take care of things in your own way." He rose to his feet, his eyes hooded. "You'll want to pay a visit to Barclay before you leave London, Northington. He's always so—informative."

Christ, how was Mowry involved in that business? He had too many damned informants.

"I'm not at all sure I appreciate your delving into my private business concerns, Mowry. There are areas in my personal life that are not open for your review."

"Certainly, unless you happen to be involved in illegal activities."

"Are you making an accusation?"

"No, a point. One hand should know what the other is doing. The Inland Revenues do not care to be cheated, nor do the Revenue cutters like chasing boats with men who shoot at them."

"None of which has anything to do with me."

Mowry's eyes narrowed slightly. "That has yet to be proven. His Majesty's taxes are expected to be paid on goods that come into this country, even goods that come by way of the back door."

Dammit, his father would destroy them all one day.

"If you're insinuating that I'm smuggling goods from my own ships into the country, you're wrong. I wouldn't take the risk for a negligible amount of money."

"Perhaps not, but it seems likely that not everyone in your firm feels the same way. Investigate it, Northington, and I think you will be surprised. Heed me well. Not every head that rolls in these situations is guilty, but if they must be sacrificed, it is done. But you know that."

"Yes," he said grimly. "I know that."

With a frosty smile, Mowry said coolly, "Excellent. I look forward to our next meeting, gentlemen."

It sounded almost like a threat.

PART IV

"All for Love, or the World Well Lost."
—John Dryden

28

It had been hours since Lord Easton had left her to her own, and Celia hadn't slept at all. She was too tense, too nervous, and there seemed to be no way out. Oh God, what would happen if she didn't leave willingly? Would he truly deport her? He could, and she'd end up in Australia or even India, or some other territory. She had no illusions that he would take sudden pity on her. There had been steel in that voice and his eyes—a family trait, no doubt.

She could tell when the sun came up, because slivers of light poked through chinks in the wall. There was no window, no avenue of escape, and she paced fretfully.

When voices outside penetrated her despair, she whirled around to face the door, and braced herself for another interview with Lord Easton.

But to her surprise, the man who entered was a friendly face. She flung herself at him, crying out with relief.

"Sir John! How did you ever find me? Oh, it

doesn't matter, nothing matters but that you've come to help me. I cannot believe that you're here—"

Harvey smiled, his hazel eyes regarding her with an expression she couldn't read. He gently put her back from him a little bit.

"Miss St. Clair—Celia, it's not quite what you think. I wish it was, but I'm afraid I cannot do anything for you. It's beyond my help."

"What do you mean? Has Lord Easton threatened you, too? Oh, he wouldn't send *both* of us away. He couldn't! It's not the same with you as it is me, and he couldn't get away with it. What has he told you? Has he told you everything?"

Sir John looked slightly embarrassed. "It's beyond my help," he said again, helplessly. "I wish you'd stayed out of this."

"Out of what? I don't know what's going on, and I'm not at all certain it has anything to do with me. Does this have something to do with that map?"

"Map?" He gave her a blank look. "I know nothing about a map. All I know is that you've managed to earn a powerful enemy."

Taken aback, she stared at him. "An enemy? If you mean Moreland, there's a reason for that."

"Reason or not, it's done."

Agitated, she snapped, "Yes, it was done ten years ago, by God, and now he wants to avoid justice!"

"Please," he said, almost desperately. "I don't need to know any more. I just have to take you with me."

"Don't you want to know why? Don't you want to know the kind of man you're helping escape justice?"

Lord Easton appeared in the doorway, his tone mild

as he said, "Really, Miss St. Clair, you aren't helping yourself with this hysteria."

"Hysteria, my lord? It's not hysteria to tell the truth, is it? Or perhaps you think it is. Why don't you tell him why you're doing this?"

"Harvey needs to know only to follow orders, not to think for himself. It's much more profitable for him that way."

It dawned on her now that this was no rescue, or random visit. Harvey was working with Easton! Somehow, and for whatever reason, they were in collusion and she was fated to suffer for it.

Drawing on a reserve of strength she hadn't known she had left, she faced Easton coolly. "I see. Very well, my lord. If I'm to leave England I will do so. I should like, however, to choose my destination, as you offered me last night."

"That can be arranged." He regarded her with a faint smile. "As long as it is across an ocean. France is out of the question, for it's much too close."

"I'll return to America. You were right, of course. It is my home and where I belong. The air there is so much more clean and fresh."

He looked amused. "I agree with your rather unsubtle views. London society does have a habit of tainting the air. But be that as it may, time is fleeting. Dover is at hand, my dear, and so, it seems, are you. By this afternoon, you should be on a ship bound for America, with a tidy little sum in your purse to make your way easier."

"You mean to purchase my silence. No, your money is not needed," she said quietly, "for I will not accept payment for the lives of two people I loved.

You may be able to send me away, but you are not able to buy redemption in whatever form it is that Lord Moreland wishes.''

Shrugging, Easton said, ''Think what you will, my dear. But be forewarned. Should you ever return to England, there will be no other offer of freedom. Stronger, shall we say, more drastic methods of dealing with you will be taken.''

Celia recognized the foolishness of more defiance at this point, not when she was faced with a man who had no compunction in making dangerous threats.

''I understand completely, my lord,'' she said with a lift of her chin, but her eyes shot defiance at him, and she was so angry she quivered with it.

Damn him! And damn Moreland, who had already cost her so much. Now it seemed that he intended to keep her from his son, though he'd had no qualms about taking her mother from her. And she was supposed to leave quietly, like a whipped cur slinking away, was she?

Oh, no, she vowed silently. It will not be that easy to rid yourself of me!

But now she must give the appearance of acquiescence to his demands, so she complied with Harvey's hesitant plea that she cooperate, though she gave him a glance of such scalding contempt that he visibly shrank with dismay.

''It's not such a bad thing,'' he said to her when Easton left to make the arrangements and they were alone again. ''And America is your home.''

''You disgust me, sir,'' she said quietly, and refused to look at him when he swore at her.

''No, damn you,'' he snarled, and reached for her

arm when she turned her back on him, all pretense at cordiality vanished. ''You'll not look at me as if I'm some St. Giles beggar, by God! Look at me. Yes, dammit, if you must fear me it's better than contempt! Do you think this is what I want? Do you think this is my idea? It's not. But I'm trapped as surely as you, and you have to know that.''

''No, you don't have to do this, Sir John. You could set me free. He's gone. It would cost you nothing and give you back some self-respect.''

He laughed harshly, released her arm and ran a hand through his hair so that it stood up on his head in golden tufts. ''Cost me nothing? My dear Celia, it would cost me *everything*. You have no idea... No, you cannot know what it is to always be on the fringe of things, and to risk it all for the sake of coin. It's the only currency that makes a difference, and without it...without it, self-respect is worthless.''

''We have widely different views on that, it seems.'' She put a hand on his arm, saw the start of surprise in his eyes as she said softly, ''I am much like you. You must know I came here with nothing, but I've been given so much. So much, that I didn't fully appreciate it until recently. My cousin has been so generous, and I've come to realize that there's much more to life than wealth. Or even vengeance.''

Hazel eyes narrowed at her, and his mouth thinned. ''We have different standards, it seems. It may be enough for you to live on the kindness of others, but it's not what I want. I'll do what I have to do to get what I want.''

''Including betray a friend?''

"You're very lovely, but I've never thought of us as friends."

"I meant Northington. Is he not your friend?"

Harvey's mouth twisted. "Northington is very much his own man. We game together and have been known to go wenching together, but he's not what either of us would call my close friend, no. Perhaps we were once closer, but that was before the Peninsular Wars, before he left and came back a different person." He shrugged, regarding her thoughtfully. "He came back to find his brother dead and his uncle dead, his father the new earl—and himself in line for the title. I would have been ecstatic. Northington was not. He seemed to consider it a tragedy, a curtailing of liberty and his own plans. Christ, I would give ten years of my life to have the same opportunity, yet he treats it with cavalier disdain, as if he detests every moment of it."

"Perhaps he does."

"You mock me now, sweet Celia, for no man could detest the lure of wealth and power. He'll be earl one day. God, an earl with unlimited resources. The Moreland Shipping Concern is worth a king's ransom as it is, even with the recent losses it's suffered. It generates so much wealth, it's hardly worth noticing when a little is lost here, a little there... I didn't think it would matter, you see, and it hasn't, really, for it's such a vast enterprise. God, when I started I never thought I'd not be able to stop...but that's not really any of your concern."

"No," she said, "I suppose it's not."

There was much more to this than she'd first thought, for Sir John seemed on the verge of some kind of confession. But of what? She wanted to ask, for it seemed as if it would be important, as if it would somehow affect her. But then he was shaking his head again, a small smile on his mouth.

"You are very lovely, Celia, very lovely indeed. And if my circumstances were different, perhaps it would be me with you instead of Northington. But now it seems that neither of us will be with you. A pity."

No, she thought, he would never have been her choice, no matter what the circumstances. And really, Colter had not been her choice either, but rather her destiny; a fanciful thought but one that seemed so true. These weeks without him had been a time of reflection, of searching her soul for the truth, and she thought now that she knew how—and why—she loved him.

Yes, she admitted it freely to herself now, she did love him, despite the circumstances, despite who he was and who she was. When had it happened? It seemed to have crept up on her, this feeling of safety when she was with him, the respect that she felt for him when she had not wanted to like him at all.

Indeed, she'd wanted to use him, to dislike him so she wouldn't feel any guilt over it, but somehow she'd fallen in love with him instead.

"What are you thinking, Celia?" Harvey asked softly, and there was an undercurrent there in his tone that set her teeth on edge. "Are you wondering, too, like me, that if we had met under a different sky things would be so much better for both of us? Ah, 'It lies not in our power to love or hate, For will in us is overruled by fate,'" he quoted. "A truer verse has rarely been written."

"Marlowe," she said. "I used to read him. But that was a long time ago, and poets' truths are not always reliable."

"No? I'd not thought you so cynical."

"There's a lot you don't know about me, Sir John." She moved to the table, leaned back against it, her arms braced on the surface to disguise the quiver in her hands. "There is a lot that not even Northington knows. Has it not pricked your curiosity to wonder why Easton is so anxious to have me leave England?"

"As he so succinctly mentioned, my duty is to obey, not ask inconvenient questions. It pays well enough that I don't let my curiosity bother me overmuch."

"That sounds safe enough."

"It isn't only my safety that worries me—and I'll admit quite frankly that's a great concern of mine—but my well-being. I like comfort. I like fine wine and whist, and I loathe the necessity of ducking my creditors. My father has threatened to cut me off without a shilling, but that hardly matters as he's done enough damage already. I must earn what I spend."

"How distressing for you."

"Yes, stand there and judge me if you like, but I don't see you taking a post as a governess. You're content enough to let Leverton pay the blunt."

It was true, and she had no defense other than it had seemed justified at the time.

But there was an intensity to Harvey's stare that finally penetrated, and she knew at once what to say. Softly she said, "You've lost someone you loved."

He recoiled as if she'd struck him, and flushed to

the roots of his fair hair. "Yes. That is what happens when one lacks money."

"It doesn't have to ruin your life, Sir John—"

"What do you know about it? Christ above, how would you know how it feels to lose the one person in this world that you love? It wasn't enough to lose her, but to stand and watch her marry another man, a man she didn't love, all for lack of money...." He laughed harshly. "It killed her, but I was the unlucky one. I lived. I lived, but every day I die a little bit more. No, Celia St. Clair, you know nothing of how it feels."

"You're wrong, Sir John. I do know something of how it feels."

He stared at her blankly, then turned away.

Far too soon, Easton returned, and though he was urbane and perfunctory, she detected a thread of tension beneath his impassive demeanor.

"Take her directly to Dover docks, Harvey, and do not delay. High tide will not be until later this afternoon, but we want to have her settled into her cabin and quite *secure* before she sails."

His meaning was unmistakable. She was to be literally a prisoner until the ship sailed from England.

Despair seeped through her determination, but Celia had not yet given up all hope.

I've come too far to just give up now! she thought fiercely, and put a pleasant smile on her face as she calmly allowed Sir John to help her into the waiting carriage.

29

It was hardly the reception he'd expected, and Colter was furious when he stormed into the entrance hall at Harmony Hill, the door banging shut behind him.

"Renfroe!" he bellowed. The man came quickly even though he had no doubt already known of his lordship's arrival from the moment he'd been seen cresting the hill.

"Yes, my lord?" Renfroe's face was carefully impassive even in the teeth of Colter's unusual anger. It was rare for his temper to be loosed, rarer still that it be loosed upon a servant.

"Was Easton here recently?" Colter was too angry to be heedful of the old man's pride. "Did you allow him in this house without my permission, by God? You? I thought you more astute than that."

"My lord, I did ask him to leave as soon as I learned of his presence, but he was here some half hour to an hour before I was informed." He coughed nervously. "With only James and Smythe at their posts, it was difficult to know how to evict him if he refused again."

"Did he refuse? Christ, all this time... He's been coming here frequently, hasn't he, and I haven't known it. It's what I deserve, I suppose, for being too involved with that other business." He beckoned. "Come with me. I want to know every time he's been here in the past year. If you can't remember, ask Barbara or James or even one of the damned dogs, but I want it written down."

"Yes, my lord."

He should have anticipated something like this, especially after this past October when he'd found those chests hidden in the cave. And Mowry knew it, damn him, as well as Barclay, who had managed to run to earth the list of smuggled goods.

It was almost humorous. He'd been investigating his father for the suspicious disappearance of cargo and the fraudulent manifests, when all the time their own goods were being smuggled into England right under his very nose. No wonder his father had been so smug. He must know it, must have laughed to himself all the while he was insisting that it be investigated, that Philip was somehow involved.

Well, he was right enough about that. Philip *was* involved. The vindictive old bastard would be most pleased to see Philip charged with it, and still be able to piously claim that he'd had nothing to do with the losses or profits.

Easton was guilty, after all. And Colter knew damn good and well that he was the man behind the note sent to Santiago.

Aghast, the gypsy had paled when Colter arrived and asked for Celia.

"But she...is she not with you, my lord? Your letter

to me was delivered by one of your stable boys.... I would never have let her leave if I was not certain you were the one who sent for her. I swear it!''

It all made more sense when Marita was questioned, though she tossed her hair and sullenly refused to answer any questions at first. Not until her father threatened to beat the truth out of her did she relent.

''Yes!'' she spat. ''I did take her with me, that pale-faced creature, like whey, she is, and so foolish. But I only did it because the man who is your friend said she was special to you, and must be tricked into joining you.'' Tears were a silver sheen in her dark eyes as she stared up at him imploringly. ''If I did not think it was what you wanted, I would never have tricked her. I swear it!''

Swearing softly, Colter's hard gaze must have terrified her into a rambling recital of all she knew, for Marita told him the details of Easton's approach to her, his sympathetic commiseration with her dislike of Celia and his suggestion that she be lured to the point where he would see her united with his nephew.

''He said it was only for a while, that you would soon tire of her as you always do, and then you would remember me and how good it was for us last summer. You do remember?''

''I remember,'' he said coldly, ''but I seem to remember it a little differently than you.'' He turned to Santiago. ''I would never dishonor you, old friend.''

Speaking in the same dialect, Santiago nodded and said, ''My daughter has too much time to dream. Perhaps she should be married soon so her husband can fill her nights with something other than illusions. My regrets are endless.''

"It is not your fault. My seal was stolen. You could not have known."

Philip Worth would know where to find the seal, just as he knew where to hide smuggled goods. It explained so much.

None of which mattered as much right now as getting to Celia. Marita, frightened by his anger and her father's threats, had told them that Celia had been taken to a small house overlooking Dover. If he didn't get there in time, it was likely Celia would vanish.

The road snaked along the rugged coast, white chalk slopes drizzling like a sticky paste from the recent rains. Dover sat in a tattered curve of the bay, and tides this time of year were roughly twelve hours apart, ships leaving on the high tide in late afternoon—or early evening. Christ, you'd think he could remember when it was so vital!

Dover Castle thrust forbidding walls into the low-lying clouds, undeterred by constant wind, looming over the town snugged against the harbor below. He was almost there. White cliffs were beacons in the lengthening shadows of dusk.

Even before he reached the town, he saw that he was too late, that ships had sailed on the high tide, canvas sails slapping against the wind, billowing out like the wings of falcons to ride the gray, tossed waves.

No one remembered a fair-haired woman of Celia's height and appearance boarding a ship, nor did anyone recall Lord Easton. All that was left was to find the house Marita had described, and hope that Celia was still there.

He found the house, and only the muzzle of his pistol convinced the landlord to admit that there had, indeed, been a young lady there earlier.

"But she is gone now, with that man!" Shaking visibly, he quailed as the long barrel stroked along his jaw. "Gone," he squeaked again, "and both men wi' her!"

"Both? That's enlightening. Come, give me descriptions of these men, and perhaps you'll not only live, but have a coin or two for your trouble."

It didn't take much to deduce who was with Easton. The devil of it was that he'd *suspected* Harvey of being near desperation. Colter could have offered a loan, or lost a large sum to him at whist, but he'd decided it would only prolong the inevitable. Harvey was an inveterate gambler, not easily cured, a man who would lose his last shilling wagering on which side of the street a cat would choose. It wouldn't have helped him for long.

He went back to Harmony Hill only to get a fresh horse, then took the London road north. During the long ride he began to think again, as he had not done for a long time, of the ancient teachings he'd picked up from the old Hindu who'd taught him the art of healing by massage. Karma. Under the law of karma, the next life was determined by the deeds of the past life. If the life was worthy, that person would be reborn in a higher form; if not, the person would live again in a lower form, possibly even that of an animal.

How, he wondered wryly, would he return? So far, he had nothing to recommend that he come back as anything more evolved than an eel. It was hardly the moment to be so introspective, but if he didn't think of the abstract while he rode, he would think of Celia, and remember her tears when he'd left her behind, her soft pleas to go with him.

He should have listened, should have overcome his concern that she'd be harmed. She was right, after all, and he should have kept her safe.

Christ, if anything happened to her he was to blame for it, and it would eat at him forever, never fade, always be at the back of his mind, one more ghost. But unlike the others, the faceless forms of the nameless dead, this ghost would be personal.

This ghost had a face and a name.

Colter swore to himself. Now he knew he could never get her out of his mind, would always feel incomplete. Celia had managed to worm her way into his very soul.

It was a hell of a time to find that out.

Philip Worth's London home held no sign of his presence, and his valet swore vehemently to Colter that he hadn't seen him.

"I swear it, Lord Northington. If he is in the city he has not come here!"

There was an air of leashed violence in him that scared not just Easton's servants, but Colter's own. He'd been to Harvey's lodgings as well, and neither of the men had been seen. When he went to his own town house, Beaton regarded him with a mixture of astonishment and agitation, his usual impassive countenance not quite enough to hide his inner turmoil.

"Excuse me for saying it, but I have never seen you in such disarray, my lord," he ventured when Colter flung his muddy garments to a low bench in the dressing room. "Your country valet has been shockingly remiss."

"Renfroe is an old family retainer, not a valet at all, as you well know. No, give me my other boots. It's too damn wet to bother with clean ones."

"My lord." Wooden-faced, Beaton stubbornly held out the clean boots, gleaming with boot polish.

Colter glanced at him as he shoved his feet into the hightop boots and reached for a clean neckcloth. Beaton held out a snowy length of linen, then arranged it in neat folds around his neck.

"Dammit, Beaton, I can do that myself," Colter said impatiently, then took pity on the valet and let him finish.

"Have my horse brought round," he said, and strode from the dressing room without answering the question in Beaton's eyes. Downstairs, he went into his study, drew out a clean sheet of paper and scrawled a note on it. He gave it to Beaton when he came to announce that his lordship's horse had been brought round.

"See that this is delivered if I do not return," he said. Beaton took the proffered note though his gaze was troubled.

"My lord, if I may be so bold—"

"No," Colter said softly, "you may not. There is little to be said now."

It was true. Whatever came after, he was done with turning his back. Done with letting it go.

The Moreland house on Curzon Street wasn't far from the Leverton house, and he would visit Celia's cousin when he was done. It was the least he could do. And by some miracle, there may be word about Celia.

Garner, the new butler who had replaced the ancient Karns, opened the door to him while a stable boy held his horse.

"I won't be here long, Garner," he said, and strode past him across the gleaming black-and-white floors to the wide staircase. He went immediately to his father's room.

The door stood slightly ajar, and he shoved it open, then came to an abrupt, disbelieving halt.

Beyond the sitting room, he heard an unmistakable soft drawl. He recognized that tone, though he had to move closer to hear what she was saying. *Celia.*

Brewster hovered anxiously over the earl, tucking the edges of a blanket around him as Celia stared at him.

Her heart pounded furiously in her chest and her mouth was dry, her hands shaking. This was the face of the man who had haunted her waking and sleeping nightmares, the man who had taken so much from her with his careless indifference.

Yet he was old, frail, a broken man now, though there was a fierce vigor in those hooded eyes that was familiar. The pockmarked flesh sagged, and one side of his face looked as if it had melted into disuse. Palsied hands gripped the gold head of a cane, and it was obvious from that dark stare that he knew her.

She wanted to rail at him, to howl her anguish and hate after all these years, but no words would come. It had taken her so long to get here, to finally drum up the courage and damn the risks, and now she couldn't speak. Oh God, she'd struggled so hard, overcome obstacles and waited and planned for so long, and now that the time was here she saw that fate had dealt with him much more harshly than any vengeance she could manage.

Just retribution had caught up with him despite her.

Drawing in a deep breath, she said finally, "I...think I made a mistake in coming here. I'll leave—"

"Do you think you can just barge into my home and tell me that it's time we talk, then leave without giving me an explanation?" The earl banged the end of his cane on the floor. "Come closer, so that I can see you, girl."

His voice was surprisingly strong, emerging from that ruined face and summoning all the old memories, the old arrogance. It was suddenly as if she had first met him again, heard his peremptory demand to see her mother.

She took two deliberate steps closer so that gray light from a bank of windows fell upon her face. For a moment he did nothing, but she saw the instant recognition in his face as his mouth worked soundlessly.

He remembers me!

Oh God, she shouldn't feel so exultant but she did. If she was to be denied vengeance, then the satisfaction of seeing his face when he realized who she was would have to suffice. He knew her. He knew the child whose life he had ruined with his cruel actions.

Moreland started up, but his wasted body wouldn't cooperate and he only rocked a little, his clawlike fingers losing their grip on the gold head of the cane so that it pitched forward to clatter on the floor. This time his voice was hoarse, sounding wrenched from him.

"Léonie! It's you...."

Celia stood frozen as the blood drained from her face. "No..."

It was more a moan than a denial, a despairing cry from her that sounded like the wail of a child.

"He doesn't really know you, it seems," a woman's voice behind her said. Celia dragged her gaze from the earl to see an elegant woman enter the room, her bearing and poise unmistakable. Then she saw Colter; he stood just outside the door, his gaze impassive.

Her heart leaped when she saw him, but he looked at her with a detached gaze, his blue eyes darkly questioning.

The same blue eyes stared out of the woman's face, but they were calm and clear.

"My husband sees your mother in you, I believe. You do look remarkably like her, you know," the countess continued in the same composed tone. "Léonie St. Remy was a most lovely woman, and my husband was obsessed with her. I once thought the obsession would fade with time, that he would forget her. Then she ran off with that American—your father, I presume." Lady Moreland smiled slightly. "Poor woman. I felt so sorry for her. When my husband decides he wants something, he does not rest until he gets it. And, of course, your mother's rejection only sharpened his determination. Isn't that right, my lord?" She turned to her husband, but Moreland's eyes were blinking rapidly, a sheen of tears filming them.

"Lady Moreland," Celia began, but the countess put up a hand to stop her.

"No, there's nothing really to say. I'm sorry about your mother. It must have been terrible for you. By the time I knew what had happened, there was no trace of you. After a while, I thought perhaps you had died as well." She paused, glanced at Colter and said with a faint smile, "I'm glad to see that you survived, Miss St. Clair. I never wanted my son to find out about it, of course, but it's obvious that I've failed in that endeavor. I did try, Colter, to spare you this, at least. Perhaps I would have if she hadn't come back."

Colter had come into the room, his gaze intent on his mother, his tone harsh.

"Are you behind Philip's actions?"

"Yes. It seemed the best thing at the time. If she'd left and gone back to America with a tidy sum, then you needed never know that your father is a murderer. Oh, yes, Miss St. Clair, I can see by your face that you thought no one knew. *I knew.* I knew because he told me, the arrogant bastard. He confessed to ease his conscience, and left me to live with the consequences."

"How could you hide it all these years?"

The countess turned to look at Colter, her brows lifted in mild inquiry. "It's not the sort of thing one discusses at dinner. There were enough rumors about him, why should I give you and Anthony one more thing to live down?"

Her gaze shifted back to the earl and her tone hardened as she said, "I made him pay for it in ways you'll never be able to understand. He killed that old man, destroyed Léonie St. Remy, and ultimately he's responsible for Anthony's death as well. Oh, Colter, it wasn't your grandfather who insisted you have the controlling shares of stock in the shipping company. It was I who made your father agree after he sent Anthony there to force him to sign. He knew his father had a fever but the shares mattered most—so I made sure he lost them.'' She smiled slightly, but there was no humor in it. ''It was the best vengeance I could manage—atonement for Anthony's death. In a weak moment, he signed them over to you as I demanded he do. Since then he's been systematically cheating his own son and his investors as often as he could get away with it. Philip has been the only restraint I've been able to use to keep him from bankrupting us. A necessary evil.''

''For Christ's sake, why didn't you tell me? Why didn't you come to me with the truth?'' Colter sounded hoarse, his expression intent.

''There was enough natural animosity between you already and I had spent years trying to keep it all quiet.'' The fine lines of her face sharpened slightly as she regarded Colter. ''Did you think I wanted you more humiliated than you were? I did not. I was all the protection you had. He'd killed one son, and I had no intention of allowing him to destroy you.''

''God...*ma mère*...''

Mother and son stared at one another, the blue eyes so alike clashing, searching, unspoken regrets and accusations almost palpable.

Celia felt suddenly like an interloper. Tension hummed in the room, and the earl had not said another word, though he made strange, garbling sounds in his throat that the man behind him tried to soothe. He held a cup to the earl's lips but Moreland knocked it away with a violent swipe of his hand. Agitated, he strained against the confines of his own body and the chair.

Lady Moreland turned at last to look at her husband. "I think," she said, "that we should send for the physician, Brewster."

Brewster looked up at them, and his eyes were faintly accusing. "Perhaps it would be best if I tended the earl in peace until he arrives, my lady."

"Yes," she said impassively. "That may be best."

It was all so strange, but Celia turned with them to leave the room, uncertain what she should say or do, or even if she should try to talk to Colter. He looked so *cold,* his expression frozen into a carefully blank mask.

When they reached the door to the sitting room, Celia glanced back. The earl was staring at her, his body tilted to one side in the chair as Brewster attempted to support him. Slack lips formed a single word that was a grating, guttural sound. "*Léonie....*"

It was the last word he was to ever say.

30

A cold wind blew across the chalky crags, swept over the barren grounds of Harmony Hill in a soft sighing moan. Winter still lay upon thc land, but already there were signs of the coming spring in the tiny buds of crocus that poked purple and yellow heads through warming soil.

Celia stood at the window looking out over the garden, waiting. It seemed she had been waiting for so many days for him to return. Oh God, he had been so distant lately when she ached for him to regard her with something other than that polite detachment that made her want to provoke him into any kind of emotion, even anger.

But there was no honest emotion, not even when they'd been wed at Gretna Green just across the border into Scotland, an "over the anvil" ceremony that was swift and legal and long overdue, if Jacqueline was to be believed. It still shocked Celia, the haste with which he had taken her from his father's home, the earl's body not yet cold in his bed, his "grieving" widow left to tend the details that were always necessary when a peer died.

He had silenced her brief protests at the impropriety with his mouth, then his quiet, controlled lovemaking, so that by the time they arrived in the tiny village, she had no more objections, only a kind of numb complaisance.

Yet it's not the same, she thought with a despairing sadness that enveloped her. He does not look at me as he once did, and I don't know what he truly thinks!

They existed in an empty life now, save for the nights when he came to her bed, usually with the smell of brandy on his breath, sometimes gentle with her and sometimes with a passion bordering on violence as he took her, his hands rough and demanding.

She had tried once to explain her lies to him, how she had not trusted even her cousin to understand the years of grief and pain and rage after her mother's death, but Colter had not let her. Instead he had stopped her, his voice fierce as he said, "He's dead now. Leave it be, Celia."

No, he would never understand, not at all. There was a wall between them she wasn't certain she'd ever be able to tear down. Why had he married her? Guilt? Or love? She had to know, and it was obvious Colter would not tell her.

So she'd sent an invitation to Jacqueline to visit. Perhaps her cousin could help her understand.

When she recognized the Leverton crest on the carriage rolling to a halt at the front door at last, Celia left the window to go and greet her cousin.

"Ma petite," Jacqueline said, sweeping into the hall to press her cold cheek against Celia's, dark hair a vivid contrast against pale. "How wonderful it is to see you again! Now come, we must have hot chocolate and you will tell me how it is to be a countess, and how happy you are with your so-handsome husband."

Celia waited until the servant left the parlor to lean forward and pour hot, fragrant chocolate into the Sévres cup that Jacqueline held out. Their eyes met briefly before her cousin's glance skidded away, as if she was afraid to look too closely into her eyes.

"How is Carolyn," she asked, a mundane question to ease the tension, "and dear Jules? They are well, I trust."

"Oh, yes, very well, and Caro sends her regrets. She is so busy lately, tending the details of the wedding and all that is to be done before— The king sent a lovely gift, a huge silver urn engraved with his crest, though what she will do with it, I am not at all sure. A vase for flowers, perhaps." Jacqueline sipped her chocolate, and the cup rattled slightly in the delicate saucer, sounding as brittle as her voice. "And you, my dearest? All is well with you?"

"I don't know. Oh, there's so much I have to say and I don't know where to begin, or even if I should, but you know it all now, or I think you do—"

Leaning forward Jacqueline put a hand on her arm. "Yes, ma petite, I know all. I found the document, the charges against Moreland, though he was Northington then. I should have confessed when you returned to London, but everything happened so fast, and Northington—oh my, now *he's* Moreland—was so anxious to wed you that there never seemed to be the right time."

"Yes, he was very anxious to marry me," Celia

said, and noted that Jacqueline's gaze shifted away again. "Perhaps you can tell me why."

"Why? Oh, it must be obvious, ma petite. He is such an impetuous, forceful man, and obviously so much in love with you. Why, he was a very *devil* until you returned!"

"Tell me the truth, please. I know there's something you aren't saying. I have to know. I *have* to know! It's so different now, and I need to know why."

Distress creased Jacqueline's face, and her hand shook slightly as she placed the cup and saucer back on the footed silver tray. "I only meant to help you, Celia, I swear it. It seemed the right thing to do, and it is, truly it is... You will be happy, anyone can see that you are both in love!"

"Oh God...." Her whisper lay between them, and in the cheery glow of the parlor fire, Celia saw the truth in her cousin's eyes.

"It wasn't for love! He married me because he had to.... Oh no, how could you? How could you do that to me?" Surging to her feet, she fought a wave of grief and nausea, sick that he would agree to it, sick that he would go through with it. What had he thought of her? It was no wonder that he'd left so quickly. "Oh God, what have you done," she moaned, and Jacqueline leaped up in distress, knocking over the chocolate pot.

Dark brown liquid splashed over her yellow silk gown and onto Celia's green silk skirts, but she ignored it.

"Ma petite, it was for the best, don't you see? People had begun to talk. No amount of explanation could account for your disappearance, and the whispers...

You were ruined! Don't you understand? And it was so obvious that you love him— Please don't hate me!"

"Hate you? I could never hate you, but now I'll never know if he is married to me because he loves me or because of his honor—and I once thought he had no honor! Oh God!"

Her laugh bordered on hysteria, and she clapped a hand over her mouth to stifle the unnatural sound.

Jacqueline knelt beside her, her hands clasping Celia's tightly, her eyes earnest and swimming with tears. "Did I not tell you once that my Jules thinks highly of him and he is never wrong about people? Oh my lovely child, after all that you've suffered...you should have told me about Léonie, for I would have understood. As will he."

"No, that's just it, don't you see? He knows. He knows and he still married me. Now I know why... after all that was said, those horrible things... even his own mother. Oh, you should have seen his face! We were there when his father—the man I have hated for so long—had another of what the physician called his seizures. Shock brought it on, his mother said, but I think it was guilt. Perhaps he did have a conscience, after all."

She rose from the settee, moved jerkily toward the fire to warm hands that had gone cold as ice. "Afterward—oh, it was all so...so *civilized,* with the countess offering me tea or chocolate, and Colter standing there like a stone statue, with no emotion or blame or accusations. But his eyes were so empty and I knew he had to wonder why I was there, but he never asked."

"Because he had to know, petite." Jacqueline's voice was soft, sympathetic. "Northington has never been what one would call oblivious to things, and he had to realize that you wanted to confront his father."

"And realize why I came to England. My entire time here has been based on lies—lies to you and to him. How can we live together with all those lies between us?"

"You won't," Jacqueline said frankly, and rose to put her hands on Celia's cheeks, palms warm and comforting. "When he returns, you will talk to him and the lies will be behind you."

"Yes, if he returns. He never told me where he was going and I don't know if he wants to come back."

"Of course he does! Celia, you mustn't torture yourself with all this guilt. Yes, you should have been honest, but it is understandable why you were not. Speak frankly to him, and I know all will be well."

Green silk rustled as Celia surveyed her stained skirts with hands that shook only slightly, and she managed a smile. "I know you're right. I've been a coward and it's time to face him and the truth. We must start our lives without lies."

"You are so strong, child, and so brave. Oh, yes, don't look so surprised. Not many would have the courage to do what you have done, and I know Léonie would be proud of you. You have her courage."

"Maman never lived a lie."

"Léonie St. Remy was practical enough to live a lie in order to survive. Do you think we were allowed to leave France during the Terror? No. We had to lie, and steal, and cheat to escape, but we did what we had to because we knew it was the only way to survive. Now.'' She came to Celia and took her arm. ''Enough of this. When he comes, you will tell him all the truths. There will be no more lies between you.''

No, there would be no more lies, Celia thought. And if there would be no more at all between them, she would deal with that, too. There was really no other choice. Like Maman, she was a survivor, but now it would be the truth that gave her freedom, not lies or vengeance, or even love. God help her, she loved him so. He must know that, must feel it when she was with him, and if it was enough, if it made up for all the rest, then they had a chance.

And if it did not...

''Let me ring for James to come and clean up the spilled chocolate,'' she turned to say to Jacqueline, and smiled a little at the look of chagrin on her cousin's face. ''If this is the worst that happens today, we should be grateful.''

''Such a lovely pot—Chelsea ware?'' Jacqueline asked as she stared down at the spreading stain and porcelain pot lying on its side on the rug, her tone curiously serene. ''An interesting pattern.''

No one answered Celia's ring, and she moved to the half-open door of the parlor to call for Renfroe. Silence muffled the entrance hall, no sounds from either the elderly butler, Barbara, the housekeeper, or from James, whom Colter had installed in the house as a sort of footman and bodyguard.

Puzzled, she moved across the gleaming floor toward the double doors that led down to the kitchens. The only sound was her footsteps, an eerie absence set her teeth on edge. It was never this quiet, this *tense,* as if waiting.

As she moved down the short, narrow stairwell to the kitchen, she heard a muted sound as of a sob, and paused, her heart thumping with alarm.

Before she could move, Renfroe appeared in front of her, his eyes wide with distress as he staggered forward.

"Whatever is the matter?" She reached out for him, but as she did, she saw from the corner of her eye a movement behind her and tried to move. It was impossible in the tight corridor, and she heard Renfroe cry out a protest as an arm slashed down to strike her against the side of her head.

Reeling, Celia tried to keep her balance, but it all happened so fast. She heard everything as if through a wall of water, moving away from her and then back, waves of sound receding and darkness slowly claiming her so that she saw nothing, heard nothing.

The raw day mirrored his mood as Colter reined in his mount on the crest of a chalky ridge that ran above the English Channel. Sea winds dampened his hair and misted on his face. Broadstairs lay below. A sandy scythe of land cupped stone buildings that staggered up the steep hill guarding the bay. On the wooded ridge, warning towers of the Revenue House kept watch for smugglers.

He found Harvey at the Albion in Broadstairs, nursing a pint and not seeming very surprised to see him.

"I've been expecting you," he said, indicating an empty chair across from him. "Was it much trouble finding me?"

"Not much. I inquired at every public house between here and Dover."

A faint grin wavered on Harvey's mouth; red-rimmed eyes met his briefly before looking away. "I suppose you've come to call me out."

"I've thought about it."

"Yes, it seems fair enough, I suppose." He lifted his tankard and drank deeply. "No need for me to be sober for it, I've not a chance either way. No match for you, old boy, and that's a fact."

Colter's eyes narrowed. Anger had eased with the past month of contemplation, but not the need for answers.

"I tracked Easton to Dover. It seems he's fled England again, gone back to France," he said when Harvey fell silent. "You should have gone with him."

Harvey blew out a wet sigh. "It's not as if we're boon companions. Christ, I don't even like the man. He was just a means to an end. A man with the blunt to ease my debts."

"And did you? Did you ease your debts, or only create more."

"Ah, therein lies the rub." His smile was rueful, a bit embarrassed. "I'm done up all over town and don't have the coin to pay for more than a few pints here and there. They get on to you after a time, see, and a gentleman can only go without paying for so long before innkeepers become nasty about it."

"You were paid to put Celia aboard a ship to America. Yet she's still here."

"Yes." Harvey nodded thoughtfully. "Yes, that was probably unwise of me, but I just couldn't do it. She was right when she told me that there are prices too great to pay in this world. I've been a bastard, a thief and probably worse, but I'm not low enough to deport a woman whose only crime was grief. It seemed that she'd suffered enough. And I knew how that felt."

"Where is he, Harvey? Easton—you know where he went."

"Yes, I suppose I do."

"Tell me where he is and I'll see that the magistrate shows mercy."

"Oh, no, old boy, I know well enough what happens to men who are so foolish as to betray their mates. Tied to a pole at low tide and red-lighted, and I like my lights still on, if you please. I'd rather take my chances at twenty paces with you. It's much more merciful and swift a death than the slow agony of drowning inch by inch."

Colter rose from the chair he'd straddled, stared down at Harvey with a sense of pity. "You're already dying inch by inch. At least make it worthwhile."

Struggling to his feet, Harvey stood swaying for a moment, face pale and jaw set. "You'll free me from life before I have to endure another day, I presume, so let's get on with it. No sense in having you accused of killing a man too far in his cups."

"Oh, no, I think it will serve my purpose far better to let you live, Harvey. It's a slower death than even that of a smuggler's fate."

The bleak illumination in his eyes was ample evidence that he recognized the truth. "Damn you," he whispered hoarsely. "Damn you!"

"Where is he, Harvey? Tell me."

After a moment, his mouth worked into a determined line and Harvey said quietly, "Still in England. Waiting for you to be careless."

And Colter knew then where Philip Worth had gone.

He rode back the way he came on a night that cleared to show millions of stars salting the sky, taking the road south from Broadstairs. He had a long way to go, too long, back through Ramsgate and Sandwich before he even got to Dover. Before he could get to Celia, who waited for him at Harmony Hill, his wife now, a bargain kept.

But he hadn't married her only to keep his bargain with Lady Leverton.

Sweet Celia, with eyes as green as the sun-struck sea, with courage and heart and qualities he'd never appreciated. He'd been stupid. It shouldn't matter why she had come to England, or that she hadn't trusted him enough to tell him about her mother and his father. God, what a sordid debacle his father had made of things!

It had been all he could do to keep from killing him.

If death hadn't come so quickly to the earl, maybe he would have. His father had caused grief wherever he'd gone, and worse, he'd left behind a legacy of hate and lies.

Maybe it was time he admitted to Celia how ashamed he was of his own father. Christ, she was more courageous than he'd ever guessed, keeping the truth to herself, determined to confront a man who had destroyed her mother and had the power to destroy her if he chose. What courage that had taken—and he'd been too caught up in his own deceptions to recognize it. It was time he told her how much he admired her. And that he loved her. They'd start over.

But first he had to ensure her safety. His father had been right about Philip Worth, perhaps because it took one rogue to recognize another. And now that Colter knew Easton had no scruples, he knew that he had to get to Celia before his uncle did.

31

Nightmarish images prodded her awake. She could see through slitted eyes the face that slowly took shape, an aristocratic face below white hair, with eyes that were too familiar, treacherous eyes that regarded her with detached curiosity.

"Ah, I see that you are awake at last," Philip Worth said, and nodded. "Very good. I began to worry that I had hit you too hard, perhaps, and that would certainly have ruined everything. But here you are, awake and in reasonably good health, so do sit up and rejoin us. Lady Leverton and I have been having a most revealing conversation."

"Pig!" Jacqueline spat in furious French. "Dog! You are a disgrace. How dare you do this!"

"Madame, I dare because I have little left to lose now. My life is at stake, and that I care to keep, even if all else eludes me at the moment. Fortune has hidden her face, it seems, but all is not yet lost if I can keep my head. So reassure yourself that you are in little danger as long as you cooperate with my requests."

He smiled, turning again to look at Celia, who lay

upon the settee in the parlor. Her head throbbed wickedly as she stared back at him.

"You should have gone to America, my dear," he said, "but since you have not, I am forced to make arrangements that will be less than pleasant for either of us. If you'd done as you were told, none of this would be necessary."

There was a silky menace in his cultured tones, malice in the clear eyes that regarded her so calmly.

"My husband will kill you if you so much as promise to harm us," Celia whispered, but Easton only laughed softly.

"That is exactly what I intend to avoid, child. Why do you think I'm here? I'd be safely in France if not for your husband—whose influence seems to reach much farther than I guessed. Every port I visited was closed to me. Damned officious men, those excise officers, and more efficient than normal in the performance of their duties. Not a one of them wanted to accept payment in lieu of arrest. I barely escaped them. I suspect Lord Mowry's hand in this, and of course, my great-nephew must be behind such rabid pursuit."

"What do you hope to gain from this farce—gratitude for abusing us?" Celia demanded more forcefully than she'd thought she could do as she pushed to a sitting position and smoothed her skirts back over her legs.

Jacqueline sat stiffly in a nearby chair, eyes huge in the glow of fire and lamps, her mouth a thin, angry slash.

Easton merely lifted a brow, the pistol in his hand a warning to both they need not attempt escape. "I need you as assurance of my safe passage from England. Once I am away, I will release you. It is a proposition that Colter will most likely view as agreeable, once given the alternatives.''

''You're mad,'' Jacqueline whispered, and Easton's lips twisted into a cruel smile.

''No, Lady Leverton, merely desperate. Beware desperate men, as we have a tendency to be unreliable at times. This pistol could discharge quite unexpectedly.''

Celia rose to her feet and the barrel of the pistol instantly swerved toward her. ''If you do shoot,'' she said calmly, ''you can only kill one of us.''

''This fires twice, an excellent model. I hardly need remind you that I possess more strength than either of you, and it would be no trouble to save powder and ball. Come here, child, since you promise to be rebellious, and secure your cousin with the sash from her dress. Tie it tightly, or I'll assume you'd rather me assure her presence by more *final* means.''

Angry, frustrated and frightened, Celia did what he told her to do, using the blue silk sash from Jacqueline's dress to tie her to the straight-backed chair by the fire. She could feel her fear, though Jacqueline said nothing, only stared balefully at Easton. While she tied the knots, Celia tried to think of a plan for escape.

Apparently Easton had already managed to secure James and Renfroe, for there was no sign of either of them. She hoped they were still alive, that he'd not been vicious enough to kill them.

Outwardly calm, Celia's insides thrummed with tension as she tied the final knot and straightened to meet Easton's narrowed stare.

"If you wish to test them, please yourself," she said, and saw the suggestion of a smile on his mouth.

"Quite a little rebel, aren't you? Rather like your mother, as I recall. She was spirited as well." He moved to test the bonds, then nodded. "Very good. Now, remove your own sash, please. I shall do the honors this time."

When she was tied with her hands in front of her, he put a burgundy cape around her shoulders to conceal her hands. "After you—and give no sign of distress or I'll shoot you. That is a promise. I may not kill you, but the pain will be severe enough to make you wish I had."

Celia had no choice but to go with him, and she saw from Jacqueline's terrified eyes that there was little hope of rescue.

Easton put her into a carriage, a fast, two-wheeled gig drawn by a pair of Colter's spirited bays, and she wished that she had the nerve to signal to Smythe of her plight.

Oh, where is Santiago when he's needed? she wondered with a spurt of real fear when the carriage door slammed shut behind her and Easton took up the reins. No one save the elderly Smythe was in sight, and of course, he knew Easton as a relative and would suspect nothing.

The afternoon light was fading, and a cold wind penetrated the closed gig and the wool lap robe Easton had carelessly tossed over her. Once out of the gates, the gig turned east along the coast; marsh marigolds had begun to bloom in the damp woodland and wet meadows, tiny bits of yellow like scattered sunlight. A ringed plover churned along a spit of sand below the road, and the gig spun just as relentlessly toward its unknown destination.

"Where are we going?" she asked, though she suspected he would not answer.

"Curiosity can be a dangerous thing, my lady," Easton said, a mocking emphasis on the title that was still so new to her.

"You're quite right, but vengeance is deadly. I should know that well enough, as I've seen for myself how fatal it can be for those who pursue it." Her fingers curled into the folds of the burgundy cape, the wind a rushing sound, the wheels whirling over chalk and sandy road an incessant hum that threatened to drown out their words. "Release me, and I'll ask Colter to withdraw his charges against you."

"My dear, naive countess, it's not up to him."

He smiled as he glanced at her, his hands competent upon the reins, the whip in his hand a cracking shot that urged the horses to a faster pace.

"I fear you've been misinformed if you think that he alone is responsible for my misfortune. There's the matter of smuggling, you see, avoiding the excise men and revenue cutters that has rather stirred up a fuss. It's not up to my great-nephew, but to his superior. It will be up to Colter to convince his superior to allow me to leave England. Would that convincing Colter alone be all I need to do...I'm sure that could be accomplished with you as the prize."

Despair formed a hard, tight knot in the pit of her stomach. Mowry had not seemed the kind of man who would be agreeable to bargains of any kind, not if it meant foiling his own plans or purpose. He would hardly consider her as a strong reason to free a man he wanted to prosecute.

The gig rocked violently to one side and she grabbed at the handstrap to remain upright on the seat. Easton gave a harsh grunt, hauling back on the reins as the gig went into a curve on the road, then rolled smoothly forward again.

Waning light turned the sea gray, easily seen now on the right as they took the coastal road toward Devon. Celia remembered the last time she had come this way, afraid then, too, when Marita had betrayed her to Easton and Sir John.

It seemed that most of her life had been lived in fear of something—fear of the past, fear of the future, fear of failure. Yet, despite it all, she survived.

There was a resilience that she hadn't realized she possessed until now, and it came to her rescue even when everything else seemed to fail her.

Even if Colter has abandoned me, she thought, then pushed the disloyal idea from her mind.

If she must save herself, then she would. This time Sir John was not there to relent, to take her back to London as he had last time. If she was to escape being put aboard a ship again just to save Easton from a well-deserved fate, she had to do it on her own. With her hands covered by the lap robe, she worked at the velvet sash around her wrists until it loosened and slithered free to the floor. Free!

A glance showed her that he had his pistol on the seat beside him. To reach it she would have to lean over him. Impossible, of course.

So she waited, watched, and when night fell and the gig went more slowly, the feeble lights flickering with scant illumination to show the rutted road, she reached slowly for the handle of the door. It was outside, so she had to slip her hand over the edge of the door, a cautious movement that required stealth.

Fumbling fingers found the latch, and she sat quietly waiting until just the right moment, until Easton was intent upon the road and the gig slowed enough so that she wouldn't kill herself with a leap. Ridges lined the road, high and narrow, dropping steeply away in places. In other spots the road dipped into softer terrain. She narrowed her eyes, staring out the window as they pressed onward. Finally she saw a break in the chalky ridge of rock that lined the road.

Spiked heads of club-rushes waved in a brisk wind, indicating soft ground to cushion her fall, seeming in the ghostly light of rising moon and lamp to be beckoning to her as she gathered her nerve.

She saw her chance as the gig slowed to take another curve. Just as Easton lifted the whip to urge the sleek matched bays to a faster pace, she snapped open the latch and flung herself out into empty air.

Even cushioned by brackish water and soft ground, she landed hard, breathless from the impact as she scrambled to her feet. There was no time to look back, no time for anything but flight, and she ran through the muddy sludge toward the rushing sound of the sea. She heard Easton's angry shouts, but he'd have to leave the gig to pursue her. Surely she could outrun him!

The enveloping cape swirled around her, impeding her movements, and as she ran she undid the braided frog that held it closed, letting it slide free of her shoulders. It billowed out, the rich burgundy like a splash of wine sailing through the air to land in a drift upon the ground.

Holding her skirts high, she fled like a marsh hare, ran as her side began to ache and her breath came in short gasps of air like a blacksmith's bellows. It was cold, the wind constant, and the hem of her skirts grew wet and heavy. Several times she stumbled and nearly fell, but she pushed herself up and surged forward again, the sense of urgency driving her on until she reached a sandy ridge.

Tussocks of marram grass studded the sand, tripping her as she ran, so that she went sprawling on the dune, tasting grit in her mouth, her hands coated with it as she tried to wipe it from her face. Breathless, aching, she waited and listened, lying under silvery light with waving grasses as graceful as dancers, a whispering sway in the wind.

Around her, it was deserted, desolate, a barren silence save for the careless indifference of nature. When she finally dared look behind her, she saw nothing but empty expanse, heard nothing but the wind.

Above, on the rutted road that led to Dover, Colter saw the stopped gig, heard the angry voice shouting. He slowed his mount and drew the pistol from the waist of his pants.

Euston turned, saw Colter in the light of moon and lamp and blanched, disbelief registering on his face.

"You—how did you get here so quickly?"

Dismounting, Colter approached him with a light, swift tread like that of a stalking cat, the pistol held at the ready.

"Where is she?"

There was a brief silence before Philip shrugged, and said, "I don't know who you mean. Where is who? You can see I've no companion with me."

Colter stepped sideways to glance inside the gig, saw the wool lap robe on the seat but nothing else to indicate Celia had been with him.

"You're coming from the direction of Harmony, so I can only assume that you were foolish enough to try to use her against me again. So help me, if you've harmed one hair on her head—"

"She was alive, well and quite energetic the last I saw of her," Philip broke in, and some of his old arrogance returned as he smiled. "I do believe you've finally formed an affection for someone, Colter. Convenient, since you married her, I suppose."

"Yes, quite convenient. Put your hands in the air where I can see them. I don't trust you not to do something rash and stupid—and I'd much rather see you dangle at the end of a rope than explain how you came to be shot."

"Hear hear now, no need for unnecessary violence. I've no weapon, as you can surely see. Not even a sword, though I would be of little use if I did have one. Never the shot or the blade that you've proven to be."

Colter beckoned him forward. "You'll ride my horse for now. I've no intention of letting you out of my sight." He loosened his neckcloth and shook it out. "Neither do I intend to leave you unbound. You're a wily old fox, and full of tricks. Sir John was meant to lure me far afield, I assume, so that you could escape. Why didn't you?"

"I believe you must know why—do you mind? If

I'm to ride a horse, I'd just as soon not freeze. My coat is in the gig."

"I'll get your coat. You stand there." Colter moved to the side of the gig and reached inside, feeling for the coat without taking his eyes from his uncle.

Christ, he was an old man, silvery hair pale under the sheen of moonlight, his bearing still straight and tall for a man of his years, but the evidence of time stamped upon his features for all to see.

Colter snagged the coat and felt along it for possible weapons then tossed it to his uncle, who caught it deftly.

"Well, my boy, what would you have me do now," he said as he shrugged into the coat, "march back to Harmony afoot?"

"As tempting as that sounds, I think I'll revise my earlier suggestion. We'll go together in the gig. It seems to be the favored transport for hostages— Who wore this?"

He held up a length of green velvet ribbon and saw the sudden wariness in Easton's posture. "Where is she, Philip?" There was menace in his voice, and danger in his eyes as he moved toward the older man. "Tell me where she is, or by God, I'll shoot you where you stand!"

"Shoot an unarmed man? Hardly fair, do you think? Give me a pistol and we'll settle this at twenty paces." Philip watched him closely. "It's better than dangling at the end of a rope for the amusement of the excise men."

Cold anger made him consider it; he'd like nothing better than to shoot him, but that would hardly help Celia.

"Tell me where she is," he said softly, "or I'll show you a few tricks I picked up from a tribe known as Apache. They're quite inventive, have ways of making a man say things that not even the Spanish Inquisitors could imagine. It's barren out here, and you wouldn't be found for days..."

"You really are a savage, aren't you." Philip's voice held thick contempt. "Your father was right."

"My father was an utter bastard. Now, tell me where you left her."

"Very well. Since you're so insistent..."

He lifted his arms as if to gesture, and there was a brief glitter of moonlight on metal that warned Colter. He threw himself to one side, brought up his pistol in a smooth motion, his thumb snapping down to release the latch that fired it. Two explosions sounded simultaneously, the acrid smell of gunpowder sharp and strong.

Philip Worth stood for an instant, a shocked look on his face, then he crumpled soundlessly to the ground near the wheel of the gig. The horses snorted and stomped, but the brake held them from bolting as Colter moved to his uncle.

The shot had been true; a stain spread on his white shirt, an obscene red flower. Kneeling, Colter knew that his uncle was dead. Damn him. It had been too easy.

His head lifted, and he stared into the world of black and silver, saw tall grasses bending in the wind, heard nothing but the sound of the endless sea.

Where was she?

32

Celia rolled over painfully, trying to get her bearings. It sounded like thunder, but the night sky was clear, with many stars. The vast bowl of sparkling points against deep blue reminded her of *his* eyes…pitiless blue at times, and at others, blazing with raw desire. Where was he?

It was cold, the wind wet and fierce, blowing the tall grasses, dampening her face and clothes. She had to move or she'd die here, left to the uncertain mercy of the elements.

Left to the certain brutality of Lord Easton.

Groaning, she struggled to sit up, hands sinking into sand and grass, the rough edges of the blades slicing soft skin. It was wet here, residue of tidal flow, no doubt. As she got clumsily to her feet, she sank softly into the ground.

It was hard work trudging through clinging sand, and she hiked up her skirts above the clumps of grass, careful not to step in a hole hollowed out by wind and sea. Ahead in the distance, faint lights flickered on a point of land. If she could reach them before Easton found her, there may be someone to help her. She may be able to escape.

Shivering almost uncontrollably, she forged on, though her legs cramped with strain, the muscles shrieking protests at the abuse. Her own breath was loud, a rasping sound, and the sea washing up to the sand was a rolling echo of her own pounding blood in her ears.

Then, behind her, she heard another pounding, a hard thud of feet that sparked panic. A glance over her shoulder was enough to show her a tall figure in pursuit.

Oh God... At any moment she expected to hear the loud report of a pistol and be slammed to the earth by the impact of a ball in her back. She began to weave this way and that over the sand, running, feet digging into the sand with a spurt of fear pressing her onward, even when she lost a shoe.

He was getting closer, for she could almost feel the earth shudder beneath her, but the sea was so loud, the blood pounding in her ears and her breath a harsh, raking sob in her throat so that she could scarcely breathe now, could only keep running.

It was inevitable, an inexorable tide that finally caught her. As the hand snatched her by the back of her dress to stop her, she swung around in the grasp, swinging fiercely, fists pummeling him with all the force she could manage, over and over, no breath left to scream or cry out, only enough strength to resist.

A hard arm slammed across her, not painfully but firmly, to pin her against him and she was crushed against an unyielding chest. Unable to move, the only weapon left was her teeth; she sank them into his hand, and heard a harsh curse.

"Christ, Celia! Vicious little hellcat—listen to me! It's Colter—have you forgotten me already?"

Slowly his words penetrated, and she sagged against him with relief.

"Oh God, Colter...oh God, he'll kill you, too! You've got to get away, you've got to...he knows... Philip—"

"Hush, love. It's all right. Philip isn't able to kill anyone." He held her tightly against him, his hand tangled in her hair, loose now somehow, a sticky mess that hung in her eyes and waved down her back. His fingers tightened to slowly tilt her head so that she was looking up at him, at the face she'd thought she would never see again.

"It's all right, my love. You're safe. No one will harm you. I'm here, and I don't intend to ever let you out of my sight again."

Her knees gave way and she collapsed so that he had to quickly tighten his grip; he lowered her to the ground.

"You're bleeding— Did he do this? God, I'd like to kill him all over again!"

"No!" Her head snapped up, eyes wide as she searched his face, mostly shadowed with his head bent, the moonlight creating a hazy aureole around him. "Tell me you didn't kill him, Colter...you'll hang for it!"

"I don't think so, love. Here...dammit, your legs look as if knives were used on them." He felt down her calf, then saw her bare foot. Lifting it, he carefully brushed away the sand, taking care not to irritate the cuts. "God...Celia. No, don't argue with me. I'm carrying you back to the carriage. You're in no condition to walk another step. Not like this."

Despite her protests, he lifted her into his arms and held her against him as he carried her effortlessly, his boots sinking into the sand but his stride steady.

She lay her head against his shoulder and put her arms around his neck, shivering from cold and reaction. Her body ached and now she felt the sting from the cuts on her legs and feet, yet somehow, she'd never felt better in her life.

The rest was a blur. Later, when she was safely in the huge canopied bed freshened with clean sheets, Barbara fussing about her and Jacqueline anxiously hovering close by, she could not bear to think of all that had happened. All that mattered now was that she was safe, and that Colter was safe—and with her again.

She wakened early in the morning, starting up with a soft cry from a troubled dream, and saw him sitting in a chair at the side of her bed, a brandy snifter in one hand.

"Go back to sleep, love," he said. "You're safe."

She needed to hear it, needed to know that he was near, and she lay back against the fat feather pillows with a soft sigh of relief.

"You should sleep," she murmured, and he shook his head.

"I'll sleep. Later."

She wanted to ask him questions, but oddly enough, she fell asleep again.

There must have been something in the hot milk

she'd been given, for she lay with her eyes closed, too sleepy to open them but awake enough now to hear whispered conversations.

"Christ," he said harshly, "I nearly got her killed. How do you think I feel?"

Jacqueline's voice was soft and patient. "I must know how you feel about her, my lord. It is important to me."

"Why? You got what you wanted, didn't you?"

There was a pause, then in a pained voice, Jacqueline said, "You don't mean that."

"No. No, I don't. Oh God—" He sounded tortured, grim. "I don't know what I'm saying half the time anymore. If you had seen her…running like a wild thing, panicked as a fox before the hounds. I don't think I'll ever get that image out of my mind. Bleeding, exhausted, yet still she had the courage to fight me. I've seen infantrymen panic under less threatening circumstances. Yet she was so valiant."

"You love her." Jacqueline's voice was soft, wondering. "You really do love her…."

"Of course I love her! Do you think I would make a bargain I didn't want to make? I've dealt with much more dangerous threats than your implied intimidation, my lady."

"Ah." In a tone reeking with satisfaction, Jacqueline said, "It would be very nice if you told her how you feel when she wakes, my lord. Very nice. Women, you see, need to hear it in order to remind themselves that a man loves them. The little things you do, yes, that is very good as well, but it's the words…the assurance, and three little words are not so very hard to say, are they? No, I do not think they are. Say them to her.''

Silence fell, expanded, soft and pressing so that Celia could almost feel it. She lay so still, unwilling to move until she heard his reply.

''Yes,'' he said at last, ''I'll say them to her.''

A faint smile curved her mouth as she drifted back to sleep, this time untroubled by dreams. It was as if she were sinking in a deep pool like a heavy stone, down into oblivion.

When she woke again, it was late; lamps had been lit, rosy glows shedding small pools of light across the room, shrouded by the heavy drapes around the bed. She looked immediately toward the chair by the bed. It was empty.

Disappointment knifed through her. Then she felt a movement beside her and turned. Colter lay next to her. He smiled a little when she let out a relieved sigh.

''Looking for someone, my love?''

''Yes,'' she murmured, ''and it seems I found him.''

He reached for the hand she held out to him, held it in his fist, his thumb raking over the backs of her fingers in a caressing stroke. ''God,'' he muttered, his eyes suddenly intent. ''I hope so.''

''Oh...oh, Colter.'' It was all she could say for a moment, the sudden enormity of it all descending like a blanket. She held her breath as he touched her face with a gentle brush of his fingers.

''We've been married over a month now,'' he said when the silence stretched too long, ''and have yet to go on our extended bridal tour. It's customary, you know, to travel to foreign places so that the beautiful bride can enjoy exotic foods, customs and people.''

He lifted her hand, fingers tucked into his palm, and licked lightly at her fingertips. She drew in a shaky breath. ''I never knew that.''

''No? Perhaps things are done differently in America. A foreign country with strange customs, in my experience.'' He smiled wickedly. ''I have acquired a new ship—a steam ship—and the Moreland Shipping Concern has a thriving market in the United States.''

''Is there a reason for telling me this?'' she asked, her heart thumping as he continued to smile at her.

''I thought perhaps you'd like to start our bridal tour with an ocean voyage. You said you've never been to Spanish California, I believe. We could visit there as well. I've made arrangements to take a year to travel with my lovely wife...would you like that?''

''Yes,'' she agreed softly, and drew her hand over his face, the stark angles and planes that were so familiar to her, so loved. Should she tell him that?

Should she tell him that, despite everything, she could not envision a world without him now? It was true, so true, and she ached at the thought of being apart from him.

''Celia...'' He caught her hand, pressed his mouth into her palm, then held her by the wrist, his tone suddenly low and fierce. ''I'm not used to caring about someone else, not like this. It will make the way I've lived different, this responsibility for another person's emotions. Christ, I'm doing this badly, but I'm not much of a hand at it. Out of practice, I suppose you could say, with elegant words.''

''But, would you mean what you say to me?'' She

ran her fingers over his mouth, saw that he hadn't shaved; a rough stubble darkened his jaw. "Elegant or not, if you feel them, say them."

"Yes, easy enough, I suppose." He tilted her chin up with his fingers, looked into her face, his eyes a deep, shadowed blue, serious and fathomless. She held her breath as he scraped his thumb over her lips. "I love you, Celia, my green-eyed little wife, my heart."

He'd said it softly, but there was a wealth of emotion in his voice, a husky intensity that reached down into her very soul. For a moment, all she could do was stare at him silently, then she leaned forward to press her forehead against his, heart in her throat and eyes as she whispered, "And I love you, my lord, my husband—my life."

As he held her against him, she moved into his embrace with a lingering sigh, the past slipping away from her at last. Now there was the future, stretching endlessly ahead.

Colter kissed her, gently at first, then with rising passion. She gave herself up to the luscious stroke of his hands over her body, beneath the nightdress, familiar and sensuous, his hands on her breasts and thighs, and she clasped him close to her as their bodies joined and became one. And now, at last, as he moved against her with a piercing sweetness, he whispered his love in her ear.

"Sweet Celia, my heart...my love, I will always love you...."

"Yes," she said, rising to meet him, her body quivering with delicious anticipation, "as I will love you—forever."

"Love conquers all; let us too yield to Love"

—Virgil

Epilogue

Sunshine filtered through heavy-leaved trees, dappling the graves that lay beneath a blanket of green. Beyond, in the distance, the roof of the White House could barely be seen. But here, in this cemetery just outside Georgetown, it was quiet and serene.

Celia knelt beside her mother's grave, sunlight gleaming on her lovely blond hair. Standing behind her, Colter didn't speak, but waited patiently. She looked so vulnerable, so sad, her slender shoulders shaking slightly with remembered grief. He wanted to ease her pain but knew there was nothing he could say.

Finally she stood up, turned toward him with a faint smile; her cheeks were still wet. "I wanted her to know how happy I am now, and that she will never be forgotten."

He held out his arm and she stepped into his embrace. The faint, familiar scent of lemon verbena wafted from her hair, and he held her tightly.

"It will be dark soon," he said softly, "and there's still one more grave to visit. Do you feel up to it?"

"Yes, yes, of course I do. I'm with child, I'm not an invalid, my love!"

"Perhaps, but you're my wife, and I've sworn never to let anything happen to you again."

She paused to look up at him, green eyes still shiny with her tears. "That's a promise you may not always be able to keep, Colter. You know that. It's enough that we live and love and have our lives ahead of us. We cannot direct fate, but we can live each day as if it will be our last, and love as much as we can."

"That," he said, "will be easy with you."

He kept his arm around her shoulders as they visited the grave of Old Peter, and Celia knelt to place flowers atop the green mound. It was a catharsis of sorts, this farewell to those who'd meant so much to her, and he understood it.

Hadn't he laid to rest his own ghosts? Even the specter of his father had at last faded from his life, a memory that he could now put from his mind. All the old ghosts were fading, and before he'd left England, he'd been able to reconcile with his mother as well. He understood the reasons for her deception, even as he loathed the necessity for it. She'd suffered humiliation for years, and the thought of one more prompted her to that infamous pact with Philip. She just hadn't realized that Easton was cut from the same cloth as her husband, both of them completely ruthless in gaining their own ends.

"Now," Celia said when she returned to him, "I'm ready to leave. It's time to let them rest, time for us to live."

Together, they left the shaded shelter of ancient oaks and walked beneath an approving sun that beamed down on them, granting peace and promising a bright tomorrow.

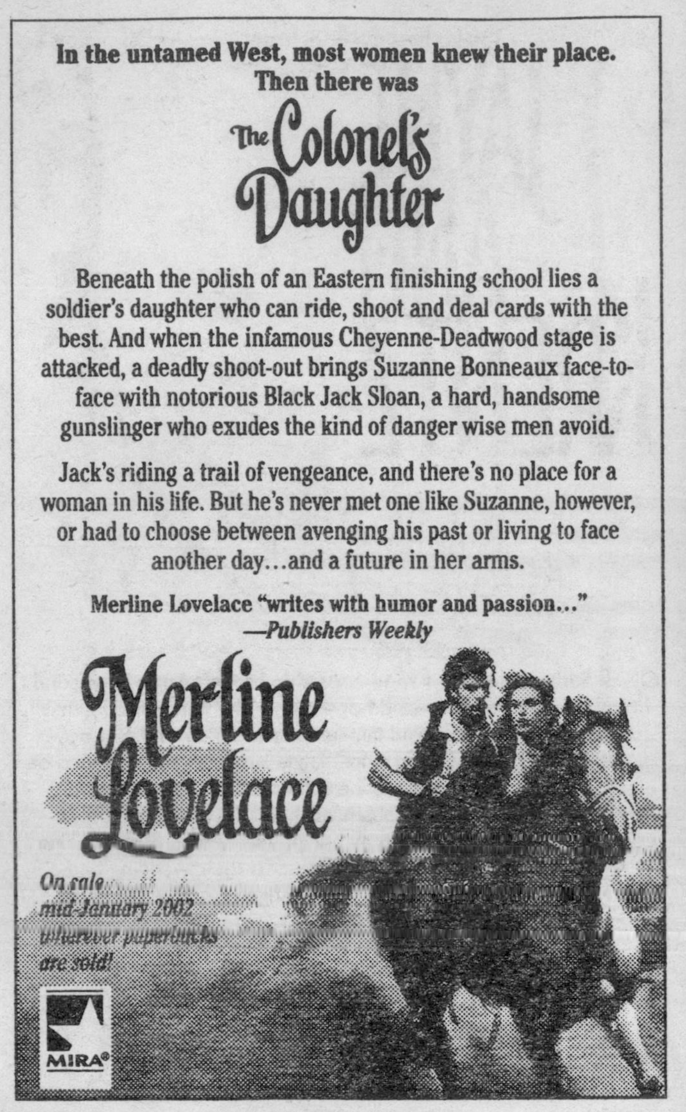
In the untamed West, most women knew their place.
Then there was
The Colonel's Daughter
Beneath the polish of an Eastern finishing school lies a soldier's daughter who can ride, shoot and deal cards with the best. And when the infamous Cheyenne-Deadwood stage is attacked, a deadly shoot-out brings Suzanne Bonneaux face-to-face with notorious Black Jack Sloan, a hard, handsome gunslinger who exudes the kind of danger wise men avoid.
Jack's riding a trail of vengeance, and there's no place for a woman in his life. But he's never met one like Suzanne, however, or had to choose between avenging his past or living to face another day…and a future in her arms.
Merline Lovelace "writes with humor and passion…"
—Publishers Weekly
Merline Lovelace
On sale mid-January 2002 wherever paperbacks are sold!
MIRA®